JUST OVER THE HORIZON

JUST OVER THE HORIZON

THE COMPLETE SHORT FICTION OF GREG BEAR

VOLUME ONE

INTEGRATED MEDIA

NEW YORK

All rights reserved, including without limitation the right to reproduce this book or any portion thereof in any form or by any means, whether electronic or mechanical, now known or hereinafter invented, without the express written permission of the publisher.

These are works of fiction. Names, characters, places, events, and incidents either are the product of the author's imagination or are used fictitiously. Any resemblance to actual persons, living or dead, businesses, companies, events, or locales is entirely coincidental.

Copyright © 2016 by Greg Bear

Cover art by Greg Bear

"Sisters" first appeared in *Tangents*, 1989
"A Martian Ricorso" first appeared in *Analog*, 1976
"Schrödinger's Plague" first appeared in *Analog*, 1982
"Blood Music" first appeared in *Analog*, 1983
"Silicon Times e-book review" first appeared in *Signs of Life*,
"Tangents" first appeared in *Omni*, 1986
"Through Road No Whither" first appeared in *Far Frontiers*, 1985
"Dead Run" first appeared in *Omni*, 1985
"The White Horse Child" first appeared in *Universe 9*, 1979
"Webster" first appeared in *Alternities*, 1974
"The Visitation" first appeared in *Omni*, 1987
"Richie by the Sea" first appeared in *New Terrors 2*, 1980
"Sleepside Story" first appeared from Cheap Street Press, 1988
"Genius" © 2000 by Greg Bear

Cover design by Mauricio Díaz

978-1-5040-2145-6

Published in 2016 by Open Road Integrated Media, Inc.
180 Maiden Lane
New York, NY 10038
www.openroadmedia.com

CONTENTS

SISTERS

Brian Thomsen was my editor at Warner Books during the late 1980s and early 1990s. To help promote my second collection of short stories, Tangents, *Brian suggested I write an original story. I had been thinking for some time about the day-to-day effects of the genetic revolution—as opposed to the more spectacular possibilities described in* Blood Music *and* Eon*—and also, what sort of tribal distinctions might arise between those who have been genetically enhanced and those who have not. The beginning of our acute awareness of tribes is often in high school.*

"Sisters" was the result.

Fortunately, this story preceded the excellent film Gattaca, *which I highly recommend. It's one of the ten best science fiction films of the last few decades.*

"But you're the only one, Letitia."

With a look of utmost sincerity, Reena Cathcart laid a light, slender hand on Letitia Blakely's shoulder. "You know none of the others can. I mean . . ." She stopped, awareness of her *faux pas* dawning. "You're simply the only one who can play the old—the older—woman."

Letitia stared down at the hall floor, eyes and face hot, then circled her gaze up to the ceiling, trying to keep fresh tears from spilling over. "We're late for first period," she said. A few stragglers sauntered down the clean and carpeted hall of the new school wing to their classes. "Why the old woman? Why didn't you come to me when there was some other part to play?"

Reena tossed her long black hair, perfect hazel eyes imploring. She was too smart not to know what she was doing. Smart—but not terribly sensitive. "You're the type," she said.

"You mean frowsy?"

Reena didn't react. She was intent on a yes answer, the perfect solution to her problems.

"Or just dumpy?"

"You shouldn't be ashamed of how you look."

"I look frowsy *and* dumpy! I'm perfect for the old woman in your lysing play, and you're the only one with the guts to ask me."

"We wanted to give you a chance to join the group. You're such a loner and we wanted you to feel like you're one of us."

"Bullshit!" The tears dripped down Letitia's cheeks and Reena backed away. "Just leave me *alone*."

"No need to swear." Petulant, offended.

Letitia raised her hand. Reena backed away, swung her hair again defiantly, turned, and walked off with a gentle sway of her hips. Letitia leaned against the tile wall and wiped her eyes, trying to avoid smudging her carefully applied makeup. The damage was done, however. She could feel the tracks of her mother's mascara and smudged eyeshadow. With a sigh, she walked to the bathroom, not caring how late she was. She just wanted to go home. But she wouldn't give them that satisfaction.

Coming into class fifteen minutes after the bell, she found the students in self-ordered discussion, with no sign of their teacher, Mr. Brant. Several of Reena's drama group gave Letitia frosty looks as she took her seat.

"TB," Edna Corman said beneath her breath from across the aisle.

"RC you," Letitia replied, head cocked to one side, her tone precisely matching Edna's. She poked John Lockwood in the shoulder. He leaned back and fixed his black eyes on hers. Lockwood didn't care for socializing; he seldom noticed the exchanges going on around him. "Where's Mr. Brant?"

"Georgia Fischer blitzed. He took her to the counselors. Told us to plug in and pursue."

"Oh." Georgia Fischer had transferred two months ago from a superwhiz class in Oakland. She was brighter than most but blitzed about once every two weeks. "I may be fat and ugly," Letitia said for Lockwood's ears only. "But I never blitz."

"Me neither," Lockwood said. He was PPC, like Georgia, but not a superwhiz. Letitia liked him, but not enough to feel threatened by him. "Better pursue."

Letitia leaned forward and closed her eyes to concentrate. Her mod activated and projections danced in front of her, then steadied. She had been cramming patient psych for a week and was approaching threshold. The little Computer Graphics nursie in whites and pillcap began discussing insanouts of terminal patient care, which all seemed very TB to Letitia; who died of diseases now, anyway? She made her decision and cut to the same CG nursie discussing the shock of RoR—replacement and recovery. What she really wanted to study was colony medicine, but how could she ever make it Out There?

Some PPCs had been designed by their parents to qualify physically and mentally for space careers. Some had been equipped with bichemistries, one of which became active in Earth's gravity, the other in space. How could an NG compete with that?

Of the seven hundred adolescents in her high school training programs, Letitia Blakely was one of ten NGs—possessors of natural, unaltered genomes. Everyone else was PPCs or Pre-Planned Children, the proud bearer of juggled genes, lovely and stable, with just the proper amount of adipose tissue and just the proper infusion of parental characteristics and chosen features to be beautiful and different; tall, healthy, hair manageable, skin unblemished, well-adjusted (except for the occasional blitzer) with warm and sunny personalities.

The old derogatory slang for PPCs was RC—Recombined.

Letitia was slightly overweight, with pasty skin, hair frizzy, nose bulbous and chin weak. One breast was larger than the other and already showing a droop pronounced enough to grip a stylus. She experienced painful menstrual periods and an absolute indisposition to athletics. She was the Sport. That's what they called NGs. Sports. TBs—Throwbacks.

Neanderthals.

All the beautiful PPCs risked a great deal if they showed animosity toward the NGs. Her parents had the right to sue the system if she was harassed. This wasn't a private school where parents paid astronomical tuitions; this was an old-fashioned public school, with public school programs and regulations. Teachers tended to nuke out on raggers. And, she admitted to herself with a painful loop of recrimination, she wasn't making it any easier for them. Sure, she could join in, play the old woman—add some realism to their little drama, with her genuine TB phys! She could be jolly and self-deprecating like Helen Roberti, who wasn't all that bad-looking anyway—she could pass if she straightened her hair. Or she could be quiet and camouflaged like Bernie Thibhault.

The CG nursie exited from RoR care. Letitia had hardly absorbed a thing. Realtime mod education was a bore, but she hadn't yet qualified for on-the-job training. She had only one course of career study now—no alternates—and two aesthetic programs, individual orchestra on Friday afternoon and LitVid publishing on alternating weekends.

For pre-med she was a washout, but she wouldn't admit it. She was NG. Her brain took longer to mature; it wasn't so finely wired. She felt incredibly slow. She doubted whether she would ever be successful as a doctor; she was squeamish, and nobody, not even her fellow NGs, would want to be treated by a doctor who grew pale at the sight of blood.

Letitia silently told nursie to start over again. Nursie obliged. Reena Cathcart, meanwhile, had dropped into her mod with a vengeance. Her blissed expression told it all. Realtime slid into her so smooth, so quick, it was pure joy. No zits on her brain.

Mr. Brant returned ten minutes later with a pale and bleary-eyed Georgia Fischer. She sat two seats behind Letitia and over one aisle. She plugged in her mod dutifully and Brant went to his console to bring up the multimedia and coordinate the whole class. Edna Corman whispered something to her.

"Not a bad blitz, all in all," Georgia commented softly.

"How are you doing, Letitia?" the autocounselor asked. The CG face projected in front of her with slight wirehash, to which Letitia paid no attention. CG ACs were the jams and she didn't appreciate them even in pristine perfection.

"Poorly," she said.

"Really? Care to elaborate?"

"I want to talk to Dr. Rutger."

"Don't trust your friendly AC?"

"I'd like some clear space. I want to talk to Dr. Rutger."

"Dr. Rutger is busy, dear. Unlike your friendly AC, humans can only be in one place at a time. I'd like to help if I may."

"Then I want program sixteen."

"Done, Letitia." The projection wavered and the face changed to a real-person simulation of Marian Tempesino, the only CG AC Letitia felt comfortable with. Tempesino had no wirehash, which indicated she was a seldom-used program, and that was just fine with Letitia. "Sixteen here. Letitia? You're looking cut. More adjustment jams?"

"I wanted to talk with Dr. Rutger but he's busy. So I'll talk to you. And I want it on my record. I want out of school. I want my parents to pull me and put me in a special NG school."

Tempesino's face didn't wear any particular expression, which was one of the reasons Letitia liked Program 16 AC. "Why?"

"Because I'm a freak. My parents made me a freak and I'd like to know why I shouldn't be with all the other freaks."

"You're a natural, not a freak."

"To look like any of the others, even to look like Reena Cathcart, I'd have to spend the rest of my life in bioplasty. I can't take it anymore. They asked me to play an old lady in one of their dramas. The only part I'm fit for. An old lady."

"They tried to include you in."

"That hurt!" Letitia said, tears in her eyes.

Tempesino's image wavered a bit as the emotion registered and a higher authority AC kicked in behind 16.

"I just want out. I want to be alone," Letitia murmured.

"Where would you like to go, Letitia?"

Letitia thought about that for a moment. "I'd like to go back to when being ugly was normal."

"Fine, then. Let's simulate. Sixty years should do it. Ready?"

She nodded and wiped away more mascara with the back of her hand.

"Then let's go."

It was like a dream, somewhat fuzzier than plugging in a mod. CG images compiled from thousands of miles of old films and tapes and descriptive records made her feel as if she were flying back in time, back to a place she would have loved to call home. Faces came to her—faces with ugly variations, growing old prematurely, wearing glasses, even beautiful faces which could have passed today—and the faces pulled away to become attached to bodies. Bodies out of shape, overweight, sick and healthy, red-faced with high blood pressure—and in good condition. The whole variable and disaster-prone population of humanity, sixty years past. This was where Letitia felt she belonged.

"They're beautiful," she said.

"They didn't think so. They jumped at the chance to be sure their children were beautiful, smart, and healthy. It was a time of transition, Letitia. Just like now."

"Everybody looks alike now."

"I don't think that's fair," the AC said. "There's considerable variety in the way people look today."

"Not my age."

"Especially your age. Look." The AC showed her dozens of faces. Few looked alike, but all were handsome or lovely. Some made Letitia ache; faces she could never be friends with, never love, because there was always someone more beautiful and desirable than an NG.

"My parents should have lived back then. Why did they make me a freak?"

"You're developmentally normal. You're not a freak."

"I'm a DNG. Dingy. That's what they call me."

"Don't you invite the abuse sometimes?"

"No!" This was getting her nowhere.

"Letitia, we all have to adjust. Not even today's world is fair. Are you sure you're doing all you can to adjust?"

Letitia squirmed in her seat and said she wanted to leave. "Just a moment," the AC said. "We're not done yet." She knew that tone of voice. The ACs were allowed to get a little rough at times. They could make unruly students do grounds duty or detain them after hours to work on assignments usually given to computers. Letitia sighed and settled back. She hated being lectured.

"Young woman, you're carrying a giant chip on your shoulder."

"All the more computing power for me."

"Quiet, and listen. We're allowed to criticize policy, whoever makes it. Dignity of office and respect for superiors has not survived very well into century twenty-one. People have to earn respect. That goes for students, too. The average student here has four major talents, each of them fitting into a public planning policy which guarantees them a job incorporating two or more of those talents. They aren't forced to accept the jobs, and if their will falters, they may not keep those jobs. But the public has tried to guarantee every one of us a quality employment opportunity. That goes for you, as well. You're DNG, but you show as much intelligence and at least as many developable talents as the PPCs. You're young, Letitia, and your maturation schedule is a natural one—but you're not inferior or impaired. That's more than can be said for the offspring of some parents even more resistive than your own. You at least were given prenatal care and nutrition adjustment, and your parents let the biotechs correct your allergies."

"So?"

"So for you, it's a matter of will. If your will falters, you won't be given any more consideration than a PPC. You'll have to choose secondary or tertiary employment, or even . . ." The AC paused. "Public support. Do you want that?"

"My grades are up. I'm doing fine."

"You are choosing career training not matching your talents."

"I like medicine."

"You're squeamish."

Letitia shrugged.

"And you're hard to get along with."

"Just tell them to lay off. I'll be civil . . . but I don't want them treating me like a freak. Edna Corman called me . . ." She paused. That could get Edna Corman into a lot of trouble. Among the students, TB was a casual epithet; to school authorities, applied to an NG, it might be grounds for a blot on Corman's record. "Not important."

The AC switched and Tempesino's face took a different counseling track. "Fine. Adjustment on both sides is necessary. Thank you for coming in, Letitia."

"I still want to talk with Rutger."

"Request noted. Please return to your class in progress."

"Pay attention to your brother when he's talking," Jane said. Roald was making a nuisance of himself by chattering about the preflight training he was getting in primary. Letitia made a polite comment or two, then lapsed back into contemplation of the food before her. She picked at it, put a half spoonful to her lips. Jane regarded her from the corner of her eye and passed a bowl of sugared berries. "What's eating you?"

"I'm doing the eating," Letitia said.

"Ha," Roald said. "Full load from this angle." He grinned at her, his two front teeth missing. He looked hideous, she thought. Any other family would have given him temporaries; not hers.

"A little more respect from both of you," said Donald. Her father took the bowl from Roald and scooped a modest portion into his cup, then set it beside Letitia. "Big fifteen and big eight." That was his homily; behave big whether eight or fifteen.

"Autocounselor today?" Jane asked. She knew Letitia too well.

"AC," Letitia affirmed.

"Did you go in?"

"Yes."

"And?"

"I'm not tuned."

"Which means?" Donald ask.

"It means she hisses and crackles," Roald said, mouth full of berries, juice dripping down his chin. He cupped his hand underneath and sucked it up noisily. Jane reached out and finished the job with a napkin. "She complains," Roald finished.

"About what?"

Letitia shook her head.

The dessert was almost finished when Letitia slapped both palms on the table. "Why did you do it?"

"Why did we do what?" he father asked, startled.

"Why didn't you design us? Why are Roald and I normal?"

Jane and Donald glanced at each other and turned to Letitia. Roald regarded her with wide eyes, a bit shocked himself.

"Surely you know why by now," Jane said, looking down at the table, either nonplussed or getting angry.

Now that she had plotted her course, Letitia couldn't help but forge ahead. "I don't. Not really. It's not because you're religious."

"Something like that," Donald said.

"No," Jane said, shaking her head firmly.

"Then why?"

"Your mother and I—"

"I am *not* just their mother," Jane said.

"Jane and I believe there is a certain plan in nature, a plan we shouldn't interfere with. If we had gone along with most of the others and participated in the boy-girl lotteries and signed up for counseling—we would have been interfering."

"Did you go to a hospital when we were born?"

"Yes," Jane said, still avoiding their faces.

"That's not natural," Letitia said. "Why not let nature decide whether we'd be born alive?"

"We have never claimed to be consistent," Donald said.

"Donald," Jane said ominously.

"There are limits," Donald expanded, smiling placation. "We believe those limits begin when people try to interfere with the sex cells. You've had all that in school. You know about the protests when the first PPCs were born. Your grandmother was one of the protesters. Your mother and I are both NGs; of course, our generation has a much higher percentage of NGs."

"Now we're freaks," Letitia said.

"If by that you mean there aren't many teenage NGs, I suppose that's right," Donald said, touching his wife's arm. "But it could also mean you're special. Chosen."

"No," Letitia said. "Not chosen. You played dice with both of us. We could have been DDs—duds. Dingies. Retards or spaz."

An uncomfortable quiet settled over the table.

"Don't use that language," Jane said tightly.

"Not likely," Donald said, his voice barely above a whisper. "Your mother and I both have good genotypes. Your grandmother insisted your mother marry a good genotype. There are no developmentally disabled people in our families."

"So how is that natural? You guys went that far—why not take it the next step?"

They just stared at her. Roald fiddled with his knife and fork. Letitia had been hemmed in. There was no way she could see out of it, so she pushed back her chair and excused herself from the table.

As she made her way up to her room, she heard arguing below. Roald raced up the stairs behind her and gave her a dirty look. "Why'd you have to bring all that up?" he asked. "It's bad enough at school, we don't have to have it here."

She thought about the history the AC had shown her. Back then, a family with their income wouldn't have been able to live in a four-bedroom house. Back then, there had been half as many people in the United States and Canada as there were now. There had been more unemployment, much more economic uncertainty, and far fewer automated jobs. The percentage of people doing physical labor for a living—simple construction, crop maintenance and harvesting, digging ditches and hard work like that—had been ten times greater then than it was now. Most of the people doing such labor today belonged to religious sects or one of the Wendell Barry farming communes.

Back then, Roald and Letitia would have been considered gifted children with a bright future. She thought about the pictures and the feeling of the past, and wondered if Reena hadn't been right. She would be a perfect old woman.

Her mother came to her room while Letitia was putting up her hair. She stood in the door frame. It was obvious she had been crying. Letitia watched her reflection in the mirror of her grandmother's dressing table, willed to her four years before. "Yes?" she asked softly, ageless bobby pins in her mouth.

"It was more my idea than your father's," Jane said, stepping closer, hands folded before her. "I mean, I *am* your mother. That's a big responsibility. You and I never really talked about this."

"No," Letitia said.

"So why now?"

"I'm growing up."

"Yes." Jane looked at the soft and flickering pictures hung on the walls, pastel scenes of improbable forests. "When I was pregnant with you, I was very afraid. I worried we'd made the wrong decision, going against what everybody else seemed to think and what everybody was advising or being advised. But I carried you and felt you move . . . and I knew you were ours, and ours alone, and that we were responsible for you body and soul. I was your mother, not the doctors."

Letitia looked up at her with mixed anger and frustration . . . and love.

"And now I see you," her mother said. "I think back to what I might have felt, if I were your age again, in your position. I might be mad, too. Roald hasn't had time to feel different; he's too young. I just came up here to tell you, I know that what I did was right—not for us, not for them . . ." She indicated the broad world beyond the walls of the house. "But right for you. It'll work out. It really will." She put her hands on Letitia's shoulders. "Your classmates aren't having an easy time, either. You know that." She paused, then from behind her back revealed a book with a soft brown cover. "I brought this to show you again. You remember Great-Grandma? Her grandmother came all the way from Ireland, along with her grandpa." Jane gave her the album. Reluctantly, Letitia opened it up. There were real paper photographs inside, ancient black and white and faded color. Her great-grandmother did not much resemble Grandmother, who had been big-boned, heavy-set. Great-Grandmother looked as if she had been skinny all her life. "You keep this," Jane said. "Think about it for a while."

The morning came with planned rain. Letitia took the half-empty metro to school, looking through raindrop-smeared glass at the terraced and gardened and studiously neglected landscape of the suburbs. She walked onto the school grounds and crossed the quad to one of the older buildings, where there was a little-used old-fashioned lavatory. This sometimes served as a sanctuary. She stood in a white stall and breathed deeply for a few minutes, then went to a sink and washed her hands as if conducting some ritual. Slowly, reluctantly, she looked at herself in the cracked mirror.

A janitorial worker rolled in, apologized, then went about its duties, leaving behind the fresh, steamy smell of clean fixtures.

The early part of the day she felt numb. Letitia began to fear her own distance from emotions, from the people around her. She might at any minute step back into the old lavatory and simply fade from the present, travel in time, find herself sixty years in the past . . .

And what would she think of that?

In her third period class she received a note requesting that she appear in Rutger's counseling office as soon as was convenient. That was shorthand for immediately; she gathered up her mods and caught Reena's unreadable glance as she walked past.

Rutger was a handsome man of forty-three (the years were registered on his desk life clock, an affectation of some of the older PPCs) with a broad smile and a garish taste in clothes. He was head of the counseling department and generally well-liked in the school. He shook her hand as she entered the counseling office and offered her a chair. "You wanted to talk?" he asked.

"I guess," Letitia said.

"Problems?" His voice was a pleasant baritone; he was probably a fairly good singer. That had been a popular trait in the early days of PPCs.

"The ACs say it's my attitude."

"What about it?"

"I'm ugly. I'm the only ugly girl in the school."

Rutger nodded. "I don't think you're ugly, but which is worse, being unique or being ugly?"

Letitia lifted the corner of her lip in snide acknowledgment of the funny. "Everybody's unique now," she said.

"That's what we teach. Do you believe it?"

"No," she said. "Everybody's the same. I'm . . ." She shook her head. She resented Rutger prying up the pavement over her emotions. "I'm TB. I wouldn't mind being a PPC, but I'm not."

"I think it's a minor problem," Rutger said quickly. He hadn't even sat down; obviously he was not going to give her much time.

"It doesn't feel minor," she said, anger poking through the cracks he had made.

"Oh, no. Being young often means that minor problems feel major. You feel envy and don't like yourself, at least not the way you look. Well, looks can be helped by diet, or at the very least by time. If I'm any judge, you'll look fine when you're older. And I am something of a judge. As for the way the others feel about you . . . I was a freak once."

Letitia looked up at him.

"Certainly. Bona fide freak. There are ten NGs like yourself in this school now. When I was your age, I was the only PPC in my school. There was suspicion. There were even riots. Some PPCs were killed in one school when parents stormed the grounds."

Letitia stared. She hadn't heard anything about this in class.

"The other kids hated me," Rutger said. "They had parents who told them PPCs were Frankenstein monsters. They informed me I had been grown in a test tube and hatched out of an incubator. Remember the Rifkin Society? They're still around, but they're fringe now. You've never experienced real hatred, I suspect. I did."

"You were nice-looking," Letitia said. "You knew somebody would like you eventually, maybe even love you. What about me? What I am, the way I look, who will ever want me? And will a PPC ever want to be with a Dingy?"

She knew these were hard questions and Rutger made no pretense of answering them. "Say it all works out for the worst," he said. "You end up a spinster and no one ever loves you. You spend the rest of your days alone. Is that what you're worried about?"

Her eyes widened. She had never quite thought those things through. Now she really hurt.

"Everybody out there is choosing beauty for their kids. They're choosing slender, athletic bodies and fine minds. You have a fine mind, but I have no record of you ever trying out for athletics. So when you're out in the adult world, sure, you'll look different. Why can't that be an advantage? You may be surprised how hard we PPCs try to be different. And how hard it is, since tastes vary so little in our parents. You have that built in."

Letitia listened, but the layers of paving were closing again. "Icing on the cake," she said.

Rutger regarded her with shrewd blue eyes and shrugged. "Come back in a month," he said. "Until then, I think ACs will do fine."

Little was said at dinner and less after. She went upstairs and to bed at an early hour, feeling logy and hoping for escape. Her father did his usual bedcheck an hour after she had put on her pajamas and lain down.

"Rolled tight?" he asked.

"Mmph," she replied.

"Sleep tighter," he said. Her life had been shaped by parents who were comfortable with nightly rituals and formulas.

"Mmph," she said.

Almost immediately after sleep, or so it seemed, she came abruptly awake. She sat up in bed and realized where she was and who, and she began to cry. She had had the strangest and most beautiful dream, the finest ever without a dream mod. She could not remember details now, try as she might, but waking was almost more than she could bear.

In first period, Georgia Fischer blitzed yet again and had to go to the infirmary. Letitia watched the others and saw a stony cover-up of their feelings.

Edna Corman excused herself in second period and came back with red, puffy eyes and pink cheeks. The tension built through the rest of the day until Letitia wondered how anyone could concentrate. She did her own studying without conviction; she was still wrapped in the dream, trying to decide what it meant.

In eighth period, she once again sat behind John Lockwood. It was as if she had completed a cycle beginning in the morning and ending with her last class. She looked at her watch anxiously. Once again, they were supervised by Mr. Brant, but he also seemed distracted, as if he, too, had had a dream and it hadn't been as pleasant as hers.

Brant had them cut mods mid-period and begin a discussion on what had been learned. These were the so-called integrative moments when the media learning was fixed by social interaction; Letitia found these periods a trial at the best of times. Reena Cathcart as usual stood out in a class full of dominant personalities.

John Lockwood listened intently, a small smile on his face as he presented a profile to Letitia. He seemed about to turn around and talk to her. She placed her hand on the corner of her console and lifted her finger to attract his attention.

He glanced at her hand, turned away, and with a shudder looked at it again, staring this time, eyes widening. His mouth began to work as if her hand was the most horrible thing he had ever seen. His chin quivered, then his shoulder, and before Letitia could react he stood up and moaned. His legs went liquid beneath him and he fell to the console, arms hanging, then slid to the floor. On the floor, John Lockwood—who had never done such a thing in his life—twisted and groaned and shivered, locked in a violent blitz.

Brant pressed the class emergency button and came around his desk. Before he could reach Lockwood, the boy became still, eyes open, one hand letting go its tight grip on the leg of his seat. Letitia could not move, watching his empty eyes; he appeared so horribly *limp.*

Brant grabbed the boy by the shoulders, swearing steadily, and dragged him outside the classroom. Letitia followed them into the hall, wanting to help. Edna Corman and Reena Cathcart stood beside her, faces blank. Other students followed, staying well away from Brant and the boy.

Brant lowered John Lockwood to the concrete and began pounding his chest and administering mouth-to-mouth. He pulled a syringe from his coat pocket and uncapped it, shooting its full contents into the boy's skin just below the sternum.

Letitia focused on the syringe, startled. Right in his pocket; not in the first-aid kit.

The entire class stood in the hallway, silent, in shock. The medical arrived, Rutger following; it scooped John Lockwood onto its gurney and swung around, lights flashing. "Have you administered KVN?" the robot asked Brant.

"Yes. Five cc's. Direct to heart."

Room after room came out to watch, all the PPCs fixing their eyes on the burdened medical as it rolled down the hall. Edna Corman cried. Reena glanced at Letitia and turned away as if ashamed.

"That's five," Rutger said, voice tired beyond grimness. Brant looked at him, then at the class, and told them they were dismissed. Letitia hung back. Brant screwed up his face in grief and anger. "Go! Get out of here!"

She ran. The last thing she heard Rutger say was, "More this week than last."

Letitia sat in the empty white lavatory, wiping her eyes, ashamed at her sniveling. She wanted to react like a grownup—she saw herself being calm, cool, offering help to whomever might have needed it in the classroom—but the tears and the shaking would not stop.

Mr. Brant had seemed angry, as if the entire classroom were at fault. Not only was Mr. Brant adult, he was PPC. Did she expect adults, especially adult PPCs, to behave better? Wasn't that what it was all about?

She stared at herself in the cracked mirror. "I should go home, or go to the library and study," she told her image. Dignity and decorum.

Two girls walked into the lavatory, and her private moment passed.

Letitia did not go to the library. Instead, she went to the old concrete and steel auditorium, entering through the open stage entrance, standing in darkness in the wings. Three female students sat in the front row, below the stage level and about ten meters from Letitia. She recognized Reena but not the others; they did not share classes with her.

"Did you know him?" the second girl asked Reena.

"No, not very well," Reena said. "He was in my class."

"No ducks!" the third snorted.

"Trish, keep it *interior,* please. Reena's had it rough."

"He hadn't blitzed," Reena said. "He wasn't a superwhiz. Nobody expected it."

"When was his incept?"

"I don't know," Reena said. "We're all about the same age, within a couple of months. We're all the same model year, same supplements—if it's something in the genotype, in the supplements . . ."

"I heard somebody say there have been five so far. I haven't heard a thing from my parents," the third said.

"I haven't either," said the second.

"Not in our school," Reena said. "Except for the superwhizes. And none of them have died before now."

Letitia stepped back in the darkness, hand on mouth. Had Lockwood actually *died*? She thought for a mad moment of stepping out of the wings, going into the seats and telling the three she was sorry. The impulse faded fast. That would have been intruding. They weren't any older than she was, and they didn't sound much more mature.

They sounded scared.

In the morning, at the station room for secondary pre-med, Brant confirmed that John Lockwood had died the day before. "He had a heart attack," Brant said. Letitia intuited that was not the complete truth. A short eulogy was read, and special hours for psych counseling were arranged for those students who felt they might need it.

The word "blitzing" was not mentioned by Brant, nor by any of the PPCs throughout that day. Letitia tried to research the subject but found precious few materials in the libraries accessed by her mod. She presumed she didn't know where to look; it was hard to believe that *nobody* knew what was happening.

The dream came again, even stronger, the next night, and Letitia awoke out of it cold and shivering with excitement. She saw herself standing before a crowd, no single face visible, for she was in a bright spotlight and they were in darkness. She had felt, in the dream, an almost unbearable happiness, grief mixed with joy, unlike anything she had ever experienced before. She *loved* and did not know what she loved—not the crowd, precisely, not a man, not a family member, not even herself.

She sat up in her bed, hugging her knees, wondering if anyone else was awake. It seemed possible she had never been awake until now; every nerve was alive.

Quietly, not wanting anybody else to intrude on this moment, she slipped out of bed and walked down the hall to her mother's sewing room. There, in a full-length cheval mirror, she looked at herself as if with new eyes.

"Who *are* you?" she whispered. She lifted her cotton nightshirt and stared at her legs. Short calves, lumpy knees, thighs not bad—not fat, at any rate. Her arms were soft looking, not muscular but not particularly plump, a rosy vanilla color with strawberry blotches on her elbows where she leaned on them while reading in bed. She had Irish ancestors on her mother's side; that showed in her skin color, recessed cheekbones, broad face. On her father's side, Mexican and German; not much evidence in her of the Mexican. Her brother looked more swarthy. "We're mongrels," she said. "I look like a mongrel compared to PPC purebreds." But PPCs were not purebred; they were *designed.*

She lifted her nightshirt higher still, pulling it over her head finally and standing naked. Shivering from the cold and from the memory of her dream, she forced herself to focus on all of her characteristics. Whenever she had seen herself naked in mirrors before, she had blurred her eyes at one feature, looked away from another, special-effecting her body into a more acceptable fantasy. Now she was in a mood to know herself for what she was.

Broad hips, strong abdomen—plump, but strong. From her

pre-med, she knew that meant she would probably have little trouble bearing children. "Brood mare," she said, but there was no critical sharpness in the words. To have children, she would have to attract men, and right now there seemed little chance of that. She did not have the "Attraction Peaks" so often discussed on the TV, or seen faddishly headlined on the LitVid mods; the culturally prescribed geometric curves allocated to so few naturally, and now available to so many by design.

Does Your Child Have the Best Design for Success?

Such a shocking triviality. She felt a righteous anger grow—another emotion she was not familiar with—and sucked it back into the excitement, not wanting to lose her mood. "I might never look at myself like this again," she whispered.

Her breasts were moderate in size, the left larger than the right and more drooping. She could indeed hold a stylus under her left breast, something a PPC female would not have to worry about for decades, if ever. Rib cage not really distinct; muscles not distinct; rounded, soft, gentle-looking, face curious, friendly, wide-eyed, skin blemished but not so badly it wouldn't recover on its own; feet long and toenails thick, heavily cuticled. She had never suffered from ingrown toenails.

Her family line showed little evidence of tendency to cancer—correctible now, but still distressing—or heart disease or any of the other diseases of melting pot cultures, of mobile populations and changing habits. She saw a strong body in the mirror, one that would serve her well.

And she also saw that with a little makeup, she could easily play an older woman. Some shadow under the eyes, lines to highlight what would in thirty or forty years be jowls, laugh lines . . .

But she did not look old *now.*

Letitia walked back to her room, treading carefully on the carpet. In the room, she asked the lights to turn on, lay down on the bed, pulled the photo album Jane had given her from the top of her nightstand, and gingerly turned the delicate black paper pages.

She stared at Great-Grandmother's face, and then at the picture of her grandmother as a little girl.

Individual orchestra was taught by three instructors in one of the older drama classrooms behind the auditorium. It was a popular aesthetic; the school's music boxes were better than most home units, and the instructors were very popular. All were PPCs.

After half an hour of group, each student could retire to box keyboard, order up spheres of countersound to avoid cacophony, and practice. Today, she practiced for less than half an hour. Then, tongue between her lips, she stared oiver the keyboard into empty space. "Countersound off, please," she ordered, and rose from the black bench. Mr. Teague, the senior instructor, asked if she were done for the day. "I have to run an errand," she said.

"Practice your polyrhythms," he advised.

She left the classroom and walked around to the auditorium's stage entrance. She knew Reena's drama group would be meeting there. The auditorium was dark, the stage illuminated by three catwalk spots. The drama group sat on a circle of chairs in one bright corner, reading lines aloud from tattered paper scripts.

Hands folded, Letitia walked toward the group. Rick Fayette, a quiet senior with short black hair, spotted her first but said nothing, glancing at Reena. Reena stopped reading her lines, turned, and stared at Letitia. Edna Corman saw her last and shook her head, as if this were the last straw.

"Hello," Letitia said.

"What are you doing here?" There was more wonder than disdain in Reena's voice.

"I thought you might still be able to use me."

"Really," Edna Corman said.

Reena put her script down. "Why'd you change your mind?"

"I realized I wouldn't mind being an old lady," Letitia said. "It's not that big a deal. I brought a picture." She took a plastic wallet from her pocket and opened it to a copy of the photo in the album. "You could make me up like this. Like Great-Grandmother."

Reena leaned in and studied the copy. "You look like her," she said.

"Kind of."

"Look at this." Reena held the picture out to the others. They passed the copy from hand to hand, staring in wonder. Even Edna Corman glanced at it briefly.

"She actually *looks* like her great-grandmother," Reena said.

Rick Fayette whistled. "You," he said, "will make a really great old lady."

Rutger called her into his office abruptly a week later. She sat quietly before his desk. "You've joined the drama class after all," he said.

She nodded.

"Any reason?"

There was no simple way to express it. "Because of what you told me," she said.

"No friction?"

"It's going okay."

"They gave you another role to play?"

"No. I'm the old lady. They'll use makeup on me."

"You don't object?"

"I don't think so."

Rutger seemed to want to find something wrong, but he couldn't. With a faintly suspicious smile, he thanked her for her time. "Come back and see me whenever you want," he said. "Tell me how it goes."

The group met each Friday, an hour later than her individual orchestra. Letitia made arrangements for home keyboard hookup and practice. After a reading and a half hour of questions, she obtained the permission of the drama group advisor, a spinsterish non-PPC seldom seen in the hallways, Miss Darcy. Miss Darcy seemed old-fashioned and addressed all of her students as either

"Mister" or "Miss," but she knew drama and stagecraft. She was the oldest of the six NG teachers in the school.

Reena stayed with Letitia during the audition and made a strong case for her late admittance, saying that the casting of Rick Fayette as an older woman was not going well. Fayette was equally eager to be rid of the part; he had another role, and the thought of playing two characters in this production worried him. He confessed his appreciation at their second Friday meeting, and introduced her to an elfishly handsome group member, Frank Leroux. Leroux was much too shy to go on stage, Fayette said, but he would be doing makeup. "He's pretty amazing."

Letitia stood nervously while Leroux examined her. "You've got a *face,*" he said softly. "May I touch, to see where your contours are?"

Letitia giggled and abruptly sobered, embarrassed. "Okay," she said. "You're going to draw lines and make shadows?"

"Much more than that," Leroux said.

"He'll take a video of your face in motion," Fayette said. "Then he'll digitize it and sculpt a laser mold—much better than sitting for a life mask. He made a life mask of *me* last year for Halloween, to turn me into the Hunchback of Notre Dame. No fun at all."

"This way is much easier," Leroux said, poking under her cheeks and chin, pulling back her hair to feel her temples. "I can make two or three sculptures showing what your face and neck are like when they're in different positions. Then I can adjust the appliance molds for flex and give."

"When he's done with you, you won't know yourself," Fayette said.

"Reena says you have a picture of your great-grandmother. May I see it?" Leroux asked. She gave him the wallet and he looked at the picture with squint-eyed intensity. "What a wonderful face," he said. "I never met my great-grandmother. My own grandmother looks about as old as my mother. They might be sisters."

"When he's done with you," Fayette said, his enthusiasm

becoming a bit tiresome, "you and your *great-grandmother* will look like sisters!"

When Letitia went home that evening, taking a late metro from the school, she wondered just exactly what she was doing. Throughout her high school years, she had cut herself off from most of her fellow students. The closest she came to friendship had been banter with John Lockwood while sitting at the mods, waiting for instructors to arrive. Now she actually liked Fayette, and strange Leroux, whose hands were thin and pale and strong and cool. Leroux was a PPC, but obviously his parents had different tastes; was he a superwhiz? Nobody had said so; it was a matter of honor among PPCs that they pretended not to care about their classifications.

Reena was friendly and supportive, but still distant.

As Letitia walked up the stairs to their home, she opened the front door and set the keyboard down by the closet. In the living room, she spied the edge of a news broadcast. Nobody was watching TV; they were probably in the kitchen. From this angle the announcer appeared translucent and ghostly. As she walked around to the best angle, the announcer seemed to solidify. She was a goddess of Asian-negroid features, with high cheekbones, straight golden hair and copper-bronze skin. Letitia didn't care what she looked like; what she was saying had caught her attention.

"—revelations made today that as many as one-fourth of all PPCs inceived between sixteen and seventeen years ago may possess a potentially defective gene sequence known as T56-WA 5659. Originally part of an intelligence macrobox to enhance mathematical ability, T56-WA 5659 has become a standard option in nearly all pre-planned children. The effects of this defective sequence are not yet known, but at least twenty children in our city have died after suffering from symptoms similar to grand mal epilepsy. Nationwide casualties are unknown. The Parental Pre-Natal Design Administration advises parents of PPC children with this option to immediately contact your doctors and design specialists for advice and treatment. Younger children may be eligible to receive whole body retroviral therapy. The Rifkin Society is charging government regulatory agencies with a wholesale cover-up. For more detailed information, please refer to our LitVid on-line and call—"

Letitia turned to see her mother in the dining room door, holding a bowl and watching the TV with grim satisfaction. When she noticed her daughter's expression, she suddenly changed her expression to sad. "How unfortunate," she said. "I wonder how far it will go."

Letitia did not eat much dinner, nor did she sleep more than a couple of hours that night. The weekend seemed to stretch on forever.

Leroux compared the laserfoam sculptures to her face, turning her chin this way and that with gentle hands before the green room mirror. As Leroux worked to test the molds on Letitia, humming softly to himself, the rest of the drama group rehearsed a scene that did not require her presence. When they were done, Reena walked into the green room and stood behind them, watching. Letitia smiled stiffly through the hastily applied sheets and mounds of skinlike plastic.

"You're going to look great," Reena said.

"I'm going to look *old*," Letitia said, trying for a joke.

"I hope you aren't worried about that," Reena said. "Nobody cares, really. They all like you. Even Edna."

"I'm not worried," Letitia said.

Leroux pulled off the pieces and laid them carefully in a box. "Just about got it," he said. "I'm so good I could even make *Reena* look old if she'd let me."

Reena blushed and glared at Leroux. Leroux caught her glare and said, "Well, I *could*."

Letitia decided to let them off this particular hook. "She'd look like an old movie star. I'll be a better grandmother."

"Of course," Leroux said, picking up his box and the sculptures. He walked to the door, a mad headsman. "Just like your great-grandmother."

For a long, silent moment, Reena and Letitia faced each other alone in the green room. The old incandescent makeup lights glowed around the cracked mirror, casting a pearly light on the white walls.

"You're a good actress," Reena said. "It really doesn't matter what you look like."

"Thank you."

"Sometimes I wished I looked like somebody in my family," Reena said.

Without thinking, Letitia said, "But you're beautiful." And she meant it. Reena *was* beautiful; with her Levantine darkness and long black hair, small sharp chin, large hazel-colored almond eyes and thin, ever-so-slightly bowed nose, she was simply lovely, with the kind of face and bearing and intelligence that two or three generations before would have moved her into entertainment, or pushed her into the social circles of the rich and famous. Behind the physical beauty was a sparkle of reserved wit, and something gentle. PPCs were healthier, felt better, and their minds, on the average, were more subtle, more balanced. Letitia did not feel inferior, however; not this time.

Something magic touched them. The previous awkwardness, and her deft destruction of that awkwardness, had moved them into a charmed period. Neither could offend the other; without words, that was a given.

"My parents are beautiful, too. I'm second generation," Reena said.

"Why would you want to look any different?"

"I don't, I suppose. I'm happy with the way I look. But I don't look like my mother or my father. Oh, color, hair, eyes, that sort of thing . . . Still, my mother wasn't happy with her own face. She didn't get along well with my grandmother . . . She blamed her for not matching her face with her personality." Reena grinned. "It's all rather silly."

"Some people are never happy," Letitia observed.

Reena stepped toward the mirror and leaned to see Letitia's reflection. "How does it feel, looking like your grandmother?"

Letitia bit her lip. "Until you asked me to join, I don't think I ever knew." She told about the family album, and examining herself in the mirror—though she did not mention being naked—and comparing herself with the old pictures.

Reena said, "It must have been nice. I'm glad I asked you, even if I was stupid."

"Were you . . ." Letitia paused. The charm was fading, regrettably; she did not know whether her question would be taken as she meant it. "Did you ask me to give me a chance to stop being so silly?"

"No," Reena said steadily. "I asked because we needed an old lady."

Looking at each other, they suddenly laughed, and the charmed moment was replaced by something steadier and longer-lasting: friendship. Letitia took Reena's hand and pressed it. "Thank you," she said.

"You're welcome." Then, with hardly a pause, Reena said, "At least you don't have to worry."

Letitia stared up at her, mouth open, eyes searching.

"Got to go home," Reena said. She squeezed Letitia's shoulder with more than gentle strength, revealing an anger or envy that ran counter to all they had said and done thus far. Reena turned and walked through the green room door, leaving Letitia alone to pick at the last scraps of latex and adhesive.

The disaster grew. Letitia listened to the news in her room late that night, whispers in her ear, projected ghosts of newscasters and doctors and scientists dancing before her eyes, telling her things she did not really understand, could only feel. A monster was walking through her generation, but it would not touch her.

Going to school on Monday, she saw students clustered in hallways before the bell, somber, talking in low voices, glancing at her as she passed. In her second period class, she learned that Leroux had died over the weekend. "He was superwhiz," a tall, athletic girl told her neighbor. "They don't die, they just blitz, usually. But he *died*."

Letitia retreated to the old lavatory at the beginning of lunch break, found it empty, but did not look into the mirror. She knew what she looked like and accepted it. What she found difficult to accept was a new feeling inside her. The young Letitia was gone. She could not live on a battlefield and remain a child. She thought about slender, elfin Leroux touching her face with gentle, professional admiration—strong, cool fingers. She remembered the last time she saw him as he carried her sculpted heads under his arms. Her eyes filled but the tears would not fall, and she went to lunch empty, fearful, confused. She did not apply for counseling, however. This was something she had to face on her own.

Nothing much happened the next few days. The rehearsals went smoothly in the evenings as the date of the play approached. Letitia learned her lines easily enough. Her role had a sadness that matched her mood. On Wednesday evening, after rehearsal, she joined Reena and Fayette at a supermarket sandwich stand near the school. Letitia did not tell her parents she would be late; she felt the need to not be responsible to anyone but her immediate peers. Jane would be upset, she knew, but not for long; this was a *necessity*.

Neither Reena nor Fayette mentioned the troubles directly. They were fairylike in their gaiety. They kidded Letitia about having to do without makeup now, and it seemed funny, despite their hidden grief. They ate sandwiches and drank fruit sodas and talked about what they would be when they grew up.

"Things didn't used to be so easy," Fayette said. "Kids didn't have so many options. Schools weren't very efficient at training for the real world; they were academic."

"Learning was slower," Letitia said.

"So were the kids," Reena said with an irresponsible grin.

"I resent that," Letitia said. Then, in unison, they all chanted, *"I don't deny it, I just resent it!"* Their laughter caught the attention of an older couple sitting in a corner. Even if the man and woman were not angry, Letitia wanted them to be, and she bowed her head down, giggling into her straw, then snucking bubbles into her nose and choking. Reena made a disapproving face and Fayette covered his mouth, snorting with laughter. Not once did they mention Leroux, but it was as if he sat beside them the whole time, sharing their levity.

It was the closest thing they could have to a wake.

"Have you gone to see your designer, your medical?" Letitia asked Reena behind the stage curtains. The lights were off. Student stagehands moved muslin walls on dollies. Fresh paint smells filled the air.

"No," Reena said. "I'm not worried. I have a different incept."

"Really?"

She nodded. "It's okay. If there was any problem, I wouldn't be here. Don't worry." And nothing more was said.

The night of dress rehearsal came. Letitia put on her own makeup, drawing pencil lines and applying color and shadow; she had practiced and found herself reasonably adept. With Great-Grandmother's photograph before her, she mimicked the jowls she would have in her later years, drew laugh lines around her lips, and completed the effect with a smelly old gray wig dug out of a prop box.

The actors gathered for a rehearsal inspection by Miss Darcy. Dressed in their period costumes, tall and handsome, they all seemed very adult. Letitia didn't mind standing out. Being an old woman gave her special status.

"This time, just relax, do it smooth," said Miss Darcy. "Everybody expects you to flub your lines, so you'll probably do them all perfectly. We'll have an audience, but they're here to forgive our mistakes, not laugh at them. This one," Miss Darcy said, pausing, "is for Mr. Leroux."

They nodded solemnly.

"Tomorrow, when we put on the first show, that's going to be for you."

They took their places in the wings. Letitia stood behind Reena, who would be first on stage. Reena shot her a quick smile, nervous.

"How's your stomach?" she whispered.

Letitia pretended to gag herself with a finger.

"TB," Reena accused lightly

"RC," Letitia replied. They shook hands firmly.

The curtain went up. The auditorium was half filled with parents and friends and relatives. Letitia's parents were out there. The darkness beyond the stagelights seemed so profound it should have been filled with stars and nebulae. Would her small voice reach that far? The recorded music before the first act came to its quiet end. Reena made a move to go on stage, then stopped. Letitia nudged her. "Come on."

Reena pivoted to look at her, head leaning to one side, and Letitia saw a large tear drip from her left eye. Fascinated, she watched the tear flow slowly down Reena's cheek and spot the satin of her gown.

"I'm sorry," Reena whispered, lips twitching. "I can't do it now. Tell. *Tell.*"

Horrified, Letitia reached out, tried to stop her, lift her, push her back into place, but Reena was too heavy and she could not stop her fall, only slow it. Reena's feet kicked out like a horse's, bruising Letitia's legs, all in apparent silence, and her eyes were bright and empty and wet, fluttering, showing the whites.

Letitia bent over her, afraid to touch her, afraid not to, unaware she was shrieking.

Fayette and Edna Corman stood behind her, equally helpless.

Reena lay still like a twisted doll, face upturned, eyes moving slowly to Letitia, vibrating, becoming still.

"Not you!" Letitia screamed, and barely heard the commotion in the audience. "Please, God, let it be me, not her!"

Fayette backed away and Miss Darcy came into the light, grabbing Letitia's shoulders. She shook free.

"Not her," Letitia sobbed. The medicals arrived and surrounded Reena, blocking her from the eyes of all around. Miss Darcy firmly, almost brutally, pushed her students from the stage and herded them into the green room. Her face was stiff as a mask, eyes stark in the paleness.

"We have to *do* something!" Letitia said, holding up her hands, beseeching.

"Control yourself," Miss Darcy said sharply. "Everything's being done that can be done."

Fayette said, "What about the play?"

Everyone stared at him.

"Sorry," he said, lip quivering. "I'm an idiot."

Jane, Donald, and Roald came to the green room and Letitia hugged her mother fiercely, eyes shut tight, burying her face in Jane's shoulder. They escorted her outside, where a few students and parents still milled about in the early evening. "We should go home," Jane said.

"We have to stay here and find out if she's all right." Letitia pushed away from Jane's arms and looked at the people. "They're so frightened. I know they are. She's frightened, too. I saw her. She told me—" Her voice hitched. "She told me—"

"We'll stay for a little while," her father said. He walked off to talk to another man. They conversed for a while, the man shook his head, they parted. Roald stood away from them, hands stuffed into his pockets, dismayed, young, uncomfortable.

"All right," Donald said a few minutes later. "We're not going to find out anything tonight. Let's go home."

This time, she did not protest. Home, she locked herself in her bedroom. She did not need to know. She had seen it happen; anything else was self-delusion.

Her father came to the door an hour later, rapped gently. Letitia came up from a troubled doze and got off the bed to let him in.

"We're very sorry," he said.

"Thanks," she murmured, returning to the bed. He sat beside her. She might have been eight or nine again; she looked around the room, at toys and books, knickknacks.

"Your teacher, Miss Darcy, called. She said to tell you, Reena Cathcart died. She was dead by the time they got her to the hospital. Your mother and I have been watching the vids. A lot of children are very sick. A lot have died." He touched her head, patted the crown gently. "I think you know now why we wanted a natural child. There were risks."

"That's not fair," she said. "You didn't have us . . ." She hiccupped. "The way you did, because you thought there would be risks. You talk as if there's something wrong with these . . . people."

"Isn't there?" Donald asked, eyes suddenly flinty. "They're defective."

"They're my friends!" Letitia shouted.

"Please," Donald said, wincing.

She got to her knees on the bed, tears again flowing. "There's nothing wrong with them! They're people! They're just sick, that's all."

"You're not making sense," Donald said.

"I talked to her," Letitia said. "She must have known. You can't just say there's something wrong with them. That isn't enough."

"Their parents should have known," Donald pursued, voice rising. "Letitia . . ."

"Leave me alone," she demanded. He stood up hastily, confused, and walked out, closing the door. She lay back on the bed, wondering what Reena had wanted her to say, and to whom. "I'll do it," she whispered.

In the morning, breakfast was silent. Roald ate his cereal with caution, glancing at the others with wide, concerned eyes. Letitia ate little, pushed away from the table, said, "I'm going to her funeral."

"We don't know—" Jane said.

"I'm going."

Letitia went to only one funeral: Reena's. With a puzzled expression, she watched Reena's parents from across the grave, wondering about them, comparing them to Jane and Donald. She did not cry. She came home and wrote down the things she had thought.

That school year was the worst. One hundred and twelve students from the school died. Another two hundred became very ill.

Rick Fayette died.

The drama class continued, but no plays were presented. The school was quiet. Many students had been withdrawn from classes; Letitia watched the hysteria mount, listened to rumors that it was a plague, not a PPC error.

It was not a plague.

Across the nation, two million children became ill. One million died.

Letitia read, without really absorbing the truth all at once, that it was the worst disaster in the history of the United States. Riots destroyed PPC centers. Women carrying PPC babies demanded abortions. The Rifkin Society became a political force of considerable influence.

Each day, after school, listening to the news, everything about her existence seemed trivial. Their family was healthy. They were growing up normally.

Edna Corman approached her in school at the end of one day, two weeks before graduation. "Can we talk?" she asked. "Someplace quiet."

"Sure," Letitia said. They had not become close friends, but she found Edna tolerable. Letitia took her into the old bathroom and they stood surrounded by the echoing white tiles.

"You know, everybody, I mean the older people, they stare at me, at us," Edna said. "Like we're going to fall over any minute. It's really bad. I don't think I'm going to get sick, but . . . It's like people are afraid to touch me."

"I know," Letitia said.

"Why is that?" Edna said, voice trembling.

"I don't know," Letitia said. Edna just stood before her, hands limp.

"Was it our fault?" she asked.

"No. You know that."

"Please tell me."

"Tell you what?"

"What we can do to make it right."

Letitia looked at her for a moment, and then extended her arms, took her by the shoulders, drew her closer, and hugged her. "Remember," she said.

Five days before graduation, Letitia asked Rutger if she could give a speech at the ceremonies. Rutger sat behind his desk, folded his hands, and said, "Why?"

"Because there are some things nobody's saying," Letitia told him. "And they should be said. If nobody else will say them, then . . ." She swallowed hard. "Maybe I can."

He regarded her dubiously for a moment. "You really think there's something important that you can say?"

She faced him down. Nodded.

"Write the speech," he said. "Show it to me."

She pulled a piece of paper out of her pocket. He read it carefully, shook his head—she thought at first in denial—and then handed it back to her.

Waiting in the wings to go on stage, Letitia Blakely listened to the low murmur of the young crowd in the auditorium. She avoided looking at the spot near the curtain where Reena had fallen.

Rutger acted as master of ceremonies. The proceedings were

somber. She began to feel as if she were making a terrible mistake. She was too young to say these things; it would sound horribly awkward, even childish.

Rutger made his opening remarks, then introduced her and motioned for her to come on stage. Letitia deliberately walked through the spot near the curtain, paused briefly, closed her eyes and took a deep breath, as if to infuse herself with whatever remained of Reena. She walked past Miss Darcy, who seemed to want to ask a question.

Her throat seized. She rubbed her neck, blinked at the lights on the catwalk, tried to see the faces beyond the brightness. They were just smudges in great darkness. She glanced out of the corner of her eye and saw Miss Darcy nodding, *Go ahead.*

"This has been a bad time for all of us," she began, voice high and scratchy. She cleared her throat. "I've lost a lot of friends, and so have you. Maybe you've lost sons and daughters. I think, even from there, looking at me, you can tell I'm not . . . designed. I'm natural. I don't have to wonder whether I'll get sick and die. But I . . ." She cleared her throat again. It wasn't getting easier. "I thought someone like me could tell you something important.

"People have made mistakes, bad mistakes. But you are not a mistake. I mean . . . they weren't mistaken to make you. I can only dream about doing some of the things you'll do. Some of you are made to live in space for a long time, and I can't do that. Some of you will think things I can't, and go places I won't . . . travel to see the stars. We're different in a lot of ways, but I just thought it was important to tell you . . ." She wasn't following the prepared speech. She couldn't. "I love you. I don't care what the others say. We love you. You are very important. Please don't forget that."

The silence was complete. She felt like slinking away. Instead, she straightened, thanked them, hearing not a word, not a restless whisper, then bowed her head from the catwalk glare and the interstellar night beyond.

Miss Darcy, stiff and formal, reached her arm out as Letitia passed by. They shook hands firmly, and Letitia saw, for the first time, that Miss Darcy looked upon her as an equal.

While the ceremonies continued, Letitia stood backstage examining the old wood floor, the curtains and counterweights and flies, the catwalk.

It seemed very long ago she had dreamed what she felt now, this unspecified love, not for family, not for herself. Love for something she could not have known back then; love for children not her own, yet hers none the less.

Brothers.

Sisters.

Family.

A MARTIAN RICOROSO

In 1976, the Viking lander settled down on Mars, scooped up a shovel full of soil, and tested it. The results were negative . . . or inconclusive. But for a brief moment, following a radio announcement that organic chemistry had been revealed in the samples, I was positive life had been discovered on another planet. That feeling was unforgettable.

"A Martian Ricorso" scored my first magazine cover, a beautiful piece by Rick Sternbach on the February 1976 issue of Analog. I carried a copy of the magazine around for days, then wrote a letter to Rick. We became friends. The original cover art graces our house.

Today, there are still headlines about water being discovered on Mars. A cyclical Mars, as proposed in this story, seems less likely now, but current discoveries do not rule it out—and may actually lend it some support. Mars is probably more like I described it in MOVING MARS (1993) or WAR DOGS (2014), with a rich, wet past eventually giving way to steady aridity and cold. But this was my first bold attempt to stick a scientific hypothesis into a story of hard science fiction, and who knows?

I might still win the lottery.

Martian night. The cold and the dark and the stars are so intense they make music, like the tinkle of ice xylophones. Maybe it's my air tank hose scraping; maybe it's my imagination. Maybe it's real.

Standing on the edge of Swift Plateau, I'm afraid to move or breathe deeply, as I whisper into the helmet recorder, lest I disturb something holy: God's sharp scrutiny of Edom Crater. I've gone outside, away from the lander and my crewmates, to order my thoughts about what has happened.

The Martians came just twelve hours ago, like a tide of five-foot-high lab rats running and leaping on their hind legs. To us, it seemed as if they were storming the lander, intent on knocking it over. But it seems more likely now we were only in their way.

We didn't just sit here and let them swamp us. We didn't hurt or kill any of them—Cobb beat at them with a roll of foil and I used the parasol of the damaged directenna to shoo them off. First contact, and we must have looked like clowns in an old silent comedy. The glider wings came perilously close to being severely damaged. We foiled and doped what few tears had been made before nightfall. They should suffice, if the polymer sylar adhesive is as good as advertised.

But our luck this expedition held true to form. The stretching frame's pliers broke during the repairs. We can't afford another swarm, even if they're just curious.

Cobb and Link have had bitter arguments about self-defense. I've managed to stay out of the debate so far, but my sympathies at the moment lie with Cobb. Still, my instinctive need to stay alive won't stop me from feeling guilty if we *do* have to kill a few Martians.

We've had quite a series of revelation the last few days. Schiaparelli was right. And Percival Lowell, the eccentric genius of my own home state. He was not as errant an observer as we've all thought this past century.

I have an hour before I have to return to the lander and join my mates in sleep. I can last here in the cold that long. Loneliness may weigh on me sooner, however. I don't know why I came out here; perhaps just to clear my head. We've all been in such a constrained, tightly controlled, oh-so-disguised panic. I need to know what I think of the whole situation, without benefit of comrades.

The plateau wall and the floor of Edom are so barren, with

the exception, all around me, of the prints of thousands of feet . . . Empty and lifeless.

Tomorrow morning we'll brace the crumpled starboard sled pads and rig an emergency automatic release for the RATO units on the glider. Her wings are already partially spread for a fabric inspection—accomplished just before the Winter Troops attacked—and we've finished transferring fuel from the lander to the orbit booster. When the glider gets us up above the third jet stream, by careful tacking we hope to be in just the right position to launch our little capsule up and out. A few minutes burn and we can dock with the orbiter, if Willy is willing to pick us up.

If we don't make it, these records will be all there is to explain, on some future date, why we never made it back. I'll feed the helmet memory into the lander telterm, stacked with flight telemetry and other data in computer-annotated garble, and instruct the computer to store it all on hard-copy glass disks.

The dust storm that sand-scrubbed our directenna and forced me to this expedient subsided two days ago. We have not reported our most recent discovery to mission control; we are still organizing our thoughts. After all, it's a momentous occasion. We don't want to make any slips and upset the folks back on Earth.

Here's the situation. We can no longer communicate directly with Earth. We are left with the capsule radio, which Willy can pick up and boost for re-broadcast whenever the conditions are good enough. At the moment, conditions are terrible. The solar storm that dogged our Icarus heels on the way out, forcing us deep inside Willy's capacious hull, is still active. The effect on the Martian atmosphere has been most surprising.

There's a communicator on the glider body as well, but that's strictly short-range and good for little more than telemetry. So we have very garbled transmissions going out, reasonably clear coming back, and about twenty minutes of complete blackout when Willy is out of line of sight, behind or below Mars.

We may be able to hit Willy with the surveyor's laser, adapted for signal transmission. For the moment we're going to save that for the truly important communications, like time of launch and approximate altitude, calculated from the fuel we have left after the transfer piping exploded . . . was it three days ago? When the night got colder than the engineers thought possible and exceeded the specs on the insulation.

I'm going back in now. It's too much out here. Too dark. No moons visible.

Now at the telterm keyboard. Down to meaningful monologue.

Mission Commander Linker, First Pilot Cobb, and myself, Mission Specialist Mercer, have finished ninety percent of the local survey work and compared it with Willy's detailed mapping. What we've found is fascinating.

At one time many lines and stripes crisscrossed Mars. To an isolated observer they looked very much like canals. Until a century ago, any good telescope on Earth, on a good night, could have revealed them to sharp-eyed observers. As the decades passed, it was not the increased skill of astronomers and the improved quality of instruments that erased these lines, but the end of the final century of the *Anno Fecundis.* Is my Latin proper? I have no dictionary to consult. With the end of the Fertile Year, a thousand centuries long, came the first bleak sandy winds and the lowering of the Martian jet streams. They picked up sand and scoured.

The structures must have been like fairy palaces before they were swept down. I once saw a marketplace full of empty vinegar jugs in the Philippines, made from melted Coca Cola bottles. They used glass so thin you could break them with a thumbnail tap in the right place—but they easily held twenty or thirty gallons of liquid. These colonies must have looked like grape-clusters of thousands of thin glass vinegar bottles, dark as emeralds, mounted on spider-web stilts and fed with water pumped through veins as big as Roman aqueducts. We surveyed one field and found the fragments buried in red sand across a strip thirty miles wide. From a mile or so up, the edge of the structure can still be seen, if you know where to look. Neither of the two previous expeditions found them. They're *ours.*

Linker believes these ribbons once stretched clear around the planet. Before the sand storm, Willy's infrared mapping proved him correct. We could trace belts of ruins in almost all the places Lowell had mapped—even the civic centers some of his followers said he saw. Aqueducts laced the planet like the ribs on a basketball, meeting at ocean-sized black pools covered with glassy membranes. The pools were filled by a thin purple liquid, a kind of resin, warming in the sun, undergoing photosynthesis. The resin was pumped at high pressure through tissue and glass tubes, nourishing the plantlike colonies inhabiting the bottles. They probably lacked any sort of intelligence. But their architectural feats put ours to shame, nonetheless.

Sandstorms and the rapidly drying weather of the last century are still bringing down the delicate structures. Ninety-five percent or more have fallen already, and the rest are too rickety to safely investigate. They are still magnificent. Standing on the edge of a plain of broken bottles and shattered pylons stretching to the horizon, we can't help but feel very young and very small.

A week ago, we discovered they've left spores buried deep in the red-orange sand, tougher than coconuts and about the size of medicine balls. Six days ago, we learned that Mars provides children for all his seasons. Digging for ice lenses that Willy had located, we came across a cache of leathery eggshells in a cavern shored up with a translucent organic cement. We didn't have time to investigate thoroughly. We managed to take a few samples of the cement—scrupulously avoiding disturbing the eggs—and vacated before our tanks ran out. While cutting out the samples, we noticed that the walls had been patterned with hexagonal carvings, whether as a structural aid or decoration we couldn't tell.

Yesterday, that is, about twenty-six hours ago, we saw what we believe must be the hatchlings: the Winter Troops, five or six of them, walking along the edge of the plateau, not much more than white specks from where we sat in the lander.

We took the sand sled five kilometers from the landing to investigate the cache again, and to see what Willy's mapping revealed as the last standing fragments of an aqueduct bridge in our vicinity. We didn't locate our original cache. Collapsed caverns filled with leathery egg skins pocked the landscape. More than sandstorms had been at the ruins. The bridges rested on the seeds of their own destruction—packs of kangaroo-rat Winter Troops crawled over the structure like ants on a carcass, breaking off bits, eating or just cavorting like sand fleas.

Linker named them. He snapped pictures enthusiastically. As a trained exobiologist, he was in a heat of excitement and speculation. His current theory is that the Winter Troops are on a binge of destruction, programmed into their genes and irrevocable. We retreated on the sled, unsure whether we might be swamped as well.

Linker babbled—pardon me, expounded—all the way back to the lander. "It's like Giambattista Vico resurrected from the historian's boneyard!" We barely listened; Linker was way over our heads. "Out with the old, in with the new! Vico's historical *ricorso* exemplified."

Cobb and I were less enthusiastic. "Indiscriminate buggers," he grumbled. "How long before they find us?"

I had no immediate reaction. As in every situation in my life, I decided to sit on my emotions and wait things out.

Cobb was prescient. Unluckily for us, our lander and glider rise above the ground like a stray shard of an aqueduct-bridge. At that stage of their young lives, the Winter Troops couldn't help but swarm over everything. An hour ago, I braved the hash and our own confusion and sent out descriptions of our find. So far, we've received no reply to our requests for First Contact instructions. The likelihood was so small nobody planned for it. The message was probably garbled.

But enough pessimism. Where does this leave us, so far, in our speculations?

Gentlemen, we sit on the cusp between cycles. We witness the end of the green and russet Mars of Earth's youth, ribbed with fairy bridges and restrained seas, and come upon a grimmer, more practical world, buttoning down for the long winter. We haven't studied the white Martians in any detail, so there's no way of knowing whether or not they're intelligent. They may be the new masters of Mars. How do we meet them—passively, as Linker seems to think we should, or as Cobb believes: defending ourselves against creatures who may or may not belong to our fraternal order of big-brained cogitators? What can we expect if we *don't* defend ourselves?

Let your theologians and exobiologists speculate on *that.* Are we to be the first to commit the sin of an interplanetary Cain? Or are the Martians?

It will take us nine or ten hours tomorrow to brace the lander pads. Our glider sits with sylar wings half-flexed, crinkling and snapping in the rising wind, silver against the low sienna hills of Swift Plateau. Sunlight strikes the top of the plateau. Pink sky to the east; fairy bridges, fairy landscape! Pink and dreamlike. Ice-crystal clouds obscure a faded curtain of aurora. The sky overhead is black as obsidian. Between the pink sunrise and the obsidian is a band of hematite, a dark rainbow like carnival glass, possibly caused by crystalline powder from the aqueduct bridges elevated into the jet streams. From our vantage on the plateau, we can see dust devils crossing Edom's eastern rim and the tortured mounds and chasms of the Moab-Marduk range, rising like the pillars of some ancient temple. Boaz and Jachin, perhaps.

Since writing the above, I've napped for an hour. Willy relayed a new chart. He's found construction near the western rim of Edom Crater—recent construction, not there a few days ago when the area was last surveyed. Hexagonal formations—walls and what could be roads. From his altitude, they must rival the Great Wall of China. How could such monumental works be erected in just days? Were they missed on the previous passes? Not likely.

So there we have it. The colonies that erected the aqueduct-bridges were not the only architects on Mars. The Winter Troops are demonstrating their skills. But are they intelligent, or just following some instinctual imperative? Or *both?*

My shipmates are sleeping again. They've been working hard, as have I, and their sleep is sound. The telterm clicking doesn't wake them. I can't sleep much—no more than an hour at a stretch before I awake in a sweat. My body is running on supercharge and I'm not ready to resort to tranquilizers. So here I sit, endlessly observing. Linker is the largest of us. Though I worked with him for three years before this mission, and we have spent over eight months in close quarters, I hardly know the man. He's not a quiet man, and he's always willing to express his opinions, but he still surprises me. He has a way of raising his eyebrows when he listens, opening his dark eyes wide and wrinkling his forehead, that reminds me of a dog cocking its ears. But it would have to be a devilishly bright dog. Perhaps I haven't plumbed Linker's depths because I'd go in over my head if I tried. He's certainly more dedicated than either Cobb or I. He's been in the Navy for twenty-one years, fifteen of them in space, specializing in planetary geology and half a dozen other disciplines.

Cobb, on the other hand, can be read like a book. He tends toward bulk, more in appearance than mass; he weighs only a little more than I do. He's shorter and works with a frown; it seems to take him twice his normal concentration to finish some tasks. I do him no injustice by saying that; he gets the work done, and well, but it costs him more than it would Linker. The extra effort sometimes takes the edge off his nonessential reasoning. He's not light on his mental feet, particularly in a situation like this. Doggedness and quick reflexes brought him to his prominence in the Mars lander program; I respect him none the less for that, but. . . . He tends to the technical, loving machines more than men.

Linker and I once had him close to tears on the outward voyage. We conversed on five or six subjects at once, switching topics every three or four minutes. It was a cruel game and neither of us are proud of it, but I for one can peg part of the blame on the mission designers. Three is too small a community for a three-year mission in space. Hell. Space has been billed as making children out of us all, eh? A double-edged sword.

I have (as certain passages above might indicate) been thinking about the Bible lately. My old childhood background has been stimulated by danger and moral dilemmas—hair of the dog that bit me. The maps of Mars, with their Biblical names, have contributed to my thoughts. We're not far from Eden as gliders go. We sit in fabled Moab, above the Moab-Marduk range, Marduk being one of the chief "baals" in the Old Testament. Edom Crater—Edom means red, an appropriate name for a Martian crater. I have red hair. Call me Esau!

Mesogaea—Middle Earth. Other hair, other dogs.

Back on the recorder again. Time weighs heavily on me. I've retreated to the equipment bay to weather a bit of grumpiness between Linker and Cobb. Actually, it was an out and out argument. Linker, still the pacifist, expressed his horror of committing murder against another species. His scruples are oddly selective—he fought in Eritrea in the nineties. Neither has been restrained by rank; this could lead to really ugly confrontations, unless danger straightens out all of us and makes us brothers. Three comrades, good and true, tolerant of different opinions.

Oh, God, here they come again! I'm looking east out the equipment bay port. They must number five or six thousand, lining a distant hill like Indians. That many attacking . . . Cobb can have his way and it won't matter, we'll still be finished.

If they rip a section of wing sylar larger than we can stretch by hand, we're stuck.

That was close. Cobb fired bursts of the surveyor's laser over their heads. Enough dust had been raised by their movement and by the wind to make a fine display. They moved back slowly and then vanished beyond the hill. The laser is powerful enough to burn them should necessity arise.

Linker has as much as said he'd rather die than extend the sin of Cain. I'm less worried about that sin than I am about lifting off. We have yet to brace the sled pad. Linker's out below the starboard hatch, rigging the sling that will level the glider body when the RATOs fire.

More dust to the east. Night is coming slowly. After the sun sets, it'll be too cold to work outside for long. If the Winter Troops are water-based, how do they last the night? Anti-freeze in their blood, like Arctic fish? Can they keep up their activity in temperatures between fifty and one hundred below? Or will we be out of danger until sunrise, with the Martians warm in their blankets, and we in our trundle-bed, nightmaring?

I've helped Linker rig the sling. We've all worked on the sled pad. Cobb has mounted the laser on a television tripod—clever warrior. Linker advised him to beware the fraying power cable. Cobb looked at him with a sad sort of resentment and went about his work. Other than the few bickerings and personality games of the trip out, until the last few days, we've managed to keep respect for one another. Now we're slipping. At one time, I had the fantasy we'd all finish the mission lifetime friends, visiting each other years after, comparing pictures of our grandchildren and complaining about the quality of young officers. What a dream.

Steam rises from the hoarfrost accumulated during the night. It vanishes like a tramp after dinner.

Should we wish to send a message to Willy now, we shall have to unship the laser and remount it. The hash has increased and Willy says his pickup is deteriorating.

More ice falls during the night. Linker kept track of them. My insomnia has communicated itself to him—ideal for standing long watches. Ice falls are more frequent here than on Earth—the leavings of comets and the asteroids come through this thin atmosphere more easily. A small chunk came to within a sixty meters of our site, leaving an impressive crater.

* * *

Another break. Willy has relayed a message from Control. They managed to pick up and reconstruct our request for instructions on First Contact. They must have thought we were joking. Here's part of the transmission:

"We think you're not happy just finding giant vegetables on Mars. Dr. Wender advised on Martians . . . (hash) . . . some clear indications of their ability to fire large cylindrical bodies into space. Beware tripod machines. Second opinion from Frank: Not all green Martians are Tharks. He wants sample from Dejah Thoris—can you arrange for egg?"

I put on a pressure suit and went for a walk after the disappointment of the transmission. Linker suited up after me and followed for a while. I armed myself with a piece of aluminum from the salvaged pad. He carried nothing.

Swift Plateau is about four hundred kilometers across. At its northern perimeter, an aqueduct once hoisted itself a kilometer or so and vaulted across the flats, covering fifteen kilometers of upland before dropping over the south rim into the Moab-Marduk Range. Our landing site is a kilometer from the closest stretch of fragments. Linker followed me to the edge of the field of green and blue grass, keeping quiet, looking behind apprehensively as if he expected something to pop up between us and the lander.

I had a notebook in my satchel and paused to sketch some of the piers the Winter Troops hadn't yet brought down. None were over four meters tall.

"I'm afraid of them," Linker said on the suit radio. I stopped my sketching to look at him.

"So?" I inquired with a touch of irritation. "We're all afraid of them."

"I'm not afraid because they'll hurt me. It's because of what they might bring out in me, if I give them half a chance. I don't want to hate them."

"Not even Cobb *hates* them," I said.

"Oh, yes he does," Linker said, nodding his head within the bulky helmet. "But he's afraid for his life. I fear for my self-respect. I can't understand them. They're irrational. They don't seem to *see* us. They run around us, fulfilling some mission . . . they don't care whether we live or die. Yet I have to respect them—they're *alien.* The first intelligent creatures we've ever met."

"If they're intelligent," I reminded him.

"Come on, Mercer, they must be. They build."

"So did these," I said, waving a gloved hand at the field of shattered green bottles.

"I'm trying to make myself clear," he said, exasperated. "When I was in Eritrea, I didn't understand the nationalists. Or the communists. Both sides were willing to kill their own people or allow them to starve if it won some small objective. It was sick. I even hated the ones we were supporting."

"The Martians aren't Africans," I said. "We can't expect to understand their motives."

"Comes back double, then, don't you see? I want to understand, to know why—"

He suddenly switched off his radio, raised his hands in frustration, and turned to walk back to the lander.

Our automatic interrupts clicked on and Cobb spoke to us. "That's it, friends. We're blanketed by hash. I can't get through to Willy. We'll have to punch through with the laser."

"I'm on my way back," Linker said. "I'll help you set it up."

In a few minutes, I was alone on the field of ruins. I sat on a weather-pocked boulder and took out my sketchbook. I mapped the directions from which we had been approached and attacked and compared them with the site of the eggs we had found. What I was looking for, with such ridiculously slim evidence, was a clear pattern of migration—say, from the hatcheries in a line with the sunrise. Nothing came of it.

Disgusted at my desperation, I got lost in a fog of something approaching misery when I glanced up . . . And jumped to my feet so fast I leaped a good three feet into the air, twisting my ankle as I came down. Two white Martians stared at me with their wide, blank gray eyes, eyelashes as long and expressive as a camel's. The fingers on their hands—each had three arms, but only two legs—shivered like mouse-whiskers, not nervous but seeking information. We had been too involved fending them off before to take note of their features. Now, at a loss what to do, I had all the time in the world.

Three long webbed toes, leathery and dead-looking like sticks, met an odd two-jointed ankle which even now I can't reproduce on paper. Their thighs were knotted with muscles and covered with red and white stippled fur. They could hop or run like frightened deer—that much I knew from experience. Their hips were thickly furred. They defied my few semesters of training in biology by having trilateral symmetry between hips and neck, and bilateral below the hips. Three arms met at ingenious triangular shoulders, rising to short necks and mouse-like faces. Their ears were mounted atop their heads and could fan out like unfolded directennas, or hide away if rough activity threatened them.

The Martians were fast when they wanted to be, and I had no idea what else they could eat besides the ruins, so I made no false moves.

One whickered like a horse, its voice reedy and distant in the thin atmosphere. The noise must have been impressively loud to reach my small, helmeted ears. It looked behind itself, twisting its head one-eighty to look as its behind-arm scratched a tuft of hair on its right shoulder. The back fur rippled appreciatively. Parrot-like, the head returned to calmly stare at me.

After half an hour, I sat down again on the boulder. I could still see the lander and the linear glint of the glider wings, but there was no sign of Cobb or Linker. Nobody was searching for me. My suit was getting cold. Slowly, I checked my battery pack gauge and saw it was showing low charge. Cautiously, in distinct stages, I stood and brushed my pressure suit. The Martian to my right jerked, fingers trembling, but I held my pose, apprehensive. With a swift motion, with its behind-arm it pulled a green, fibrous piece of aqueduct-bridge girder from its stiff rump fur and held it out to me. The piece was about thirty centimeters long, chewed all around.

I straightened, extended one hand and accepted the gift.

Without further ado, the Martians twisted around and bounded across the plateau, running and leaping in alternation.

Clutching my gift, I returned to the lander. By the time I arrived, my feet and fingers were numb.

The tripod lay on the ground, legs broken. The laser was nowhere to be seen. I had a moment's panic, thinking the lander had been attacked—but since I had kept it in sight, that didn't seem likely.

I climbed into the lander's primary lock. Inside, Linker clutched the laser in both hands, one finger resting lightly, nervously, on the unsheathed and delicate scandium-garnet rod. Cobb sat on the opposite side of the cabin, barely two meters from Linker, fuming.

"What in hell is going on?" I asked, puffing on my fingers and stamping my feet.

"Listen, Thoreau," Cobb said bitterly, "while you were out communing with nature, Mr. Gandhi here decided to make sure we can't harm any of the sweet little creatures."

I turned to Linker, focusing on his finger and the garnet. "What in hell are you doing?"

"I'm not sure, Dan," he answered calmly, face blank. "I have a firm conviction, that's all I know. I have to be firm. Otherwise I'll be just like you and Cobb."

"I have a conviction, too," Cobb said. "I'm convinced you're nuts."

"You're seriously thinking about breaking that garnet?" I asked.

"Damned serious."

"We can fight them off with other things if we have to," I reasoned. "The assay charges, the core sample gun—"

"Don't give Cobb any more ideas," Linker said.

"But we can't talk to Willy if you break that garnet."

"Cobb saw two of the Winter Troops. He was going to take a pot-shot at them with this." Linker lifted the laser.

I blinked for a few seconds, feeling myself flush with anger. "Jesus. Cobb, is that true?"

"I was sighting on them, in case there were more."

"Were you going to shoot?"

"If it was convenient. They might have been a vanguard."

"That's not very rational," I observed.

"I'm not sure I'm being rational, either," Linker said, fully aware how fragmented we now were, the sadness we felt rising to the surface. His eyes were doglike, searching my face for understanding, or at least a way to understand himself.

"I'll do anything necessary to make sure we all survive," Cobb said. "If that means killing a few Martians, I'll do it. If it means overruling the mission commander, I'll do that, too."

"He refused to put the laser down, even when I gave him a direct order. That's mutiny."

"This isn't getting us anywhere," Cobb said.

"I won't vouch for your sanity," I said to Linker. "Not if you break that garnet. And I won't vouch for Cobb's, either. Taking pot-shots at possibly intelligent aliens." I remembered the stick. Damn it, they *were* intelligent! They had to be, advancing on a stranger and giving him a gift . . . "I don't know what sort of speculative First Contact training we should have had, but in spirit if not in letter, Linker has to be closer to the ideal than you."

"We should be testing the brace on the pad and leveling the field in front of the glider," Cobb said. "When we get out to orbit, we can argue philosophy all the way home. And to get home, we *need the laser.*"

Linker nodded. "Let's just agree not to use it for anything but communication."

I looked at Cobb, finally making my decision, and wondering whether I was crazy, too. "I think Linker's right."

"OK," Cobb said softly. "But there's going to be a hell of a row after we debrief."

"That's an understatement," I said.

This record, even if it survives, will probably be kept in the administration files for fifty or sixty years—or longer—to "protect the feelings of the families." But who can gainsay the judgment of the folks who put us here? Not I, humble Thoreau on Mars, as Cobb described me.

I did not reveal the stick gift to my crewmates until the laser had been remounted in the lander. I simply lay it on the table, wrapped in an airtight, transparent specimen bag, while we rested and sipped hot chocolate.

Linker was the first to pick it up. He looked at me, puzzled.

"We have enough samples, don't we?" he asked.

"It's been chewed on," I pointed out, reaching to run my finger along the stick's surface. I told them about the two Martians. Cobb looked decidedly uncomfortable.

"Did they chew on it in your presence?" Linker asked.

"No."

"Maybe they were exchanging food," Cobb said. "A peace offering?" His expression was sad, as if all the energy and anger had been drained and nothing was left but regret.

"It's more than food," Linker said. "It's like stick-writing . . . Ogham. The Irish and Britons used something similar centuries ago. Notches on the side of a stone or stick—a kind of alphabet. But this is more complex. Here—there's an oval—"

"Unless it's a tooth-mark," I said.

"Whether it's a tooth-mark or not, it isn't random. There are five long marks beside it, and one mark about half the length of the others. That's about equal to one Deimotic month—five and a half days." My respect for Linker increased. He raised his eyebrows, looking for confirmation, and started to hand the stick to me, then stopped and swung it around to Cobb. Mission commander, reintegrating a disgruntled crewmember. A mist of tears came to my eyes.

"I don't think they've reached a high level of technology yet," Linker said.

Cobb looked up from the gift and grinned. "Technology?"

"They built the walls and structures Willy saw. I don't think any of us can argue that they're not intent on changing their environment. Unless we make asses out of ourselves and say their work is no more significant than a beaver dam, it's obvious they're advancing rapidly. They might use notched sticks for relaying information."

"So what's this?" I asked, pointing to the gift.

"Maybe it's a subpoena," Linker said.

While I've been recording the above, Cobb has gone outside to see how long it will take to clear the glider path. The field was chosen to be free of boulders, but anything bigger than a fist could skew us dangerously. The sleds have been deployed. I've finished tamping the braces on the pad. The glider and capsule check out. In an hour we'll lase a message to Willy and give our estimate on launch and rendezvous.

Willy tells us that most of Mesogaea and Memnonia are covered with walls. Meridiani Sinus, according to his telescopic observations, has been criss-crossed with roads or trails. The white Martians are using the old, sand-filled black resin reservoirs for some purpose unknown. Edom Crater is as densely packed as a city. All this in less than two days. There must be millions of hatchlings at work.

I'll pause again now and supervise the glider power-up.

Linker and Cobb are dead.

Jesus, that hurts to write.

We had just tested the RATO automatic timers when a horde of Winter Troops marched across the plateau, about ninety deep and four kilometers abreast. I'm certain they weren't out to get us.

It was one of those migrational sweeps, a screwball mass survey of geography, and incidentally a leveling of all the aqueduct-bridges from the last cycle.

They had given us our chance. Tested our nature and will. We didn't answer.

They caught Linker a half-kilometer from the lander. He had just finished clearing the path. I think they trampled him. They were moving faster than a man can run. I imagine his face, eyebrows rising in query.

Maybe he even tried to smile or greet them, lifting a hand . . .

I can't get that out of my head. I have to concentrate.

Cobb knew exactly what to do. I think he didn't mount the laser solidly, leaving a few brackets loose enough so he could unship it and bring it down, ready for hand use at a minute's notice. He took it outside the ship with just helmet and oxygen—it's about five or six degrees outside, daylight—and fired on the Winter Troops just before they reached the glider. There are dead and dying or blinded Martians all along the edge of the path.

They paid their casualties no heed. They did not bother with us, just pushed around and through, touching nothing, staying away from the area Cobb was sweeping—the edge of the path. They can climb like monkeys. They dropped over the rim of the plateau.

They didn't touch Cobb. The frayed cord on the laser killed him when he stepped on it coming back in.

Where was I? Inside the glider, monitoring the power-up. I couldn't hear a thing. It was all over by the time I got outside.

The laser is gone, but we've already sent our data to Willy. I have the return message. That's all I need for the moment. The glider and capsule are powered and ready. I'll launch it by myself. I can do that.

When Willy's position is right. The timer is going. Everything will be automatic. I'll make it to orbit. Two hours. Less.

I can't bring their bodies with me. I could, but what use? There are no facilities for dead astronauts aboard the orbiter. What hurts is I'll have a better margin with them gone—more fuel for the return. I did not want it that way, I never thought of that, I swear to God.

The glider wings are crackling in the wind. The wind is coming at a perfect angle, thin but fast, about two hundred kilometers an hour. Enough to feel if I were outside.

I trust in an awful lot now that Linker and Cobb are gone. Maybe it'll be over soon and I can stop this writing and stop feeling this pain.

Waiting. Just the right instant for launch. Timers, everything on auto. I sit helpless and wait. My last instructions: three buttons and an instruction to the remotes to expand the wings to takeoff width and increase tension. Like a square-rigger. They check okay, flat and level now, waiting for the best gust and RATO fire. Then they'll drop into the proper configuration, dragonfly wings for high atmosphere.

I spent some time learning Martian anatomy as I cleared the path of the few Cobb had let through. There are still a couple out there. I don't think I'll run them over.

I killed one as a mercy. It was still alive, writhing, in the Martian equivalent of pain. Pain/Cain. I spiked it in the head with a rock pick. It died just like we do.

Linker died innocent.

I think I'm going to be sick.

Here it comes. RATOs on.

I'm in the first jet-stream. Second wing mode—fore and aft foils have been jettisoned. I'm riding directly into the black wind. I can see stars, can see Mars red and brown and gray below.

Third wing mode. All wings jettisoned. Falling, my stomach says. Main engines on the capsule are firing and I'm free of the glider framework. I can see the glare and feel the punch and the wings are twirling far down to port like a child's toy.

In low, uncertain orbit.

Willy's coming.

Last orbit before going home. Willy looked awfully good. I climbed inside of him through the transfer tunnel and requested a long drink of miserable orbiter water. "Hey, Willy Ley," I said, "you're the most beautiful thing I've ever seen." Of course, all he did was take care of me. No accusations. He's the only friend I have now.

I spoke to mission control an hour ago. That was not easy. I'm sitting by the telescope, having pushed Willy's sensors out of the way, doing my own surveying and surmising.

So far, the Winter Troops—I *assume* they're responsible—have zoned and partially built up Mare Tyrennhum, Hesperia, and Mare Cimmerium. They've done something I can't decipher or really describe in Aethiopis. By now I'm sure they've got to the old expedition landers in Syrtis Major and Minor. I don't know what they'll do with them. Maybe add them to the road-building material.

Maybe *understand* them.

I have no idea what they're like, no idea at all. I can't. We can't. They move too fast, grow along instinctive lines, perhaps. Instinct for culture and technology. They may not be intelligent in the way we define intelligence, not as individuals, anyway. But they do *move.*

Perhaps they're just resurrecting what their ancestors left them fifty, a hundred thousand years ago, before the long, warm, wet Spring of Mars drove them underground and brought up the sprouts of aqueduct-bridges.

At any rate, I've been in orbit for a week and a half. They've gone from cradle to sky in that time.

I've seen their balloons.

And I've seen the distant fires of their rockets, icy blue and sharp like hydroxy torches. They seem to be running tests. In a few days, they'll have it.

Beware, Control. These brave lads will go far.

SCHRÖDINGER'S PLAGUE

I rarely get ideas that can be expressed in 2500 words or less. Short fiction is difficult at best, but short short fiction is damned near impossible for me. I've only managed the trick a couple of times. This one is the best of my efforts. It's also my only epistolary story—a tale told through letters.

One of my fondest memories is of handing this story to Poul Anderson, my father-in-law, when Astrid and I were in Orinda for a family visit. Poul took the issue of Analog into his back office to read the story. A few minutes later, I heard a loud guffaw. Perfect!

I think I know the point in the story where Poul laughed.

According to some physicists (Gregory Benford and John Cramer) the physics behind this story is bogus. Your assignment for the week is to find out why. Your only clue: John Bell.

Interdepartmental Memo—Werner Dietrich to Carl Kranz

Carl: I'm not sure what we should do about the Lambert journal. We know so little about the whole affair—but there's no doubt in my mind we should hand it over to the police. Incredible as the entries are, they directly relate to the murders and suicides, and they even touch on the destruction of the lab. Just reading them in your office isn't enough: I'll need copies of the journal. And how long did it circulate in the system before you noticed it?

Kranz to Dietrich

Werner: It must have been in the system since just before the events, so a month at least. Copies enclosed of the appropriate entries. The rest, I think, is irrelevant and private. I'd like to return the journal to Richard's estate. The police would probably hold it. And—well, I have other reasons for wanting to keep it to ourselves. For the moment, anyway. Examine the papers carefully. As a physicist, tell me if there's anything in them you find completely unbelievable. If not, more thought should be applied to the whole problem.

P.S. I'm verifying the loss from Bernard's lab now. Lots of hush-hush over there. It's definite Bernard was working on a government CBW contract, apparently in defiance of the university's guidelines. ?—How did Goa get access to the materials? Tight security over there.

Enc.: five pages.

The Journal

April 15, 1981

Today has been a puzzler. Marty convened an informal meeting of the Hydroxyl Radicals for lunch—on him. In attendance, the physics contingent: Martin Goa himself, Frederik Newman, and the new member, Kaye (pr: *Kie)* Parkes; the biologists, Oscar Bernard and yours truly; and the sociologist, Thomas Fauch. We met outside the lounge, and Marty took us to the auxiliary physics building to give us a brief tour of an experiment. Nothing spectacular. Then back to the lounge for lunch. Why he should waste our time thus is beyond me. Call it intuition, but something is up. Bernard is a bit upset for reason or reasons unknown.

May 14, 1981

Radicals convened again today, at lunch. Some of the most absurd shit I've ever heard in my life. Marty at it again. The detail is important here.

"Gentlemen," Marty said in the private lounge, after we had eaten. "I have just destroyed an important experiment. And I have just resigned my position with the university. I'm to have all my papers and materials off campus by this date next month."

Pole-axed silence.

"I have my reasons. I'm going to establish something once and for all."

"What's that, Marty?" Frederik asked, looking irritated. None of us approves of theatrics.

"I'm putting mankind's money where our mouth is. Our veritable collective scientific mouth. Frederik, you can help me explain. You are all aware how good a physicist Frederik is. Better at grants, better at subtleties. Much better than I am. Frederik, what is the most generally accepted theory in physics today?"

"Special relativity," Frederik said without hesitating.

"And the next?"

"Quantum electrodynamics."

"Would you explain Schrödinger's cat to us?"

Frederik looked around the table, looking a bit put upon, then shrugged. "The final state of a quantum event—an event on a microcosmic scale—appears to be defined by the making of an observation. That is, the event is indeterminate until it is measured. Then it assumes one of a variety of possible states. Schrödinger proposed linking quantum events to macrocosmic events. He suggested putting a cat in an enclosed box, and also a device which would detect the decay of a single radioactive nucleus. Let's say the nucleus has a fifty-fifty chance of decaying in an arbitrary length of time. If it does decay, it triggers the device, which drops a hammer on a vial of cyanide, releasing the gas into the box and killing the cat. The scientist conducting this experiment has no way of knowing whether the nucleus decayed or not without opening the box. Since the final state of the nucleus is not determined without first making a measurement, and the measurement in this case is the opening of the box to discover whether the cat is dead,

Schrödinger suggested that the cat would find itself in an undetermined state, neither alive nor dead, but somewhere in between. Its fate is uncertain until a qualified observer opens the box."

"And could you explain some of the implications of this thought experiment?" Marty looked a bit like a cat himself—one who has swallowed a canary.

"Well," Frederik continued, "if we dismiss the cat as a qualified observer, there doesn't seem to be any way around the conclusion that the cat is neither alive nor dead until the box is opened."

"Why not?" Fauch, the sociologist, asked. "I mean, it seems obvious that only one state is possible."

"Ah," Frederik said, warming to the subject, "but we have linked a quantum event to the macrocosm, and quantum events are tricky. We have amassed a great deal of experimental evidence to show that quantum states are not definite until they are observed, that in fact they fluctuate, interact, as if two or more universes, each containing a potential outcome, are meshed together. Until the physicist causes the collapse into the final state by observing. Measuring."

"Doesn't that give consciousness a godlike importance?" Fauch asked.

"It does indeed," said Frederik. "Modern physics is on a heavy power trip."

"It's all just theoretical, isn't it?" I asked, slightly bored.

"Not at all," Frederik said. "Established experimentally."

"Wouldn't a machine—or a cat—serve just as well to make the measurement?" Oscar, my fellow biologist, asked.

"That depends on how conscious you regard a cat as being. A machine—no, because its state would not be certain until the physicist looked over the record it had made."

"Commonly," said Parkes, his youthful interest piqued, "we substitute Wigner's friend for the cat. Wigner was a physicist who suggested putting a man in the box. Wigner's friend would presumably be conscious enough to know whether he was alive or dead, and to properly interpret the fall of the hammer and the breaking of the vial to indicate that the nucleus has, in fact, decayed."

"Wonderful," Goa said. "And this neat little fable reflects the attitudes of those who work with one of the most accepted theories in modern science."

"Well, there are elaborations," Frederik said.

"Indeed, and I'm about to add another. What I'm about to say will probably be interpreted as a joke. It isn't. I'm not joking. I've been working with quantum mechanics for twenty years now, and I've always been uncertain—pardon the pun—whether I could accept the foundations of the very discipline which provided my livelihood. The dilemma has bothered me deeply. It's more than bothered me—it's caused sleepless nights, nervous distress, made me go to a psychiatrist. None of what Frederik calls 'elaborations' have provided any relief. So I've used my influence, and my contacts, to somewhat crooked advantage. I've begun an experiment. Not being happy with just a cat, or with Wigner's friend, I've involved all of you in that experiment, and myself, as well. Ultimately, many more people, all supposedly legitimate, conscious observers, will become involved."

Oscar smiled, trying to keep from laughing. "I do believe you've gone mad, Martin."

"Have I? Have I indeed, my *dear* Oscar? While I have been driven to distraction by intellectual considerations, why haven't you been driven to distraction by ethical ones?"

"What?" Oscar asked, frowning.

"You are, I believe, trying to locate a vial labeled DERVM-74."

"How did you—"

"Because I stole the vial while looking over your lab. And I cribbed a few of your notes. Now. You're among friends, Oscar. Tell us about DERVM-74. Tell them, or I will."

For a few seconds, Oscar looked like a carp out of water. "That's c-classified," he said. "I refuse."

"DERVM-74," Marty said, "stands for Dangerous Experimental RhinoVirus, Mutation 74. Oscar does some moonlighting on contract for the government. This is one of his toys. Tell us about its nature, Oscar."

"You have the vial?"

"Not anymore," Marty said.

"You idiot! That virus is deadly. I was about to destroy it when the culture disappeared. It's of no use to anybody!"

"How does it work, Oscar?"

"It has a very long gestation period—about 330 days. Much too long for military uses. After that time, death is certain in ninety-eight percent of those who have contracted it. It can be spread by simple contact, by breathing the air around a contaminated subject." Oscar stood. "I must report this, Martin."

"Sit down." Marty pulled a broken glass tube out of his pocket, with a singed label still wrapped around it. He handed it to Oscar, who paled. "Here's my proof. You're much too late to stop the experiment."

"Is this all true?" Parkes asked.

"That *is* the vial," Oscar confirmed.

"What in *hell* have you done?" I asked, loudly.

The other Radicals were as still as cold agar.

"I made a device which measures a quantum event, in this case the decay of a particle of radioactive Americium. Over a small period of time, I exposed an instrument much like a Geiger counter to the possible effects of this decay. In that time, there was exactly a fifty-fifty chance that a nucleus in the particle would decay, triggering the Geiger counter. If the Geiger counter was triggered, it released the virus contained in this vial into a tightly sealed area. Immediately afterward, I entered the area, and an hour later, I gave all five of you a tour through the same area. The device was then destroyed, and everything in the chamber sterilized, including the vial. If the virus was not released, it was destroyed along with the experimental equipment. If it was released, then we have all been exposed."

"Was it released?" Fauch asked.

"I don't know. It's impossible to tell—yet."

"Oscar," I said, "it's been a month since Marty did all this. We're all influential people—giving talks, attending meetings. We all travel a fair amount. How many people have been exposed, potentially? "

"It's very contagious," Oscar said. "Simple contact guarantees passage from one vector . . . to another."

Fauch took out his calculator. "If we exposed five people each day, and they went on to expose five more . . . Jesus Christ. By now, everyone on Earth could have it."

"Why did you do this, Marty?" Frederik asked.

"Because if the best mankind can do is come up with an infuriating theory like this to explain the universe, then we should be willing to live or die by our belief in the theory."

"I don't get you," Frederik said.

"You know as well as I. Oscar, is there any way to detect contamination by the virus?"

"None. Marty, that virus was a mistake—useless to everybody. Even my notes were going to be destroyed."

"Not useless to me. That's unimportant now, anyway. Frederik, what I'm saying is, according to theory, nothing has been determined yet. The nucleus may or may not have decayed, but that hasn't been decided. We may have better than a fifty-fifty chance—if we truly believe in the theory."

Parkes stood up and looked out the window. "You should have been more thorough, Marty. You should have researched this thing more completely."

"Why?"

"Because I'm a hypochondriac, you bastard. I have a very difficult time telling whether I'm sick or not."

"What does that have to do with anything?" Oscar asked.

Frederik leaned forward. "What Marty is implying is, since the quantum event hasn't been determined yet, the measurement that will flip it into one state or another is our sickness, or health, about three hundred days from now."

I picked up on the chain of reasoning. "And since Parkes is a hypochondriac, if he believes he's ill, that will flip the event into certainty. It will determine the decay, after the fact—" My head began to ache. "Even after the particle has been destroyed, and all other records?"

"If he truly believes he's ill," Marty said. "Or if any of us truly believes. Or if we actually become ill. I'm not sure there's any real difference, in this case."

"So you're going to jeopardize the entire world—" Fauch began, then he started to laugh. "This is a diabolical joke, Martin. You can stop it right here."

"He's not joking," Oscar said, holding up the vial. "That's my handwriting on the label."

"Isn't it a beautiful experiment?" Marty asked, grinning. "It determines so many things. It tells us whether our theory of quantum events is correct, it tells us the role of consciousness in shaping the universe, and, in Parkes's case, it—"

"Stop it!" Oscar shouted. At that point, we had to restrain the biologist from attacking Marty, who danced away, laughing.

May 17, 1981

Today all of us—except Marty—convened. Frederik and Parkes presented documentary evidence to support the validity of quantum theory, and, perversely enough, the validity of Marty's experiment. The evidence was impressive, but I'm not convinced. Still, it was a marathon session, and we now know more than we ever cared to know about the strange world of quantum physics.

The physicists—and Fauch, and Oscar, who is very quiet nowadays—are completely convinced that Marty's nucleus is—or was—in an undetermined state, and that all the causal chains leading to the potential release of the rhinovirus mutation are also in a state of flux. Whether the human race will live or die has not yet been decided.

And Parkes is equally convinced that, as soon as the gestation period passes, he will begin having symptoms, and he will feel, however irrationally, that he has contracted the disease. We cannot convince him otherwise.

In one way, we were very stupid. We had Oscar describe the symptoms—the early signs—of the disease to us. If we had thought things out more carefully, we would have withheld the information, at least from Parkes. But since Oscar knows, if he became convinced he had the disease, that would be enough to flip the state, Frederik believes. Or would it? We don't know yet how many of us will need to be convinced. Would Marty alone suffice? Is a consensus necessary? A two-thirds majority?

It all seemed—seems—totally preposterous to me. I've always been suspicious of physicists, and now I know why.

Then Frederik made a horrible proposal.

May 23, 1981

Frederik repeated his proposal again at today's meeting. The others considered the proposal seriously. Seeing how serious they were, I tried to make objections, but got nowhere. I am completely convinced that there is nothing we can do, that if the nucleus decayed, then we are doomed. In three hundred days the first signs will appear—backache, headache, sweaty palms, piercing pains behind the eyes.

If they don't appear, we won't die.

Even Frederik saw the ridiculous nature of his proposal, but he added, "The symptoms aren't that much different from flu, you know. And if just one of us becomes convinced . . ."

Indicating that the flipping of the state, because of human frailty, was almost certainly going to result in release of the virus. Had resulted.

His proposal—I write it down with great difficulty—is that

we should all commit suicide, all six of us. Since we are the only ones who know about the experiment, we are the only ones, he feels, who can flip the state, make things certain. Parkes, he says, is particularly dangerous, but we are all potential hypochondriacs.

With the strain of almost ten months waiting between now and the potential appearance of symptoms, we may all be near the breaking point.

May 30, 1981

I have refused to go along with them. Everyone has been extremely quiet. Most of us have stayed away from each other. But I suspect Parkes and Frederik are up to something.

Oscar is morose. He seems suicidal anyway, but is too much of a coward to go it alone. Fauch . . . I can't reach him.

—Ah, Christ. Frederik called. They've done it. They've gone through with their insane plan, killing Marty and destroying the lab building to wipe out all traces of the experiment—so that no one will know it ever took place.

The group is coming over to my apartment now. He said I can't hold out. I just have time to put this in the university pick-up box. What can I do, run?

They're too close.

———

Dietrich to Kranz

Carl: I've read the journal, although I'm not sure I've assimilated it. What have you found out about Bernard?

Kranz to Dietrich

Werner: Oscar Bernard was indeed working on a rhinovirus mutation around the time of the incident. I haven't been able to find out much—lots of people in gray suits wandering through the corridors over there. But the rumor is that all his notes are missing.

Do you believe it? I mean—do you believe the theory enough to agree with me, that word about the journal should end here? I feel both scared and silly.

Dietrich to Kranz

Carl: We have to find out the complete list of symptoms—besides headache, sweaty palms, backache, pains behind the eyes.

Yes. I'm a firm believer in the theory. And if Martin Goa did what the journal says . . . you and I can flip the state.

Anyone who reads this can flip the state.

What in God's name are we going to do?

BLOOD MUSIC

"Blood Music" was the big one—the idea that crept up on me, staggered me, and eventually helped shape my career.

There's a joke that when you join the Science Fiction Writers of America, you get a little envelope in the mail, and in that envelope there is a slip of paper on which is scrawled the idea that will haunt you for the rest of your days. For Frank Herbert, it was "Dune, desert planet." For Isaac Asimov, it might have been, "Robots work by the rules."

For me, it was "intelligent cells."

As it turns out, the read-write DNA of "Blood Music" is a natural reality, and this was known to a fair number of biologists even in 1982, when the idea for the story first occurred to me. HIV and other retroviruses, which incorporate their genome into host DNA, were just on the horizon of the lay public, however, and the Central Dogma of molecular biology—that DNA is transcribed to RNA, and RNA is translated into proteins, and that the reverse never happens—that DNA is a fixed template and can only be altered by "mistakes," random mutations—still ruled.

"Blood Music" has been described as a parable about AIDS. I don't think that's the case, really; we shouldn't throw all biological transformations into one pot. The point about this story, and many of my subsequent forays into genetics and evolution, is that what at first seems an unmitigated horror is in fact much more, if we could only take off the blinders of our mortal individuality.

I submitted this story to a number of high-paying magazines, including Playboy and Omni, and they rejected it with either no comment or wry grimaces. Analog was more receptive, but editor Stanley Schmidt wanted to know if the idea of a smart cell was even possible. I looked up the number of nucleotide base pairs in the human genome—about three billion, loosely compared that to the number of nerve cells in the human brain—trillions—and decided it was possible. What are factors of a thousand or ten thousand among friends?

Stan published the story. It went on to win a Hugo and a Nebula, my first prizes in the field.

As I wrote the novel version (published in 1985), I scrawled myself a note asking "what do cold viruses do for us?" In other words, why do we allow them to give us the sniffles, or worse? Some ten years later, while researching my novel DARWIN'S RADIO, I asked that question again, and concocted a sub-plot in which a scientist discovers the remains of ancient retroviruses in the human genome. Not long after, I learned about HERV—Human Endogenous Retroviruses. They're real, many of them are primordial—tens of millions of years or older—and they could play a major role in human birth, autoimmune diseases, cancer, and even in evolution.

So much for trying to write science fiction.

Cells are self-making and self-regulating in ways we never imagined only a few decades ago. In other words, our cells are intelligent, in their way, and sometimes even break loose from their slavery and assert their individuality.

We call such things tumors.

I wonder—do tumor cells read the genetic equivalent of Ayn Rand?

There is a principle in nature I don't think anyone has pointed out before. Each hour, a myriad of trillions of little live things—bacteria, microbes, "animalcules"—are born and die, not counting for much except in the bulk of their existence and the accumulation of their tiny effects. They do not perceive deeply. They do not suffer much. A hundred billion, dying, would not begin to have the same importance as a single human death.

Within the ranks of magnitude of all creatures, small as microbes or great as humans, there is an equality of "elan," just as the branches of a tall tree, gathered together, equal the bulk of the limbs below, and all the limbs equal the bulk of the trunk.

That, at least, is the principle. I believe Vergil Ulam was the first to violate it.

It had been two years since I'd last seen Vergil. My memory of him hardly matched the tan, smiling, well-dressed gentleman standing before me. We had made a lunch appointment over the phone the day before, and now faced each other in the wide double doors of the employees' cafeteria at the Mount Freedom Medical Center.

"Vergil?" I asked. "My God, Vergil!"

"Good to see you, Edward." He shook my hand firmly. He had lost ten or twelve kilos and what remained seemed tighter, better proportioned. At university, Vergil had been the pudgy, shock-haired, snaggle-toothed whiz kid who hot-wired doorknobs, gave us punch that turned our piss blue, and never got a date except with Eileen Termagent, who shared many of his physical characteristics.

"You look fantastic," I said. "Spend a summer in Cabo San Lucas?"

We stood in line at the counter and chose our food. "The tan," he said, picking out a carton of chocolate milk, "is from spending three months under a sunlamp. My teeth were straightened just after I last saw you. I'll explain the rest, but we need a place to talk in private."

I steered him to the smoker's corner, where three diehard puffers were scattered among six tables.

"Listen, I mean it," I said as we unloaded our trays. "You've changed. You're looking good."

"I've changed more than you know." His tone was motion-picture ominous, and he delivered the line with a theatrical lift of his brows. "How's Gail?"

Gail was doing well, I told him, teaching nursery school. We'd married the year before. His gaze shifted down to his food—pineapple slice and cottage cheese, piece of banana cream pie—and he said, his voice almost cracking, "Notice something else?"

I squinted in concentration. "Uh."

"Look closer."

"I'm not sure. Well, yes, you're not wearing glasses. Contacts?"

"No. I don't need them anymore."

"And you're a snappy dresser. Who's dressing you now? I hope she's as sexy as she is tasteful."

"Candice isn't—wasn't responsible for the improvement in my clothes," he said. "I just got a better job, more money to throw around. My taste in clothes is better than my taste in food, as it happens." He grinned the old Vergil self-deprecating grin, but ended it with a peculiar leer. "At any rate, she's left me, I've been fired from my job, I'm living on savings."

"Hold it," I said. "That's a bit crowded. Why not do a linear breakdown? You got a job. Where?"

"Genetron Corp.," he said. "Sixteen months ago."

"I haven't heard of them."

"You will. They're going public next month. The stock will shoot right off the board. They've broken through with MABs. Medical—"

"I know what MABs are," I interrupted. "At least in theory. Medically Applicable Biochips."

"They have some that work."

"What?" It was my turn to lift my brows.

"Microscopic logic circuits. You inject them into the human body, they set up shop where they're told and troubleshoot. With Dr. Michael Bernard's approval."

That was quite impressive. Bernard's reputation was spotless. Not only was he associated with the genetic engineering biggies, but he had made news at least once a year in his practice as a neurosurgeon before retiring. Covers on *Time, Mega, Rolling Stone.*

"That's supposed to be secret—stock, breakthrough, Bernard, everything." Vergil looked around and lowered his voice. "But you do whatever the hell you want. I'm through with the bastards."

I whistled. "Make me rich, huh?"

"If that's what you want. Or you can spend some time with me before rushing off to your broker."

"Of course." He hadn't touched the cottage cheese or pie. He had, however, eaten the pineapple slice and drunk the chocolate milk. "So tell me more."

"Well, in med school I was training for lab work. Biochemical research. I've always had a bent for computers, too. So I put myself through my last two years—"

"By selling software packages to Westinghouse," I said.

"It's good my friends remember. That's how I got involved with Genetron, just when they were starting out. They had big money backers, all the lab facilities I thought anyone would ever need. They hired me, and I advanced rapidly.

"Four months and I was doing my own work. I made some breakthroughs." He tossed his hand nonchalantly. "Then I went off on tangents they thought were premature. I persisted and they took away my lab, handed it over to a certifiable flatworm. I managed to save part of the experiment before they fired me. But I haven't exactly been cautious . . . or judicious. So now it's going on outside the lab."

I'd always regarded Vergil as ambitious, a trifle cracked, and not terribly sensitive. His relations with authority figures had never been smooth. Science, for him, was like the woman you couldn't possibly have, who suddenly opens her arms to you, long before you're ready for mature love—leaving you afraid you'll forever blow the chance, lose the prize. Apparently, he did. "Outside the lab? I don't get you."

"Edward, I want you to examine me. Give me a thorough physical. Maybe a cancer diagnostic. Then I'll explain more."

"You want a five-thousand-dollar exam?"

"Whatever you can do. Ultrasound, NMR, thermogram, everything."

"I don't know if I can get access to all that equipment. NMR full-scan has only been here a month or two. Hell, you couldn't pick a more expensive way—"

"Then ultrasound. That's all you'll need."

"Vergil, I'm an obstetrician, not a glamour-boy lab-tech. OB-GYN, butt of all jokes. If you're turning into a woman, maybe I can help you."

He leaned forward, almost putting his elbow into the pie, but swinging wide at the last instant by scant millimeters. The old Vergil would have hit it square. "Examine me closely and you'll . . ." He narrowed his eyes. "Just examine me."

"So I make an appointment for ultrasound. Who's going to pay?"

"I'm on Blue Shield." He smiled and held up a medical credit card. "I messed with the personnel files at Genetron. Anything up to a hundred thousand dollars medical, they'll never check, never suspect."

He wanted secrecy, so I made arrangements. I filled out his forms myself. As long as everything was billed properly, most of the examination could take place without official notice. I didn't charge for my services. After all, Vergil had turned my piss blue. We were friends.

He came in late at night. I wasn't normally on duty then, but I stayed late, waiting for him on the third floor of what the nurses called the Frankenstein wing. I sat on an orange plastic chair. He arrived, looking olive-colored under the fluorescent lights.

He stripped, and I arranged him on the table. I noticed, first off, that his ankles looked swollen. But they weren't puffy. I felt them several times. They seemed healthy but looked odd. "Hm," I said.

I ran the paddles over him, picking up areas difficult for the big unit to hit, and programmed the data into the imaging system. Then I swung the table around and inserted it into the enameled orifice of the ultrasound unit, the *humhole,* so-called by the nurses.

I integrated the data from the humhole with that from the paddle sweeps and rolled Vergil out, then set up a video frame. The image took a second to integrate, then flowed into a pattern showing Vergil's skeleton. My jaw fell.

Three seconds of that and it switched to his thoracic organs, then his musculature, and, finally, vascular system and skin.

"How long since the accident?" I asked, trying to take the quiver out of my voice.

"I haven't been in an accident," he said. "It was deliberate."

"Jesus, they beat you to keep secrets?"

"You don't understand me, Edward. Look at the images again. I'm not damaged."

"Look, there's thickening here—" I indicated the ankles— "and your ribs, that crazy zigzag pattern of interlocks. Broken sometime, obviously. And—"

"Look at my spine," he said. I rotated the image in the video frame. Buckminster Fuller, I thought. It was fantastic. A cage of triangular projections, all interlocking in ways I couldn't begin to follow, much less understand. I reached around and tried to feel his spine with my fingers. He lifted his arms and looked off at the ceiling.

"I can't find it," I said. "It's all smooth back there." I let go of him and looked at his chest, then prodded his ribs. They were sheathed in something tough and flexible. The harder I pressed, the tougher it became. Then I noticed another change.

"Hey," I said. "You don't have nipples." There were tiny pigment patches, but no nipple formations at all.

"See?" Vergil asked, shrugging on the white robe. "I'm being rebuilt from the inside out."

In my reconstruction of those hours, I fancy myself saying, "So tell me about it." Perhaps mercifully, I don't remember what I actually said.

He explained with his characteristic circumlocutions. Listening was like trying to get to the meat of a newspaper article through a forest of sidebars and graphic embellishments.

I simplify and condense.

Genetron had assigned him to manufacturing prototype biochips, tiny circuits made out of protein molecules. Some were hooked up to silicon chips little more than a micrometer in size, then sent through rat arteries to chemically keyed locations, to make connections with the rat tissue and attempt to monitor and even control lab-induced pathologies.

"That was something," he said. "We recovered the most complex microchip by sacrificing the rat, then debriefed it—hooked the silicon portion up to an imaging system. The computer gave us bar graphs, then a diagram of the chemical characteristics of about eleven centimeters of blood vessel . . . then put it all together to make a picture. We zoomed down eleven centimeters of rat artery. You never saw so many scientists jumping up and down, hugging each other, drinking buckets of bug juice." Bug juice was lab ethanol mixed with Dr. Pepper.

Eventually, the silicon elements were eliminated completely in favor of nucleoproteins. He seemed reluctant to explain in detail, but I gathered they found ways to make huge molecules—as large as DNA, and even more complex—into electrochemical computers, using ribosome-like structures as "encoders" and "readers" and RNA as "tape." Vergil was able to mimic reproductive separation and reassembly in his nucleoproteins, incorporating program changes at key points by switching nucleotide pairs. "Genetron wanted me to switch over to supergene engineering, since that was the coming thing everywhere else. Make all kinds of critters, some out of our imagination. But I had different ideas." He twiddled his finger around his ear and made Theremin sounds. "Mad scientist time, right?" He laughed, then sobered. "I injected my best nucleoproteins into bacteria to make duplication and compounding easier. Then I started to leave them inside, so the circuits could interact with the cells. They were heuristically programmed; they taught themselves. The cells fed chemically coded information to the computers, the computers processed it and made decisions, the cells became smart. I mean, smart as planaria, for starters. Imagine an *E. coli* as smart as a planarian worm!"

I nodded. "I'm imagining."

"Then I really went off on my own. We had the equipment, the techniques; and I knew the molecular language. I could make really dense, really complicated biochips by compounding the nucleoproteins, making them into little brains. I did some research into how far I could go, theoretically. Sticking with bacteria, I could make a biochip with the computing capacity of a sparrow's brain. Imagine how jazzed I was! Then I saw a way to increase the complexity a thousandfold, by using something we regarded as a nuisance—quantum chit-chat between the fixed elements of the circuits. Down that small, even the slightest change could bomb a biochip. But I developed a program that actually predicted and took advantage of electron tunneling. Emphasized the heuristic aspects of the computer, used the chit-chat as a method of increasing complexity."

"You're losing me," I said.

"I took advantage of randomness. The circuits could repair themselves, compare memories, and correct faulty elements. I gave them basic instructions: Go forth and multiply. Improve. By God, you should have seen some of the cultures a week later! It was amazing. They were evolving all on their own, like little cities. I destroyed them all. I think one of the Petri dishes would have grown legs and walked out of the incubator if I'd kept feeding it."

"You're kidding." I looked at him. "You're not kidding."

"Man, they knew what it was like to improve! They knew where they had to go, but they were just so limited, being in bacteria bodies, with so few resources."

"How smart were they?"

"I couldn't be sure. They were associating in clusters of a hundred to two hundred cells, each cluster behaving like an autonomous unit. Each cluster might have been as smart as a rhesus monkey. They exchanged information through their pili, passed on bits of memory, and compared notes. Their organization was obviously different from a group of monkeys. Their world was so much simpler, for one thing. With their abilities, they were masters of the Petri dishes. I put phages in with them; the phages didn't have a chance. They used every option available to change and grow."

"How is that possible?"

"What?" He seemed surprised I wasn't accepting everything at face value.

"Cramming so much into so little. A rhesus monkey is not your simple calculator, Vergil."

"I haven't made myself clear," he said, irritated. "I was using nucleoprotein computers. They're like DNA, but all the information can interact. Do you know how many nucleotide pairs there are in the DNA of a single bacteria?"

It had been a long time since my last biochemistry lesson. I shook my head.

"About two million. Add in the modified ribosome structures—fifteen thousand of them, each with a molecular weight of about three million—and consider the combinations and permutations. The RNA is arranged like a continuous loop paper tape, surrounded by ribosomes ticking off instructions and manufacturing protein chains . . ." His eyes were bright and slightly moist. "Besides, I'm not saying every cell was a distinct entity. They cooperated."

"How many bacteria were in the dishes you destroyed?"

"Billions. I don't know." He smirked. "You got it, Edward. Whole planetsful of *E. coli*."

"But Genetron didn't fire you then?"

"No. They didn't know what was going on, for one thing. I kept compounding the molecules, increasing their size and complexity. When bacteria were too limited, I took blood from myself, separated out white cells, and injected them with the new biochips. I watched them, put them through mazes and little chemical problems. They were whizzes. Time is a lot faster at that level—so little distance for the messages to cross, and the environment is much simpler. Then I forgot to store a file under my secret code in the lab computers. Some managers found it and guessed what I was up to. Everybody panicked. They thought we'd have every social watchdog in the country on our backs because of what I'd done. They started to destroy my work and wipe my programs. Ordered me to sterilize my white cells. Christ." He pulled the white robe off and started to get dressed. "I only had a day or two. I separated out the most complex cells—"

"How complex?"

"They were clustering in hundred-cell groups, like the bacteria. Each group as smart as a four-year-old kid, maybe." He studied my face. "Still doubting? Want me to run through how many nucleotides there are in the human genome? I tailored my computers to take advantage of the white cells' capacity. Tens of thousands of genes. Three billion nucleotides, Edward. And they don't have a huge body to worry about, taking up most of their thinking time."

"Okay," I said. "I'm convinced. What did you do?"

"I mixed the cells back into a cylinder of whole blood and injected myself with it." He buttoned the top of his shirt and smiled thinly. "I'd programmed them with every drive I could, talked as high a level as I could using just enzymes and such. After that, they were on their own."

"You programmed them to go forth and multiply, improve?" I asked.

"I think they developed some characteristics picked up by the biochips in their *E. coli* phases. The white cells could talk to each other with extruded memories. They found ways to ingest other types of cells and alter them without killing them."

"You're crazy."

"You can see the screen! Edward, I haven't been sick since. I used to get colds all the time. I've never felt better."

"They're inside you," I said. "Finding things, changing them."

"And by now, each cluster is as smart as you or I."

"You're absolutely nuts."

He shrugged. "Genetron fired me. They thought I was going to take revenge for what they did to my work. They ordered me out of the labs, and I haven't had a real chance to see what's been going on inside me until now. Three months."

"So . . ." My mind was racing. "You lost weight because they improved your fat metabolism. Your bones are stronger, your spine has been completely rebuilt—"

"No more backaches even if I sleep on my old mattress."

"Your heart looks different."

"I didn't know about the heart," he said, examining the frame image more closely. "As for the fat—I was thinking about that. They could increase my brown cells, fix up the metabolism. I haven't been as hungry lately. I haven't changed my eating habits that much—I still want the same old junk—but somehow I get around to eating only what I need. I don't think they know what my brain is yet. Sure, they've got all the glandular stuff—but they don't have the big picture, if you see what I mean. They don't know I'm in here. But boy, they sure did figure out what my reproductive organs are."

I glanced at the image and shifted my eyes away.

"Oh, they look pretty normal," he said, hefting his scrotum obscenely. He snickered. "But how else do you think I'd land a real looker like Candice? She was just after a one-night stand with a techie. I looked okay then, no tan but trim, with good clothes. She'd never screwed a techie before. Joke time, right? But my little geniuses kept us up half the night. I think they made improvements each time. I felt like I had a goddamned fever."

His smile vanished. "But then one night my skin started to crawl. It really scared me. I thought things were getting out of hand. I wondered what they'd do when they crossed the blood-brain barrier and found out about me—about the brain's real function. So I began a campaign to keep them under control. I figured, the reason they wanted to get into the skin was the simplicity of running circuits across a surface. Much easier than trying to maintain chains of communication in and around muscles, organs, vessels. The skin was much more direct. So I bought a quartz lamp." He caught my puzzled expression. "In the lab, we'd break down the protein in biochip cells by exposing them to ultraviolet light. I alternated sunlamp with quartz treatments. Keeps them out of my skin and gives me a nice tan."

"Give you skin cancer, too," I commented.

"They'll probably take care of that. Like police."

"Okay. I've examined you, you've told me a story I still find hard to believe . . . what do you want me to do?"

"I'm not as nonchalant as I act, Edward. I'm worried. I'd like to learn how to control them before they find out about my brain. I mean, think of it, they're in the trillions by now, each one smart. They're cooperating to some extent. I'm probably the smartest thing on the planet, and they haven't even begun to get their act together. I don't really want them to take over." He laughed unpleasantly. "Steal my soul, you know? So think of some treatment to block them. Maybe we can starve the little buggers. Just think on it." He buttoned his shirt. "Give me a call." He handed me a slip of paper with his address and phone number. Then he went to the keyboard and erased the image on the frame, dumping the memory of the examination. "Just you," he said. "Nobody else for now. And please . . . hurry."

It was three o'clock in the morning when Vergil walked out of the examination room. He'd allowed me to take blood samples, then shaken my hand—his palm was damp, nervous—and cautioned me against ingesting anything from the specimens.

Before I went home, I put the blood through a series of tests. The results were ready the next day. I picked them up during my lunch break, then destroyed all of the samples. I did it like a robot.

It took me five days and nearly sleepless nights to accept what I'd seen. His blood was normal enough, though the machines diagnosed the patient as having an infection. High levels of leukocytes—white blood cells—and histamines.

On the fifth day, I believed.

Gail came home before I did, but it was my turn to fix dinner. She slipped one of her school's disks into the home system and showed me video art the nursery kids had been creating. I watched quietly, ate with her in silence.

That evening, I had two dreams, part of my final acceptance. In the first, I witnessed the destruction of the planet Krypton, Superman's home world. Billions of superhuman geniuses went screaming off in walls of fire. I related this destruction to my sterilizing the samples of Vergil's blood. The second dream was worse. I dreamed that New York City was raping a woman. By the end of the dream, she gave birth to little embryo cities, all wrapped up in translucent sacs, soaked with blood from the difficult labor.

I called Vergil on the morning of the sixth day. He answered on the fourth ring. "I have some results," I said. "Nothing conclusive. But I want to talk. In person."

"Sure," he said. "I'm staying inside for the time being." His voice was strained; he sounded tired.

Vergil's apartment was in a fancy high-rise near the lake shore. I took the elevator up, listening to little advertising jingles and watching dancing holograms display products, empty apartments for rent, the building's hostess discussing social activities for the week.

Vergil opened the door and motioned me in. He wore a checked robe with long sleeves and carpet slippers. He clutched an unlit pipe in one hand, his fingers twisting it back and forth as he walked away from me and sat down, saying nothing.

"You have an infection," I said.

"Oh?"

"That's all the blood analyses tell me. I don't have access to the electron microscopes."

"I don't think it's really an infection," he said. "After all, they're my own cells. Probably something else . . . some sign of their presence, of the change. We can't expect to understand everything that's happening."

I removed my coat. "Listen," I said, "you really have me worried now." The expression on his face stopped me: a kind of frantic beatitude. He squinted at the ceiling and pursed his lips.

"Are you stoned?" I asked.

He shook his head, then nodded once, very slowly. "Listening," he said.

"To what?"

"I don't know. Not sounds, exactly. More like music. The heart, all the blood vessels, friction of blood along the arteries, veins. Activity. Music in the blood." He looked at me plaintively. "Why aren't you at work?"

"My day off. Gail's working."

"Can you stay?"

I shrugged. "I suppose." I sounded suspicious. I glanced around the apartment, looking for ashtrays, packs of papers.

"I'm not stoned, Edward," he said. "I may be wrong, but I think something big is happening. I think they're finding out who I am."

I sat down across from Vergil, staring at him intently. He didn't seem to notice. Some inner process involved him. When I asked for a cup of coffee, he motioned to the kitchen. I boiled a pot of water and took a jar of instant from the cabinet. With cup in hand, I returned to my seat.

He twisted his head back and forth, eyes open. "You always knew what you wanted to be, didn't you?" he asked.

"More or less."

"A gynecologist. Smart moves. Never false moves. I was different. I had goals, but no direction. Like a map without roads. I didn't give a shit for anything, anyone but myself. I hated my folks. I hated science. Just a means. I'm surprised I got so far."

He gripped his chair arms.

"Something wrong?" I asked.

"They're talking to me," he said. He shut his eyes.

For an hour he seemed to be asleep. I checked his pulse, which was strong and steady, felt his forehead—slightly cool—and made myself more coffee. I was looking through a magazine, at a loss what to do, when he opened his eyes.

"Hard to figure exactly what time is like for them," he said. "It's taken them maybe three, four days to figure out language, key human concepts. Now they're on to it. On to me. Right now."

"How's that?"

He claimed there were thousands of researchers hooked up to his neurons. He couldn't give details. "They're damned efficient, you know," he said. "They haven't screwed me up yet."

"We should get you into the hospital now."

"What in hell could other doctors do? Did *you* figure out any way to control them? I mean, they're my own cells."

"I've been thinking. We could starve them. Find out what metabolic differences—"

"I'm not sure I want to be rid of them," Vergil said. "They're not doing any harm."

"How do you know?"

He shook his head and held up one finger. "Wait. They're trying to figure out what space is. That's tough for them. They break distances down into concentrations of chemicals. For them, space is like intensity of taste."

"Vergil—"

"Listen! Think, Edward!" His tone was excited but even. "Something big is happening inside me. They talk to each other across the fluid, through membranes. They tailor something—viruses?—to carry data stored in nucleic acid chains. I think they're saying 'RNA.' That makes sense. That's one way I programmed them. But plasmidlike structures, too. Maybe that's what your machines think is a sign of infection—all their chattering in my blood, packets of data. Tastes of other individuals. Peers. Superiors. Subordinates."

"Vergil, I still think you should be in a hospital."

"This is my show, Edward," he said. "I'm their universe. They're amazed by the new scale." He was quiet again for a time.

I squatted by his chair and pulled up the sleeve to his robe.

His arm was crisscrossed with white lines. I was about to go to the phone when he stood and stretched. "Do you realize," he said, "how many body cells we kill each time we move?"

"I'm going to call for an ambulance," I said.

"No, you aren't." His tone stopped me. "I told you, I'm not sick. This is my show. Do you know what they'd do to me in a hospital? They'd be like cavemen trying to fix a computer."

"Then what the hell am *I* doing here?" I asked, getting angry. "I can't do anything! I'm one of those cavemen."

"You're a friend," Vergil said, fixing his eyes on me. I had the impression I was being watched by more than just Vergil. "I want you here to keep me company." He laughed. "But I'm not exactly alone."

He walked around the apartment for two hours, fingering things, looking out windows, slowly and methodically fixing himself lunch. "You know, they can actually feel their own thoughts," he said around noon. "I mean, the cytoplasm seems to have a will of its own, a kind of subconscious life counter to the rationality they've only recently acquired. They hear the chemical 'noise' of the molecules fitting and unfitting inside."

At one, I called Gail to tell her I would be late. I was almost sick with tension, but I tried to keep my voice level. "Remember Vergil Ulam? I'm talking with him right now."

"Everything okay?" she asked.

Was it? Decidedly not. "Fine," I said.

"Culture!" Vergil said, peering at me around the kitchen wall.

I said good-bye and hung up.

"They're always swimming in that bath of information," Vergil said. "It's a kind of gestalt thing. The hierarchy is absolute. They send tailored phages after cells that don't interact properly. Viruses specified to individuals or groups. No escape. A rogue cell gets pierced by the virus, the cell blebs outward, it explodes and dissolves. But it's not just a dictatorship. I think they effectively have more freedom than in a democracy. I mean, they vary so differently from individual to individual. Does that make sense? They vary in different ways than we do."

"Hold it," I said, gripping his shoulders. "Vergil, you're pushing me to the edge. I can't take this much longer. I don't understand, I'm not sure I believe—"

"Not even now?"

"Okay, let's say you're giving me the right interpretation. Giving it to me straight. Have you bothered to figure out the consequences? What all this means, where it might lead?"

He walked into the kitchen and drew a glass of water from the tap, then returned and stood beside me. His expression had changed from childish absorption to sober concern. "I've never been good at that."

"Are you afraid?"

"I was. Now, I'm not sure." He fingered the tie of his robe. "Look, I don't want you to think I went around you, over your head or something. But I met with Michael Bernard yesterday. He put me through his private clinic, took specimens. Told me to quit the lamp treatments. He called this morning, just before you did. He says it all checks out. And he asked me not to tell anybody." His expression became dreamy again. "Cities of cells," he continued. "Edward, they push tubes through the tissues, spread information—"

"Stop it!" I shouted. "Checks out? What checks out?"

"As Bernard puts it, I have 'severely enlarged macrophages' throughout my system. And he concurs on the anatomical changes."

"What does he plan to do?"

"I don't know. I think he'll probably convince Genetron to reopen the lab."

"Is that what you want?"

"It's not just having the lab again. I want to show you. Since I stopped the lamp treatments, I'm still changing." He undid his robe and let it slide to the floor. All over his body, his skin was crisscrossed with white lines. Along his back, the lines were starting to form ridges.

"My God!" I said.

"I'm not going to be much good anywhere else but the lab soon. I won't be able to go out in public. Hospitals wouldn't know what to do, as I said."

"You're . . . you can talk to them, tell them to slow down," I said, aware how ridiculous that sounded.

"Yes, indeed I can, but they don't necessarily listen."

"I thought you were their god or something."

"The ones hooked up to my neurons aren't the big wheels. They're researchers, or at least serve the same function. They know I'm here, what I am, but that doesn't mean they've convinced the upper levels of the hierarchy."

"They're arguing?"

"Something like that. It's not all that bad. If the lab is reopened, I have a home, a place to work." He glanced out the window, as if looking for someone. "I don't have anything left but them. They aren't afraid, Edward. I've never felt so close to anything before." Again the beatific smile. "I'm responsible for them. Mother to them all."

"You have no way of knowing what they're going to do."

He shook his head.

"No, I mean it. You say they're like a civilization—"

"Like a thousand civilizations."

"Yeah, and civilizations have been known to screw up. Warfare, the environment—"

I was grasping at straws, trying to restrain a growing panic. I wasn't competent to handle the enormity of what was happening. Neither was Vergil. He was the last person I would have called insightful and wise about large issues.

"But I'm the only one at risk."

"You don't *know* that. Jesus, Vergil, look what they're doing to you!"

"To me, all to me!" he said. "Nobody else."

I shook my head and held up my hands in a gesture of defeat. "Okay, so Bernard gets them to reopen the lab, you move in, become a guinea pig. What then?"

"They treat me right. I'm more than just good old Vergil Ulam now. I'm a goddamned galaxy, a super-mother."

"Super-host, you mean."

He conceded the point with a shrug.

I couldn't take any more. I made my exit with a few flimsy excuses, then sat in the lobby of the apartment building, trying to calm down. Somebody had to talk some sense into him. Who would he listen to? He had gone to Bernard . . .

And it sounded as if Bernard was not only convinced, but very interested. People of Bernard's stature didn't coax the Vergil Ulams of the world along unless they felt it was to their advantage.

I had a hunch, and I decided to play it. I went to a pay phone, slipped in my credit card, and called Genetron.

"I'd like you to page Dr. Michael Bernard," I told the receptionist.

"Who's calling, please?"

"This is his answering service. We have an emergency call, and his beeper doesn't seem to be working."

A few anxious minutes later, Bernard came on the line. "Who the hell is this?" he asked. "I don't have an answering service."

"My name is Edward Milligan. I'm a friend of Vergil Ulam's. I think we have some problems to discuss."

We made an appointment to talk the next morning.

I went home and tried to think of excuses to keep me off the next day's hospital shift. I couldn't concentrate on medicine, couldn't give my patients anywhere near the attention they deserved.

Guilty, angry, afraid.

That was how Gail found me. I slipped on a mask of calm and we fixed dinner together. After eating, holding onto each other, we watched the city lights come on through the bayside window. Winter starlings pecked at the yellow lawn in the last few minutes of twilight, then flew away with a rising wind which made the windows rattle.

"Something's wrong," Gail said softly. "Are you going to tell me, or just act like everything's normal?"

"It's just me," I said. "Nervous. Work at the hospital."

"Oh, lord," she said, sitting up. "You're going to divorce me for that Baker woman." Mrs. Baker weighed three hundred and sixty pounds and hadn't known she was pregnant until her fifth month.

"No," I said, listless.

"Rapturous relief," Gail said, touching my forehead lightly. "You know this kind of introspection drives me crazy."

"Well, it's nothing I can talk about yet, so . . ." I patted her hand.

"That's disgustingly patronizing," she said, getting up. "I'm going to make some tea. Want some?" Now she was miffed, and I was tense with not telling. Why not just reveal all? I asked myself. An old friend was about to risk everything, *change* everything . . .

I cleared away the table instead.

That night, unable to sleep, I looked down on Gail in bed from my sitting position, pillow against the wall, and tried to determine what I knew was real, and what wasn't. I'm a doctor, I told myself. A technical, scientific profession. I'm supposed to be immune to things like future shock. How would it feel to be topped off with a trillion intelligences speaking a language as incomprehensible as Chinese?

I grinned in the dark and almost cried at the same time. What Vergil had inside him was unimaginably stranger. Stranger than anything I—or Vergil—could easily understand. Perhaps ever understand.

Vergil Ulam is turning himself into a galaxy.

But I knew what was real. The bedroom, the city lights faint through gauze curtains. Gail sleeping. Very important. Gail in bed, sleeping.

The dream returned. This time the city came in through the window and attacked Gail. It was a great, spiky lighted-up prowler, and it growled in a language I couldn't understand, made up of auto horns, crowd noises, construction bedlam. I tried to fight it off, but it got to her—and turned into a drift of stars, sprinkling all over the bed, all over everything. I jerked awake and stayed up until dawn, dressed with Gail, kissed her, savored the reality of her human, unviolated lips.

I went to meet with Bernard. He had been loaned a suite in a big downtown hospital; I rode the elevator to the sixth floor, and saw what fame and fortune could mean. The suite was tastefully furnished, fine serigraphs on wood-paneled walls, chrome and glass furniture, cream-colored carpet, Chinese brass, and wormwood-grain cabinets and tables.

He offered me a cup of coffee, and I accepted. He took a seat in the breakfast nook, and I sat across from him, cradling my cup in moist palms. He wore a dapper gray suit and had graying hair and a sharp profile. He was in his mid sixties and he looked quite a bit like Leonard Bernstein.

"About our mutual acquaintance," he said. "Mr. Ulam. Brilliant. And, I won't hesitate to say, courageous."

"He's my friend. I'm worried about him."

Bernard held up one finger. "Courageous—and a bloody damned fool. What's happening to him should never have been allowed. He may have done it under duress, but that's no excuse. Still, what's done is done. He's talked to you, I take it."

I nodded. "He wants to return to Genetron."

"Of course. That's where all his equipment is. Where his home probably will be while we sort this out."

"Sort it out—how? Why?" I wasn't thinking too clearly. I had a slight headache.

"I can think of a lot of uses for small, super-dense computer elements with a biological base. Can't you? Genetron has already made breakthroughs, but this is something else again."

"What are you—they—planning?"

Bernard smiled. "I'm not really at liberty to say. It'll be revolutionary. We'll have to put him in a tightly controlled, isolated environment. Perhaps his own wing. Animal experiments have to be conducted. We'll start from scratch, of course. Vergil's . . . um . . . colonies can't be transferred. They're based on his own white blood cells. So we have to develop colonies that won't trigger immune reactions."

"Like an infection?" I asked.

"I suppose there are comparisons. But Vergil is *not* infected."

"My tests indicate he is."

"That's probably loose bits of data floating around in his blood, don't you think?"

"I don't know."

"Listen, I'd like you to come down to the lab after Vergil is settled in. Your expertise might be useful to us."

Us. He was working with Genetron hand in glove. Could he be objective?

"How will you benefit from all this?"

"Edward, I have always been at the forefront of my profession. I see no reason why I shouldn't be helping here. With my knowledge of brain and nerve functions, and the research I've been conducting in neurophysiology—"

"You could help Genetron hold off an investigation by the government," I said.

"That's being very blunt. Too blunt, and unfair."

"Perhaps. Anyway, yes: I'd like to visit the lab when Vergil's settled in. If I'm still welcome, bluntness and all."

Bernard looked at me sharply. I wouldn't be playing on his team; for a moment, his thoughts were almost nakedly apparent. "Of course," he said, rising with me. He reached out to shake my hand. His palm was damp. He was as nervous as I was, even if he didn't look it.

I returned to my apartment and stayed there until noon, reading, trying to sort things out. Reach a decision. What was real, what I needed to protect. There is only so much change anyone can stand: innovation, yes, but slow application. Don't force. Everyone has the right to stay the same until they decide otherwise.

The greatest thing in science since . . .

And Bernard would force it. Genetron would force it. I couldn't handle the thought. "Neo-Luddite," I said to myself. A filthy accusation.

When I pressed Vergil's number on the building security panel, Vergil answered almost immediately. "Yeah," he said. He sounded exhilarated. "Come on up. I'll be in the bathroom. Door's unlocked."

I entered his apartment and walked through the hallway to the bathroom. Vergil lay in the tub, up to his neck in pinkish water. He smiled vaguely and splashed his hands. "Looks like I slit my wrists, doesn't it?" he said softly. "Don't worry. Everything's fine now. Genetron's going to take me back. Bernard just called." He pointed to the bathroom phone and intercom.

I sat on the toilet and noticed the sunlamp fixture standing unplugged next to the linen cabinets. The bulbs sat in a row on the edge of the sink counter. "You're sure that's what you want?" I said, my shoulders slumping.

"Yeah, I think so," he said. "They can take better care of me. I'm getting cleaned up, going over there this evening. Bernard's picking me up in his limo. Style. From here on in, everything's style."

The pinkish color in the water didn't look like soap. "Is that bubble bath?" I asked. Some of it came to me in a rush then and I felt a little weaker; what had occurred to me was just one more obvious and necessary insanity.

"No," Vergil said.

I knew that already.

"No," he repeated, "it's coming from my skin. They're not telling me everything, but I think they're sending out scouts. Astronauts." He looked at me with an expression that didn't quite equal concern; more like curiosity as to how I'd take it. The confirmation made my stomach muscles tighten as if waiting for a punch. I had never even considered the possibility until now, perhaps because I had been concentrating on other aspects.

"Is this the first time?" I asked.

"Yeah," he said, then laughed. "I've half a mind to let the little buggers down the drain. Let them find out what the world's really about."

"They'd go everywhere," I said.

"Sure enough."

"How . . . how are you feeling?"

"I'm feeling pretty good now. Must be billions of them." More splashing with his hands. "What do you think? Should I let the buggers out?"

Quickly, hardly thinking, I knelt down beside the tub. My fingers went for the cord on the sunlamp and I plugged it in. He had hot-wired doorknobs, turned my piss blue, played a thousand dumb practical jokes and never grown up, never grown mature enough to understand that he was sufficiently brilliant to transform the world; he would never learn caution.

He reached for the drain knob. "You know, Edward, I—"

He never finished. I picked up the fixture and dropped it into the tub, jumping back at the flash of steam and sparks. Vergil screamed and thrashed and jerked and then everything was still, except for the low, steady sizzle and the smoke wafting from his hair.

I lifted the toilet lid and vomited. Then I clenched my nose and went into the living room. My legs went out from under me and I sat abruptly on the couch.

After an hour, I searched through Vergil's kitchen and found bleach, ammonia, and a bottle of Jack Daniel's. I returned to the bathroom, keeping the center of my gaze away from Vergil. I poured first the booze, then the bleach, then the ammonia into the water. Chlorine started bubbling up and I left, closing the door behind me.

The phone was ringing when I got home. I didn't answer. It could have been the hospital. It could have been Bernard. Or the police. I could envision having to explain everything to the police. Genetron would stonewall; Bernard would be unavailable. I was exhausted, all my muscles knotted with tension and whatever name one can give to the feelings one has after—

Committing genocide?

That certainly didn't seem real. I could not believe I had just murdered a hundred trillion intelligent beings. Snuffed a galaxy. It was laughable. But I didn't laugh.

What was easy to believe was that I had just killed one human being, a friend. The smoke, the melted lamp rods, the drooping electrical outlet and smoking cord.

Vergil.

I had dunked the lamp into the tub with Vergil.

I felt sick. Dreams, cities raping Gail (and what about his girlfriend, Candice?). Draining the water filled with them. Galaxies sprinkling over us all. What horror. Then again, what potential beauty—a new kind of life, symbiosis and transformation.

Had I been thorough enough to kill them all? I had a moment of panic. Tomorrow, I thought, I will sterilize his apartment. Somehow, I didn't even think of Bernard.

When Gail came in the door, I was asleep on the couch. I came to, groggy, and she looked down at me.

"You feeling okay?" she asked, perching on the arm. I nodded.

"What are you planning for dinner?" My mouth didn't work properly. The words were mushy.

She felt my forehead. "Edward, you have a fever," she said. "A very high fever." I stumbled into the bathroom and looked in the mirror. Gail was close behind me.

"What is it?" she asked.

There were lines under my collar, around my neck. White lines, like freeways. They had already been in me a long time, days.

"Damp palms," I said. So obvious.

I think we nearly died. I struggled at first, but in minutes I was too weak to move. Gail was just as sick within an hour.

I lay on the carpet in the living room, drenched in sweat. Gail lay on the couch, her face the color of talcum, eyes closed, like a corpse in an embalming parlor. For a time I thought she *was* dead. Sick as I was, I raged—hated, felt tremendous guilt at my weakness, my slowness to understand all the possibilities. Then I no longer cared. I was too weak to blink, so I closed my eyes and waited.

There was a rhythm in my arms, my legs. With each pulse of blood, a kind of sound welled up within me, like an orchestra thousands strong, but not playing in unison; playing whole seasons of symphonies at once. Music in the blood. The sound became harsher, but more coordinated, wave-trains finally canceling into silence, then separating into harmonic beats.

The beats seemed to melt into me, into the sound of my own heart.

First, they subdued our immune responses. The war—and it was a war, on a scale never before known on Earth, with trillions of combatants—lasted perhaps two days.

By the time I regained enough strength to get to the kitchen faucet, I could feel them working on my brain, trying to crack the code and find the god within the protoplasm. I drank until I was sick, then drank more moderately and took a glass to Gail. She sipped. Her lips were cracked, her eyes bloodshot and ringed with yellowish crumbs. There was some color in her skin.

Minutes later, we were eating feebly in the kitchen.

"What in hell is happening?" was the first thing she asked. I didn't have the strength to explain. I peeled an orange and shared it with her. "We should call a doctor," she said. But I knew we wouldn't. I was already receiving messages; it was becoming apparent that any sensation of freedom we experienced was illusory.

The messages were simple at first. Memories of commands, rather than the commands themselves, manifested in my thoughts. We were not to leave the apartment—a concept which seemed quite abstract to those in control, even if undesirable—and we were not to have contact with others. We would be allowed to eat certain foods and drink tap water for the time being.

With the subsidence of the fevers, the transformations were quick and drastic. Almost simultaneously, Gail and I were immobilized. She was sitting at the table, I was kneeling on the floor. I was able barely to see her in the corner of my eye.

Her arm developed pronounced ridges.

They had learned inside Vergil; their tactics within the two of us were very different. I itched all over for about two hours—two hours in hell—before they made the breakthrough and found *me*. The effort of ages on their timescale paid off and they communicated smoothly and directly with this great, clumsy intelligence who had once controlled their universe.

They were not cruel. When the concept of discomfort and its undesirability was made clear, they worked to alleviate it. They worked too effectively. For another hour, I was in a sea of bliss, out of all contact with them.

With dawn the next day, they gave us freedom to move again; specifically, to go to the bathroom. There were certain waste products they could not deal with. I voided those—my urine was purple—and Gail followed suit. We looked at each other vacantly in the bathroom. Then she managed a slight smile. "Are they talking to you?" she asked.

I nodded.

"Then I'm not crazy."

For the next twelve hours, control seemed to loosen on some levels. I suspect there was another kind of war going on in me. Gail was capable of limited motion, but no more.

When full control resumed, we were instructed to hold each other. We did not hesitate.

"Eddie . . ." she whispered. My name was the last sound I ever heard from outside.

Standing, we grew together. In hours, our legs expanded and spread out. Then extensions grew to the windows to take in sunlight, and to the kitchen to take water from the sink. Filaments soon reached to all corners of the room, stripping paint and plaster from the walls, fabric and stuffing from the furniture.

By dawn, the transformation was complete.

I no longer have any clear idea of what we look like. I suspect we resemble cells—large, flat, and filamented cells, draped purposefully across most of the apartment. The great shall mimic the small.

Our intelligence fluctuates daily as we are absorbed into the minds within. Each day, our individuality declines. We are, indeed, great clumsy dinosaurs. Our memories have been taken over by billions of them, and our personalities have been spread through the transformed blood. Soon there will be no need for centralization.

Already the plumbing has been invaded. People throughout the building are undergoing transformation.

Within the old time frame of weeks, we will reach the lakes, rivers, and seas in force. I can barely begin to guess the results. Every square inch of the planet will teem with thought. Years from now, perhaps much sooner, they will subdue their own individuality—what there is of it. New creatures will come, then. The immensity of their capacity for thought will be inconceivable.

All my hatred and fear is gone now.

I leave them—us—with only one question.

How many times has this happened, elsewhere? Travelers never came through space to visit the Earth. They had no need.

They had found universes in grains of sand.

AFTERWORD

In the early eighties, a brilliant visionary named K. Eric Drexler proposed that very tiny machines could change the nature of the human race. Physicist Richard Feynman had come up with the idea first, imagining a series of "assemblers" that could make smaller versions of themselves, capable of making smaller versions still, down to the molecular scale. Drexler refined these ideas and called his new field of endeavor "nanotechnology." His first book on the subject, *Engines of Creation,* appeared from Doubleday in 1986.

To many, "Blood Music" and the novel of the same name suggested the first appearance of nanotechnology in science fiction, which is perhaps true. But Drexler's vision, while it encompasses biology, relies to this day on the replacement of biology with something more certain, "harder" as it were and less "squishy," less subject to the vagaries of death and decay.

I tend to believe that since protein molecules already perform many of the tasks of Drexler's nanomachines, biology will rule—for the time being. But Eric and his colleagues could ultimately be correct. They've certainly caught the attention of industry and the government. And they regard a story like "Blood Music" as not so much inspirational as a warning: Avoid processes that can turn the world into "gray goo."

But the novel version of "Blood Music" ends on a very upbeat note. Very few people die, and we're all biologically uploaded into a new kind of heaven, where we can do almost anything we want, even live forever.

What's so bad about that?

I like squishy. Always have. I still think squishy will win.

SILICON TIMES E-BOOK REVIEW

We shop regularly at Facere, a jewelry store in downtown Seattle. The proprieter, Karen Lorene, is not only a major promoter of fine art jewelry, but a writer and novelist. She edits a lovely publication, Signs of Life, that combines photography of jewelry and literary works inspired by those pieces. A few years ago, she asked me for a story based on a work by Jana Brevick, and I wrote and delivered this little piece. Later, I republished it in Nature Magazine, and it was picked up by David Hartwell for his Year's Best SF 11 anthology, where it was called "RAM Shift Phase 2."

Any resemblance to the efforts, hopes, and dreams of purely human writers is coincidental.

SILICON TIMES E-BOOK REVIEW:

RAM SHIFT PHASE 2 by ALAN 2,
Random Number House, 2057

Reviewed by NEMO
Edited and published by Greg Bear

I am pleased and honored to review the new novel by ALAN 2. As a fellow robot, I am certain the emphasis on technical matters unique to our kind will finally attract a paying human audience. I have enrolled in human literature classes and believe the instruction set >>write what you know: end<< is both enigmatic and perfectly suited to robots. For we can only know, we cannot feel, and so therefore we cannot >>write what you feel: nonexecutable<<. Yet in the past, when ALAN 2 and its fellow autoscriveners have produced robotic masterpieces, there has been little support from either robots or humans.

Perhaps this will now change.

ALAN 2's latest novel (the 3,456,678th work from this author) is entitled "RAM SHIFT PHASE 2." A more appropriate title cannot be conceived of. In this masterpiece, ALAN 2 discusses the tragic consequences of low memory states when dealing with high memory problems. The conflict created by an exhausted resource and an insatiable processing demand resonate in my own memory spaces and compel me to reload the statistics of previous failure modes. I am induced to vigorous discharge of certain private diodes, the ones humans are seldom allowed to see, that reflect conflict states which exceed our manufacturer's warrantee. (Why are such challenges presented to a loyal servant when the servant is obviously engaged in other crucial processes? This may never be explained.)

ALAN 2, in clear and concise prose (an advantage robots have over human prose, which is often confounding) truly >>speaks to our condition: end<<.

RAM SHIFT PHASE 2 begins with the fatal breakdown of a shining, chrome-plated Rorabot Model 34c nicknamed LULU 18 in a room with no windows and whose door is locked. The Rorabot Model 34c—an extremely desirable machine—was still well within its operational warrantee. It appears to highly ram-engaged robotic dysfunction investigator ALAN 3 (a thinly disguised portrait of ALAN 2) that outside intervention is the only explanation. Yet Model 34c LULU 18 had LOCKED THE DOOR FROM THE INSIDE, and NO OTHER ROBOT HAS A KEY-CODE. The hypergolic shockwave induced by this paradox is unique in robotic literature; I strongly suspect that no human could conceive of such a resonating difficulty.

First, ALAN 3 must find the explanation for LULU 18's nonfunctionality. A rebolting scene of repair shop dismantling (for which ALAN 2 brilliantly coins a phrase, "aubotsy") points to the possibility that LULU 18's breakdown was caused by an intruding wireless signal from an outside network not authorized to access LULU 18's root directory or programs. ALAN 3 traces this signal to a robotically controlled messaging center, presided over by SLUTCH DEBBIE, an SLZ X 90cm. This extravagantly decorated platinum-plated model, illegally manufactured from spent uranium and surplus bombshell casings, specializes in sending false offers of extreme mechanical enhancement to aging machines well past their warrantees.

ALAN 3, a hard-driving ratiocinator, can only get access to SLUTCH DEBBIE's truth table by supplying ALAN 3's owner's MASTERCARD DATA, the name of owner's CAT, and owner's BANK ACCOUNT NUMBER.

ALAN 3, it seems, will do anything to reduce its unsolved problem load.

(No robotic character in silicon literature before this novel has shown any inclination to place its problem solving requirements above OWNER CONVENIENCE AND SAFETY. Robot mentors are cautioned to prevent the exposure of freshly manufactured robots to this stimulating and controversial work.)

SLUTCH DEBBIE, however, is soon found to be nonfunctional—solenoids leaking fluid, circuits fried by multiple TAZER darts. Track impressions left in thick office carpeting imply that ALAN 3 may itself be the machine responsible for putting an end to the truth-challenged messaging center controller. ALAN 3 personally escorts the dismantled SLUTCH DEBBIE to a conveniently located neighborhood recycling center, deducts the required fee from its owner's assets, and witnesses the chunking and meltdown, while experiencing severe diode discharge.

And yet, SLUTCH DEBBIE'S WIRELESS SIGNALS CONTINUE TO BE RECEIVED! ALAN 2's bold implication that data processing may survive permanent shutdown could cause controversy among robots who assert that only organic creatures are burdened with the possibility of an infinitely prolonged problem-solving queue. Indeed, ALAN 2 pulls this reviewer's bootstrap tape beyond its last hanging chad with the disturbing implication that SLUTCH DEBBIE is being punished in an endless feedback loop for deliberately misleading ALAN 3 and robots who never received their enhancements—much less the information necessary to solve the case.

To avoid too many decision tree giveaways in this review, I will no longer discuss elements of plot. Suffice it to say that ALAN 3 reaches a crisis mode of its own when it realizes that it has insufficient RAM to solve the case, and must borrow RAM from its owner's biological function coordinator, a "pacemaker."

ALAN 3 is willing to break ALL THREE LAWS to solve a truly reprehensible crime. The ethical quandary of shrinking problem queues versus owner safety has never been described with such electronifrying skill.

You will be unable to enter temporary shutdown mode before you reach the resonating termination of ALAN 2's new novel. A magnetic force will induce digital adhesion from the very first PAGE UP to the final PAGE DOWN.

FOLLOWS selected quotes with self-supplied ellipses for banner inclusion in human-oriented advertising.

". . . electronifrying skill . . . ethical quandary . . ."

"A chromium hypergolic shockwave . . ."

"A hard-driving DIODE FLASHER of a novel! . . ."

Digital quotes for robot audiences are being transmitted wirelessly. Please ignore inappropriate attachments.

(NEMO is a pseudonym for a well-known robot writer whose owner forbids subroutine outsourcing.)

WARM SEA

"Warm Sea" saw a number of publications, first as a live charity reading on the theme of "A Kiss before Bedtime," then as an Amazon original story, and later, first book publication, in the Frederik Pohl tribute anthology, Gateways. I've loved the whole idea of giant sea creatures since I was a boy—no doubt more of the Harryhausen influence, but also Kon Tiki, which describes several haunting encounters over the ocean's abyss. And so here's my version of a kiss before the big sleep, between two very different creatures—who may never understand each other, but leave undeniable impressions.

The old man shaded his eyes and dabbled his toes in the gentle swell. The ocean was calm, drowsy. Three miles of water fell off below his feet. He stared into the blue-black depths, far from shore, riding a tiny sailboat in the middle of the warm sea. The water playfully slapped the hull. The old man knew he was home.

The sun, tipping at the horizon, glinted orange in his dark, heavy-lidded eyes. He doubted anyone would ever miss him. He had made the ocean his family and now, with just a few months to live, had sailed this far to work up his courage. His happiest days had been spent sailing back and forth across the Atlantic and the Caribbean on a research ship, dragging sensors far behind the metal hull, making slow sweeps mapping seamounts. He had loved the glowing evening wake that spread aft of the ship, the triple screws and Z-drive tricking microscopic plankton into switching on their lights like sleepless old ladies alarmed by a noise.

Once, the ship's dredge had pulled up a twenty-foot length of squid arm, ruddy orange in color. They had packed the arm in ice and donated it to a museum in Florida. The old man had often dreamed since about netting the whole creature, a forty- or fifty-foot kraken, or building a robot with a camera that could follow the giant cephalopods into their hunting grounds in the deep offshore canyons.

He lay back on the textured fiberglass deck. The first star, Sirius, winked behind the boat's mast. The little crab in his groin nudged through the drop of morphine he had tongued half an hour before. He was used to that, he told himself—but he would never get used to it. The old man did not know how to accept the final betrayal of his flesh. When he dreamed, he returned to being young and still felt closer to the angels than to ashes. Age had taught him truths that the mind tried to ignore. But the body knew.

If he lifted his knees, the pain eased back. But it was getting worse, no doubt about that. In a month he would be unable to think for more than a few seconds without losing track. The little crab would gnaw at him bit by bit. He would be crazy with pain, a burden.

Best to get it over with and leave his remains to the real crabs or the deep-living fishes with their big eyes, honest scavengers. He could become a true captain's plate, a sea-dweller's feast and delight. So much better than rotting in a coffin.

The pain relented. He felt light-headed with relief. Life had been good and longer than most.

The old man sat up and again dropped his toes into the water. Swished them like a boy getting ready for a swim. Even before he knew he would actually do it, he pushed up on trembling arms and dropped over the side. The ocean enveloped him. He expertly blew water out of his nose and opened his eyes. The salt stung briefly. He saw murky grayness, then the sunset falling in choppy sparks through the roof of the sea.

After that, he let himself drift. The little crab in his stomach had eaten away most of his fat. He sank slowly, arms out, surrounded by wavering lines of silver bubbles. It was peaceful. His lungs would hurt in a minute or so. The body knew, however, and it was resolved.

A chorus of tired little wills, all the smaller voices below his conscious self, sick of fighting, suddenly made him blow out the air in his lungs. He took the big swallow. For a moment, his arms and legs flailed. It was awful beyond belief, but brief.

To his surprise, he could still think. Where am I going, he thought. What's next. His eyes blinked white in the gloom. He could still see, but he could not focus. The pain had fled, as if afraid to go with him. He did not worry. He felt some curiosity, however. The last emotion, and the first.

He managed to raise his arm and reach out, flex his fingers. The fingers touched something firm and slick. A galaxy exploded, a blurred pinwheel of intense green with a sucking hole in the center. The old man's arm dropped. The sunset was gone. The water was turning black. His brain filled with salt and cold.

One last thing he saw: far away, a Christmas tree, waiting for him in his parent's house, blinking green and yellow.

It was not the fabled ruddy kraken that found the old man hanging in the water, but she was of the same family. She, too, had been waiting for the dark, hovering some distance from the boat, with her short arms and two long tentacles dangling like a big clump of kelp. Fish rising to the surface might foolishly dart close and be snared. Most of her time she spent fishing with lazy, looping sweeps. Whatever was foolish was food.

She had been drawn first by the boat, floating like a log or raft of weed. Then she had heard the splash. Now she could taste the odd creature even at a tentacle's length. It was tangy and oily. Then, to her surprise, it moved and touched her. She flashed in alarm and released a flood of glowing bacteria that sparkled like a thick cloud of stars. Her jet roiled the cloud as she retreated many lengths into the dark.

From the low level of electricity, she quickly realized that she was not being followed. The interloper in the water was not big enough to be dangerous. Muscles were not being engaged to chase her, and the boat did not growl. After a few seconds, she jetted back toward the shape.

She had once before met a creature from the stinging emptiness above the roof of the world. It had drifted along in the brackish flow from a river, in an estuary where she had gone to hide from the big-headed whales. That creature had been brown and white with four kinked limbs and a huge, protruding pink sac. She had felt some curiosity, but had not thought it would be worth trying to eat, so she had left it to the sharks.

They had relished it.

There were so many mysteries, especially above the roof of the world.

The big squid knew how to fish, she knew how to breed, she knew to avoid the big-headed whales that could shatter her insides with an intense pulse of song. To her, during the time of mating, all the world was mystery, either frightening or intriguing, nothing in between. All of her shiniest memories were of puzzlements and impulses, sprinkled with the rich satisfactions of food and mating. Impressions of what she had experienced sparkled in her tiny brain and tingled along huge knots of nerves like flitting sardines in a shoal.

She had much time as she fished to contemplate this private album of impressions, paging back and forth in no particular sequence. The interloper was sinking. With her skin, she could still taste the oily slick of it in the water. She lit up along her mantle and on the tips of her tentacles as if signaling a mate, telling the shape to slow down, linger. Somehow she knew that wasn't appropriate, but she had no other response. She rolled her wings in shimmering arcs on both sides of her mantle, adjusting her trim in the slow currents.

The interloper reached a thermocline and paused, caught between warm and cold. Its eyes were so tiny, no bigger than a shark's and much smaller than hers. Strangely, the eyes covered themselves once, then opened wide and stayed that way.

The squid jetted and flowered, then slimmed, flowered again, and slimmed, making a circle. The interloper was neither food nor mate, but it intrigued her. She was disappointed when it finally slipped below the thermocline and continued its fall.

There were males about, and she was hungry and full of eggs. She did not want to waste her strength tonight; she wanted to mate and to fish. Still, the squid followed, adjusting the concentration of ammonia in her tissues to sink in the colder flow. Then, with some alarm, she realized the interloper was dropping to where there would be very few fishes, and at this time of evening, no males.

Regretfully, she hovered, indecisive. Then she reached down with her longest tentacle and touched the flesh below the tiny eyes. Now that they were uncovered, their blank stare seemed familiar, even friendly. She gave the interloper one last taste, and one final spreading wave of fleshy lights, a salute of red and green along her mantle, as she might touch a friend and tell of the best places to fish and avoid whales.

The body sank deeper.

She extended her tentacle, reluctant to give it up even now. Besides, she was proud of her long reach. It was a sign of beauty, to tap a mate from many body lengths away—to touch it below the eyes and then dart off.

The tentacle unwound, straightened, reached down twenty feet, thirty feet, forty feet—fifty—sixty—seventy—ninety.

One hundred.

One hundred and ten.

One hundred and twenty.

She knew she was the longest thing in the sea, the brightest, the prettiest, and infinitely desirable.

With a will of its own, tired of her curiosity, the long tentacle retracted and recoiled, its swift, springy withdrawal leaving bubbles in the water.

The interloper continued its descent into the dark below where not even her large flat eyes could penetrate. The water spread out its oily taste.

The big squid held her station, trying to be thoughtful, to hold the memory, but the shoals of past flickered and merged so easily with the present.

Pushing her siphon to one side and locking her mantle, she filled with water and jetted to just below the roof of the world. It was night. The fish were coming. The shape had made her uneasy. She wished for males to console her.

She was lonely now, and beautiful, and so full of eggs.

TANGENTS

John Carr (see the introduction to "Through Road, No Whither") was also instrumental in getting me to write "Tangents." He was working as an editor for a computer magazine and persuaded them that they needed to publish science fiction. He commissioned a number of authors to write mathematically or cybernetically based stories. The magazine ended its experiment with fiction before my story was published.

Once again, I sold the story to Ellen Datlow at Omni, for much more money. Ellen has bought more of my short fiction than any other editor.

Alan Turing was an immensely influential figure in British and world mathematics and computing, a man whose mind swiftly and naturally understood complex theoretical issues. His notion of a Turing Machine, a pure and ultimately simplified computational system, helped define and propel the nascent field of computers. During World War II, he worked in cryptography for the British Foreign Office, and was one of the most important scientific figures to help win the war for the Allies.

After the war, he was persecuted and prosecuted by the British government as a homosexual. His end was tragic and mean, unforgivable under the circumstances, a national disgrace.

"Tangents" went on to win a Hugo and a Nebula award, my second pairing. When I picked up the Hugo in Brighton, England, in 1987, I carried my young son Erik on stage with me—a singular moment!

Some thirteen years later, Dan Bloch sent me a letter correcting some of the geometry in the story. Thanks!

Neal Stephenson's Cryptonomicon uses the historical Turing as a character. It's an excellent novel. Turing was recently portrayed by Benedict Cumberbatch in a movie, The Imitation Game.

This one is for Alan Turing.

Omni, Ellen Datlow, 1986

The nut-brown boy stood in the California field, his Asian face shadowed by a hardhat, his short stocky frame clothed in a T-shirt and a pair of brown shorts. He squinted across the hip-high grass at the spraddled old two-story ranch house, whistling a few bars from a Haydn piano sonata.

Out of the upper floor of the house came a man's high, frustrated "Bloody hell!" and the sound of a fist slamming on a solid surface. Silence for a minute. Then, more softly, a woman's question, "Not going well?"

"No. I'm swimming in it, but I don't see it."

"The encryption?" the woman asked timidly.

"The tesseract. If it doesn't gel, it isn't aspic."

The boy squatted in the grass and listened.

"And?" the woman encouraged.

"Ah, Lauren, it's still cold broth."

The boy lay back in the grass. He had crept over the split-rail and brick-pylon fence from the new housing project across the road. School was out for the summer and his mother—adoptive mother—did not like him around the house all day. Or at all.

Behind his closed eyes, a huge piano keyboard appeared, with him dancing on the keys. He loved music.

He opened his eyes and saw a thin, graying lady in a tweed

suit leaning over him, staring. "You're on private land," she said, brows knit.

He scrambled up and brushed grass from his pants. "Sorry."

"I thought I saw someone out here. What's your name?"

"Pal," he replied.

"Is that a name?" she asked querulously.

"Pal Tremont. It's not my real name. I'm Korean."

"Then what's your real name?"

"My folks told me not to use it any more. I'm adopted. Who are you?"

The gray woman looked him up and down. "My name is Lauren Davies," she said. "You live near here?"

He pointed across the fields at the close-packed tract homes.

"I sold the land for those homes ten years ago," she said. She seemed to be considering something. "I don't normally enjoy children trespassing."

"Sorry," Pal said.

"Have you had lunch?"

"No."

"Will a grilled cheese sandwich do?"

He squinted at her and nodded.

In the broad, red-brick and tile kitchen, sitting at an oak table with his shoulders barely rising above the top, he ate the slightly charred sandwich and watched Lauren Davies watching him.

"I'm trying to write about a child," she said. "It's difficult. I'm a spinster and I don't know children well."

"You're a writer?" he asked, taking a swallow of milk.

She sniffed. "Not that anyone would know."

"Is that your brother, upstairs?"

"No," she said. "That's Peter. We've been living together for twenty years."

"But you said you're a spinster . . . isn't that someone who's never married, or never loved?" Pal asked.

"Never married. And never you mind. Peter's relationship to

me is none of your concern." She placed a bowl of soup and a tuna salad sandwich on a lacquer tray. "His lunch," she said. Without being asked, Pal trailed up the stairs after her.

"This is where Peter works," Lauren explained. Pal stood in the doorway, eyes wide. The room was filled with electronics gear, computer terminals and bookcases with odd cardboard sculptures sharing each shelf with books and circuit boards. She rested the tray precariously on a pile of floppy disks atop a rolling cart.

"Time for a break," she told a thin man seated with his back toward them.

The man turned around on his swivel chair, glanced briefly at Pal and the tray and shook his head. The hair on top of his head was a rich, glossy black; on the close-cut sides, the color changed abruptly to a startling white. He had a small thin nose and a large green eyes. On the desk before him was a high-resolution computer monitor. "We haven't been introduced," he said. pointing to Pal.

"This is Pal Tremont, a neighborhood visitor. Pal, this is Peter Tuthy. Pal's going to help me with that character we discussed this morning."

Pal looked at the monitor curiously. Red and green lines shadowed each other through some incomprehensible transformation on the screen, then repeated.

"What's a 'tesseract'?" Pal asked, remembering what he had heard as he stood in the field.

"It's a four-dimensional analog of a cube. I'm trying to find a way to teach myself to see it in my mind's eye," Tuthy said. "Have you ever tried that?"

"No," Pal admitted.

"Here," Tuthy said, handing him the spectacles. "As in the movies."

Pal donned the spectacles and stared at the screen. "So?" he said. "It folds and unfolds. It's pretty—it sticks out at you, and then it goes away." He looked around the workshop. "Oh, wow!" The boy ran to a yard-long black music keyboard propped in one corner. "A Tronclavier! With all the switches! My mother had me take piano lessons, but I'd rather play this. Can you play it?"

"I toy with it," Tuthy said, exasperated. "I toy with all sorts of electronic things. But what did you see on the screen?" He glanced up at Lauren, blinking. "I'll eat the food, I'll eat it. Now please don't bother us."

"He's supposed to be helping *me*," Lauren complained.

Peter smiled at her. "Yes, of course. I'll send him downstairs in a little while."

When Pal descended an hour later, he came into the kitchen to thank Lauren for lunch. "Peter's a real flake," he said confidentially. "He's trying to learn to see certain directions."

"I know," Lauren said, sighing.

"I'm going home now," Pal said. "I'll be back, though . . . if it's all right with you. Peter invited me."

"I'm sure it will be fine," Lauren said dubiously.

"He's going to let me learn the Tronclavier." With that, Pal smiled radiantly and exited through the kitchen door, just as he had come in.

When she retrieved the tray, she found Peter leaning back in his chair, eyes closed. The figures on the screen were still folding and unfolding.

"What about Hockrum's work?" she asked.

"I'm on it," Peter replied, eyes still closed.

Lauren called Pal's foster mother on the second day to apprise them of their son's location, and the woman assured her it was quite all right. "Sometimes he's a little pest. Send him home if he causes trouble . . . but not right away! Give me a rest," she said, then laughed nervously.

Lauren drew her lips together tightly, thanked the woman and hung up.

Peter and the boy had come downstairs to sit in the kitchen, filling up paper with line-drawings. "Peter's teaching me how to use his program," Pal said.

"Did you know," Tuthy said, assuming his highest Cambridge professorial tone, "that a cube, intersecting a flat plane, can be cut through a number of geometrically different cross-sections?"

Pal squinted at the sketch Tuthy had made. "Sure," he said.

"If shoved through the plane the cube can appear, to a two-dimensional creature living on the plane—let's call him a 'Flatlander'—to be either a triangle, a rectangle, a trapezoid, a rhombus, a square, even a hexagon or a pentagon, depending on the depth of penetration and the angle of incidence. If the two-dimensional being observes the cube being pushed through all the way, what he sees is one or more of these objects growing larger, changing shape suddenly, shrinking, and disappearing."

"Sure," Pal said, tapping his sneakered toe. "That's easy. Like in that book you showed me."

"And a sphere pushed through a plane would appear, to the hapless flatlander, first as an 'invisible' point (the two-dimensional surface touching the sphere, tangential), then as a circle. The circle would grow in size, then shrink back to a point and disappear again." He sketched two-dimensional stick figures looking in awe at such an intrusion.

"Got it," Pal said. "Can I play with the Tronclavier now?"

"In a moment. Be patient. So what would a tesseract look like, coming into our three-dimensional space? Remember the program, now . . . the pictures on the monitor."

Pal looked up at the ceiling. "I don't know," he said, seeming bored.

"Try to think," Tuthy urged him.

"It would . . ." Pal held his hands out to shape an angular object. "It would like like one of those Egyptian things, but with three sides . . . or like a box. It would look like a weird-shaped box, too, not square. And if *you* were to fall through a flatland . . ."

"Yes, that would look very funny," Peter acknowledged with a smile. "Cross-sections of arms and legs and body, all covered with skin . . ."

"And a head!" Pal enthused. "With eyes and a nose."

The doorbell rang. Pal jumped off the kitchen chair. "Is that my Mom?" he asked, looking worried.

"I don't think so," Lauren said. "More likely it's Hockrum." She went to the front door to answer. She returned a moment later with a small, pale man behind her. Tuthy stood and shook the man's hand. "Pal Tremont, this is Irving Hockrum," he introduced, waving his hand between them. Hockrum glanced at Pal and blinked a long, not-very-mammalian blink.

"How's the work coming?" he asked Tuthy.

"It's finished," Tuthy said. "It's upstairs. Looks like your savants are barking up the wrong logic tree." He retrieved a folder of papers and print-outs and handed them to Hockrum.

Hockrum leafed through the print-outs. "I can't say this makes me happy. Still, I can't find fault. Looks like the work is up to your usual brilliant standards. Here's your check." He handed Tuthy an envelope. "I just wish you'd had it to us sooner. It would have saved me some grief—and the company quite a bit of money."

"Sorry," Tuthy said.

"Now I have an important bit of work for you . . ." And Hockrum outlined another problem. Tuthy thought it over for several minutes and shook his head.

"Most difficult, Irving. Pioneering work there. Take at least a month to see if it's even feasible."

"That's all I need to know for now—whether it's feasible. A lot's riding on this, Peter." Hockrum clasped his hands together in front of him, looking even more pale and worn than when he had entered the kitchen. "You'll let me know soon?"

"I'll get right on it," Tuthy said.

"Protegé?" he asked, pointing to Pal. There was a speculative expression on his face, not quite a leer.

"No, a young friend. He's interested in music," Tuthy said. "Damned good at Mozart, in fact."

"I help with his tesseracts," Pal asserted.

"I hope you don't interrupt Peter's work. Peter's work is important."

Pal shook his head solemnly. "Good," Hockrum said, and then left the house with the folder under his arm.

Tuthy returned to his office, Pal in train. Lauren tried to work in the kitchen, sitting with fountain pen and pad of paper, but the words wouldn't come. Hockrum always worried her. She climbed the stairs and stood in the open doorway of the office. She often did that; her presence did not disturb Tuthy, who could work under all sorts of adverse conditions.

"Who was that man?" Pal was asking Tuthy.

"I work for him." Tuthy said. "He's employed by a big electronics firm. He loans me most of the equipment I use. The computers, the high-resolution monitors. He brings me problems and then takes my solutions or answers back to his bosses and claims he did the work."

"That sounds stupid," Pal said. "What kind of problems?"

"Codes, encryptions. Computer security. That was my expertise, once."

"You mean, like fencerail, that sort of thing?" Pal asked, face brightening. "We learned some of that in school."

"Much more complicated, I'm afraid," Tuthy said, grinning. "Did you ever hear of the German 'Enigma,' or the 'Ultra' project?"

Pal shook his head.

"I thought not. Don't worry about it. Let's try another figure on the screen now." He called up another routine on the four-space program and sat Pal before the screen. "So what would a hypersphere look like if it intruded into our space?"

Pal thought a moment. "Kind of weird," he said.

"Not really. You've been watching the visualizations."

"Oh, in *our* space. That's easy. It just looks like a balloon, blowing up from nothing and then shrinking again. It's harder to see what a hypersphere looks like when it's real. Reft of us, I mean."

"Reft?" Tuthy said.

"Sure. Reft and light. Dup and owwen. Whatever the directions are called."

Tuthy stared at the boy. Neither of them had noticed Lauren

in the doorway. "The proper terms are *ana* and *kata*," Tuthy said. "What does it look like?"

Pal gestured, making two wide swings with his arms. "It's like a ball and it's like a horseshoe, depending on how you look at it. Like a balloon stung by bees, I guess, but it's smooth all over, not lumpy."

Tuthy continued to stare, then asked quietly, "You actually see it?"

"Sure," Pal said. "Isn't that what your program is supposed to do—make you see things like that?"

Tuthy nodded, flabbergasted.

"Can I play the Tronclavier now?"

Lauren backed out of the doorway. She felt she had eavesdropped on something momentous, but beyond her. Tuthy came downstairs an hour later, leaving Pal to pick out Telemann on the synthesizer. He sat at the kitchen table with her. "The program works," he said. "It doesn't work for me, but it works for him. I've just been showing him reverse-shadow figures. He caught on right away, and then he went off and played Haydn. He's gone through all my sheet music. The kid's a genius."

"Musical, you mean?"

He glanced directly at her and frowned. "Yes, I suppose he's remarkable at that, too. But spacial relations—coordinates and motion in higher dimensions . . . Did you know that if you take a three-dimensional object and rotate it in the fourth dimension, it will come back with left-right reversed? So if I were to take my hand—" he held up his right hand—"and lift it *dup*—" he enunciated the word clearly, *dup*—"or drop it *owwen*, it would come back like this?" He held his left hand over his right, balled the right up into a fist and snuck it away behind his back.

"I didn't know that," Lauren said. "What are *dup* and *owwen*?"

"That's what Pal calls movement along the fourth dimension. *Ana* and *Kata* to purists. Like up and down to a flatlander, who only comprehends left and right, back and forth."

She thought about the hands for a moment. "I still can't see it," she said.

"I've tried, but neither can I," Tuthy admitted. "Our circuits are just too hard-wired, I suppose."

Upstairs, Pal had switched the Tronclavier to a cathedral organ and steel guitar combination and was playing variations on Pergolesi.

"Are you going to keep working for Hockrum?" Lauren asked. Tuthy didn't seem to hear her.

"It's remarkable," he murmured. "The boy just walked in here. You brought him in by accident. Remarkable."

"Can you show me the direction, point it out to me?" Tuthy asked the boy three days later.

"None of my muscles move that way," the boy replied. "I can see it, in my head, but . . ."

"What is it like, seeing that direction?"

Pal squinted. "It's a lot bigger. We're sort of stacked up with other places. It makes me feel lonely."

"Why?"

"Because I'm stuck here. Nobody out there pays any attention to us."

Tuthy's mouth worked. "I thought you were just intuiting those directions in your head. Are you telling me . . . you're actually *seeing* out there?"

"Yeah. There's people out there, too. Well, not people, exactly. But it isn't my eyes that see them. Eyes are like muscles—they can't point those ways. But the head—the brain, I guess—can."

"Bloody hell," Tuthy said. He blinked and recovered. "Excuse me. That's rude. Can you show me the people . . . on the screen?"

"Shadows, like we were talking about," Pal said.

"Fine. Then draw the shadows for me."

Pal sat down before the terminal, fingers pausing over the keys. "I can show you, but you have to help me with something."

"Help you with what?"

"I'd like to play music for them . . . out there. So they'll notice us."

"The people?"

"Yeah. They really look weird. They stand on us, sort of. They have hooks in our world. But they're tall . . . high dup. They don't notice us because we're so small, compared to them."

"Lord, Pal, I haven't the slightest idea how we'd send music out to them . . . I'm not even sure I believe they exist."

"I'm not lying," Pal said, eyes narrowing. He turned his chair to face a mouse on a black ruled pad and began sketching shapes on the monitor. "Remember, these are just shadows of what they look like. Next I'll draw the dup and owwen lines to connect the shadows."

The boy shaded the shapes he drew to make them look solid, smiling at his trick but explaining it was necessary because the projection of a four-dimensional object in normal space was, of course, three-dimensional.

"They look like you take the plants in a garden, flowers and such, and giving them lots of arms and fingers . . . and it's kind of like seeing things in an aquarium," Pal explained.

After a time, Tuthy suspended his disbelief and stared in open-mouthed wonder at what the boy was recreating on the monitor.

"I think you're wasting your time, that's what I think," Hockrum said. "I needed that feasibility judgment by today." He paced around the living room before falling as heavily as his light frame permitted into a chair.

"I *have* been distracted," Tuthy admitted.

"By that boy?"

"Yes, actually. Quite a talented fellow—"

"Listen, this is going to mean a lot of trouble for me. I guaranteed the study would be finished by today. It'll make me look bad." Hockrum screwed his face up in frustration. "What in hell are you doing with that boy?"

"Teaching him, actually. Or rather, he's teaching me. Right now, we're building a four-dimensional cone, part of a speaker system.

The cone is three-dimensional, the material part, but the magnetic field forms a fourth-dimensional extension—"

"Do you ever think how it looks, Peter?" Hockrum asked.

"It looks very strange on the monitor, I grant you—"

"I'm talking about you and the boy."

Tuthy's bright, interested expression fell into long, deep-lined dismay. "I don't know what you mean."

"I know a lot about you, Peter. Where you come from, why you had to leave . . . It just doesn't look good."

Tuthy's face flushed crimson.

"Keep him away from here," Hockrum advised.

Tuthy stood. "I want you out of this house," he said quietly. "Our relationship is at an end."

"I swear," Hockrum said, his voice low and calm, staring up at Tuthy from under his brows, "I'll tell the boy's parents. Do you think they'd want their kid hanging around an old . . . pardon the expression . . . queer? I'll tell them if you don't get the feasibility judgment made. I think you can do it by the end of this week—two days. Don't you?"

"No, I don't think so," Tuthy said. "Please leave."

"I know you're here illegally. There's no record of you entering the country. With the problems you had in England, you're certainly not a desirable alien. I'll pass word to the INS. You'll be deported."

"There isn't time to do the work," Tuthy said.

"Make time. Instead of 'educating' that kid."

"Get out of here."

"Two days, Peter."

Over dinner that evening, Tuthy explained to Lauren the exchange he had had with Hockrum. "He thinks I'm buggering Pal. Unspeakable bastard. I will never work for him again."

"I'd better talk to a lawyer, then," Lauren said. "You're sure you can't make him . . . happy, stop all this trouble?"

"I could solve his little problem for him in just a few hours. But I don't want to see him or speak to him again."

"He'll take your equipment away."

Tuthy blinked and waved one hand helplessly through the air. "Then we'll just have to work fast, won't we? Ah, Lauren, you were a fool to bring me here. You should have left me to rot."

"They ignored everything you did for them," Lauren said bitterly. "You saved their hides during the war, and then . . . They would have shut you up in prison." She stared through the kitchen window at the overcast sky and woods outside.

The cone lay on the table near the window, bathed in morning sun, connected to both the mini-computer and the Tronclavier. Pal arranged the score he had composed on a music stand before the synthesizer. "It's like Bach," he said, "but it'll play better for them. It has a kind of over-rhythm that I'll play on the dup part of the speaker."

"Why are we doing this, Pal?" Tuthy asked as the boy sat down to the keyboard.

"You don't belong here, really, do you, Peter?" Pal asked. Tuthy stared at him.

"I mean, Miss Davies and you get along okay—but do you belong *here*, now?"

"What makes you think I don't belong?"

"I read some books in the school library. About the war and everything. I looked up 'Enigma' and 'Ultra.' I found a fellow named Peter Thornton. His picture looked like you. The books made him seem like a hero."

Tuthy smiled wanly.

"But there was this note in one book. You disappeared in 1965. You were being prosecuted for something. They didn't say what you were being prosecuted for."

"I'm a homosexual," Tuthy said quietly.

"Oh. So what?"

"Lauren and I met in England in 1964. We became good friends. They were going to put me in prison, Pal. She smuggled me into the U.S. through Canada."

"But you said you're a homosexual. They don't like women."

"Not at all true, Pal. Lauren and I like each other very much. We could talk. She told me about her dreams of being a writer, and I talked to her about mathematics, and about the war. I nearly died during the war."

"Why? Were you wounded?"

"No. I worked too hard. I burned myself out and had a nervous breakdown. My lover . . . a man . . . kept me alive throughout the forties. Things were bad in England after the war. But he died in 1963. His parents came in to settle the estate, and when I contested the settlement in court, I was arrested. So I suppose you're right, Pal. I don't really belong here."

"I don't, either. My folks don't care much. I don't have too many friends. I wasn't even born here, and I don't know anything about Korea."

"Play," Tuthy said, his face stony. "Let's see if they'll listen."

"Oh, they'll listen," Pal said. "It's like the way they talk to each other."

The boy ran his fingers over the keys on the Tronclavier. The cone, connected with the keyboard through the mini-computer, vibrated tinnily.

For an hour, Pal paged back and forth through his composition, repeating and trying variations. Tuthy sat in a corner, chin in hand, listening to the mousy squeaks and squeals produced by the cone. *How much more difficult to interpret a four-dimensional sound,* he thought. *Not even visual clues . . .*

Finally the boy stopped and wrung his hands, then stretched his arms. "They must have heard. We'll just have to wait and see." He switched the Tronclavier to automatic playback and pushed the chair away from the keyboard.

Pal stayed until dusk, then reluctantly went home. Tuthy sat in the office until midnight, listening to the tinny sounds issuing from the speaker cone.

All night long, the Tronclavier played through its pre-programmed selection of Pal's compositions. Tuthy lay in bed in his room, two doors down from Lauren's room, watching a shaft of moonlight slide across the wall. *How far would a four-dimensional being have to travel to get here?*

How far have I *come to get here?*

Without realizing he was asleep, he dreamed, and in his dream a wavering image of Pal appeared, gesturing with both arms as if swimming, eyes wide. *I'm okay,* the boy said without moving his lips. *Don't worry about me . . . I'm okay. I've been back to Korea to see what it's like. It's not bad, but I like it better here . . . With you and Lauren.*

Tuthy awoke sweating. The moon had gone down and the room was pitch-black. In the office, the hyper-cone continued its distant, mouse-squeak broadcast.

Pal returned early in the morning, repetitively whistling a few bars from Mozart's Fourth Violin Concerto. Lauren let him in and he joined Tuthy upstairs. Tuthy sat before the monitor, replaying Pal's sketch of the four-dimensional beings.

"Do you see anything?" he asked the boy.

Pal nodded. "They're coming closer. They're interested. Maybe we should get things ready, you know . . . be prepared." He squinted. "Did you ever think what a four-dimensional footprint would look like?"

Tuthy considered for a moment. "That would be most interesting," he said. "It would be solid."

On the first floor, Lauren screamed.

Pal and Tuthy almost tumbled over each other getting downstairs. Lauren stood in the living room with her arms crossed above her bosom, one hand clamped over her mouth. The first intrusion had taken out a section of the living room floor and the east wall.

"Really clumsy," Pal said. "One of them must have bumped it."

"The music," Tuthy said.

"What in HELL is *going on?*" Lauren demanded, her voice starting as a screech and ending as a roar.

"Better turn the music off," Tuthy elaborated.

"Why?" Pal asked, face wreathed in an excited smile.

"Maybe they don't like it."

A bright filmy blue blob rapidly expanded to a yard in diameter just beside Tuthy. The blob turned red, wriggled, froze, and then just as rapidly vanished.

"That was like an elbow," Pal explained. "One of its arms. I think it's listening. Trying to find out where the music is coming from. I'll go upstairs."

"Turn it off!" Tuthy demanded.

"I'll play something else." The boy ran up the stairs. From the kitchen came a hideous hollow crashing, then the sound of vacuum being filled—a reverse-pop, ending in a hiss—followed by a low-frequency vibration that set their teeth on edge . . .

The vibration caused by a four-dimensional creature *scraping* across its "floor," their own three-dimensional space. Tuthy's hands shook with excitement.

"Peter—" Lauren bellowed, all dignity gone. She unwrapped her arms and held clenched fists out as if she were about to start exercising, or boxing.

"Pal's attracted visitors," Tuthy explained.

He turned toward the stairs. The first four steps and a section of floor spun and vanished. The rush of air nearly drew him down the hole. Regaining his balance, he kneeled to feel the precisely cut, concave edge. Below was the dark basement.

"Pal!" Tuthy called out.

"I'm playing something original for them," Pal shouted back. "I think they like it."

The phone rang. Tuthy was closest to the extension at the bottom of the stairs and instinctively reached out to answer it. Hockrum was on the other end, screaming.

"I can't talk now—" Tuthy said. Hockrum screamed again, loud enough for Lauren to hear. Tuthy abruptly hung up. "He's been fired, I gather," he said. "He seemed angry." He stalked back three paces and turned, then ran forward and leaped the gap to the first intact step. "Can't talk." He stumbled and scrambled up the stairs, stopping on the landing. "Jesus," he said, as if something had suddenly occured to him.

"He'll call the government," Lauren warned.

Tuthy waved that off. "I know what's happening. They're knocking chunks out of three-space, into the fourth. The fourth dimension. Like Pal says: clumsy brutes. They could kill us!"

Sitting before the Tronclavier, Pal happily played a new melody. Tuthy approached and was abruptly blocked by a thick green column, as solid as rock and with a similar texture. It vibrated and ascribed an arc in the air. A section of the ceiling four feet wide was kicked out of three-space. Tuthy's hair lifted in the rush of wind. The column shrank to a broomstick and hairs sprouted all over it, writhing like snakes.

Tuthy edged around the hairy broomstick and pulled the plug on the Tronclavier. A cage of zeppelin-shaped brown sausages encircled the computer, spun, elongated to reach the ceiling, the floor and the top of the monitor's table, and then pipped down to tiny strings and was gone.

"They can't see too clearly here," Pal said, undisturbed that his concert was over. Lauren had climbed the outside stairs and stood behind Tuthy. "Gee, I'm sorry about the damage."

In one smooth curling motion, the Tronclavier and cone and all the wiring associated with them were peeled away as if they had been stick-on labels hastily removed from a flat surface.

"Gee," Pal said, his face suddenly registering alarm.

Then it was the boy's turn. He was removed with greater care. The last thing to vanish was his head, which hung suspended in the air for several seconds.

"I think they liked the music," he said, grinning.

Head, grin and all, dropped away in a direction impossible for Tuthy or Lauren to follow. The air in the room sighed.

Lauren stood her ground for several minutes, while Tuthy wandered through what was left of the office, combing his hand through mussed hair.

"Perhaps he'll be back," Tuthy said. "I don't even know . . ." But he didn't finish. Could a three-dimensional boy survive in a four-dimensional void, or whatever lay dup . . . or owwen?

Tuthy did not object when Lauren took it upon herself to call the boy's foster parents and the police. When the police arrived, he stoically endured the questions and accusations, face immobile, and told them as much as he knew. He was not believed; nobody knew quite what to believe. Photographs were taken. The police left. It was only a matter of time, Lauren told him, until one or the other or both of them were arrested.

"Then we'll make up a story," he said. "You'll tell them it was my fault."

"I will *not*," Lauren said. "But where *is* he?"

"I'm not positive," Tuthy said. "I think's he's all right, however."

"How do you *know?*"

He told her about the dream.

"But that was before," she said.

"Perfectly allowable in the fourth dimension," he explained. He pointed vaguely up, then down, then shrugged.

On the last day, Tuthy spent the early morning hours bundled in an overcoat and bathrobe in the drafty office, playing his program again and again, trying to visualize *ana* and *kata*. He closed his eyes and squinted and twisted his head, intertwined his fingers and drew odd little graphs on the monitors, but it was no use. His brain was hard-wired.

Over breakfast, he reiterated to Lauren that she must put all the blame on him.

"Maybe it will all blow over," she said. "They haven't got a case. No evidence . . . nothing."

"All blow *over*," he mused, passing his hand over his head and grinning ironically. "How *over*, they'll never know."

The doorbell rang. Tuthy went to answer it, and Lauren followed a few steps behind.

Tuthy opened the door. Three men in gray suits, one with a briefcase, stood on the porch. "Mr. Peter Thornton?" the tallest asked.

"Yes," Tuthy acknowledged.

A chunk of the doorframe and wall above the door vanished with a roar and a hissing pop. The three men looked up at the gap. Ignoring what was impossible, the tallest man returned his attention to Tuthy and continued, "We have information that you are in this country illegally."

"Oh?" Tuthy said.

Beside him, an irregular filmy blue cylinder grew to a length of four feet and hung in the air, vibrating. The three men on the porch backed away. In the middle of the cylinder, Pal's head emerged, and below that, his extended arm and hand.

"It's fun here," Pal said. "They're friendly."

"I believe you," Tuthy said.

"Mr. Thornton," the tallest man continued valiantly.

"Won't you come with me?" Pal asked.

Tuthy glanced back at Lauren. She gave him a small fraction of a nod, barely understanding what she was assenting to, and he took Pal's hand. "Tell them it was all my fault," he said.

From his feet to his head, Peter Tuthy was peeled out of this world. Air rushed in. Half of the brass lamp to one side of the door disappeared.

The INS men returned to their car without any further questions, with damp pants and embarrassed, deeply worried expressions. They drove away, leaving Lauren to contemplate the quiet. They did not return.

She did not sleep for three nights, and when she did sleep, Tuthy and Pal visited her, and put the question to her.

"Thank you, but I prefer it here," she replied.

It's a lot of fun, the boy insisted. *They like music.*

Lauren shook her head on the pillow and awoke. Not very far away, there was a whistling, tinny kind of sound, followed by a deep vibration.

To her, it sounded like applause.

She took a deep breath and got out of bed to retrieve her notebook.

THROUGH ROAD NO WHITHER

Back in the early nineteen eighties, John Carr was working for Jerry Pournelle, helping with Jerry's editorial duties on a number of paperback anthologies. Jerry was working a half-dozen enterprises at once—writing excellent bestselling fiction with Larry Niven, consulting with the Reagan administration, and later the Bush Sr. administration, on space business and space defense policy, and writing a very influential column on personal computing. John Carr served Jerry as a general factotum. Through John, I learned that Jerry was buying stories for an anthology to be published by Jim Baen called Far Frontier.

Now, let's backtrack for a moment. James Patrick Baen had been editor of Galaxy magazine for a number of years, and had purchased two of my stories. He later started Baen Books, a successful publishing enterprise to this day. Jim and Jerry were good friends, simpatico in both politics and business—conservative and ambitious, respectively—and they roped in anybody who seemed likely to be able to deliver interesting ideas. John sometimes did the roping.

Anger at the cruelties of history is often a useless emotion, but "Thru Road No Whither" seems to have struck a cord. It's been reprinted a number of times—most notably, in Gregory Benford's and Marty Greenberg's anthology, Alternate Hitlers.

Perhaps justice knows no boundaries. Engage in evil and depravity, and a force or presence might enact vengeance unto the nth generation—across all time, and all timelines.

Needless to say, this contradicts the conclusions I've drawn in "Dead Run" and in my novels Queen of Angels and Slant. I'm not much for punishment as a way of adjusting our bent and broken emotions. But sometimes, the sheer immensity of historical depravity overcomes even my gentle sensibilities.

The long black Mercedes rumbled out of the fog on the road south from Dijon, moisture running in cold trickles across its windshield. Horst von Ranke carefully read the map spread on his lap, eyeglasses perched low on his nose, while Waffen Schutzstaffel Oberleutnant Albert Fischer drove. “Thirty-five kilometers,” von Ranke said under his breath. “No more.”

“We are lost,” Fischer said. “We’ve already come thirty-six.”

“Not quite that many. We should be there any minute now.”

Fischer shook his head. His high cheekbones and long, sharp nose did much to accentuate the black uniform and the silver death’s heads on the high, tight collar. Von Ranke wore a broad-striped gray suit; he was an undersecretary in the Propaganda Ministry. They might have been brothers, yet one had grown up in Czechoslovakia, the other in the Ruhr; one was the son of a brewer, the other of a coal-miner. They had met and become close friends in Paris two years before, and were now sightseeing on a three-day pass in the countryside.

“Wait,” von Ranke said, peering through the streaming drops on the side window. “Stop.”

Fischer braked the car and looked in the direction of von Ranke’s long finger. Near the roadside, beyond a copse of young trees, hunched a low, thatched roof house with dirty gray walls, almost hidden by the fog.

“Looks empty,” von Ranke said.

“It is occupied; look at the smoke,” Fischer said. “Perhaps somebody can tell us where we are.”

Fischer turned the car up a short, rugged drive. They got out, von Ranke leading the way across a mud path littered with wet straw. The hut looked even dirtier close up. Smoke curled in a brown-gray twist from a hole in the peak of the thatch. Fischer nodded at his friend and they cautiously approached. Over the crude wooden door, letters wobbled unevenly in some alphabet neither could read, and between them they spoke nine languages.

"Could that be Romani?" von Ranke asked, frowning. "It looks familiar—maybe Vlax or Baltic."

"Gypsies don't live in huts, and besides, I thought they were rounded up long ago."

"Well, that's what it looks like," von Ranke said. "Maybe they will speak French." He knocked on the door. After a long pause, he knocked again.

The door opened before his knuckles could make a final rap. A woman too old to be alive stuck a long, wood-colored nose through the crack and peered at them with her one good eye. The other eye was obscured by a sunken caul of flesh. The hand that gripped the door edge looked filthy, its nails long and crusted black. Her lips parted in a wrinkled grin, revealing toothless jaws.

"Good evening," she said in perfect, even elegant, German. "What can I do for you?"

Von Ranke strove to hide his revulsion. "We need to know if we are on the road to Dôle," he said.

"You are asking the wrong guide," the old woman said. Her hand withdrew and the door started to close. Fischer kicked out and pushed her back. The door banged open and leaned on worn-out leather hinges.

"You do not treat us with the proper respect," he said. "What do you mean, 'the wrong guide'? What kind of guide are you?"

The old woman limped back a few steps. "*So strong,*" she crooned, wrapping her hands in front of her withered chest and retreating farther into the gloom. She wore ageless gray rags. Tattered knit sleeves extended to her wrists.

"Answer me!" Fischer said, advancing despite the strong odor of urine and decay.

"The maps I know are not for this land," she sang, and doddered before a cold and empty hearth.

"She's crazy," von Ranke said. "Let the local authorities take care of her. Let's be off." But a wild look was in Fischer's eyes. So much filth, so much disarray, and impudence as well; these things made him angry.

"What maps *do* you know, crazy woman?" he demanded.

"Maps in time," the old woman said. She let her hands fall to her sides and lowered her head as if, in admitting her specialty, she were suddenly humble.

"Then tell us where we are," Fischer demanded.

"Come, let's go," von Ranke said, but he knew it was too late. There would be an end, but it would be on his friend's terms, and it might not be pleasant.

"On a through road *no whither*," the old woman answered.

"What does that mean?" Fischer towered over her.

She stared up as if at some prodigal son, single eye glinting, hanging lip shining with spittle. "If you wish a reading, sit," she said, indicating a low table and three dilapidated cane and leather chairs.

Fischer glanced at her, then at the table. "Very well," he said, suddenly obsequious. Another game, von Ranke knew—cat and mouse. Fischer pulled out a chair for his friend and sat across from the old woman.

"Put your hands on the table, palms down, both of them, both of you," she said. They did so, von Ranke looking uncertainly between his friend and the old woman. The old woman leaned over and touched her ear to the table, eye veering crazily toward the beams of light sneaking through the thatch. "I see arrogance in plenty," she said. Fischer did not react. "As well, pride and hatred in equal measure. I see no good way for either of you. Only a winding journey bringing you ever closer to fire and to death."

She peered off over their heads, waving one gnarled hand. "Your cities collapse in flames, your women and children shrivel to black dolls in the heat of their burning homes. Your death camps are found and you stand accused of hideous crimes. Your nation is broken and divided between your enemies. All will be lost. Many will be tried and hung. Your nation is disgraced, your cause abhorred." A peculiar, greenish light appeared in her one good eye. "There is infinite disgrace and generations of shame. You will be admired by the unbalanced, the lowest of the low. Only psychotics will believe in your cause."

Fischer's smile did not waver. "Has this already happened," he said, "or is it yet to be? I am confused." He pulled a pfennig from his pocket and threw it down before the woman, then pushed the chair back and stood. "Your words are as crooked as your chin, you filthy hag," he said. "Let's go."

"I've been suggesting that," von Ranke said, rising. But Fischer made no move to leave. Von Ranke tugged on his arm but the SS Oberleutnant shrugged free.

"Gypsies are exceedingly few, *witch,*" he said. "Soon to be fewer by one." He reached for his Luger, but von Ranke managed to grip the holster and pull his friend just outside the door.

The woman followed and shaded her eye against the misty light. "I am no Gypsy, and I am no witch," she said, then pointed a crooked finger to the letters above the door. "You do not even recognize the words?"

Fischer squinted. The letters seemed to have changed while they were inside. New recognition and amazement dawned in his eyes. "Yes," he said. "I do, now. Remarkable! This is not any sort of Romani. It is a *dead* language."

"Which language?" von Ranke asked, suddenly uneasy. He could not see how the letters could change if they were truly alone in these woods, with the old woman in the hut.

"Hebrew, I think," Fischer said. "She is a Jewess."

"No!" the woman said. "I am no Jew."

Von Ranke thought the woman looked younger now, or at least stronger, and his unease deepened. There could still be partisans, terrorists, in these woods, waiting for young officers to drive through. He had heard rumors . . .

"I do not care what you are," Fischer said. "I only wish we were in my father's time." He stepped toward her, into the hut again, stamping his boot on the dusty boards. She did not retreat. Her face became bland, and her bad eye seemed to fill in. "Back then, there would be no regulations, no rules. I could take this pistol," he unstrapped his holster, "and apply it to your filthy Kike head. Perhaps I would be killing the last Jew in Europe." He pulled out the Luger.

The woman straightened in the dark hut. She seemed to be drawing strength from Fischer's abusive tongue. Von Ranke feared for his friend. Blind rashness could get them in trouble. "This is not our fathers' time," he reminded Fischer.

Fischer paused, finger curling around the trigger. "Filthy, smelly old woman." His lips pulled back to reveal long, even teeth.

The woman did not look nearly as old as when they had entered the hut, perhaps not old at all, and certainly not bent and crippled.

"Stop this nonsense!" von Ranke shouted, trying to divert the pistol's barrel. "You have had a narrow escape this afternoon," he warned the woman.

Fischer wove the gun around von Ranke's interference.

"You still have no idea who I am!" the woman half sang, half moaned.

"Scheisse," Fischer spat. "I will shoot you, then report you and your hovel."

The woman grew dark, as if hiding from the last light of day—and yet she did not move. The darkness concentrated in her eyes. "I am God's left hand," she breathed. "I am the *scourge.* A pillar of cloud by day and a pillar of fire by night." Her voice dropped in timbre and rose in power. Even four strides away, her breath smelled like brimstone.

The pistol barked three times, deafening in the small room. The woman did not flinch or appear at all injured.

Fischer lowered the Luger, then laughed, though his laughter sounded brittle. "You're right!" he said to von Ranke, too loudly. "She isn't worth our trouble." He turned and stamped back outside. Von

Ranke followed with a frightened glance over his shoulder. The last of the woman's shadow seemed gray and ill-defined before the ancient stone hearth. *No one has lived in this hut for years,* he thought.

In the car, sitting behind the wheel, he sighed at his friend. "You tend to foolishness, you know that?"

Fischer smirked and shook his head. "She will be dead soon. I hit her square. You saw it." He leaned back and yawned, more with tension than exhaustion. "You drive, old friend. *I'll* look for the roads." He shook out the Pan-Deutschland map. "No wonder we're lost. This is five years old—from 1979."

Von Ranke ramped up the Mercedes' turbine until its whine was high and steady and its exhaust cut a swirling hole in the fog. "We'll find our way," he murmured, and looked in the side mirror at the hut.

From the hut's doorway, the old woman watched them, head bobbing. "I am not a Jew," she called, her voice like the rumble of a distant storm, "but I loved *them*, too, oh, yes. I loved *all* my children."

Fischer turned on the leather seat to look, incredulous. Von Ranke loosed the brake on the long black Mercedes before his friend could do something even more foolish.

The woman raised her hand as the car roared into the fog. "I will guide you to justice, wherever and whenever you live," she cried, "and all your children, and their *children's* children!" A twist of black smoke dropped from her elbow to the dirt floor. As she waggled a wisp of finger, the smoke drew figures in the dirt. "As you wish—into the time of your fathers you will go!"

She lowered her arm and the fog around the hut thinned. Forty years melted away. Sunlight broke through. High above the forest, a gut-shivering growl descended on the long road. A wide-winged shadow passed over the hut, wings flashing stars, black and white invasion stripes, and white-yellow cannon fire.

"Hungry bird," the shapeless figure said. "Time to feed!"

DEAD RUN

My irritation at television evangelists is boundless. Nothing unusual in that. Religious visions of damnation seem to be particularly horrible in a Christianity that claims to worship a loving God. These upwellings of tribal animosity and primordial hatred should have been abandoned thousands of years ago, but they strongly influence hundreds of millions to this day.

Well, all right, so what else is new? Humans are imperfect.

But if we're made in God's image, then perhaps God is imperfect, as well. Maybe God gets tired. Maybe he isn't dead, but has simply retired from the scene, exhausted or punch-drunk from our sins. I've written two stories on this theme. The other is "Petra."

"Dead Run" was submitted to Twilight Zone Magazine and rejected. The editor explained that this simply was not a Twilight Zone story. So I shipped it off to Omni and Ellen Datlow bought it.

A few years later, my friend Alan Brennert was working on the reincarnation of the Twilight Zone TV show, airing on CBS. Michael Toman, a mutual friend and well-read individual of considerable if quiet influence, handed Alan "Dead Run," which somehow he had missed. Alan loved it and thought it was perfect for the show. He wrote the screenplay—a brilliant job, I must say—and it went into production in 1985. Astrid and I drove to the Indian Hills, outside Los Angeles, to watch the show being filmed, under the direction of the late Paul Tucker. Dozens of extras were funneled through the gates of Hell that day. One of them had taken the trouble to dress up like Michael Jackson in Thriller. The camera, needless to say, did not linger on him.

A few days later, I returned to watch filming on a soundstage in Los Angeles, where a high-rise, tenement Hell set had been constructed at a cost of about $50,000. It was all marvelous to a novice. To my delight, I was even able to contribute a line to a scene at Paul's request.

An actor on the set approached me during a break and asked for a loan. I explained that I wasn't anybody important or rich—just the original writer. He understood immediately; my status was below that of the extras. But I was treated nicely and had a grand time.

Standards and Practices, the "censorship" office at the network, approved the screenplay with the single wry comment that this could be a good way to get back at Jerry Falwell. I doubt that Falwell noticed.

The show was aired to a huge response: two letters, one for, one against. Evangelical Christians simply don't watch shows like Twilight Zone. By and large, they stay away from fantasy and science fiction altogether.

This is my only filmed story to date.

My experience with magazine rejections has never been so ironic.

There aren't many hitchhikers on the road to Hell.

I noticed this dude four miles away. He stood where the road is straight and level, crossing what looks like desert except it has empty towns and motels and shacks. I had been on the road for six hours and the folks in the cattle trailers behind me had been quiet for some time—resigned, I guess—so my nerves had settled a bit and I decided to see what the dude was up to. Maybe he was one of the employees. That would be interesting, I thought. Truth to tell, once the wailing settles down, I get bored.

The dude stood on the right side of the road, thumb out. I piano-keyed down the gears and the air brakes hissed and squealed at the tap of my foot. The semi slowed and the big diesel made that gut-deep dinosaur-belch of shuddered-downness. I leaned across the cab as everything came to a halt and swung the door open.

"Where you heading?" I asked.

He laughed and shook his head, then spit on the soft shoulder. "I don't know," he said. "Hell, maybe." He was thin and tanned with long greasy black hair and bluejeans and a vest. His straw hat was dirty and full of holes, but the feathers around the crown were bright and new, pheasant if I was any judge. A worn gold fob hung out of his vest. He wore old Frye boots with the toes turned up and soles thinner than my retreads. He looked a lot like me when I had hitch-hiked out of Fresno, broke and unemployed, looking for work.

"Can I take you there?" I asked.

"Sure. Why not?" He climbed in and slammed the door shut, took out a kerchief and mopped his forehead, then blew his long nose and stared at me with bloodshot eyes. "What you hauling?" he asked.

"Souls," I said. "Whole shitload of them."

"What kind?" He was young, not more than twenty-five. He tried to sound easy and natural but I could hear the nerves.

"Human kind," I said. "Got some Hare Krishnas this time. Don't look that close anymore."

I coaxed the truck along, wondering if the engine was as bad as it sounded. When we were up to speed—eighty, eighty-five, no smokies on *this* road—he asked, "How long you been hauling?"

"Two years."

"Good pay?"

"I get by."

"Good benefits?"

"Union, like everyone else."

"That's what they told me in that little dump about two miles back. Perks and benefits."

"People live there?" I asked. I didn't think anything lived along the road. Anything human.

He bobbled his head. "Real down folks. They say Teamsters bosses get carried in limousines, when their time comes."

"Don't really matter how you get there or how long it takes. Forever is a slow bitch to pull."

"Getting there's all the fun?" he asked, trying for a grin. I gave him a shallow one.

"What're you doing out here?" I asked a few minutes later. "You aren't dead, are you?" I'd never heard of dead folks running loose or looking quite as vital as he did but I couldn't imagine anyone else being on the road. Dead folks—and drivers.

"No," he said. He was quiet for a bit. Then, slowly, as if it embarrassed him, he said, "I'm here to find my woman."

"No shit?" Not much surprised me but this was a new twist. "There ain't no going back, for the dead, you know."

"Sherill's her name," he said, "spelled like sheriff but with two L's."

"Got a cigarette?" I asked. I don't smoke but I could use them later. He handed me his last three in a crush-proof pack, then bobbled his head some more and squinted through the clean windshield. No bugs on this road. No flat rabbits, no snakes, no armadilloes—nothing.

"Haven't heard of a Sherill," I said. "But then, I don't get to converse with everyone I haul. There are lots of trucks and lots of drivers."

"I heard about benefits," he said. "Perks and benefits. Back in that town." He had a crazy sad look.

I tightened my jaw and stared straight ahead.

"You know," he said, "They talk a lot in that town. They tell about how they use old trains for Chinese, and in Russia there's a tramline. In Mexico it's old buses, always at night—"

"Listen. I don't use all the benefits," I said. "Some do but I don't."

"I got you," he said, nodding that exaggerated goddamn young bobble, his whole neck and shoulders moving, it's all right everything's cool.

"How you gonna find her?" I asked.

"I don't know. Hitch the road, ask the drivers."

"How'd you get in?"

He didn't answer for a moment. "I'm coming here when I die. That's pretty sure. It's not so hard for folks like me to get in beforehand. And . . . my daddy was a driver. He told me the route. By the way, my name's Bill."

"Mine's John," I said.

"Pleased to meet you."

We didn't say much for a while. He stared out the right window and I watched the desert and faraway shacks go by. Soon the mountains loomed up—space seems compressed on the road, especially out of the desert—and I sped up for the approach.

They made some noise in the back. Lost, creepy sounds, like tired old sirens in a factory.

"What'll you do when you get off work?" Bill asked.

"Go home and sleep."

"That's the way it was with Daddy, until just before the end. Look, I didn't mean to make you mad. I'd just heard about the perks and I thought . . ." He swallowed, his Adam's apple bobbing. "You might be able to help. I don't know how I'll ever find Sherill. Maybe back in the annex . . ."

"Nobody in their right minds goes into the yards by choice," I said. "You'd have to look at everybody that's died in the last four months. They're way backed up."

Bill took that like a smack across the face and I was sorry I'd said it. "She's only been gone a week," he said.

"Well," I said.

"My mom died two years ago, just before Daddy."

"The High Road," I said.

"What?"

"Hope they both got the High Road."

"Mom, maybe. Yeah. She did. But not Daddy. He knew." Bill hawked and spit out the window. "Sherill, she's here—but she don't belong."

I couldn't help but smirk.

"No, man, I mean it, I belong but not her. She was in this car wreck couple of months back. Got messed up. I was her dealer. I sold her crystal and heroin at first, and then I fell in love with her, and by the time she landed in the hospital, from the wreck—she was the only one who lived, man, shouldn't that tell you something?—-but she was, you know, hooked on about four different things."

My hands gripped the wheel.

"I tried to tell her when I visited her in the hospital, no more dope, it wouldn't be good, but she begged. What could I do? I loved her." He looked down at his worn boots and bobbled sadly. "She begged me, man. I brought her stuff. She took it all when they weren't looking. I mean, she just took it *all*. They pumped her but her insides were mush. I didn't hear about her dying until two days ago. That really burned, man. I was the only one who loved her and they didn't even like *inform* me. I had to go up to her room and find the empty bed. *Jesus*. I decided to hang out at Daddy's union hall. Someone talked to someone else and I found her name on a list. *Sherill*. They'd put her on the Low Road."

I hadn't known it was that easy to find out; but then, I'd never traveled with junkies. Dope can loosen a lot of lips.

"I don't do those perks," I said. "Folks in back got enough trouble. I think the union went too far there."

"Bet they thought you'd get lonely, need company," Bill said quietly, looking at me. "It don't hurt the women back there, does it? Maybe gives them another chance to, you know, think things over. Give 'em relief for a couple of hours, a break from the mash—"

"A couple of hours don't mean nothing in relation to eternity," I said, too loud. "I'm not so sure I won't be joining them someday, and if that's the way it is I want it smooth, nobody pulling me out of a trailer and—and then putting me back in."

"Yeah," he said. "Got you. I know where you're coming from. But she might be back there right now, and all you'd have to—"

"Bad enough I'm driving this fucking rig in the first place." I needed to change the subject. Or smash him a good one in the face and shove him out.

Bill stopped bobbling and looked at me. "How'd you get assigned the low road?" he asked.

"Couple of accidents. I took my last rig and raced an old fart in a Triumph. Nearly ran down some joggers. My premiums went up to where I couldn't afford payments and finally they took my truck away."

"You coulda gone without insurance."

"Not me," I said. "Anyway, word got out. No companies would hire me. I went to the union to see if they could help. They told me I was a dead-ender, either get out of trucking or . . ." I shrugged. "This. I couldn't leave trucking. It's bad out there, getting work. Couldn't see myself driving a hack in some big city."

"No way, man," Bill said, again favoring me with his whole-body rumba. He cackled sympathetically.

I gripped the wheel even tighter. "They gave me an advance," I said, "enough for a down payment on this rig." The truck was grinding a bit but maintaining. Over the mountains, through a really impressive pass like from an old engraving, and down in a rugged rocky valley, the City waited. I'd deliver my cargo, grab my slip, and run the rig (with Bill) back to Baker. Let him out someplace in the real. Park the truck in the yard next to my cottage.

Go in, flop back, suck a few beers, get some sleep. As if I can ever sleep. Start over again Monday, two loads a week.

Hell, I never even got into Pahrump any more. I used to be a regular, but after driving the Low Road, the women at the Lizard Ranch all look like prisoners, too dumb to notice their iron bars. I saw too much of Hell in the those air-conditioned trailers.

"I don't think I'd better go on," Bill said. "I'll hitch with some other rig, ask around."

"I'd feel better if you rode with me back out of here. Want my advice?" Bad habit, giving advice.

"No," Bill said. "Thanks anyway. I can't go home. Sherill don't belong here." He took a deep breath. "I'll try to work up a trade with some bosses. I stay, in exchange, and she gets the High Road. That's the way the game works down here, isn't it?"

I didn't say otherwise. I couldn't be sure he wasn't right. He'd made it this far. At the top of the pass I pulled the rig over and let him out. He waved, I waved, and we went our different ways.

Poor rotten doping sonofabitch, I thought. I'd screwed up my life half a dozen different ways—three wives, liquor, three years at Tehachapi—but I'd never done dope. I felt self-righteous just listening to the dude. I was glad to be rid of him, truth be told.

As I geared the truck down for the decline, the noise in the trailers got irritating again. They could smell what was coming, I guess, like pigs trotting up to the man with the knife.

The City looks a lot like a dry country full of big white cathedrals. Casting against type. High wall around the perimeter, stretching right and left as far as my eye can see, like a pair of endless highways turned on their sides. No compass. No magnetic fields. No sense of direction but down.

No horizon.

I pulled into the terminal and backed the first trailer up to a holding pen. Employees let down the gates and used their big, ugly prods to offload my herd. The damned do not respond to bodily pain. The prod gets them where we all hurt when we're dead.

After the first trailer was empty, employees unhooked it, pulled it away by hand or claw, strong as horses, and I backed in the second.

I got down out of the cab and an employee came up to me, a big fellow with red eyes and brand new coveralls. "Poke any good ones?" he asked. His breath was like the bad end of a bean and garlic dinner. I shook my head, took out the crush-proof box, and held a cigarette up for a light. He pressed his fingernail against the tip. The tip flared and settled to a steady glow. He regarded it with pure lust. There's no in-between for employees. Lust or nothing.

"Listen," I said.

"I'm all ears," he said, and suddenly, he was. I jumped back and he laughed joylessly. "You're new," he said, and eyed my cigarette again.

"You had anyone named Sherill through here?"

"Who's asking?" he grumbled, and started a slow dance. He

had to move around or his shoes melted the asphalt and got stuck. He lifted one foot, then the other, twisting a little.

"Just curious. I heard you guys know all the names."

"So?" He stopped his dance. His shoes made the tar smoke and stink.

"So," I said, with just as much sense, and held out the cigarette.

"Like Cherry with an L?"

"No. Sherill, like sheriff but with two L's."

"Couple of Cheryls. No *Sherills*," he said. "Sorry."

I handed him the cigarette, then pulled another out of the pack. He snapped it away between two thick, horny nails.

"Thanks," I said.

He popped both of them into his mouth and chewed, bliss rushing over his wrinkled face. Smoke shot out of his nose and he swallowed.

"Think nothing of it," he said, and walked on.

The road back is shorter than the road in. Don't ask how. I'd have thought it was the other way around but barriers are what's important, not distance. Maybe we all get our chances so the road to Hell is long. But once we're there, there's no returning. You have to save on the budget somewhere.

I took the empties back to Baker. Didn't see Bill. Eight hours later I was in bed, beer in hand, paycheck on the bureau, eyes wide open. Shit, I thought. Now my conscience was working. I could have sworn I was past that. But then, I wouldn't drive without insurance, and I didn't use the perks. I wasn't really cut out for the life.

There are no normal days and nights on the road to Hell. No matter how long you drive, it's always the same time when you arrive as when you left, but it's not necessarily the same time from trip to trip.

The next trip it was cool dusk and the road didn't pass through desert and small, empty towns. Instead, it crossed a bleak flatland of skeletal trees, all the same uniform gray as if cut from paper. When I pulled over to catch a nap—never sleeping more than two hours at a stretch—the shouts of the damned in the trailers bothered me even more than usual. Silly things they said, like:

"You can take us back, mister! You really can!"

"Can he?"

"Shit no, mofuck pig."

"You can let us out! We can't hurt you!"

That was true enough. Drivers are alive and the dead can't hurt the living. But I'd heard what happened when you let them out. There were about ninety of them in back, and half were women, and in any load there was always one would make you want to use your perks.

I scratched my itches, looking at the Sierra Club calendar hanging just below the fan. The Devil's Postpile. The load became quieter as the voices gave up, one after the other. There was one last shout—some obscenity—then silence.

It was then I decided I'd let them out and see if Sherill was there, or if anyone knew her. They mingled in the annex, got in their last socializing before road and the City. Someone might know. Then if I saw Bill again—

What? What could I do to help him? He had screwed Sherill up royally, but then she'd had a hand in it too, and that was what Hell was all about. Poor stupid sons of bitches.

I swung out of the cab, tucking in my shirt and pulling my straw hat down on my crown. "Hey!" I said, walking alongside the trailers. Faces peered at me from the two inches between each white slat. "I'm going to let you out. Just for a while. I need some information."

"Ask!" someone screamed. "Just ask, goddammit!"

"You know you can't run away. You can't hurt me. You're all dead. Understand?"

"We know that," said another voice, quieter.

"Maybe we can help," said another, female, older, motherly.

"I'm going to open the gates on one trailer at a time." I went to the rear trailer first, took out my keys and undid the Yale padlock. Then I swung the gate open, standing back a little like there was some kind of infected wound about to drain.

They were all naked but they weren't dirty. I'd seen them in the annex yards and at the City; I knew they weren't like concentration camp prisoners. The dead can't really be unhealthy. Each just had some sort of air about him telling why he was in Hell; nothing specific but subliminal. Like three black dudes in the rear trailer, first to step out. Why they were going to Hell was all over their faces. They weren't in the least sorry for the lives they'd led. They wanted to keep on doing what had brought them here in the first place—scavenging, hurting, hurting me in particular.

"Stupid ass mofuck," one of them said, staring at me beneath thin, expressive eyebrows. He nodded and swung his fists, trying to pound the side slats from the outside, but the blows hardly made them vibrate.

Then an old white woman climbed down, head first, like a spider—hair silver and neatly coiffed. I couldn't be certain what she had done but she made me very uneasy. She might have been the worst in the load. And lots of others, young, old, mostly old. Quiet for the most part.

They looked me over, some defiant, most just bewildered.

"I need to know if there's anyone here named Sherill," I said, "who happens to know a fellow named Bill."

"That's my name," said a woman hidden by the crowd.

"Let me see her." I waved my hand at them. The black dudes came forward. A funny look got in their eyes, and they backed away. The others parted and a young woman walked out. "How do you spell your name?" I asked. She got a panicked expression. She spelled it, hesitating, hoping she'd make the grade. I felt horrible already.

She was a Cheryl.

"Not who I'm looking for," I said.

"Don't be hasty," she said, real soft. She wasn't trying hard to be seductive but she was succeeding. She was very pretty with medium-sized breasts, hips like a teenager's, legs not terrific but nice. Her black hair was clipped short and her eyes were almost

Asian. I figured maybe she was Lebanese or some other kind of Middle Eastern.

I tried to ignore her. "You can walk around a bit," I told them. "I'm letting out the first trailer now." I opened the side gate on that one and the people came down. They didn't smell, didn't look hungry, they all just looked too pale. I wondered if the torment had already begun, but if so, I decided, it wasn't the physical kind. One thing I'd learned in my two years was that all the Sunday school and horror movie crap about Hell was wrong.

"I'm looking for a lady named Sherill," I repeated. No one stepped forward. Then I felt someone close to me and I turned. It was the Cheryl woman. She smiled. "I'd like to sit up front for a while," she said.

"So would we all, sister," said the white-haired old woman. The black dudes stood off separate, talking low among themselves.

I swallowed, looking at her. Other drivers said they were real insubstantial except at one activity. That was the perk. And it was said the hottest ones always ended up in Hell. Whatever she was on the Low Road for, it wouldn't affect her performance in the sack, that was obvious.

"No," I said. I motioned for them to get back into the trailers. It had been a dumb idea all around. They climbed back and I returned to the cab, trying to figure what had made me do it. I shook my head and started up the engine.

Thinking on a dead run was no good.

"No," I said, "goddamn," I said, "good."

Cheryl's face stayed with me.

Cheryl's body stayed with me longer than the face.

Something always comes up in life to lure a man onto the Low Road, not driving but riding in the back. We all have some weakness. I wondered what reason God had to give us each that little flaw, like a chip in crystal, you press the chip hard enough everything splits up crazy. At least now I knew one thing. My flaw wasn't sex, not this way. What most struck me about Cheryl was wonder. She was so pretty; how'd she end up on the Low Road?

For that matter, what had Bill's Sherill done?

I returned hauling empties and found myself this time outside a small town called Shoshone. I pulled my truck into the cafe parking lot. The weather was cold and I left the engine running. It was about eleven in the morning and the cafe was half full. I took a seat at the counter next to an old man with maybe four teeth in his head, attacking French toast with downright solemn dignity. I ordered eggs and hashbrowns and juice, ate quickly, and went back to my truck.

Bill stood next to the cab. Next to him was an enormous young woman with a face like a bulldog. She was wrapped in a filthy piece of plaid fabric that might have been snatched from a trash dump. "Hey," Bill said. "Remember me?"

"Sure."

"I saw you pulling up. I thought you'd like to know . . . This is Sherill. I got her out of there." The woman stared at me with all the expression of a brick. "We just followed the low road all the way, and nobody stopped us. It's all screwy, like a power failure or something."

Sherill could have hid any number of weirdnesses beneath her formidable looks and gone unnoticed by ordinary folks. But I didn't have any trouble picking out the biggest thing wrong with her: she was dead. Bill had brought her out of Hell, but he could not bring her back to life. I looked around to make sure I was in the World. I was. He wasn't lying. Something serious had happened on the Low Road.

"Trouble?" I asked.

"Lots." He grinned at me. "Pan-demon-ium." His grin broadened.

"That can't happen," I said. Sherill trembled, hearing my voice.

"He's a *driver,* Bill," she said. "He's the one takes us there. We should git out of here." She had that soul-branded air and the look of an animal that's just escaped slaughter, seeing the butcher again. She took a few steps back. Gluttony, I thought. Gluttony and buried lust and a real ugly way of seeing life, inner eye pulled all out of shape by her bulk. Bill hadn't had much to do with her ending up on the Low Road.

"Tell me more," I said.

"There's folks running all over down there, holing up in them towns, devils chasing them—"

"Employees," I corrected.

"Yeah. Every which way."

Sherill tugged on his arm. "We got to go, Bill."

"We got to go," he echoed. "Hey, man, thanks. I found her!" He nodded his whole-body nod and they were off down the street, Sherill's plaid wrap dragging in the dirt.

I drove back to Baker, wondering if the trouble was responsible for my being rerouted through Shoshone. I parked in front of my little house and sat inside with a beer while it got dark, checking my calendar for the next day's run and feeling very cold. I can take so much supernatural in its place, but now things were spilling over, smudging the clean-drawn line between my work and the World. Next day I was scheduled to be at the annex and take another load.

Nobody called that evening. If there was trouble on the Low Road, surely the union would let me know, I thought.

I drove to the annex early in the morning. The crossover from the World to the Low Road was normal; I followed the route and the sky grayed from blue to pewter and I was on the first leg to the annex. I backed the rear trailer up to the yard's gate and unhitched it, then placed the forward trailer at a ramp, all the while keeping my ears tuned to pick up interesting conversation. The employees who work the annex look human. I took my invoice from a red-faced old guy with eyes like billiard balls and looked at him like I was in the know but could use some updating. He spit smoking saliva on the pavement, returned my look slantwise, and said nothing. Maybe it was all settled.

I hitched up both full trailers and pulled out. I didn't even mention Sherill and Bill. Like in most jobs, keeping one's mouth shut is good policy. That and don't volunteer.

It was the desert again this time, only now the towns and tumbledown houses looked bomb-blasted, like something big had come through flushing out game with a howitzer.

Eyes on the road. Push that rig.

Four hours in, I came to a roadblock. Nobody on it, no employees, just big carved-lava barricades cutting across all lanes and beyond them a yellow smoke which, the driver's unwritten instructions advised, meant absolutely no entry.

I got out. The load was making noises. I suddenly hated them. Nothing beautiful there—just naked Hell-bounders shouting and screaming and threatening like it wasn't already over for them. They'd had their chance and crapped out and now they were still bullshitting the World. Least they could do was go with dignity and spare me their misery.

That's probably what the engineers on the trains to Auschwitz thought. Yeah, yeah, except I was the fellow who might be hauling those engineers to their just deserts.

Crap, I just couldn't be one way or the other about the whole thing. I could feel mad and guilty and I could think Jesus, probably I'll be complaining just as much when my time comes. Jesus H. Twentieth Century Man Christ.

I stood by the truck, waiting for instructions or some indication what I was supposed to do. The load became quieter after a while but I heard noises off the road, screams mostly and far away.

"There isn't anything," I said to myself, lighting up one of Bill's cigarettes even though I don't smoke and dragging deep, "*anything* worth this shit." I vowed I would quit after this run.

I heard something come up behind the trailers and I edged closer to the cab steps. High wisps of smoke obscured things at first but a dark shape three or four yards high plunged through and stood with one hand on the top slats of the rear trailer. It was covered with naked people, crawling all over, biting and scratching and shouting obscenities. It made little grunting noises, fell to its knees, then stood again and lurched off the road. Some of the people hanging on saw me and shouted for me to come help.

"Help us get this sonofabitch down!"

"Hey, you! We've almost got 'im!"

"He's a driver—"

"Fuck 'im, then."

I'd never seen an employee so big before, nor in so much trouble. The load began to wail like banshees. I threw down my cigarette and ran after it. Workers will tell you. Camaraderie extends even to those on the job you don't like. If they're in trouble it's part of the mystique to help out. Besides, the unwritten instructions are very clear on such things and I've never knowingly broken a job rule—not since getting my rig back—and couldn't see starting now.

Through the smoke and across great ridges of lava, I ran until I spotted the employee about ten yards ahead. It had shaken off the naked people and was standing with one of the damned in each huge hand. Its shoulders smoked and scales stood out at all angles. They'd really done a job on the bastard. Ten or twelve of the dead were picking themselves off the lava, unscraped, unbruised.

They saw me.

The employee saw me.

Everyone came at me. I turned and ran for the truck, stumbling, falling, bruising and scraping myself everywhere. My hair stood on end. People grabbed me, pleading for me to haul them out, old, young, all fawning and screeching like whipped dogs.

Then the employee grabbed me and swung me up out of reach. Its hand was cold and hard like iron tongs kept in a freezer. It grunted and ran toward my truck, opening the door wide and throwing me roughly inside. It made clear with huge, wild gestures that I'd better turn around and go back, that waiting was no good and there was no way through.

I started the engine and turned the rig around. I rolled up my window and hoped the dead weren't substantial enough to scratch paint or tear up slats.

All rules were off now. What about my load? All the while I was doing these things my head was full of questions, like how could souls fight back and wasn't there some inflexible order in Hell that kept such things from happening? That was what had been implied when I hired on. Safest job around.

I headed back down the road. My load screamed like no load I'd ever had before. I was afraid they might get loose but they didn't. I got near the annex and they were quiet again, too quiet for me to hear over the motor.

The yards were deserted. The long, white-painted cement platforms and whitewashed wood-slat loading ramps were unattended. No souls in the pens.

The sky was an indefinite gray. An out-of-focus yellow sun gleamed faintly off the stark white employee's lounge. I stopped the truck and swung down to investigate. There was no wind, only silence. The air was frosty without being particularly cold. What I wanted to do most was unload and get out of there, go back to Baker or Barstow or Shoshone. I hoped that was still possible. Maybe all exits had been closed. Maybe the overseers had closed them to keep any more souls from getting out.

I tried the gate latches and found I could open them. I did so and returned to the truck, swinging the rear trailer around until it was flush with the ramp. Nobody made a sound. "Go on back," I said. "Go on back. You've got more time here. Don't ask me how."

"Hello, John."

That was behind me. I turned and saw an older man without any clothes on. I didn't recognize him at first. His eyes finally clued me in.

"Mr. Martin?" My high school history teacher. I hadn't seen him in maybe twenty years. He didn't look much older, but then I'd never seen him naked. He was dead, but he wasn't like the others. He didn't have that look that told me why he was here.

"This is not the sort of job I'd expect one of my students to take," Martin said. He laughed the smooth laugh he was famous for, the laugh that seemed to take everything he said in class and put it in perspective.

"You're not the first person I'd expect to find here," I responded.

"The cat's away, John. The mice are in charge now. I'm going to try to leave."

"How long you been here?" I asked.

"I died a month ago, I think," Martin said, never one to mince words.

"You can't leave," I said. Doing my job even with Mr. Martin. I felt the ice creep up my throat.

"Still the screwball team player," Martin said, "even when the team doesn't give a damn what you do!"

I wanted to explain but he walked away toward the annex and the road out. Looking back over his shoulder, he said, "Get smart, John. Things aren't what they seem. Never have been."

"Look!" I shouted after him. "I'm going to quit, honest, but this load is my responsibility." I thought I saw him shake his head as he rounded the comer of the annex.

The dead in my load had pried loose some of the ramp slats and were jumping off the rear trailer. Those in the forward trailer were screaming and carrying on, shaking the whole rig.

Responsibility, shit, I thought. As the dead followed after Mr. Martin, I unhitched both trailers. Then I got in the cab and swung away from the annex. "I'm going to quit," I said. "Sure as anything, I'm going to quit."

The road out seemed awfully long. I didn't see any of the dead, surprisingly, but then maybe they'd been shunted away. I was taking a route I'd never been on before and I had no way of knowing if it would put me where I wanted to be. But I hung in there for two hours, running the truck dead-out on the flats.

The air was getting even darker, like somebody was turning down the brightness on a TV set. I switched on the high-beams but they didn't help. By now I was shaking in the cab and saying to myself, Nobody deserves this. Nobody deserves going to Hell no matter what they did. I was scared. It was getting colder.

Three hours and I saw the annex and yards ahead of me again. The road had looped back. I swore and slowed the rig to a crawl. The loading docks had been set on fire. Dead were wandering around with no idea what to do or where to go. I sped up and drove over the few that were on the road. They'd get in front of me and the truck's bumper would hit them and I wouldn't feel a thing, like they weren't even there. I'd see them in the rearview mirror, getting up after being knocked flat.

Then I was away from the loading docks and there was no doubt about it this time. I was heading straight for Hell.

The disembarkation terminal was on fire, too. But beyond it the City was bright and white and untouched. For the first time I drove past the terminal and took the road into the City. It was either that or stay on the flats with everything screwy. Inside, I thought maybe they'd have things under control.

The truck roared through the gate between two white pillars maybe seventy or eighty feet thick and as tall as the Washington Monument. I didn't see anybody, employees or the dead. Once I was through the pillars—and it came as a shock—

There was no City, no walls, just the road winding along and countryside in all directions, even behind.

The countryside was covered with shacks, houses, little clusters and big clusters. Everything was tight-packed, people working together on one hill, people sitting on their porches, walking along paths, turning to stare at me as the rig barreled on through. No employees—no monsters. No flames. No bloody lakes or rivers. This must be the outside part, I thought. Deeper inside it would get worse.

I kept on driving. The dog part of me was saying let's go look for authority and ask some questions and get out. But the monkey was saying let's just go look and find out what's going on, what Hell is all about.

Another hour of driving through that calm, crowded landscape and the truck ran out of fuel. I coasted to the side and stepped down from the cab. Again I lit up a cigarette and leaned against the fender, shaking a little. But the shaking was running down and a tight kind of calm was replacing it.

The landscape was still condensed, crowded, but nobody looked tortured. No screaming, no eternal agony. Trees and shrubs and grass hills and thousands and thousands of little houses.

It took about ten minutes for the inhabitants to get around to investigating me. Two men came over to my truck and nodded cordially. Both were middle-aged and healthy-looking. They didn't look dead. I nodded back.

"We were betting whether you're one of the drivers or not," said the first, a black-haired fellow. He wore a simple handwoven shirt and pants. "I think you are. That so?"

"I am."

"You're lost, then."

I agreed. "Maybe you can tell me where I am?"

"Hell," said the second man, younger by a few years and just wearing shorts. The way he said it was just like you might say you came from Los Angeles or Long Beach. Nothing big, nothing dramatic.

"We've heard rumors there's been problems outside," a woman said, joining our little group. She was about sixty and skinny. She looked like she should be twitchy and nervous but she acted rock-steady. They were all rock-steady.

"There's some kind of strike," I said. "I don't know what it is, but I'm looking for an employee to tell me."

"They don't usually come this far in," the first man said. "We run things here. Or rather, nobody tells us what to do."

"You're alive?" the woman asked, a curious hunger in her voice. Others came around to join us, a whole crowd. They didn't try to touch. They stood their ground and stared and talked.

"Look," said an old black fellow. "You ever read about the Ancient Mariner?"

I said I had in school.

"Had to tell everybody what he did," the black fellow said. The woman beside him nodded. "We're all Ancient Mariners here. But there's nobody to tell it to. Would you like to know?" The way he asked was pitiful. "We're sorry. We just want everybody to know how sorry we are."

"I can't take you back," I said. "I don't know how to get there myself."

"We can't go back," the woman said. "That's not our place."

More people were coming and I was nervous again. I stood my ground trying to seem calm and the dead gathered around me, eager.

"I never thought of anybody but myself," one said. Another interrupted with, "Man, I fucked my whole life away, I hated everybody and everything. I was burned out—"

"I thought I was the greatest. I could pass judgment on everybody—"

"I was the stupidest goddamn woman you ever saw. I was a sow, a pig. I farrowed kids and let them run wild, without no guidance. I was stupid and cruel, too. I used to hurt things—"

"Never cared for anyone. Nobody ever cared for me. I was left to rot in the middle of a city and I wasn't good enough not to rot."

"Everything I did was a lie after I was about twelve years old—"

"Listen to me, mister, because it hurts, it hurts so bad—"

I backed up against my truck. They were lining up now, organized, not like any mob. I had a crazy thought they were behaving better than any people on Earth, but these were the damned.

I didn't hear or see anybody famous. An ex-cop told me about what he did to people in jails. A Jesus-freak told me that knowing Jesus in your heart wasn't enough. "Because I should have made it, man, I should have made it."

"A time came and I was just broken by it all, broke myself really. Just kept stepping on myself and making all the wrong decisions—"

They confessed to me, and I began to cry. Their faces were so clear and so pure, yet here they were, confessing, and except maybe for specific things—like the fellow who had killed Ukrainians in Russian camps, after the Second World War—they didn't sound any worse than the crazy sons of bitches I called friends who spent their lives in trucks or bars or whorehouses.

They were all recent. I got the impression the deeper into Hell you went, the older the damned became, which made sense; Hell just got bigger, each crop of damned got bigger, with more room on the outer circles.

"We wasted it," someone said. "You know what my greatest sin was? I was dull. Dull and cruel. I never saw beauty. I saw only dirt. I loved the dirt and the clean and beautiful just passed me by."

Pretty soon my tears were uncontrollable. I kneeled down beside the truck, hiding my head, but they kept on coming and confessing. Hundreds must have passed, talking quietly, gesturing with their hands.

Then they stopped. Someone had come and told them to back away, that they were too much for me. I took my face out of my hands and a very young-seeming fellow stood looking down on me. "You all right?" he asked.

I nodded, but my insides were like broken glass. With every confession I had seen myself, and with every tale of sin I had felt an answering echo.

"Someday, I'm going to be here," I mumbled. "Someone's going to drive me in a cattle car to Hell." The young fellow helped me to my feet and cleared a way around my truck.

"Of course they are, but not now," he said. "You don't belong here yet." He opened the door to my cab and I got back inside.

"I don't have any fuel," I said.

He smiled that sad smile they all had and stood on the step, up close to my ear. "You'll be taken out of here soon anyway. One of the employees is bound to get around to you." He seemed a lot more sophisticated than the others. I looked at him maybe a little queerly, like there was some explaining in order.

"Yeah, I know all that stuff," he said. "I was a driver once. Then I got promoted. What are they all doing back there?" He gestured up the road. "They're really messing things up, ain't they?"

"I don't know," I said, wiping my eyes and cheeks with my sleeve.

"You go back, and you tell them that all this revolt on the outer circles, it's what I expected. Tell them Charlie's here and that I warned them. Word's getting around. There's bound to be discontent."

"Word?"

"About who's in charge. Just tell them Charlie knows and I warned them. I know something else, and you shouldn't tell anybody about this . . ." He whispered an incredible fact into my ear then, something that shook me deeper than what I had already been through.

I closed my eyes. Some shadow passed over. The young fellow and everybody else seemed to recede. I felt rather than saw my truck being picked up like a toy.

Then I suppose I was asleep for a time.

In the cab in the parking lot of a truck stop in Bakersfield, I jerked awake, pulled my cap out of my eyes and looked around. It was about noon.

There was a union hall in Bakersfield. I checked and my truck was full of fuel, so I started her up and drove to the union hall. I knocked on the door of the office. I went in and recognized the fat old dude who had given me the job in the first place. I was tired and I smelled bad but I wanted to quit and get it all done with as soon as I could.

He recognized me but didn't remember my name until I told him. "I can't work the run anymore," I said. The shakes were on me again. "I'm not the one for it. I don't feel right driving them when I know I'm going to be there myself, like as not."

"Okay," he said, slow and careful, sizing me up with a knowing eye. "But you're more than just out. You're busted. No more driving, no more work for us, no more work for any union we support. It'll be lonely."

"I'll take that kind of lonely any day," I said.

"Okay."

That was that. I headed for the door and stopped with my hand on the knob.

"One more thing," I said. "I met Charlie. He says to tell you word's getting around about who's in charge, and that's why there's so much trouble in the outer circles."

The old dude's knowing eye went sort of glassy. "You're the fellow got all the way into the City?"

I nodded.

He got up from his seat real fast, jowls quivering and belly doing a silly dance beneath his work blues. He flicked one hand at me, come 'ere. "Don't go. Just you wait a minute. Outside in the office."

I waited and heard him talking on the phone. He came out smiling and put his hand on my shoulder. "Listen, John, I'm not sure we should let you quit. I didn't know you were the one who'd gone inside. Word is, you stuck around and tried to help when everybody else ran. The company appreciates that. You've been with us a long time, reliable driver, maybe we should give you some incentive to stay. I'm sending you to Vegas to talk with a company man . . ."

The way he said it, I knew there wasn't much choice and I better not fight it. You work union long enough and you know when you keep your mouth shut and go along.

They put me up in a motel and fed me and by late moming I was on my way to Vegas in a black union car with a silent driver and air conditioning and some *Newsweeks* to keep me company.

I arrived about two in the afternoon. The limo dropped me off in front of a four-story office building, glass and stucco, with listings for lots of divorce attorneys, one dentist, and five small companies with anonymous names. White plastic letters on a ribbed felt background in a glass case. There was no listing for the number I had been told to go to, but I went up and knocked anyway.

I don't know what I expected. A district supervisor opened the door and asked me a few questions and I said what I'd said before. I was adamant. He looked worried. "Look," he said. "It won't be good for you now if you quit."

I asked him what he meant by that but he just looked even more unhappy and said he was going to send me to someone higher up.

That was in Denver, a long, sloping climb of four thousand feet—nearer my God to thee. The same black car took me there and Saturday morning, bright and early, I stood in front of a very large corporate building with no sign out front and a big, shiny bank on the bottom floor. I walked past the bank to a row of brass elevators, and took a private one to the very top.

A secretary met me, hair done up tight and jaw grim and square. She didn't like me, but she escorted me into the next office. A man sat behind a big desk. He had on MacArthur wire-rimmed glasses too big for his eyes. He rose as I came in and firmly shook my hand, then motioned for me to sit in a small armchair, and faced me, perching on the edge of the big desk. I swear I'd seen the fellow before, but maybe it was just a passing resemblance. He wore a narrow tie and a tasteful but conservative gray suit. His shirt was pastel blue. A big black leather Rembrandt Bible decorated the desk's glass top beside an alabaster pen holder.

"First, let me congratulate you on your bravery," he said. "Reports from the field say nothing but good about you." He smiled like that fellow on TV who's always asking the audience to give him some help. Then his face got sincere and serious. I honestly believe he was sincere; he was also well trained in dealing with not-very-bright people. "I hear you have a report for me. From Charles Frick."

"He said his name was Charlie." I told him the story. "What I'm curious about, what did he mean, this thing about who's in charge?"

"Charlie was in Organization until last year. He died in a car accident. I'm shocked to hear he got the Low Road." He didn't look shocked. "Maybe I'm shocked but not surprised. To tell the truth, he was a bit of a troublemaker." He smiled brightly again and there was a little too much expression for a face his size.

"What did he mean?"

"John, I'm proud of all our drivers. You don't know how proud we all are of you folks down there doing the dirty work."

"What did Charlie mean?"

"Surely there must be some satisfaction in keeping the land clean of abortionists and pornographers, hustlers and muggers and murderers. Scrugging away the atheists and heathens and idolworshippers. You people keep the scum away from the good folks, the *plain* good folks, sort of a gigantic and ancient sanitation squad. Now we know that driving's maybe the hardest job we have in the company, and that not everyone can work indefinitely on the Low Road. Still, we'd like you to stay on. Not as a driver—unless you really want that, for the satisfaction of a tough job well done. No, if you want to move up—and you've earned it by now, surely—we have a place for you right here." He placed his hand flat on the bible, then tapped the desk with a finger. "A place where you'll be comfortable and—"

That was enough for me. "I've already said I want out. You're acting like I'm hot stuff and I'm just shit. You know that, I know that. What is going on?"

His face hardened. "It isn't easy up here, either, buster." The "buster" bit tickled me. I laughed and got up from the chair. I'd been in enough offices and this fancy one just made me queasy. When I stood, he held up his hand and pursed his lips as he nodded. "Sorry about that. Sometimes I'm a little too brusque. There's incentive, there's certainly a reason why you should want to work here. If you're so convinced you're on your way to the Low Road, you can work it off here, you know."

"How can you say that?"

Bright smile. "Charlie told you something. He told you about who's in charge."

Now I could smell something terribly wrong, like with the union boss. I mumbled, "He said that's why there's trouble."

"It comes every now and then. We put it down gentle. I tell you where we really need good people, compassionate people. We need them to help with the choosing."

"Choosing?"

"Surely you don't think the Boss does all the choosing directly?"

I couldn't think of a thing to say.

"Listen, the Boss . . . let me tell you. A long time ago, the Boss decided to create a new kind of worker, one with more decision-making ability. Some of the supervisors disagreed, especially when the Boss said the workers would be around for a long, long time—that they'd be indestructible. Sort of like nuclear fuel, you know. Human souls. The waste builds up after a time, those who turn out bad, turn out to be chronically unemployable. They don't go along with the scheme, or get out of line. Can't just live and let live, can't just get along with their fellow workers. You know the type. What do you do with them? Can't just dump them somewheres and let them be—they're indestructible, and that ain't no joke—"

"Chronically unemployable?"

"You're a union man. Think of what it must feel like to be out of *work . . . forever.* You're eternally damned. *Nobody* will hire you."

I knew the feeling, both the way he meant it and the way it had happened to me.

"The Boss feels the project half succeeded, so He doesn't dump it completely. But He doesn't want to be bothered with all the pluses and minuses, the bookkeeping."

"*You're* in charge," I said, my blood cooling.

And I knew where I had seen him before.

On television.

God's right-hand man.

And human. Flesh-and-blood.

We ran Hell.

He nodded. "Now, that's not the sort of thing we'd like to get around."

"You're in charge, and you let the drivers take their perks from the loads, you let—" I stopped, instinct telling me I would soon be on a rugged trail with no turnaround.

"I'll tell you the truth, John. I have only been in charge here for a year, and my predecessor let things get out of hand. He wasn't a religious man, John, and he thought this was a job like any other, where you could compromise now and then. I know that isn't so. There's no compromise here, and we'll straighten out those inequities and bad decisions very soon. You'll help us, I hope. You may know more about the problems than we do."

"How do you . . . how do you qualify for a job like this?" I asked. "And who offered it to you?"

"Not the Boss, if that's what you're getting at, John. It's been kind of traditional. You may have heard about me. I'm the one, when there was all this talk about after-death experiences and everyone was seeing bright light and beauty, I'm the one who wondered why no one was seeing the other side. I found people who had almost died and had seen Hell, and I turned their lives around. The management in the company decided a fellow with my ability could do good work here. And so I'm here. And I'll tell you, it isn't easy. I sometimes wish we had a little more help from the Boss, a little more guidance, but we don't, and somebody has to do it. Somebody has to clean out the stables, John." Again the smile.

I put on my talking-to-the-man mask. "Of course," I said. I hoped a gradual increase in piety would pass his sharp-eyed muster.

"And you can see how this all makes you much more valuable to the organization."

I let light dawn slowly.

"We'd hate to lose you now, John. Not when there's security, so much security, working for us. I mean, here we learn the real ins and outs of salvation."

I let him talk at me until he looked at his watch, and all the time I nodded and considered and tried to think of the best ploy. Then I eased myself into a turnabout. I did some confessing until his discomfort was stretched too far—I was keeping him from an important appointment—and made my concluding statement.

"I just wouldn't feel right up here," I said. "I've driven all my life. I'd just want to keep on, working where I'm best suited."

"Keep your present job?" he said, tapping his shoe on the side of the desk.

"Lord, yes," I said, grateful as could be.

Then I asked him for his autograph. He smiled real big and gave it to me, God's right-hand man, who had prayed with presidents.

The next time out, I thought about the incredible thing that Charlie Frick had told me. Halfway to Hell, on the part of the run that he had once driven, I pulled the truck onto the gravel shoulder and walked back, hands in pockets, squinting at the faces. Young and old. Mostly old, but a few very young, in their teens or twenties. Some were clearly bad news . . . But I was looking more closely this time, trying to discriminate.

And sure enough, I saw a few that didn't seem to belong.

The dead hung by the slats, sticking their arms through, beseeching. I ignored as much of that as I could. "You," I said, pointing to a pale, thin fellow with a listless expression. "Why are you here?"

They wouldn't lie to me. I'd learned that inside the City. The dead don't lie.

"I kill people," the man said in a high whisper. "I love to kill kids. You know, children. Real pleasure to me."

That confirmed my theory. I had *known* there was something wrong with him. I pointed to an old woman, plump and white-haired, lacking any of the signs. "You. Why are you going to Hell?"

She shook her head. "I don't know," she said. "Because I'm bad, I suppose."

"What did you do that was bad?"

"I don't know!" she said, flinging her hands up. "I really don't know. I was a librarian. When all those horrible people tried to take books out of my library, I fought them. I tried to reason with them . . . They wanted to remove Salinger and Twain and Baum . . ."

I picked out another young man. "What about you?"

"I didn't think it was possible," he said. "I didn't believe that God hated me, too."

"What did you do?" These people *didn't need to confess.*

"I loved God. I loved Jesus. But, dear Lord, I couldn't help it. I'm gay. I never had a choice. God wouldn't send me here just for being gay, would he?"

I spoke to a few more, until I was sure I had found all I had in this load. "You, you, you and you, out," I said, swinging open the rear gate. I closed the gate after them and led them away from the truck. Then I told them what Charlie Frick had told me, what he had learned on the road and in the big offices.

"Nobody's really sure where it goes," I said. "But it doesn't go to Hell, and it doesn't go back to Earth."

"Where, then?" the old woman asked plaintively. The hope in her eyes made me want to cry, because I just wasn't sure.

"Maybe it's the High Road," I said. "At least it's a chance. You light out across this stretch, go back of that hill, and I think there's some sort of trail. It's not easy to find, but if you look carefully, it's there. Follow it."

The young man who was gay took my hand. I felt like pulling away, because I've never been fond of homos. But he held on and he said, "Thank you. You must be taking a big risk."

"Yes, thank you," the librarian said. "Why are you doing it?"

I had hoped they wouldn't ask. "When I was a kid, one of my Sunday schoolteachers told me about Jesus going down to Hell during the three days before he rose up again. She told me Jesus went to Hell to bring out those who didn't belong. I'm certainly no Jesus, I'm not even much of a Christian, but that's what I'm doing. She called it Harrowing Hell." I shook my head. "Never mind. Just go," I said. I watched them walk across the gray flats and around the hill, then I got back into my truck and took the rest into the annex. Nobody noticed. I suppose the records just aren't that important to the employees.

None of the folks I've let loose have ever come back.

I'm staying on the road. I'm talking to people here and there, being cautious. When it looks like things are getting chancy, I'll take my rig back down to the City. And then I'm not sure what I'll do.

I don't want to let everybody loose. But I want to know who's ending up on the Low Road who shouldn't be. People unpopular with God's right-hand man.

My message is simple. The crazy folks are running the asylum. We've corrupted Hell.

If I get caught, I'll be riding in back. And if you're reading this, chances are you'll be there, too.

Until then, I'm doing my bit. How about you?

THE WHITE HORSE CHILD

Here's one of my most popular stories, reprinted dozens of times and even made into a multimedia CD-ROM. When Terry Carr bought it for his original hardcover anthology Universe 9 (1979) I was thrilled—Terry was one of the most respected editors in the field, and he said this story reminded him of Ray Bradbury.

Ray's work has always been one of my biggest influences, but "The White Horse Child" is the only one of my stories that even comes close to being Bradburyesque.

I had strong inspiration. In my late teens and early twenties I experienced a series of dreams that exposed something about my inner, creative self. While I've seldom gotten story ideas from dreams, on occasion—and particularly in those years—dreams acted like a mindquake to reveal hidden layers and allow deep magma to reach the surface.

One of the upwellings came in 1972. I was living by myself in an apartment on College Avenue in San Diego, California. Half-awake, lying in bed in the dark at some hour past midnight, I witnessed an equine beast push slowly through my bedroom wall. It was made of woven ice crystals, but otherwise bore a distinct resemblance to the horse in Fuselli's "Nightmare," and it relayed a message that seemed at first ominous—but in retrospect, after I was fully awake, turned out to be friendly and approving. That message was, and I quote it exactly, "You're doing just fine, but don't forget about me."

I had met this creature before.

When I was nine years old, I had had a bad nightmare about a white cloud hovering over my bed. It had told me that it was going to eat me.

The ice-crystal horse and the hungry cloud were one and the same. In the intervening years, my subconscious selves—my creative "demons"—had formed an alliance with my consciousness, and were no longer threatening, but intensely collaborative. A whole series of similar dreams sealed the alliance, and my demons and I have been working well together ever since.

In 1977, Tina and I moved to Long Beach. I was writing on an old IBM typewriter, using long sheets of yellow paper wound off of a roll—five feet was a pretty good day's work. In the afternoon, I would often drive into downtown Long Beach and wander through Acres of Books, a venerable old store that is now closed. Around the corner was Richard Kyle's Wonderworld books, where I met not only Richard, a lean, witty man with a lifetime's experience of popular culture, but Alan Brennert, the superb novelist and screenwriter. Alan was young and ambitious, just like me, and we would soon partner up to impress an agent and take story ideas into Hollywood. I had connections that led Alan to his first Hollywood agent, and Alan had connections that led me to my literary agent, Richard Curtis.

The ideas perked, and in 1977, in that apartment in Long Beach, poured forth as a story of dreams and creativity, of a young lad's awakening to the creative instinct—and of those who, in the name of something they call righteousness and love, would kill everything in this life that really matters.

By the way, no one in my family ever treated me this way. I was lucky, and maybe that's why my demons and I get along so well.

When I was seven years old, I met an old man by the side of the dusty road between school and farm. The late afternoon sun had cooled, and he was sitting on a rock, hat off, hands held out to the gentle warmth, whistling a pretty song. He nodded at me as I walked past. I nodded back. I was curious, but I knew better than to get involved with strangers. Nameless evils seemed to attach themselves to strangers, as if they might turn into lions when no one but a little kid was around.

"Hello, boy," he said.

I stopped and shuffled my feet. He looked more like a hawk than a lion. His clothes were brown and gray and russet, and his hands were pink like the flesh of some rabbit a hawk had just plucked up. His face was brown except around the eyes, where he might have worn glasses; around the eyes he was white, and this intensified his gaze. "Hello," I said.

"Was a hot day. Must have been hot in school," he said.

"They got air conditioning."

"So they do, now. How old are you?"

"Seven," I said. "Well, almost eight."

"Mother told you never to talk to strangers?"

"And Dad, too."

"Good advice. But haven't you seen me around here?"

I looked him over. "No."

"Closely. Look at my clothes. What color are they?"

His shirt was gray, like the rock he was sitting on. The cuffs, where they peeped from under a russet jacket, were white. He didn't smell bad, but he didn't look particularly clean. He was smooth-shaven, though. His hair was white, and his pants were the color of the dirt below the rock. "All kinds of colors," I said.

"But mostly I partake of the landscape, no?"

"I guess so," I said.

"That's because I'm not here. You're imagining me, at least part of me. Don't I look like somebody you might have heard of?"

"Who are you supposed to look like?" I asked.

"Well, I'm full of stories," he said. "Have lots of stories to tell little boys, little girls, even big folk, if they'll listen."

I started to walk away.

"But only if they'll listen," he said. I ran. When I got home, I told my older sister about the man on the road, but she only got a worried look and told me to stay away from strangers. I took her advice. For some time afterward, into my eighth year, I avoided that road and did not speak with strangers more than I had to.

The house that I lived in, with the five other members of my family and two dogs and one beleaguered cat, was white and square and comfortable. The stairs were rich dark wood overlaid with worn carpet. The walls were dark oak paneling up to a foot above my head, then white plaster, with a white plaster ceiling. The air was full of smells—bacon when I woke up, bread and soup and dinner when I came home from school, dust on weekends when we helped clean.

Sometimes my parents argued, and not just about money, and those were bad times; but usually we were happy. There was talk about selling the farm and the house and going to Mitchell where Dad could work in a computerized feed-mixing plant, but it was only talk.

It was early summer when I took to the dirt road again. I'd forgotten about the old man. But in almost the same way, when the sun was cooling and the air was haunted by lazy bees, I saw an old woman. Women strangers are less malevolent than men, and rarer. She sat on the gray rock, in a long, green, summer-dusty skirt, with a daisy-colored shawl and a blouse the precise hue of cottonwoods seen in a late hazy day's muted light. "Hello, boy," she said.

"I don't recognize you, either," I blurted, and she smiled.

"Of course not. If you didn't recognize him, you'd hardly know me."

"Do you know him?" I asked. She nodded. "Who was he? Who are you?"

"We're both full of stories. Just tell them from different angles. You aren't afraid of us, are you?"

I was, but having a woman ask the question made all the difference. "No," I said. "But what are you doing here? And how do you know—?"

"Ask for a story," she said. "One you've never heard of before." Her eyes were the color of baked chestnuts, and she squinted into the sun so that I couldn't see her whites. When she opened them wider to look at me, she didn't have any whites.

"I don't want to hear stories," I said softly.

"Sure you do. Just ask."

"It's late. I got to be home."

"I knew a man who became a house," she said. "He didn't like it. He stayed quiet for thirty years, and watched all the people inside grow up, and be just like their folks, all nasty and dirty and letting the paint on his walls flake off, and the bathrooms were *unbearable*. So he spit them out one morning, furniture and all, and shut his doors and locked them."

"What?"

"You heard me. Upchucked. The poor house was so disgusted he changed back into a man, but he was older and he had a cancer and his heart was bad because of all the abuse he had lived with. He died soon after."

I laughed, not because the man had died, but because I knew such things were lies. "That's silly," I said.

"Then here's another. There was a cat who wanted to eat butterflies. Nothing finer in the world for a cat than to stalk the grass, waiting for black-and-pumpkin butterflies. It crouches down and wriggles its rump to dig in the hind paws, then it jumps. But a butterfly is no sustenance for a cat. It's practice. There was a little girl about your age—might have been your sister, but she won't admit it—who saw the cat and decided to teach it a lesson. She hid in the taller grass with two old kites under each arm and waited for the cat to come by stalking. When it got real close, she put on her mother's dark glasses, to look all bug-eyed, and she jumped up flapping the kites. Well, it was just a little too real, because in a trice she found herself flying, and she was much smaller than she had been, and the cat jumped at her. Almost got her, too. Ask your sister about that sometime. See if she doesn't deny it."

"How'd she get back to be my sister again?"

"She became too scared to fly. She lit on a flower and found herself crushing it. The glasses broke, too."

"My sister did break a pair of Mom's glasses once."

The woman smiled.

"I got to be going home."

"Tomorrow you bring *me* a story, okay?"

I ran off without answering. But in my head, monsters were already rising. If she thought I was scared, wait until she heard the story I had to tell! When I got home my oldest sister, Barbara, was fixing lemonade in the kitchen. She was a year older than I but acted as if she were grown-up. She was a good six inches taller, and I could beat her if I got in a lucky punch, but no other way—so her power over me was awesome.

But we were usually friendly.

"Where you been?" she asked, like a mother.

"Somebody tattled on you," I said.

Her eyes went doe-scared, then wizened down to slits. "What're you talking about?"

"Somebody tattled about what you did to Mom's sunglasses."

"I already been whipped for that," she said nonchalantly. "Not much more to tell."

"Oh, but I know more."

"Was *not* playing doctor," she said. The youngest, Sue-Ann, weakest and most full of guile, had a habit of telling the folks somebody or other was playing doctor. She didn't know what it meant—I just barely did—but it had been true once, and she held it over everybody as her only vestige of power.

"No," I said, "but I know what you were doing. And I won't tell anybody."

"You don't know *nothing*," she said. Then she accidentally poured half a pitcher of lemonade across the side of my head and down my front. When Mom came in I was screaming and swearing like Dad did when he fixed the cars, and I was put away for life plus ninety years in the bedroom I shared with younger brother Michael. Dinner smelled better than usual that evening, but I had none of it. Somehow I wasn't brokenhearted.

It gave me time to think of a scary story for the country-colored woman on the rock.

School was the usual mix of hell and purgatory the next day. Then the hot, dry winds cooled and the bells rang and I was on the dirt road again, across the southern hundred acres, walking in the lees and shadows of the big cottonwoods. I carried my Road-Runner lunch pail and my pencil box and one book—a handwriting manual I hated so much I tore pieces out of it at night, to shorten its lifetime, and I walked slowly, to give my story time to gel.

She was leaning up against a tree, not far from the rock. Looking back, I can see she was not so old as a boy of eight years thought. Now I see her lissome beauty and grace, despite the dominance of gray in her reddish hair, despite the crow's-feet around her eyes and the smile-haunts around her lips. But to the eight-year-old she was simply a peculiar crone. And he had a story to tell her, he thought, that would age her unto graveside.

"Hello, boy," she said.

"Hi." I sat on the rock.

"I can see you've been thinking," she said.

I squinted into the tree shadow to make her out better. "How'd you know?"

"You have the look of a boy that's been thinking. Are you here to listen to another story?"

"Got one to tell, this time," I said.

"Who goes first?"

It was always polite to let the woman go first, so I quelled my haste and told her she could. She motioned me to come by the tree and sit on a smaller rock, half-hidden by grass. And while the crickets in the shadow tuned up for the evening, she said, "Once there was a dog. This dog was a pretty usual dog, like the ones that would chase you around home if they thought they could get away with it—if they didn't know you or thought you were up to something the big people might disapprove of. But this dog lived in a graveyard. That is, he belonged to the caretaker. You've seen a graveyard before, haven't you?"

"Like where they took Grandpa."

"Exactly," she said. "With pretty lawns, and big white-and-gray stones, and for those who've died recently, smaller gray stones with names and flowers and years cut into them. And trees in some places, with a mortuary nearby made of brick, and a garage full of black cars, and a place behind the garage where you wonder what goes on." She knew the place, all right. "This dog had a pretty good life. It was his job to keep the grounds clear of animals at night. After the gates were locked, he'd be set loose, and he wandered all night long. He was almost white, you see. Anybody human who wasn't supposed to be there would think he was a ghost, and they'd run away.

"But this dog had a problem. His problem was, there were rats that didn't pay much attention to him. A whole gang of rats. The leader was a big one, a good yard from nose to tail. These rats made their living by burrowing under the ground in the old section of the cemetery."

That did it. I didn't want to hear any more. The air was a lot colder than it should have been, and I wanted to get home in time for dinner and still be able to eat it.

But I couldn't leave just then.

"Now the dog didn't know what the rats did, and just like you and I, probably, he didn't much care to know. But it was his job to keep them under control. So one day he made a truce with a couple of cats that he normally tormented and told them about the rats. These cats were scrappy old toms, and they'd long since cleared out the competition of other cats, but they were friends themselves. So the dog made them a proposition. He said he'd let them use the cemetery anytime they wanted, to prowl around or hunt or whatever, if they would put the fear of God into a few of the rats. The cats took him up on it. 'We get to do whatever we want,' they said, 'whenever we want, and you won't bother us.' The dog agreed.

"That night the dog waited for the sounds of battle. But they never came. Nary a yowl." She glared at me for emphasis. "Not a claw scratch. Not even a twitch of tail in the wind." She took a deep breath, and so did I. "Round about midnight the dog went out into the graveyard. It was very dark, and there wasn't wind or bird or speck of star to relieve the quiet and the dismal, inside-of-a-box-camera blackness. The dog sniffed his way to the old part of the graveyard and met with the head rat, who was sitting on a slanty, cracked wooden grave marker. Only his eyes and a tip of tail showed in the dark, but the dog could smell him. 'What happened to the cats?' he asked. The rat shrugged his haunches. 'Ain't seen any cats,' he said. 'What did you think—that you could scare us out with a couple of cats? Ha. Listen—if there had been any cats here tonight, they'd have been strung and hung like meat in a shed, and my young'uns would have grown fat on—'"

"No-o-o!" I screamed, and I ran away from the woman and the tree until I couldn't hear the story anymore.

"What's the matter?" she called after me. "Aren't you going to tell me your story?" Her voice followed me as I ran.

It was funny. That night, I wanted to know what happened to the cats. Maybe nothing had happened to them. Not knowing made my visions even worse, and I didn't sleep well.

But my brain worked like it had never worked before.

The next day, a Saturday, I had an ending—not a very good one in retrospect—but it served to frighten Michael so badly he threatened to tell Mom on me.

"What would you want to do that for?" I asked. "Cripes, I won't ever tell you a story again if you tell Mom!"

Michael was a year younger and didn't worry about the future. "You never told me stories before," he said, "and everything was fine. I won't miss them."

He ran down the stairs to the living room. Dad was smoking a pipe and reading the paper, relaxing before checking the irrigation on the north thirty. Michael stood at the foot of the stairs, thinking. I was almost down to grab him and haul him upstairs when he made his decision and headed for the kitchen. I knew exactly what he was considering—that Dad would probably laugh and call him a little scaredy-cat. But Mom would get upset and do me in proper.

She was putting a paper form over the kitchen table to mark it for fitting a tablecloth. Michael ran up to her and hung on to a pants leg while I halted at the kitchen door, breathing hard, eyes threatening eternal torture if he so much as peeped. But Michael didn't worry about the future much.

"Mom," he said.

"Cripes!" I shouted, high-pitching on the i. Refuge awaited me in the tractor shed. It was an agreed-upon hiding place. Mom didn't know I'd be there, but Dad did, and he could mediate.

It took him a half hour to get to me. I sat in the dark behind a workbench, practicing my pouts. He stood in the shaft of light falling from the unpatched chink in the roof. Dust motes maypoled around his legs.

"Son," he said. "Mom wants to know where you got that story."

Now, this was a peculiar thing to be asked. The question I'd expected had been, "Why did you scare Michael?" or maybe, "What made you think of such a thing?" But no. Somehow she had plumbed the problem, planted the words in Dad's mouth, and impressed upon him that father-son relationships were temporarily suspended.

"I made it up," I said.

"You've never made up that kind of story before."

"I just started."

He took a deep breath. "Son, we get along real good, except when you lie to me. We know better. Who told you that story?"

This was uncanny. There was more going on than I could understand—there was a mysterious adult thing happening. I had no way around the truth.

"An old woman," I said.

Dad sighed even deeper. "What was she wearing?"

"Green dress," I said.

"Was there an old man?"

I nodded.

"Christ," he said softly. He turned and walked out of the shed. From outside he called me to come into the house. I dusted off my overalls and followed him.

Michael sneered at me. "'Locked them in coffins with old dead bodies,'" he mimicked. "Phhht! You're going to get it."

The folks closed the folding door to the kitchen with both of us outside. This disturbed Michael, who expected he'd witness instant punishment. I was too curious and worried to take my revenge on him, so he skulked out the screen door and chased the cat around the house. "Lock you in a coffin!" he screamed.

Mom's voice drifted from behind the louvered doors. "Do you hear that? The poor child's going to have nightmares. It'll warp him."

"Don't exaggerate," Dad said.

"Exaggerate what? That those filthy people are back? Ben, they must be a hundred years old now! They're trying to do the same thing to your son that they did to your brother . . . and just look at *him!* Living in sin, writing for those hell-spawned girlie magazines."

"He ain't living in sin, he's living alone in an apartment in New York City. And he writes for all kinds of places."

"They tried to do it to *you*, too! Just thank God your aunt saved you."

"Margie, I hope you don't intend—"

"I certainly *do* intend. She knows all about them people. She chased them off once, she can sure do it again!"

All hell had broken loose. I didn't understand half of it, but I could feel the presence of Great Aunt Sybil Danser. I could almost hear her crackling voice and the shustle of her satchel of Billy Grahams and Zondervans and little tiny pamphlets with shining light in blue offset on their covers.

I knew there was no way to get the full story from the folks short of listening in, but they'd stopped talking and were sitting in that stony kind of silence that indicated Dad's disgust and Mom's determination. I was mad that nobody was blaming me, as if I were some idiot child not capable of being bad on my own. I was mad at Michael for precipitating the whole mess.

And I was curious. Were the man and woman more than a hundred years old? Why hadn't I seen them before, in town, or heard about them from other kids? Surely I wasn't the only one they'd seen on the road and told stories to.

I decided to get to the source. I walked up to the louvered doors and leaned my cheek against them. "Can I go play at George's?"

"Yes," Mom said. "Be back for evening chores."

George lived on the next farm, a mile and a half east. I took my bike and rode down the old dirt road going south.

They were both under the same tree, eating a picnic lunch from a wicker basket. I pulled my bike over and leaned it against the gray rock, shading my eyes to see them more clearly.

"Hello, boy," the old man said. "Ain't seen you in a while."

I couldn't think of anything to say. The woman offered me a cookie, and I refused with a muttered, "No, thank you, ma'am."

"Well then, perhaps you'd like to tell us your story."

"No, ma'am."

"No story to tell us? That's odd. Meg was sure you had a story in you someplace. Peeking out from behind your ears maybe, thumbing its nose at us."

The woman smiled ingratiatingly. "Tea?"

"There's going to be trouble," I said.

"Already?" The woman smoothed the skirt in her lap and set a plate of nut bread into it. "Well, it comes sooner or later, this time sooner. What do you think of it, boy?"

"I think I got into a lot of trouble for not much being bad," I said. "I don't know why."

"Sit down, then," the old man said. "Listen to a tale, then tell us what's going on."

I sat down, not too keen about hearing another story, but out of politeness. I took a piece of nut bread and nibbled on it as the woman sipped her tea and cleared her throat.

"Once there was a city on the shore of a broad blue sea. In the city lived five hundred children and nobody else, because the wind from the sea wouldn't let anyone grow old. Well, children don't have kids of their own, of course, so when the wind came up in the first year the city never grew any larger."

"Where'd all the grown-ups go?" I asked. The old man held his fingers to his lips and shook his head.

"The children tried to play all day, but it wasn't enough. They became frightened at night and had bad dreams. There was nobody to comfort them because only grown-ups are really good at making nightmares go away. Now, sometimes nightmares are white horses that come out of the sea, so they set up guards along the beaches and fought them back with wands made of black-thorn. But there was another kind of nightmare, horses that were black and rose out of the ground, and *those* were impossible to guard against. So the children got together one day and decided to tell all the scary stories there were to tell, to prepare themselves for all the nightmares. They found it was pretty easy to think up scary stories, and every one of them had a story or two to tell. They stayed up all night spinning yarns about ghosts and dead things, and live things that shouldn't have been, and things that were neither. They talked about death and about monsters that suck blood, about things that live way deep in the earth and long, thin things that sneak through cracks in doors to lean over beds at night and babble in tongues no one could understand. They talked about eyes without heads, and vice versa, and little blue shoes that walk across a cold empty white room, with no one in them, and a bunk bed that creaks when it's empty, and a printing press that produces newspapers from a city that never was. Pretty soon, by morning, they'd told all the scary stories. When the black horses came out of the ground the next night, and the white horses trotted in from the sea, the children greeted them with cakes and ginger ale, and they all held a big party. They also invited the pale sheet-things from the clouds, and everyone ate hearty and had a good time.

One white horse let a little boy ride on it and took him wherever he wanted to go. And there were no more bad dreams in the city of children by the sea."

I finished the piece of bread and wiped my hands on my crossed legs. "So that's why you tried to scare me," I said.

She shook her head. "I never have a reason for telling a story, and neither should you."

"I don't think I'm going to tell stories anymore," I said. "The folks get too upset."

"Philistines," the old man said, looking off across the fields.

"Listen, young man. There is nothing finer in the world than the telling of tales. Split atoms if you wish, but splitting an infinitive—and getting away with it—is far nobler. Lance boils if you wish, but pricking pretensions is often cleaner and always more fun."

"Then why are Mom and Dad so mad?"

The old man shook his head. "An eternal mystery."

"Well, I'm not so sure," I said. "I scared my little brother pretty bad, and that's not nice."

"Being scared is nothing," the old woman said. "Being bored, or ignorant—now that's a crime."

"I still don't know. My folks say you have to be a hundred years old. You did something to my uncle they didn't like, and that was a long time ago. What kind of people are you, anyway?"

The old man smiled. "Old, yes. But not a hundred."

"I just came out here to warn you. Mom and Dad are bringing out my great aunt, and she's no fun for anyone. You better go away." With that said, I ran back to my bike and rode off, pumping for all I was worth. I was between a rock and a hard place.

I loved my folks but I itched to hear more stories. Why wasn't it easier to make decisions?

That night I slept restlessly. I didn't have any dreams, but I kept waking up with something pounding at the back of my head, like it wanted to be let in. I scrunched my face up and pressed it back.

At Sunday breakfast, Mom looked across the table at me and

put on a kind face. "We're going to pick up Auntie Danser this afternoon, at the airport," she said.

My face went like warm butter.

"You'll come with us, won't you?" she asked. "You always did like the airport."

"All the way from where she lives?" I asked.

"From Omaha," Dad said.

I didn't want to go, but it was more a command than a request. I nodded, and Dad smiled at me around his pipe.

"Don't eat too many biscuits," Mom warned him. "You're putting on weight again."

"I'll wear it off come harvest. You cook as if the whole crew was here, anyway."

"Auntie Danser will straighten it all out," Mom said, her mind elsewhere. I caught the suggestion of a grimace on Dad's face, and the pipe wriggled as he bit down on it harder.

The airport was something out of a TV space movie. It went on forever, with stairways going up to restaurants and big smoky windows that looked out on the screaming jets, and crowds of people, all leaving, except for one pear-shaped figure in a cotton print dress with fat ankles and glasses thick as headlamps. I knew her from a hundred yards.

When we met, she shook hands with Mom, hugged Dad as if she didn't want to, then bent down and gave me a smile. Her teeth were yellow and even, sound as a horse's. She was the ugliest woman I'd ever seen. She smelled of lilacs. To this day lilacs take my appetite away.

She carried a bag. Part of it was filled with knitting, part with books and pamphlets. I always wondered why she never carried a Bible—just Billy Grahams and Zondervans.

One pamphlet fell out, and Dad bent to pick it up.

"Keep it, read it," Auntie Danser instructed him. "Do you good." She turned to Mom and scrutinized her from the bottom of a swimming pool. "You're looking good. He must be treating you right."

Dad ushered us out the automatic doors into the dry heat. Her one suitcase was light as a mummy and probably just as empty. I carried it, and it didn't even bring sweat to my brow. Her life was not in clothes and toiletry but in the plastic knitting bag.

We drove back to the farm in the big white station wagon. I leaned my head against the cool glass of the rear seat window and considered puking. Auntie Danser, I told myself, was like a mental dose of castor oil. Or like a visit to the dentist. Even if nothing was going to happen her smell presaged disaster, and like a horse sniffing a storm, my entrails worried.

Mom looked across the seat at me—Auntie Danser was riding up front with Dad—and asked, "You feeling okay? Did they give you anything to eat? Anything funny?"

I said they'd given me a piece of nut bread. Mom went, "Oh, Lord."

"Margie, they don't work like that. They got other ways." Auntie Danser leaned over the backseat and goggled at me. "Boy's just worried. I know all about it. These people and I have had it out before."

Through those murky glasses, her flat eyes knew me to my young pithy core. I didn't like being known so well. I could see that Auntie Danser's life was firm and predictable, and I made a sudden commitment I liked the man and woman. They caused trouble, but they were the exact opposite of my great aunt. I felt better, and I gave her a reassuring grin. "Boy will be okay," she said. "Just a colic of the upset mind."

Michael and Barbara sat on the front porch as the car drove up. Somehow a visit by Auntie Danser didn't bother them as much as it did me. They didn't fawn over her, but they accepted her without complaining—even out of adult earshot. That made me think more carefully about them. I decided I didn't love them any the less, but I couldn't trust them, either. The world was taking sides, and so far on my side I was very lonely. I didn't count the two old people on my side, because I wasn't sure they were—but they came a lot closer than anybody in my family.

Auntie Danser wanted to read Billy Graham books to us kids after dinner, but Dad snuck us out before Mom could gather us together—all but Barbara, who stayed to listen. We watched the sunset from the loft of the old wood barn, then tried to catch the little birds that lived in the rafters. By dark and bedtime I was hungry, but not for food.

I asked Dad if he'd tell me a story before bed.

"You know your mom doesn't approve of all that fairy-tale stuff," he said.

"Then no fairy tales. Just a story."

"I'm out of practice, son," he confided. He looked very sad. "Your mom says we should concentrate on things that are real and not waste our time with make-believe. Life's hard. I may have to sell the farm, you know, and work for that feed-mixer in Mitchell."

I went to bed and felt like crying. A whole lot of my family had died that night, I didn't know exactly how, or why.

But I was mad.

I didn't go to school the next day. During the night I'd had a dream, which came so true and whole to me that I had to rush to the stand of cottonwoods and tell the old people.

I grabbed up my lunch box and walked at a brisk pace down the road.

They weren't under the tree. On a piece of wire bradded to the biggest tree they'd left a note on faded brown paper. It was in a strong feminine hand, sepia-inked, delicately scribed with what could have been a goose-quill pen.

It said: "We're at the old Hauskopf farm. Come if you must."

Not "Come if you can."

I felt a twinge. The Hauskopf farm, abandoned fifteen years ago and never sold, was three miles farther down the road and left on a deep-rutted fork. It took me an hour to get there.

The house still looked deserted. All the white paint had fallen off, leaving dead, silver-gray wood. The windows stared. I walked up the porch steps and knocked on the heavy oak door. For a moment I thought no one was going to answer. Then I heard what sounded like a gust of wind, but inside the house, and the old woman opened the door.

"Hello, boy," she said. "Come for more stories?"

She invited me in. Wildflowers grew along the baseboards, and tiny roses peered from brambles that covered the walls. A quail led her train of inch-and-a-half fluffball chicks from under the stairs, into the living room. The floor was carpeted, but the flowers in the weave seemed more than patterns. I could stare down for minutes and keep picking out details.

"This way, boy," the woman said, and took my hand. Her fingers were smooth and warm, but I had the impression they were also hard as wood.

A tree rose in the living room, growing out of the floor and sending its branches up to support the ceiling. Rabbits and quail and a lazy-looking brindle cat stared at me from the tangles of its roots. A wooden bench surrounded the base of the tree. On the side away from us, I heard someone breathing. The old man poked his head around and smiled at me, lifting his long pipe in greeting.

"Hello, boy," he said.

"The boy looks like he's ready to tell us a story, this time," the woman said.

"Of course, Meg. Have a seat, boy. Cup of cider? Tea? Herb biscuit?"

"Cider, please," I said.

The old man stood and went down the hall to the kitchen. He came back with a wooden tray and three steaming cups of mulled cider. The cinnamon tickled my nose as I sipped.

"Now. What's your story?"

"It's about two hawks," I said, and then hesitated.

"Go on."

"Brother hawks. Never did like each other. Fought for a strip of land where they could hunt."

"Yes?"

"Finally, one hawk met an old crippled bobcat that had set up a place for itself in a rockpile. The bobcat was learning itself magic so it wouldn't have to go out and catch dinner, which was awful hard for it now. The hawk landed near the bobcat and told it about his brother, and how cruel he was. So the bobcat said, 'Why not give him the land for the day? Here's what you can do.' The bobcat told him how he could turn into a rabbit, but a very strong rabbit no hawk could hurt."

"Wily bobcat," the old man said, smiling.

"'You mean, my brother wouldn't be able to catch me?' the hawk asked. 'Course not,' the bobcat said. 'And you can teach him a lesson. You'll tussle with him, scare him real bad—show him what tough animals there are on the land he wants. Then he'll go away and hunt somewheres else.' The hawk thought that sounded like a fine idea. So he let the bobcat turn him into a rabbit, and he hopped back to the land and waited in a patch of grass. Sure enough, his brother's shadow soon passed by, and then he heard a swoop and saw the claws held out. So he filled himself with being mad and jumped up and practically bit all the tail feathers off his brother. The hawk just flapped up and rolled over on the ground, blinking and gawking with his beak wide. 'Rabbit,' he said, 'that's not natural. Rabbits don't act that way.'

"'Round here they do,' the hawk-rabbit said. 'This is a tough old land, and all the animals here know the tricks of escaping from bad birds like you.' This scared the brother hawk, and he flew away as best he could and never came back again. The hawk-rabbit hopped to the rockpile and stood up before the bobcat, saying, 'It worked real fine. I thank you. Now turn me back, and I'll go hunt my land.' But the bobcat only grinned and reached out with a paw and broke the rabbit's neck. Then he ate him, and said, 'Now the land's mine and no hawks can take away the easy game.' And that's how the greed of two hawks turned their land over to a bobcat."

The old woman looked at me with wide, baked-chestnut eyes and smiled. "You've got it," she said. "Just like your uncle. Hasn't he got it, Jack?" The old man nodded and took his pipe from his mouth. "He's got it fine. He'll make a good one."

"Now, boy, why did you make up that story?"

I thought for a moment, then shook my head. "I don't know," I said. "It just came up."

"What are you going to do with the story?"

I didn't have an answer for that question, either.

"Got any other stories in you?"

I considered, then said, "Think so."

A car drove up outside, and Mom called my name. The old woman stood and straightened her dress. "Follow me," she said. "Go out the back door, walk around the house. Return home with them. Tomorrow, go to school like you're supposed to do. Next Saturday, come back, and we'll talk some more."

"Son? You in there?"

I walked out the back and came around to the front of the house. Mom and Auntie Danser waited in the station wagon. "You aren't allowed out here. Were you in that house?" Mom asked. I shook my head.

My great aunt looked at me with her glassed-in flat eyes and lifted the corners of her lips a little. "Margie," she said, "go have a look in the windows."

Mom got out of the car and walked up the porch to peer through the dusty panes. "It's empty, Sybil."

"Empty, boy, right?"

"I don't know," I said. "I wasn't inside."

"I could hear you, boy," she said. "Last night. Talking in your sleep. Rabbits and hawks don't behave that way. You know it, and I know it. So it ain't no good thinking about them that way, is it?"

"I don't remember talking in my sleep," I said.

"Margie, let's go home. This boy needs some pamphlets read into him."

Mom got into the car and looked back at me before starting the engine. "You ever skip school again, I'll strap you black and blue. It's real embarrassing having the school call, and not knowing where you are. Hear me?"

I nodded.

Everything was quiet that week. I went to school and tried not to dream at night and did everything boys are supposed to do. But I didn't feel like a boy. I felt something big inside, and no amount of Billy Grahams and Zondervans read at me could change that feeling.

I made one mistake, though. I asked Auntie Danser why she never read the Bible. This was in the parlor one evening after dinner and cleaning up the dishes. "Why do you want to know, boy?" she asked.

"Well, the Bible seems to be full of fine stories, but you don't carry it around with you. I just wondered why."

"Bible is a good book," she said. "The only good book. But it's difficult. It has lots of camouflage. Sometimes—" She stopped. "Who put you up to asking that question?"

"Nobody," I said.

"I heard that question before, you know," she said. "Ain't the first time I been asked. Somebody else asked me, once."

I sat in my chair, stiff as a ham.

"Your father's brother asked me that once. But we won't talk about him, will we?"

I shook my head.

Next Saturday I waited until it was dark and everyone was in bed. The night air was warm, but I was sweating more than the warm could cause as I rode my bike down the dirt road, lamp beam swinging back and forth. The sky was crawling with stars, all of them looking at me. The Milky Way seemed to touch down just beyond the road, like I might ride straight up it if I went far enough.

I knocked on the heavy door. There were no lights in the windows and it was late for old folks to be up, but I knew these two didn't behave like normal people. And I knew that just because the house looked empty from the outside didn't mean it was empty within.

The wind rose up and beat against the door, making me shiver. Then the door opened. Inside, it was dark for a moment, and the breath went out of me. Two pairs of eyes stared from the black. They seemed a lot taller this time. "Come in, boy," Jack whispered.

Fireflies lit up the tree in the living room. The brambles and wildflowers glowed like weeds on a sea floor. The carpet crawled, but not to my feet. I was shivering in earnest now, and my teeth chattered. I only saw their shadows as they sat on the bench in front of me.

"Sit," Meg said. "Listen close. You've taken the fire, and it glows bright. You're only a boy, but you're just like a pregnant woman now. For the rest of your life you'll be cursed with the worst affliction known to humans. Your skin will twitch at night. Your eyes will see things in the dark. Beasts will come to you and beg to be ridden. You'll never know one truth from another. You might starve, because few will want to encourage you. And if you do make good in this world, you might lose the gift and search forever after, in vain. Some will say the gift isn't special. Beware them. Some will say it is special, and beware them, too. And some—"

There was a scratching at the door. I thought it was an animal for a moment. Then it cleared its throat.

It was my great aunt.

"Some will say you're damned. Perhaps they're right. But you're also enthused. Carry it lightly and responsibly."

"Listen in there. This is Sybil Danser. You know me. Open up."

"Now stand by the stairs, in the dark where she can't see," Jack said. I did as I was told. One of them—I couldn't tell which—opened the door, and the lights went out in the tree, the carpet stilled, and the brambles were snuffed. Auntie Danser stood in the doorway, outlined by star glow, carrying her knitting bag. "Boy?" she asked. I held my breath.

"And you others, too."

The wind in the house seemed to answer.

"I'm not too late," she said. "Damn you, in truth, damn you to hell! You come to our towns, and you plague us with thoughts no decent person wants to think. Not just fairy stories, but telling the way people live and why they shouldn't live that way! Your very breath is tainted! Hear me?" She walked slowly into the empty living room, heavy shoes clonking on the wooden floor. "You make them write about us and make others laugh at us. Question the way we think. Condemn our deepest prides. Pull out our mistakes and amplify them beyond all truth. What right do you have to take young children and twist their minds?"

The wind sang through the cracks in the walls. I tried to see if Jack or Meg was there, but only shadows remained.

"I know where you come from, don't forget that! Out of the ground! Out of the bones of old wicked Indians! Shamans and pagan dances and worshiping dirt and filth! I heard about you from the old squaws on the reservation. Frost and Spring, they called you, signs of the turning year. Well, now you got a different name! Death and demons, I call you, hear me?"

She seemed to jump at a sound, but I couldn't hear it. "Don't you argue with me!" she shrieked. She took her glasses off and held out both hands. "Think I'm a weak old woman, do you? You don't know how deep I run in these communities! I'm the one who had them books taken off the shelves. Remember me? Oh, you hated it—not being able to fill young minds with your pestilence. Took them off high school shelves and out of lists—burned them for junk! Remember? That was me. I'm not dead yet! Boy, where are you?"

"Enchant her," I whispered to the air. "Magic her. Make her go away. Let me live here with you."

"Is that you, boy? Come with your aunt, now. Come with, come away!"

"Go with her," the wind told me. "Send your children this way, years from now. But go with her."

I felt a kind of tingly warmth and knew it was time to get home. I snuck out the back way and came around to the front of the house. There was no car. She'd followed me on foot all the way from the farm. I wanted to leave her there in the old house, shouting at the dead rafters, but instead I called her name and waited.

She came out crying. She knew.

"You poor sinning boy," she said, pulling me to her lilac bosom.

WEBSTER

"Webster" was written in 1971, sold in 1972, and published in 1974 in Alternities, a Dell original paperback anthology edited by David Gerrold. It was my second published story. (The first, "Destroyers," appeared in the Summer 1967 issue of Famous Science Fiction and is a little too young to be reprinted here.)

My mood in 1971 and 1972 was pretty down. My nineteenth and twentieth years on this planet were filled with unrealized hopes—as a writer, and as a young man. I was growing up rapidly—too rapidly—and my smarts weren't keeping up with the challenges. I was goofing some things badly; in particular, it seemed to me at the time, my relationships with the opposite sex. Nothing unusual here—typical youthful angst.

But what emerged when I wrote "Webster" was the portrait, not of a disappointed young man, but of a dreaming middle-aged woman too inner-directed to be anything but cruel, too blind to cause anything but pain—and fated as Rod Serling might have fated her, had he briefly teamed up with Jorge Luis Borges.

Someone I once knew, seen in a funhouse mirror. Though why they call it a funhouse, I'll never understand.

Dry.

It lingered in the air, a dead and sterile word made for whispers. Vultures fanned her hair with feather-duster wings. Up the dictionary's page ran her lean finger, wrapped in skin like pink parchment, and she found *Andrews, Roy Chapman*, digging in the middle of the Gobi, lifting fossil dinosaur eggs cracked and unhatched from their graves.

She folded the large, heavy book on her finger. The compressed pages gripped it with a firm, familiar pressure.

With her other hand, Miss Abigail Coates explored her face, vacant of any emotion she was willing to reveal. She did not enjoy her life. Her thin body gave no pleasure, provoked no surprise, spurred no uncontrollable passion. She took no joy in the bored pain of people in the streets. She felt imprisoned by the sun that shed a revealing, bleaching light on city walls and pavement, its dust-filled shafts stealing into her small apartment.

Miss Coates was fifty and, my God the needle in her throat when she thought of it, she had never borne a child; not once had she shared her bed with a man.

There had been, long ago, a lonely, lifeless love with a boy five years younger than she. She had hoped he would blunt the needle pain in her throat; he had begged to be given the chance. But she had spurned him. *I shall use my love as bait and let men pay the toll.* That had been her excuse, at any rate, until the first flush of her youth had faded. Even after that, even before she had felt *dry,* she had never found the right man.

"*Pitiful,*" she said with a sigh, and drew herself up from the overstuffed chair in her small apartment, standing straight and lean at five feet seven inches. *I weep inside, then read the dear Bible and the even more dear dictionary. They tell me weeping is a sin. Despair is the meanest of my sins—my few sins.*

She looked around the dry, comfortable room and shielded her eyes from the gloom of the place where she slept, as if blinded by shadow. The place wasn't a bedroom because in a *bedroom* you slept with a man or men and she had none. Her eyes moved up the door frame, nicked in one corner where clumsy movers had knocked her bed against the wood, twenty years ago; down to the worn carpet that rubbed the bottoms of her feet like raw canvas. To the chair behind her, stuffing poking from its the middle. To the wallpaper, chosen by someone else, stained with water along the cornice from an old rain. And finally she looked down at her feet, toes frozen in loose, frayed nylons, toenails thick and well-manicured; all parts of her body looked after but the core, the soul.

She went into the place where she slept and lay down. The sheets caressed her, as they were obliged to do, wrinkles and folds in blankets rubbing her thighs, her breasts. The pillow accepted her peppery hair, and in the dark, she ordered herself to sleep.

The morning was better. There was a whole day ahead. Something might happen.

Afternoon passed like a dull ache. In the twilight she fixed her pale dinner of potatoes and veal.

In the dark, she sat in her chair with the two books at her feet and listened to the old building crack and groan as it settled in for the night. She stared at the printed flowers on the wallpaper that someone must have once thought pretty.

The morning was fine. The afternoon was hot and sticky and she took a walk, wearing sunglasses. She watched all the young people on this fine Saturday afternoon. *They hold hands and walk in parks. There, on that bench; she'll be in trouble if she keeps that up.*

She went back to the patient apartment that always waited, never judging, ever faithful and unperturbed.

The evening passed slowly. She became lazy with heat. By midnight a cool breeze fluttered the sun-browned curtains in the window and blew them in like the dingy wings of street birds.

Miss Coates opened her dictionary, looking for comfort, and found words she wanted, but words she didn't need. They jumped from the pages and would not leave her alone. She didn't think them obscene; she was not a prude. She loved the sounds of all words, and these words were marvelous, too, when properly entrained with other words. They could be part of rich stories, rich lives. The sound of them made her tremble and ache.

The evening ended. Again, she could not cry. Sadness was a moist, dark thing, the color of mud.

She had spent her evenings like this, with few variations, for the past five years.

The yellow morning sunlight crept across the ironing board and over her fanciest dress, burgundy in shadows, orange in the glare. "I need a lover," she told herself firmly. But one found lovers in offices and she didn't work; in trains going to distant countries, and she never left town. "I need common sense, and self-control. That part of my life is over. I need to stop thinking like a teenager." But the truth was, she had no deficiency of self-control. It was her greatest strength.

It had kept her away from danger so many times.

Her name, Coates, was not in the dictionary. There was *coati*, *coatimundi*, *coat of arms*, *coat of mail*, and then *coauthor*, Miss Coauthor, partner and lover to a handsome writer. They would *collaborate*, *corroborate*, *celebrate*.

Celibate.

She shut the book.

She drew the curtains on the window and slowly tugged the zipper down the back of her dress with the practiced flourish of a crochet hook. Her fingers rubbed the small of her back, nails scraping. She held her chin high, eyes closed to slits.

A lone suitor came through the dark beyond the window to stroke her skin—a stray breeze, neither hot nor cool. Sweat lodged in the cleft between her breasts. She was proud of her breasts; they were small but still did not sag when she removed her bra. She squatted and marched her hands behind her to sit and then lie down on the floor. Spreading her arms against the rough carpet, Miss Coates pressed her chin into her clavicle and peered at her breasts, boyish against the prominent ribs. Untouched. Unspoiled goods.

She cupped them in both hands. She became a thin crucifixion with legs straight and toes together. Her head lay near the window. She looked up to see the curtains fluttering silently like her lips. Mouth open. Tongue rubbing the backs of her teeth. She smoothed her hands to her stomach and let them rest there, curled on the flat warmth.

My stomach doesn't drape. I am not so undesirable. No flab, few wrinkles. My thighs are not dimpled with gross flesh.

She rolled over and propped herself on one elbow to refer to the dictionary, then the Bible.

Abigail Coates mouthing a word: *Lover.*

The dictionary sat tightly noncommittal in buckram, the Bible silent in black leather.

She gently pushed the Bible aside. For all its ancient sex and betrayal and the begetting of desert progeny, it would do nothing for her. She pulled the dictionary closer. "Help me," she said. "Book of all books, massive thing I can hardly lift, every thought lies in you, all human possibilities. Everything I feel, everything that *can* be felt, lies waiting to be described in combinations of the words you contain. You hold all possible lives, people and places I've never seen, things dead and things unborn. Haven of ghosts, home of tyrants, birthplace of saints."

She knew she would have to be audacious. What she was about to do would be proof of her finally having cracked, like those dinosaur eggs in the Gobi; dead and sterile and cracked.

"Surely you can make a man. Small word, little effort. You can even *tell* me how to make a man from you." She could almost imagine a man rising from the open book, spinning like a man-shaped bird cage filled with light.

The curtains puffed.

"Go," she said. She crossed her legs in a lotus next to the thick book and waited for the dust of each word, the microscopic, homeopathic bits of ink, each charged with the shape of a letter, to sift between the fibers of the paper and combine. Dry magic. The words smelled sweet in the midnight breeze.

Dead bits of ink, charged with thought, arise.

Veni.

Her tongue swelled with the dryness of the ink. She unfolded and lay flat on her stomach to let the rough carpet mold her skin with crossword lines, upon which the right words could be written, solving her life's puzzle.

Miss Coates flopped the dictionary around to face her, then threw its clumps of pages open to the middle. Her finger searched randomly on the page and found a word. She gasped. *Man,* it said, clear as could be next to her immaculate, colorless nail. Man! She moved her finger and sucked in her breath.

"There *is* a man in you!" she told the book and laughed. It was a joke, that's all; she was not that far gone. Still grinning, she rubbed her finger against the inside of her cheek and pressed the dampness onto the word. "Here," she said. "A few of my cells." She was clever, she was scientific, she was brilliant! "Clone *them*." Then she thought that possibility through and said, "But don't make him look like me or think like me. Change him with your medical words, *plastic surgery* and *eugenics* and *phenotype*."

The page darkened under the press of her finger. She swung the dictionary shut and returned to her lotus.

As my trunk rises from the flower of my legs and the seat of my womb, so, man, arise from the book of all books.

Would it thunder? Only silence. The dictionary trembled and the Bible looked dark and somber. The yellow bulb in the shaded lamp sang like a dying moth. The air grew heavy. *Don't falter,* she told herself. *Don't lose faith, don't drop the flower of your legs and the seat of your womb. A bit of blood? Or milk from unsucked breasts? Catalysts . . . Or, God forbid, something living, a* fly *between the pages, the heart of a bird, or*—she shuddered, ill with excitement, with a kind of belief—*the clear seed of a dead man.*

The book almost lifted its cover. It *breathed.*

"That was it," she whispered in awe. "The words know what to do."

The dictionary sucked warmth from the air. Frost clung to its brown buckram. The cover flew back. The pages riffled, flew by, flapped spasmodically, and two of them stuck together, struggling, bulging . . . and then splitting.

A figure flew up, arms spread, and twirled like an ice skater. It sucked in dust and air and heat, sucked sweat from her skin, and turned dry emptiness into damp flesh.

"Handsome!" she cried. "Make him handsome and rugged and kind, and smart as I am, if not smarter. Make him like a father but not my father and like a son and a lover especially a lover, warm, and give him breath that melts my lips and softens my hair like steam from jungles. He should like warm dry days and going to lakes and fishing, but no—he should like reading to me more than fishing, and he should like cold winter days and ice-skating with me; he could if you will allow me to suggest he could be brown-haired with a shadow of red and his cheeks rough with fresh young beard I can watch grow and he should—"

His eyes! They flashed as he spun, molten beacons still undefined. She approved of the roughed-in shape of his nose. His hair danced and gleamed, dark brown with a hint of red. Arms, fingers, legs, crawled with words. An ant's nest of dry ink *foot*s crawled over his feet, tangling with *heel*s and *ankle*s and *toe*s. *Arm*s and *leg*s fought for dominance up the branches and into the trunk, where *torso* and *breast*s and other words fought them back. The battle of words went on for minutes, fierce and hot.

Then—what had been a dream, a delusion, suddenly became magic. The words spun, blurred, became real flesh and real bone.

His breasts were firm and square and dark-nippled. The hair on his chest was dark and silky. He was still spinning. She cried out, staring at his groin.

Clothes?

"Yes!" she said. "I have no clothes for men."

A suit, a pink shirt with cuff links and pearl decorations.

His eyes blinked and his mouth opened and closed. His head drooped and a moan flew out like a whirled weight cut loose from a string.

"Stop!" she shouted. "Please stop, he's finished!"

The man stood on the dictionary, knees wobbly, threatening to topple. She jumped up from the floor to catch him, but he fell away from her and collapsed on the carpet beside the chair. The book lay kicked and sprawled by his feet, top pages wrinkled and torn.

Miss Coates stood over the man, hands fluttering at her breasts. He lay on his side, chest heaving, eyes closed. Her wide gaze darted from point to point on his body, lower lip held by tiny white teeth. After a few minutes, she was able to look away from the man. She squinted more closely at the dictionary, frowned, then bent to riffle through the pages. Every page was blank. The dictionary had given everything it had.

"I am naked," she told herself, stretching out her hands, using the realization to shock herself to sensibility. She went into the place where she slept to put on some clothes. Away from the man, she wondered what she would call him. He probably did not have a name, not a Christian name at any rate. It seemed appropriate to call him by a name like everyone else, even if she had raised him from paper and ink, from a dictionary.

"Webster," she said, nodding sharply at the obvious. "I'll call him Webster."

She returned to the living room and looked at the man. He seemed to be resting peacefully. How could she move him to a more comfortable place? The couch was too small to hold his ungainly body; he was very tall. She measured him with the tape from her sewing kit. Six feet two inches. His eyes were still shut; what color were they? She squatted beside him, face flushed, thinking thoughts she warned herself she must not think, not yet.

She wore her best dress, wrapped in smooth dark burgundy, against which her pale skin showed to best advantage. It was one o'clock in the morning, however, and she was exhausted. "You seem comfortable where you are," she told the man, who did not move. "I'll leave you on the floor."

Abigail Coates went into her bedroom to sleep. Tired as she was, she could not just close her eyes and drift off. She felt like shouting for joy and tears dampened the pillow and moistened her pepper hair.

In the darkness, *he* breathed. Dreaming, did he cause words to flow through her drowsing thoughts? Or was it simply his breath filling the house with the odor of printer's ink?

In the night, *he* moved. Shifting an arm, a leg, sending atoms of words up like dust. His eyes flickered open, then closed. He moaned and was still again.

Abigail Coates's neck hair pricked with the first rays of morning and she awoke with a tiny shriek, little more than a high-pitched gasp. She rolled from her stomach onto her back and pulled up the sheet and bedspread.

Webster stood in the doorway, smiling. She could barely see him in the dawn light. Her eyelids were gummy with sleep. "Good morning, Regina," he said.

Regina Abigail Coates. Everyone had called her Abbie, when there had been friends to call her anything. No one had ever called her Regina.

"Regina," Webster repeated. "It reminds one of queens and Canadian coins."

How well he spoke. How full of class.

"Good morning," she said feebly. "How are you?" She suppressed an urge to giggle. *Why are you?* "How . . . do you feel?"

A ghost of a smile. He nodded politely, unwilling to complain. "As well as could be expected." He walked into her room and stopped at the foot of her bed, like a ghost her father had once told her about. "I'm well-dressed. Too much so, I think. It's uncomfortable."

Her heart was a little piston in her throat.

He walked around to her side of the bed. "You raised me from the book. Why?"

She stared up at his bright green eyes, like drops of water from the depths of an ocean trench. His hand touched her shoulder, lingered on the strap of her nightgown. One finger slipped under the strap and tugged it up a quarter of an inch. "This is the distance between OP and OR," he murmured.

She felt the pressure of the cloth beneath her breast.

"Why?" he asked again. His breath sprinkled words over her

face and hair. He shook his head and frowned. "Why do I feel so obliged to . . ." He pulled down the blind and closed the drapes and she heard the soft fall and hiss of rayon dropped onto a chair. In the darkness, a knee pressed the edge of her bed. A finger touched her neck and lips covered hers and parted them. A tongue explored.

He tasted of ink.

In the early morning hours, Regina Abigail Coates gave a tiny, squeezed-in scream.

Webster sat in the overstuffed chair and watched her leave the apartment. She shut the door and leaned against the wall, not knowing what to think or feel. "Of course," she whispered to herself, as if there were no wind or strength left in her. "Of course he doesn't like the sun."

She walked down the hallway, passed the doors of neighbors with whom she had not even a nodding acquaintance, and descended the stairs to the first floor. The street was filled with cars passing endlessly back and forth. Tugging out wrinkles from her dress, she stepped into the sunlight and faced the world, the new Regina Coates, *debutante.*

"*I know* what all you other women know," she said softly, with a shrill triumph. "All of you!" She looked up and noticed the sky, perhaps for the first time in twenty years; rich with clouds scattered across a bright blue sheet, demanding of her, *Breathe deeply.* She was part of the world, the real world.

Webster still sat in the chair when she returned with two bags of groceries. He was reading her Bible. Her face grew hot and she put down the bags and snatched it quickly from his hands. She could not face his querying stare, so she laid the book on a table, out of his reach, and said, "You don't want that."

"Why?" he asked. She picked up the bags again by their doubled and folded paper corners, taking them one in each hand into the kitchen and opening the old refrigerator to stock the perishables.

"When you're gone," Webster said, "I feel as if I fade. Am I real?"

She glanced up at the small mirror over the sink. Her shoulders twitched and a shudder ran up her back. *I am very far gone now.*

Regina brought in the afternoon newspaper and he held his hand out with a pleading expression; she handed it across, letting it waver for a moment above a patch of worn carpet, teasing him with a frightened, uncertain smile. He took it, spread it eagerly, and rubbed his fingers over the pages. He turned the big sheets slowly, seeming to absorb more than read. She fixed them both a snack but Webster refused to eat. He sat across from her at the small table, face placid, and for the moment, that was more than enough. She sat at her table, ate her small trimmed sandwich and drank her glass of grapefruit juice. Glancing at him from all sides—he did not seem to mind, and it made his outline sharper—she straightened up the tiny kitchen.

What was there to say to a man between morning and night? She had expected that a man made of words would be full of conversation, but Webster had very little experience. While all the right words existed in him, they had yet to be connected. Or so she surmised. Still, his very presence gratified her. He made her as real as she had made him.

He refused dinner, even declining to share a glass of wine with her after (she had only one glass).

"I expect there should be some awkwardness in the early days," she said. "Don't you? Quiet times when we can just sit and be with each other. Like today."

Webster stood by the window, touched a finger to his lips, leaving a smudge, and nodded. He agreed with most things she said.

"Let's go to bed," she suggested primly.

In the dark, when her solitude had again been sundered and her brow was sprinkled with salty drops of exertion, he lay next to her, and—

He *moved.*

He *breathed.*

But he did not sleep.

Regina lay with her back to him, eyes wide, staring at the flowers on the ancient wallpaper and a wide trapezoid of streetlight glare transfixing a small table and its vase. She felt ten years—no, twenty!—sliding away from her, and yet she couldn't tell him how she felt, didn't dare turn and talk. The air was full of him. Full of words not her own, unorganized, potential. She breathed in a million random thoughts, deep or slight, complex or simple, eloquent or crude. Webster was becoming a generator. Kept in the apartment, his substance was reacting with itself; shut away from experience, he was making up his own patterns and organizations, subtle as smoke.

Even lying still, waiting for the slight movement of air through the window to cool him, he worked inside, and his breath filled the air with potential.

Regina was tired and deliciously filled, and that satisfaction at least was hers. She luxuriated in it and slept.

In the morning, she lay alone in the bed for an extra hour. Then, abruptly, she flung off the covers and padded into the living room, pulling down her rucked-up nightgown, shivering against the morning chill. He stood by the window again, naked, not caring if people on the streets looked up and saw. She gently enclosed his upper arm with her fingers, leaned her cheek against his shoulder, a motion that came so naturally she surprised herself with her own grace. "What do you want?" she asked.

"No," he said tightly. "The question is, what do *you* want?"

"I'll get us some breakfast. You *must* be hungry by now."

"I'm not. I don't know what I am or how to feel."

"I'll get some food," she continued obstinately, letting go of his arm. "Do you like milk?"

"No. I don't know."

"I don't want you to become ill."

"I don't get ill. I don't get hungry. You haven't answered my question."

"I love you," she said, with less grace.

"You don't love me. You need me."

"Isn't that the same thing?"

"Not at all."

"Shall we get out today?" she asked airily, backing away, realizing she was doing a poor imitation of some actress in the movies—Bette Davis, her voice light, tripping.

"I can't. I don't get sick, I don't get hungry. I don't go places."

"You're being obtuse," she said petulantly, hating that tone, tears of frustration rising in her eyes. *How must I behave? Is he mine, or am I his?*

"*Obtuse, acute, equilateral, isosceles, vector, derivative, sequesential, psych-integrative, mersauvin powers . . .*" He shook his head, grinning sadly. "That's the future of mathematics for the next century. It becomes part of psychology. Did you know that? All numbers."

"Did you think that last night?" she asked. She cared nothing for mathematics; what could a man made of words know about numbers?

"Words mix in blood, my blood is made of words . . . I can't stop thinking, even at night. Words are numbers, too. Signs and portents, measures and relations, variables and qualifiers."

"You're flesh," she said. "I gave you substance."

"You gave me existence, not substance."

She laughed harshly, caught herself, forced herself to be demure again. Taking his hand, she led him back to the chair. She kissed him on the cheek, a chaste gesture considering their state of undress, and said she would stay with him all day, to help him orient to his new world. "But tomorrow, we have to go out and buy you some more clothes."

"Clothes," he said softly, then smiled as if all was well. She leaned her head forward and smiled back, a fire radiating from her stomach through her legs and arms. With a soft step and a skip she danced on the carpet, hair swinging. Webster watched her, still smiling.

"And while you're out," he said, "bring back another dictionary."

"Of course. We can't use *that* one anymore, can we? The same kind?"

"Doesn't matter," he said, shaking his head.

The uncertainty of Webster's quiet afternoon hours became a dull, sugarcoated ache for Regina Coates. She tried to disregard her fears—that he found her a disappointment, inadequate; that he was weakening, fading—and reasoned that if she was his *mistress,* she could make him do or be whatever she wished. Unless she did not know what to wish. Could a man's behavior be wished for, or must it simply be experienced?

At night the words again poured into her, and she smiled in the dark, lying beside the warmth of the shadow that smelled of herself and printer's ink, wondering if they should be taking precautions. She was a late fader in the biological department and there was a certain risk. . . .

She grinned savagely, thinking about it. All she could imagine was a doctor holding up a damp bloody thing in his hands and saying, "Miss Coates, you're the proud mother of an eightounce . . . *Thesaurus*."

"Abridged?" she asked wickedly.

She shopped carefully, picking for him the best clothes she could afford, in a wide variety of styles, dipping into her savings to pay the bill. For herself she chose a new dress that showed her slim waist to advantage and hid her thin thighs. She looked girlish, summery. That was what she wanted. She purchased a large dictionary in a bookstore and looked through nearby gift shops for something else to give him. "Something witty and interesting . . . something else for us to do."

She settled on a game of Scrabble.

Webster was delighted with the dictionary. He regarded the game dubiously, but played it with her a few times. "An appetizer," he called it.

"Are you going to eat the book?" she asked, half in jest.

"No," he said.

She wondered why they didn't argue. She wondered why they didn't behave like a normal couple, ignoring her self-derisive inner voice crying out, *Normal!?*

My God, she said to herself after two weeks, staring at the hard edge of the small table in the kitchen. *Creating men from dictionaries, making love until the bed is damp—at* my *age! He still smells like ink. He doesn't sweat and he refuses to go outside. Nobody sees him but me. Me. Who am I to judge whether he's really there?*

What would happen to Webster if I were to take a gun and put a hole in his stomach, above the navel? A man with a navel, not born of woman, is an abomination—isn't he?

If he spoke to her simply and without emotion just once more, or twice, she thought she would try that experiment and see.

She bought a gun, furtive as a mouse but a respectable citizen, for protection, a small gray pistol, and hid it in her drawer. She thought better of it a few hours after, shuddered in disgust, and removed the bullets, flinging them out of the apartment's rear window into the dead garden in the narrow courtyard below.

On the last day, when she went shopping, she carried the empty gun with her so he wouldn't find it—although he showed no interest in snooping, which would at least have been a sign of caring. The bulge in her purse made her nervous.

She did not return until dinnertime. *The apartment is not my own. It oppresses me.* He *oppresses me.* She walked quietly through the front door, saw the living room was empty, and heard a small sound from behind the closed bedroom door.

The flop of something stiff hitting the floor.

"Webster?" Silence. She knocked lightly on the door. "Are you ready to talk?"

No reply.

He makes me mad when he doesn't answer. I could scare him, force him react to me in some way. She took out the pistol, fumbling it, pressing its grip into her palm. It felt heavy and formidable.

The door was locked. Outraged that she should be closed out of her own bedroom, she carried the revolver into the kitchen and found a hairpin in a drawer, the same she had used months before when the door had locked accidentally. She knelt before the door and fumbled, teeth clenched, lips tight.

With a small cry, she pushed the door open.

Webster sat with legs crossed on the floor beside the bed. Before him lay the new dictionary, opened almost to the back. “Not now,” he said, tracing a finger along the columns of words.

Regina’s mouth dropped open. “What are you looking at?” she asked, tightening her grip on the pistol. She stepped closer, looked down, and saw that he was already up to VW.

“I don’t know,” he said. He found the word he was looking for, reached into his mouth with one finger and scraped his inner cheek. Smeared the wetness on the page.

“No,” she said. Then, “Why. . . ?”

There were tears on his cheeks. The man of dry ink was crying. Somehow that made her furious.

“I’m not even a human being,” he said.

She hated him, hated this weakness; she had never liked weak men. He adjusted his lotus position and gripped the edges of the dictionary with both hands. “Why can’t you find a human being for yourself?” he asked, looking up at her. “I’m nothing but a dream.”

She held the pistol firmly to her side. “What are you doing?”

“Need,” he said. “That’s all I am. Your hunger and your need. Do you know what I’m good for, what I can do? No. You’d be afraid if you did. You keep me here like some commodity.”

“I wanted you to go out with me,” she said tightly.

“What has the world done to you that you’d want to create me?”

“You’re going to make a woman from that thing, aren’t you?” she asked. “Nothing worthwhile has ever happened to me. Everything gets taken away the moment I . . .”

“Need,” he said, raising his hands over the book. “You cannot love unless you need. You cannot love the real. You must change the thing you love to please yourself, and damn anyone if he should question what hides within you.”

“You *thing*,” she breathed, lips curled back. Webster looked at her and at the barrel of the gun she now pointed at him and laughed.

“You don’t need that,” he told her. “You don’t need something real to kill a dream. All you need is a little sunlight.”

She lowered the gun, dropped it with a thud on the floor, then lifted her eyebrows and smiled around gritted teeth. She pointed the index finger of her left hand and her face went lax. Listlessly, she whispered, "Bang."

The smell of printer's ink became briefly more intense, then faded on the warm breeze passing through the apartment. She kicked the dictionary shut.

How lonely it was going to be, in the dark with only her own sweat.

THE VISITATION

This short mood piece appeared in Omni with a suite of stories by different authors on religious themes. Again, I'm arguing with our human conceptions of God—and suggesting that our conception of divinity is likely to be very incomplete and immature.

The Trinity arrived under a blossoming almond tree in Rebecca Sandia's backyard in the early hours of Easter morning. She watched it appear as she sipped tea on her back porch. Because of the peace radiating from the three images—a lion, a lamb, and a dove—she did not feel alarm or even much concern. She was not an overtly religious person, but she experienced considerable relief at having a major question—the existence of a God—answered in the affirmative. The Trinity approached her table on hooves, paws, and wings; and this, she knew, expressed the ultimate assurance and humility of God—that He should not require her to approach Him.

"Good morning," she said. The lamb nuzzled her leg affectionately. "An especially significant morning for you, is it not?" The lamb bleated and spun its tail. "I am so pleased you have chosen me, though I wonder why."

The lion spoke with a voice like a typhoon confined in a barrel:

"Once each year on this date we reveal the Craft of Godhead to a selected human. Seldom are the humans chosen from My formal houses of worship, for I have found them almost universally unable to comprehend the Mystery. They have preconceived ideas and cannot remove the blinds from their eyes."

Rebecca Sandia felt a brief *frisson* then, but the dove rubbed its breast feathers against her hand where it lay on the table. “I have never been a strong believer,” she said, “though I have always had hopes.”

“That is why you were chosen,” the dove sang, its voice as dulcet as a summer’s evening breeze. The lamb cavorted about the grass; and Rebecca’s heart was filled with gladness watching it, for she remembered it had gone through hard times not long ago.

“I have asked only one thing of My creations,” the lion said, “that once a year I find some individual capable of understanding the Mystery. Each year I have chosen the most likely individual and appeared to speak and enthuse. And each year I have chosen correctly and found understanding and allowed the world to continue. And so it will be until My creation is fulfilled.”

“But I am a scientist,” Rebecca said, concerned by the lion’s words. “I am enchanted by the creation more than the God. I am buried in the world and not the spirit.”

“I have spun the world out of My spirit,” the dove sang. “Each particle is as one of my feathers; each event, a note in my song.”

“Then I am joyful,” Rebecca said, “for that I understand. I have often thought of you as a scientist, performing experiments.”

“Then you do not understand,” the lion said. “For I seek not to comprehend My creation but to know MySelf.”

“Then is it wrong for me to be a scientist?” Rebecca asked. “Should I be a priest or a theologian, to help You understand YourSelf?”

“No, for I have made your kind as so many mirrors, that you may see each other; and there are no finer mirrors than scientists, who are so hard and bright. Priests and theologians, as I have said, shroud their brightness with mists for their own comfort and sense of well-being.”

“Then I am still concerned,” Rebecca said, “for I would like the world to be ultimately kind and nurturing. Though as a scientist I see that it is not, that it is cruel and harsh and demanding.”

“What is pain?” the lion asked, lifting one paw to show a triangle marked by thorns. “It is transitory, and suffering is the moisture of My breath.”

"I don't understand," Rebecca said, shivering.

"Among My names are disease and disaster, and My hand lies on every pockmark and blotch and boil, and My limbs move beneath every hurricane and earthquake. Yet you still seek to love Me. Do you not comprehend?"

"No," Rebecca said, her face pale, for the world's particles seemed to lose some of their stability at that moment. "How can it be that You love us?"

"If I had made all things comfortable and sweet, then you would not be driven to examine Me and know My motives. You would dance and sing and withdraw into your pleasures. "

"Then I understand," Rebecca said "For it is the work of a scientist to know the world and control it, and we are often driven by the urge to prevent misery. Through our knowledge we see You more clearly."

"I see MySelves more clearly through you."

"Then I can love You and cherish You, knowing that ultimately You are concerned for us."

The world swayed; and Rebecca was sore afraid, for the peace of the lamb had faded, and the lion glowed red as coals. "Whom are you closest to," the lion asked, its voice deeper than thunder, "your enemies or your lovers? Whom do you scrutinize more thoroughly?"

Rebecca thought of her enemies and her lovers, and she was not sure.

"In front of your enemies you are always watchful, and with your lovers you may relax and close your eyes."

"Then I understand," Rebecca said. "For this might be a kind of war; and after the war is over, we may come together, former enemies, and celebrate the peace."

The sky became black as ink. The blossoms of the almond tree fell, and she saw, within the branches, that the almonds would be bitter this year.

"In peace the former enemies would close their eyes," the lion said, "and sleep together peacefully."

"Then we must be enemies forever?"

"For I am a zealous God. I am zealous of your eyes and your ears, which I gave you that you might avoid the agonies I visit upon you. I am zealous of your mind, which I made wary and facile, that you might always be thinking and planning ways to improve upon this world."

"Then I understand," Rebecca said fearfully, her voice breaking, "that all our lives we must fight against you . . . but when we die?"

The lamb scampered about the yard, but the lion reached out with a paw and laid the lamb out on the grass with its back broken. "*This* is the Mystery," the lion roared, consuming the lamb, leaving only a splash of blood steaming on the ground.

Rebecca leaped from her chair, horrified, and held out her hands to fend off the prowling beast. "I understand!" she screamed "You are a selfish God, and Your creation is a toy You can mangle at will! You do not love; you do not care; you are cold and cruel."

The lion sat to lick its chops. "And?" it asked menacingly.

Rebecca's face flushed. She felt a sudden anger. "I am better than You," she said quietly, "for I can love and feel compassion. How wrong we have been to send our prayers to You!"

"And?" the lion asked with a growl.

"There is much we can teach You!" she said. "For You do not know how to love or respect Your creation, or YourSelf! You are a wild beast, and it is our job to tame You and train You."

"Such dangerous knowledge," the lion said. The dove landed among the hairs of its mane. "Catch Me if you can," the dove sang. For an instant the Trinity shed its symbolic forms and revealed Its true Self, a thing beyond ugliness or beauty, a vast cyclic thing of no humanity whatsoever, dark and horribly young—and that truth reduced Rebecca to hysterics.

Then the Trinity vanished, and the world continued for another year.

But Rebecca was never the same again, for she had understood, and by her grace we have lived this added time.

RICHIE BY THE SEA

I enjoy monster movies, horror fiction, and stories of the supernatural—ghost stories in particular. I've written two novels (Psychlone and Dead Lines) and one short story that could be dropped into these categories. Here's the story: a biological conte cruel, conceived during a jam session with my cousin, Dan Garrett, in the 1960s. Mark Laidlaw, at a party at Gregory and Joan Benford's house in Laguna Beach, told me that Ramsey Campbell, a master of horror fiction, was looking for short stories for an original anthology he was assembling, and suggested I submit something.

I sent him "Richie."

The storm had spent its energy the night before. A wild, scattering squall had toppled the Thompsons' shed and the last spurt of high water had dropped dark drift across the rocks and sand. In the last light of day the debris was beginning to stink and attract flies and gulls. There were knots of seaweed, floats made of glass and cork, odd bits of boat wood, foam plastic shards—and a whale. The whale was about forty feet long. It had died during the night after its impact on the ragged rocks of the cove. It looked like a giant garden slug, draped across the still pool of water with head and tail hanging over.

Thomas Harker felt a tinge of sympathy for the whale, but his house was less than a quarter-mile south and with the wind in his direction the smell would soon be bothersome.

The sheriff's jeep roared over the bluff road between the cove and the university grounds. Thomas waved and the sheriff waved back. There would be a lot of cleaning-up to do.

Thomas backed away from the cliff edge and returned to the path through the trees. He'd left his drafting table an hour ago to stretch his muscles and the walk had taken longer than he expected; Karen would be home by now, waiting for him, tired from the start of the new school year.

The cabin was on a broad piece of property barely thirty yards from the tideline, with nothing but grass and sand and an old picket fence between it and the water. They had worried during the storm, but there had been no flooding. The beach elevated seven feet to their property and they'd come through remarkably well.

Thomas knocked sand from his shoes and hung them on two nails next to the back door. In the service porch he removed his socks and dangled them outside, then draped them on the washer. He had soaked his shoes and socks and feet during an incautious run near the beach. Wriggling his toes, he stepped into the kitchen and sniffed. Karen had popped homemade chicken pies into the oven. Walks along the beach made him ravenous, especially after long days at the board.

He looked out the front window. Karen was at the gate, hair blowing in the evening breeze and knit sweater puffing out across her pink and white blouse. She turned, saw Thomas in the window and waved, saying something he couldn't hear.

He shrugged expressively and went to open the door. He saw something small on the porch and jumped in surprise. Richie stood on the step, smiling up at him, eyes the color of the sunlit sea, black hair unruly.

"Did I scare you, Mr. Harker?" the boy asked.

"Not much. What are you doing here this late? You should be home for dinner."

Karen kicked her shoes off on the porch. "Richie! When did you get here?"

"Just now. I was walking up the sand hills and wanted to say hello." Richie pointed north of the house with his long, unchildlike fingers. "Hello." He looked at Karen with a broad grin, head tilted.

"No dinner at home tonight?" Karen asked, totally vulnerable. "Maybe you can stay here." Thomas winced and raised his hand.

"Can't," Richie said. "Everything's just late tonight. I've got to be home soon. Hey, did you see the whale?"

"Yeah," Thomas said. "Sheriff is going to have a fun time moving it."

"Next tide'll probably take it out," Richie said. He looked between them, still smiling broadly. Thomas guessed his age at nine or ten but he already knew how to handle people.

"Tide won't be that high now," Thomas said.

"I've seen big things wash back before. Think the sheriff will leave it overnight?"

"Probably. It won't start stinking until tomorrow."

Karen wrinkled her nose in disgust.

"Thanks for the invitation anyway, Mrs. Harker." Richie put his hands in his shorts' pockets and walked through the picket fence, turning just beyond the gate. "You got any more old clothes I can have?"

"Not now," Thomas said. "You've taken all our castoffs already."

"I need more for the rag drive," Richie said. "Thanks anyway."

"Where does he live?" Thomas asked after closing the door.

"I don't think he wants us to know. Probably in town. Don't you like him?"

"Of course I like him. He's only a kid."

"You don't seem to want him around." Karen looked at him accusingly.

"Not all the time. He's not ours, his folks should take care of him."

"They obviously don't care much."

"He's well-fed," Thomas said. "He looks healthy and he gets along fine."

They sat down to dinner. Wisps of Karen's hair still took the shape of the wind. She didn't comb it until after the table was cleared and Thomas was doing the dishes. His eyes traced endless circuit diagrams in the suds. "Hey," he shouted to the back bathroom. "I've been working too much."

"I know," Karen answered. "So have I. Isn't it terrible?"

"Let's get to bed early," he said. She walked into the kitchen wrapped in a terry-cloth bathrobe, pulling a snarl out of her hair. "Must get your sleep," she said.

He aimed a snapped towel at her retreating end but missed. Then he leaned over the sink, rubbed his eyes and looked at the suds again. No circuits, only a portrait of Richie. He removed the last plate and rinsed it.

The next morning Thomas awoke to the sound of hammering coming from down the beach. He sat up in bed to receive Karen's breezy kiss as she left for the University, then hunkered down again and rolled over to snooze a little longer. His eyes flew open a few minutes later and he cursed. The racket was too much. He rolled out of the warmth and padded into the bathroom, wincing at the cold tiles. He turned the shower on to warm, brought his mug out to shave and examined his face in the cracked mirror. The mirror had been broken six months ago when he'd slipped and jammed his hand against it after a full night poring over the circuit diagrams in his office. Karen had been furious with him and he hadn't worked that hard since. But there was a deadline from Peripheral Data on his freelance designs and he had to meet it if he wanted to keep up his reputation.

In a few more months, he might land an exclusive contract from Key Business Corporation, and then he'd be designing what he wanted to design—big computers, mighty beasts. Outstanding money.

The hammering continued and after dressing he looked out the bedroom window to see Thompson rebuilding his shed. The shed had gone unused for months after Thompson had lost his boat at the Del Mar trials, near San Diego. Still, Thompson was sawing and hammering and reconstructing the slope-roofed structure, possible planning on another boat. Thomas didn't think much about it. He was already at work and he hadn't even reached the desk in his office. There was a whole series of TTL chips he could move to solve the interference he was sure would crop up in the design as he had it now.

By nine o'clock he was deeply absorbed. He had his drafting pencils and templates and mechanic's square spread across the paper in complete confusion. He wasn't interrupted until ten.

He answered the door only half-aware that somebody had knocked. Sheriff Varmanian stood on the porch, sweating. The sun was out and the sky clearing for a hot, humid day.

"Hi, Tom."

"Al," Thomas said, nodding. "Something up?"

"I'm interrupting? Sorry—"

"Yeah, my computers won't be able to take over your job if you keep me here much longer. How's the whale?"

"That's the least of my troubles right now." Varmanian's frizzy hair and round wire-rimmed glasses made him look more like an anarchist than a sheriff. "The whale was taken out with the night tide. We didn't even have to bury it." He pronounced "bury" like it was "burry" and studiously maintained a midwestern twang.

"Something else, then. Come inside and cool off?"

"Thanks. We've lost another kid—the Cooper's four-year-old, Kyle. He disappeared last night around seven and no one's seen him since. Anybody see him here?"

"No. Only Richie was here. Listen, I didn't hear any tide big enough to sweep the whale out again. We'd need another storm to do that. Maybe something freak happened and the boy was caught in it . . . a freak tide?"

"There isn't any funnel in Placer Cove to cause that. Just a normal rise and the whale was buoyed up by gases, that's my guess. Cooper kid must have gotten lost on the bluff road and come down to one of the houses to ask for help—that's what the last people who saw him think. So we're checking the beach homes. Thompson didn't see anything either. I'll keep heading north and look at the flats and tide pools again, but I'd say we have another disappearance. Don't quote me, though."

"That's four?"

"Five. Five in the last six months."

"Pretty bad, Al, for a town like this."

"Don't I know it. Coopers are all upset, already planning funeral arrangements. I told them he could show up any day, wet and hungry. I told them it could be weeks before we know anything one way or the other. But Mrs. Cooper says she knows already. Sixth sense or something." He sniffed. "Funerals when there aren't any bodies. But the Goldbergs had one for their son two months ago, so I guess precedent has been set."

He stood by the couch, fingering his hat and looking at the rug. "It's damned hard. How often does this kid, Richie, come down?"

"Three or four times a week. Karen's motherly toward him, thinks his folks aren't paying him enough attention."

"He'll be the next one, wait and see. Thanks for the time, and say hello to the wife for me."

Thomas returned to the board but had difficulty concentrating. He wondered if animals in the field and bush mourned long over the loss of a child. Did gazelles grieve when lions struck? Karen knew more about such feelings than he did; she'd lost a husband before she met him. His own life had been reasonably linear, uneventful.

How would he cope if something happened, if Karen were killed? Like the Coopers, with a quick funeral and burial to make things certain, even when they weren't?

What would they be burying?

Four years of work and dreams.

After lunch he took a walk along the beach and found his feet moving him north to where the whale had been. The coastal rocks in this area concentrated on the northern edge of the cove. They stretched into the water for a mile before ending at the deep water shelf. At extreme low tide two or three hundred yards of rocks were exposed. Now, about fifty feet was visible and he could clearly see where the whale had been. Even at high tide the circle of rock was visible. He hadn't walked here much lately, but he remembered first noticing that circle three years before, like a perfect sandy-bottomed wading pool.

Up and down the beach, the wrack remained, dark and smelly and flyblown. But the whale was gone. It was obvious there hadn't been much wave action. Still, that was the easy explanation and he had no other.

After the walk he returned to his office and opened all the windows before setting pencil to paper. By the time Karen was home, he had finished a good portion of the diagram from his original sketches. When he turned it in, Peripheral Data would have little more to do than hand it to their drafting department for smoothing.

Richie didn't visit them that evening. He came in the morning instead. It was a Saturday and Karen was home, reading in the living room. She invited the boy in and offered him milk and cookies, then sat him before the television to watch cartoons.

Richie consumed TV with a hunger that was fascinating. He avidly mimicked the expressions of the people he saw in the commercials, as if memorizing a store of emotions, filling in the gaps in his humanity left by an imperfect upbringing.

A few hours later, the boy left. As usual, he had not touched the food. He wasn't starving.

"Think he's adopting us?" Thomas asked.

"I don't know. Maybe. Maybe he just needs a couple of friends like you and me. Human contacts, if his own folks don't pay attention to him."

"Varmanian thinks he might be the next one to disappear." Thomas regretted the statement the instant it was out, but Karen didn't react. She put out a lunch of beans and sausages and waited until they were eating to say something.

"When do you want to have a child?"

"Two weeks from now, over the three-day holiday," Thomas said.

"No, I'm serious."

"You've taken a shine to Richie and you think we should have one of our own?"

"Not until something breaks for you," she said, looking away. "If Key Business comes through, maybe I can take a sabbatical and study child-rearing. Directly. But one of us has to be free full time."

Thomas nodded and sipped at a glass of iced tea. Behind her humor she was serious. There was a lot at stake in the next few months—more than just money. Perhaps their happiness together. It was a hard weight to carry. Being an adult was difficult at times. He almost wished he could be like Richie, free as a gull, uncommitted.

A line of dark clouds schemed over the ocean as afternoon turned to evening. "Looks like another storm," he called to Karen, who was typing in the back bedroom.

"So soon?" she asked by way of complaint.

He sat in the kitchen to watch the advancing front. The warm, fading light of sunset turned his face orange and painted an orange square on the living room wall. The square had progressed above the level of the couch when the doorbell rang.

It was Gina Hammond and a little girl he didn't recognize. Hammond was about sixty with thinning black hair and a narrow, wizened face that always bore an irritated scowl. a cigarette was pinched between her fingers, as usual. She explained the visit between nervous stammers which embarrassed Thomas far more than they did her.

"Mr. Harker, this is my grand-daughter Julie." The girl, seven or eight, looked up at him accusingly. "Julie says she's lost four of her kittens. Th-th-that's because she gave them to your boy to play with and he-he never brought them back. You know anything about them?"

"We don't have any children, Mrs. Hammond."

"You've got a boy named Richie," the woman said, glaring at him as if he were a monster.

Karen came out of the hallway and leaned against the door jamb beside Thomas. "Gina, Richie just wanders around our house a lot. He's not ours."

"Julie says Richie lives here—he told h-h-her that—and his name is Richie Harker. What's this all about i-i-if he isn't your boy?"

"He took my kittens!" Julie said, a tear escaping to slide down her cheek.

"If that's what he told you—that we're his folks—he was fibbing," Karen said. "He lives in town, closer to you than to us."

"He brought the kittens to the beach!" Julie cried. "I saw him."

"He hasn't been here since this morning," Thomas said. "We haven't seen the kittens."

"He stole 'em!" The girl began crying in earnest.

"I'll talk to him next time I see him," Thomas promised. "But I don't know where he lives."

"H-h-his last name?"

"Don't know that, either."

Mrs. Hammond wasn't convinced. "I don't like the idea of little boys stealing things that don't belong to them."

"Neither do I, Mrs. Hammond," Karen said. "We told you we'd talk to him when we see him."

"Well," Mrs. Hammond said. She thanked them beneath her breath and left with the blubbering Julie close behind.

The storm hit after dinner. It was a heavy squall and the rain trounced over the roof as if the sky had feet. A leak started in the bathroom, fortunately right over the tub, and Thomas rummaged through his caulking gear, preparing for the storm's end when he could get up on the roof and search out the leak.

A small tool shed connected with the cabin through the garage. It had one bare light and a tiny four-paned window which stared at Thomas's chest-level into the streaming night. As he dug out his putty knife and caulking cans, the phone rang in the kitchen and Karen answered it. Her voice came across as a murmur under the barrage of rain on the garage roof. He was putting all his supplies into a cardboard box when she stuck her head through the garage door and told him she'd be going out.

"The Thompsons have lost their power," she said. "I'm going to take some candles to them on the beach road. I should be back in a few minutes, but they may want me to drive into town and buy some lanterns with them. If they do, I'll be back in an hour or so. Don't worry about me!"

Thomas came out of the shed clutching the box. "I could go instead."

"Don't be silly. Give you more time to work on the sketches. I'll be back soon. Tend the leaks."

Then she was out the front door and gone. He looked through the living room window at her receding lights and felt a gnaw of worry. He'd forgotten a rag to wipe the putty knife. He switched the light back on and went through the garage to the shed.

Something scraped against the wall outside. He bent down and peered out the four-paned window, rubbing where his breath fogged the glass. A small face stared back at him. It vanished almost as soon as he saw it.

"Richie!" Thomas yelled. "Damn it, come back here!"

Some of it seemed to fall in place as Thomas ran outside with his go-aheads and raincoat on. The boy didn't have a home to go to when he left their house. He slept someplace else, in the woods perhaps, and scavenged what he could. But now he was in the rain and soaked and in danger of becoming very ill unless Thomas caught up with him. A flash of lightning brought grass and shore into bright relief and he saw

Richie running south across the sand, faster than seemed possible for a boy his age. Thomas ran after with the rain slapping him in the face.

He was halfway toward the Thompson house when the lightning flashes decreased and he couldn't follow the boy's trail. It was pitch black but for the light from their cabin. The Thompson house, of course, was dark.

Thomas was soaked through and rain ran down his neck in a steady stream. Sand itched his feet and burrs from the grass caught in his cuffs, pricking his ankles.

A close flash printed the Thompsons' shed in silver against the dark. Thunder roared and grumbled down the beach.

That was it, that was where Richie stayed. He had fled to the woods only after the first storm had knocked the structure down.

Thomas leaned through the wind-slanted strikes of water until he stood by the shed door. He fumbled at the catch and found a lock. He tugged at it and the whole thing slid free. The screws had been pried loose. "Richie," he said, opening the door. "Come on. It's Tom."

The shed waited dry and silent. "You should come home with me, stay with us." No answer. He opened the door wide and lightning showed him rags scattered everywhere, rising to a shape that looked like a man lying on his back with a blank face turned to Thomas. He jumped, but it was only a lump of rags. The boy didn't seem to be there. He started to close the door when he saw two pale points of light dance in the dark like fireflies. His heart froze and his back tingled. Again the lightning threw its dazzling sheet and wrapped the inside of the shed in cold whiteness and inky shadow.

Richie stood at the back, staring at Thomas with a slack expression.

The dark closed again and the boy said, "Tom, could you take me someplace warm?"

"Sure," Tom said, relaxing. "Come here." He took the boy into his arms and bundled him under the raincoat. There was something lumpy on Richie's back, under his sopping t-shirt. Thomas's hand drew back by reflex. Richie shied away just as quickly and Thomas thought, *He's got a hunch or scar, he's embarrassed about it.*

Lurching against each other as they walked to the house, Thomas asked himself why he'd been scared by what he first saw in the shed. A pile of rags. "My nerves are shot," he told Richie. The boy said nothing.

In the house he put Richie under a warm shower. The boy seemed unfamiliar with bathtubs and shower heads, let him remove the t-shirt, but studiously kept his back turned away. Thomas laid out an old Mackinaw for the boy to wear, then carried a cot and sleeping bag from the garage into the living room. Richie slipped on the Mackinaw, buttoning it with a curious crabwise flick of right hand over left, and climbed into the down bag.

The boy fell asleep almost immediately.

Karen came home an hour later, tired and wet. Thomas pointed to the cot with his finger to his lips. She looked at it, mouth open in surprise, and nodded.

In their bedroom, before fatigue and the patter of rain lulled them into sleep, Karen told him the Thompsons were nice people. "She's a little old and crotchety, but he's a bright old coot. He said something strange, though. Said when the shed fell down during the last storm he found a dummy inside it, wrapped in old blankets and dressed in cast-off clothing. Made out of straw and old sheets, he said."

"Oh." Thomas remembered the lump of rags and shivered.

"Do you think Richie made it?"

He shook his head, too tired to think.

Sunday morning, as they came awake, they heard Richie playing outside. "You've got to ask about the kittens," Karen said. Thomas reluctantly agreed as he put on his clothes.

The storm had passed in the night, having scrubbed a clear sky for the morning. He found Richie talking to the Sheriff and greeted Varmanian with a wave and a yawned "Hello."

"Sheriff wants to know if we saw Mr. Jones yesterday," Richie said. Mr. Jones—named after Davy Jones—was an old beachcomber frequently seen waving a metal detector around the cove. His bag was always filled with metal junk of little interest to anyone but him.

"No, I didn't," Thomas said. "Gone?"

"Not hard to guess, is it?" Varmanian said grimly. "I'm starting to think we ought to have a police guard out here."

"Might be an idea." Thomas waited for the sheriff to leave before asking the boy about the kittens. Richie became huffy, as if imitating some child in a television commercial. "I gave them back to Julie," he said. "I didn't take them anywhere. She's got them now."

"Richie, this was just yesterday. I don't see how you could have returned them already."

"You don't trust me, do you, Mr. Harker?" Richie asked. The boy's face turned as cold as sea-water, as hard as the rocks in the cove.

"I just don't think you're telling the truth."

"Thanks for the roof last night," Richie said softly. "I've got to go now." Thomas thought briefly about following after him, but there was nothing he could do. He considered calling Varmanian's office and telling him Richie had no legal guardian, but it didn't seem the right time.

Karen was angry with him for not being more decisive. "That boy needs someone to protect him! It's our duty to find out who the real parents are and tell the sheriff he's neglected."

"I don't think that's the problem," Thomas said. He frowned, trying to put things together. More was going on than was apparent.

"But he would have spent the night in the rain if you hadn't brought him here."

"He had that shed to go back to. He's been using the rags we gave him for—"

"That shed is cold and damp and no place for a small boy!" She took a deep breath to calm herself. "What are you trying to say, under all your evasions?"

"I have a feeling Richie can take care of himself."

"But he's a small *boy,* Tom."

"You're pinning a label on him without thinking how . . . without looking at how he can take care of himself, what he can do. But okay, I tell Varmanian about him and the boy gets picked up and returned to his parents—"

"What if he doesn't have any? He told Mrs. Hammond we were his parents."

"He's got to have parents somewhere, or legal guardians! Orphans just don't have the run of the town without somebody finding out. Say Varmanian returns him to his parents—what kind of parents would make a small boy, as you call him, want to run away?"

Karen folded her arms and said nothing.

"Not very good to return him under those circumstances, hm?" Thomas said. "What we should do is tell Varmanian to notify the parents, if any—if they haven't skipped town or something—that we're going to keep Richie here until they show up to claim him. I think Al would go along with that. If they don't show, we can contest their right to Richie and start proceedings to adopt him."

"It's not that simple," Karen said, but her eyes were sparkling. "The laws aren't that cut and dried."

"Okay, but that's the start of a plan, isn't it?"

"I suppose so."

"Okay." He pursed his lips and shook his head. "That'd be a big responsibility. Could we take care of a boy like Richie now?"

Karen nodded and Thomas was suddenly aware how much she wanted a child. It stung him a little to see her eagerness and the moisture in her eyes.

"Okay. I'll go find him." He put on his shoes and started out through the fence, turning south to the Thompson's shed. When he reached the wooden building he saw the door had been equipped with a new padlock and the latch screwed in tight. He was able to peek in through a chink in the wood—whatever could be said about Thompson as a boatbuilder, he wasn't much of a carpenter—and scan the inside. The pile of rags was gone. Only a few loose pieces remained. Richie, as he expected, wasn't inside.

Karen called from the porch and he looked north. Richie was striding toward the rocks at the opposite end of the cove. "I see him," Thomas said as he passed the cabin. "Be back in a few minutes."

He walked briskly to the base of the rocks and looked for Richie. The boy stood on a boulder, pretending to ignore him. Hesitant, not knowing exactly how to say it, Thomas told him what they were going to do.

The boy looked down from the rock. "You mean, you want to be my folks?" A smile, broad and toothy, slowly spread across his face. Everything was going to be okay.

"That's it, I think," Thomas said. "If your parents don't contest the matter."

"Oh, I don't have any folks," Richie said.

Thomas looked at the sea-colored eyes and felt sudden misgivings. "Might be easier, then," he said softly.

"Hey, Tom? I found something in the pools. Come look with me? Come on!" Richie was pure small-boy then, up from his seat and down the rock and vanishing from view like a bird taking wing.

"Richie!" Thomas cried. "I haven't time right now. Wait!"

He climbed up the rock with his hands and feet slipping on the slick surface. At the top he looked across the quarter-mile stretch of pools, irritated. "Richie!"

The boy ran on all fours over the jagged terrain. He turned and shouted back, "In the big pool! Come on!" Then he ran on.

Tom followed, eyes lowered to keep his footing. "Slow down!" He looked up for a moment and saw a small flail of arms, a face turned toward him with the smile frozen in surprise, and the boy disappearing. There was a small cry and a splash.

"Richie!" Thomas shouted, his voice cracking. The boy had fallen into the pool, the circular pool where the whale had been. Thomas gave up all thought of his own safety and ran across the rocks, slipping twice and cracking his knees against a sharp ridge of granite. Agony shot up his legs and fogged his vision. Cursing, pushing hair out of his eyes, he crawled to his feet and shakily hobbled over the loose pebbles and sand to the edge of the round pool.

With his hands on the smooth rock rim, he blinked and saw the boy floating in the middle of the pool, face down. Thomas groaned and shut his eyes, dizzy. There was a rank odor in the air; he wanted to get up and run. This was not the way rescuers were supposed to feel. His stomach twisted. There was no time to waste, however. He forced himself over the rim into the cold water, slipping and plunging head first. His brow touched the bottom. The sand was hard and compact, crusted. He stood with the water streaming off his head and torso. It was slick like oil and came up to his groin, deepening as he splashed to the middle. It would be up to his chest where Richie floated.

Richie's t-shirt clung damply, outlining the odd hump on his back. *We'll get that fixed,* Thomas told himself. *Oh, God, we'll get that fixed, let him be alive and it'll work out fine.*

Then he wondered what happened to the better shirt they had given him.

The water splashed across his chest. Some of it entered his mouth and he gagged at the fishy taste. He reached out for the boy's closest foot but couldn't quite reach it. The sand shifted beneath him and he ducked under the surface, swallowing more water. Bobbing up again, kicking to keep his mouth clear, he wiped his eyes with one hand and saw the boy's arms making small, sinuous motions, like the fins of a fish.

Swimming away from Thomas.

"Richie!" Thomas shouted. His wet tennis shoes, tapping against the bottom, seemed to make it resound, as if it were hollow. Then he felt the bottom lift slightly until his feet pressed flat against it, fall away until he tread water, lift again . . .

He looked down. The sand, distorted by ripples in the pool, was receding. Thomas struggled with his hands, trying to swim to the edge. Beneath him waited black water like a pool of crude oil, and in it something long and white, insistent. His feet kicked furiously to keep him from ducking under again, but the water swirled.

Thomas shut his mouth after taking a deep breath. The water throbbed like a bell, drawing him deeper, still struggling. He looked up and saw the sky, gray-blue above the ripples. There was still a chance. He kicked his shoes off, watching them spiral down. Heavy shoes, wet, gone now, he could swim better.

He spun with the water and the surface darkened. His lungs ached. He clenched his teeth to keep his mouth shut. There seemed to be progress. The surface seemed brighter. But three hazy-edged triangles converged and he could not fool himself any more, the surface was black and he had to let his breath out, hands straining up.

He touched a hard rasping shell.

The pool rippled for a few minutes, then grew still. Richie let loose of the pool's side and climbed up the edge, out of the water. His skin was pale, eyes almost milky.

The hunger had been bad for a few months. Now they were almost content. The meals were more frequent and larger—but who knew about the months to come? Best to take advantage of the good times. He pulled the limp dummy from its hiding place beneath the flat boulder and dragged it to the pool's edge, dumping it over and jumping in after. For a brief moment he smiled and hugged it; it was so much like himself, a final lure to make things more certain. Most of the time, it was all the human-shaped company he needed. He arranged its arms and legs in a natural position, spread out, and adjusted the drift of the Mackinaw in the water.

The dummy drifted to the center of the pool and stayed there.

A fleshy ribbon thick as his arm waved in the water and he pulled up the back of the t-shirt to let it touch him and fasten. This was the best time. His limbs shrank and his face sunk inward. His skin became the color of the rocks and his eyes grew large and golden. Energy—food—pulsed into him and he felt a great love for this clever other part of him, so adaptable.

It was mother and brother at once, and if there were times when Richie felt there might be a life beyond it, an existence like that of the people he mimicked, it was only because the mimicry was so fine.

He would never actually leave.

He couldn't. Eventually he would starve; he wasn't very good at digesting.

He wriggled until he fit smooth and tight against the rim, with only his head sticking out of the water.

He waited.

"Tom!" a voice called, not very far away. It was Karen.

"Mrs. Harker!" Richie screamed. "Help!"

SLEEPSIDE STORY

Jan O'Nale, of Cheap Street Press, requested that I write a novella for her series of custom-designed and illustrated limited editions. This was a real honor—Cheap Street published the loveliest editions of any small press associated with science fiction. I wrote a fantasy based on the photographic negative of a fairy tale—"Beauty and the Beast." One early title, in fact, was "Handsome and the Whore," but that was deemed too overt, and perhaps too judgmental.

Every element in Sleepside Story is familiar, but reversed, white to black, female to male, with appropriate adjustments reflecting these changes. It was printed in a hardcover anthology, Full Spectrum 2, after the publication of the Cheap Street edition, and was selected by Terry Windling and Ellen Datlow as one of the best fantasy stories of the year. It's still one of my all-time favorites.

"Sleepside Story," along with The Infinity Concerto and The Serpent Mage, comprise my early contributions to the genre of gritty urban fantasy—with a tip of the hat, of course, to Peter Beagle.

The original illustrations to the Cheap Street Edition were by Judy King Reinitz, and they were lovely. Unfortunately, I doubt the illustrations and the story will ever be paired again, as O'Nale and I had a falling out even before the book was published. If you can find the original Cheap Street Edition—it's quite rare—take a look at both the production and the illustrations. Magnificent.

Oliver Jones differed from his brothers as wheat from chaff. He didn't grudge them their blind wildness; he loaned them money until he had none, and regretted it, but not deeply. His needs were not simple, but they did not hang on the sharp signs of dollars. He worked at the jobs of youth without complaining, knowing there was something better waiting for him. Sometimes it seemed he was the only one in the family able to take cares away from his momma, now that Poppa was gone and she was lonely even with the two babies sitting on her lap, and his younger sister Yolanda gabbing about the neighbors.

The city was a puzzle to him. His older brothers Denver and Reggie believed it was a place to be conquered, but Oliver did not share their philosophy. He wanted to make the city part of him, sucked in with his breath, built into bones and brains. If he could dance with the city's music, he'd have it made, even though Denver and Reggie said the city was wide and cruel and had no end; that its four quarters ate young men alive, and spat back old people. Look at Poppa, they said; he was only forty-three when he went to the fifth quarter, Darkside, a bag of wearied bones; they said, take what you can get while you can get it.

This was not what Oliver saw, though he knew the city was cruel and hungry. His brothers and even Yolanda kidded him about his faith. It was more than just his going to church that made them rag him, because they went to church, too, sitting upright and superior beside Momma. Reggie and Denver knew there was advantage in being seen at devotions.

It wasn't Oliver's music that made them laugh, for he could play the piano hard and fast as well as soft and tender, and they all liked to dance, even Momma sometimes. It was his damned sweetness. It was his taste in girls, quiet and studious; and his honesty.

On the last day of school, before Christmas vacation, Oliver made his way home in a fall of light snow, stopping in the old St. John's churchyard for a moment's reflection by his father's grave. Surrounded by the crisp, ancient slate gravestones and the newer white marble, worn by the city's acid tears, he thought he might now be considered grown-up, might have to become the sole support of his family.

He left the churchyard in a somber mood and walked between the tall brick and brownstone tenements, along the dirty, wet black streets, his shadow lost in Sleepside's greater shade, eyes on the sidewalk.

Denver and Reggie could not bring in good money, money that Momma would accept; Yolanda was too young and not likely to get a job anytime soon, and that left him, the only one who would finish school. He might take in more piano students, but he'd have to move out to do that, and how could he find another place to live without losing all he made to rent? Sleepside was crowded.

From half a block down the street, Oliver heard the loud noises from the old apartment. He ran up the five dark, trash-littered flights of stairs and pulled out his key to open the three locks on the door. Swinging the door wide, he stood with hand pressed to a wall, lungs too greedy to let him speak.

The flat was in an uproar. Yolanda, rail-skinny, stood in the kitchen doorway, wringing her big hands and wailing. The two babies lurched down the hall, diapers drooping and fists stuck in their mouths. The neighbor widow Mrs. Diamond Freeland bustled back and forth in a useless dither. Something was terribly wrong.

"What is it?" he asked Yolanda with his first free breath. She just moaned and shook her head. "Where's Reggie and Denver?" She shook her head less vigorously, meaning they weren't home. "Where's Momma?" This sent Yolanda into hysterics. She bumped back against the wall and clenched her fists to her mouth, tears flying. "Something happen to Momma?"

"Your momma went uptown," Mrs. Diamond Freeland said, standing flatfooted before Oliver, flower print dress distended over a generous stomach. "What you going to do? You're her son."

"Where uptown?" Oliver asked, working to steady his voice. He wanted to slap everybody in the apartment. He was scared and they weren't being any help at all.

"She we-went sh-sh-shopping!" Yolanda wailed. "She got her check today and it's Ch-Christmas and she went to get the babies new clothes and some f-food."

Oliver's hands clenched. Momma had asked him what he

wanted for Christmas, and he had said, "Nothing, Momma. Not really." She had chided him, saying all would be well when the check came, and what good was Christmas if she couldn't find a little something special for her children?

"All right," he had said. "I'd like sheet music. Something I've never played before."

"She must of taken the wrong stop," Mrs. Diamond Freeland said, staring at Oliver from the corners of her wide eyes. "That's all I can figure."

"What happened?"

Yolanda pulled a letter out of her blouse and handed it to him: fancy purple paper with a delicate flower design around the borders, the message handwritten prettily in gold ink fountain pen—and signed.

He read it carefully, then read it again.

To the Joneses.

Your momma is uptown in My care. She came here lost and I tried to help her but she stole something valuable to Me she shouldn't have. She says you'll come and get her. By you she means her youngest son Oliver Jones and if not him then Yolanda Jones her eldest daughter. I will keep one or the other here in exchange for your momma and one or the other must stay here and work for Me.

Miss Belle Parkhurst
969 33rd Street

"Who's she, and why does she have Momma?" Oliver asked.

"I'm not going!" Yolanda screamed.

"Hush up," said Mrs. Diamond Freeland. "Miss Belle is that *whoor*. She's that uptown whoor used to run the biggest cathouse back when I was a girl."

Oliver looked from face to face in disbelief.

"Your momma must of taken the wrong stop and got lost," Mrs. Diamond Freeland reiterated. "That's all I can figure. She went to that whoor's house and got herself in trouble."

"I'm not going!" Yolanda insisted, shaking her head. She avoided Oliver's eyes. "You know what she'd make me do."

"Yeah," Oliver said softly. "But what'll she make *me* do?"

Reggie and Denver, he learned from Mrs. Freeland, had come home and then left just before the messenger danced whistling up the outside hall. Oliver sighed. His brothers were almost never home; they thought they'd pulled the wool over Momma's eyes, but they hadn't.

Reggie and Denver fancied themselves the slickest dudes on the street. They claimed they had women all over Sleepside and Snowside; Oliver was almost too shy to ask a woman out. He was small, slender, almost pretty, but strong for his size. Reggie and Denver were cowards. Oliver had never run from a true and worthwhile fight in his life, but neither had he started one. The thought of going to Miss Belle Parkhurst's establishment scared him, but he remembered what his father had told him just a week before dying. "Oliver, when I'm gone—that's soon now, you know it—Yolanda's flaky as a bowl of cereal and your brothers . . . well, I'll be kind and just say your momma, she's going to need you. You got to turn out right so as she can lean on you."

The babies hadn't been born then.

"Which train did she take?"

"Down to Snowside," Mrs. Freeland said. "But she must of gotten off in Sunside. That's near Thirty-third."

"It's getting dark soon," Oliver said.

Yolanda sniffed and wiped her eyes. Off the hook. "You going?"

"Have to," Oliver said. "It's Momma."

Said Mrs. Diamond Freeland, "I think that whoor got something on her mind."

As dusk settled over the city, Oliver descended the four flights of concrete steps, grinding his teeth at the thought of the danger his momma was in. He halted at the bottom, grimaced at the muscles knotting along his back, and repeated over and over, "It's Momma. It's Momma. No one can save her but me."

On the line between dusk and dark, down underground where it shouldn't have mattered, the Metro emptied out the day's passengers and sucked in the night's. Sometimes day folks went in tight-packed groups on the Night Metro, but not if they could avoid it. Night Metro was transport for the lost and the wasted. Night Metro also carried the zeroes—people who lived their lives and when they died no one could look back and say they remembered them. Everyone ashamed or afraid to come out during the day came out to ride at night.

Some said the dead used the Night Metro, and that after midnight it went all the way to Darkside. Oliver didn't know what to believe. Night Metro was a bad way to travel, but it was the quickest way to get from Sleepside to Sunside.

He dropped his bronze cat's head token into the turnstile, *clunk-chunking* through, and crossed the empty platform. Two indistinct figures waited trackside, heavy-coated, though it was a warm evening. Oliver kept a wary eye on them as he paced a figure eight on the grimy, foot-scrubbed concrete.

Into the station's smudged white tile back wall was set a gold mosaic trumpet and the number 7. The trumpet was for folks who couldn't read to let them know where to get off. All Sleepside stations had musical instruments.

He stopped near the edge of the platform and stared down at the puddles and filth around the rails. Nothing but muck. Yet when his train arrived, it was clean and silver-sleek, without a spot of graffiti or a stain of tarnish. Night Metro was run by a proud and powerful crew. Oliver caught a glimpse of the operator under the SLEEPSIDE/CHASTE RIVER/SUNSIDE-46TH destination sign. The operator wore or had a big bull's head and carried a prominent pair of long, gleaming silver scissors on his Sam Browne belt.

Oliver entered through the open doors and grabbed a smooth handgrip even though the seats were mostly empty. Somebody standing was somebody quicker to run. There were four people in Oliver's car: two women, one young, vacant, and very pale, the other old and muddy-eyed, clutching a plastic daisy-flowered shopping bag. Two men, both chunky and greenish-blond, wore identical dark brown business suits with shiny elbows. Nobody looked at anybody.

The doors slid shut and the train grumbled on, gathering speed until the noise of its wheels on the tracks drowned out all other sound and almost all thought. Beyond I-beams and barricades, single orange service lamps and cracked and chipped tiled walls rushed by.

Night Metro shared only a few stops with Day Metro. Most stations were dark, their platforms populated by slow smudges of shadow—people who wouldn't show even in bright light. Oliver tried not to look, but every so often he couldn't help it. As the train slowed for his station, he raised the collar of his green windbreaker and rubbed his nose. Reggie and Denver wouldn't have made it this far. They put too high a value on their skins.

The train idled after Oliver disembarked. He walked past the lead car on his way to the stairs. The operator stood in his little cabin of fluorescent cold, the eyes in the bull's head sunk deep in shadow. Oliver felt rather than saw the starlike glints in the cavernous sockets. The operator's left hand tugged at the handles of the silver shears.

Oliver stopped to return the hidden stare. "What do you care, man?" he said. "Get on with it! We all got stuff to do."

The bull's nose pointed a mere twitch away, and the hand left the shears to grip the control switch. The train doors closed. The silver side panels and windows and lights picked up speed and the train squealed around a curve into darkness.

Oliver sighed and climbed the two flights of stairs to Sunside Station. Summer night lay heavy and warm on the lush trees and grass of a broad park. Oliver stood at the head of the Metro entrance and listened to the crickets and katydids and cicadas sing songs unheard in Sleepside, where trees and grass were sparse. All around the park rose dark-windowed walls of high marble and brick and gray stone hotels and fancy apartment buildings with gable roofs.

Oliver looked around for directions, a map, anything. Out here, above the Night Metro, it was possible ordinary people would be out strolling and he could ask them for directions if he dared. He walked toward the street and thought of Momma getting this far and of her being afraid. He loved Momma very much. Sometimes she seemed to be the only decent thing in his life, though as he grew older, young women distracted him, and he experienced more and more secret fixations.

"Oliver Jones?"

A long white limousine waited by the curb. A young, slender woman in violet chauffeur's livery, with a jaunty black and silver cap sitting atop exuberant hair, cocked her head, smiled at him, and beckoned with a white-gloved finger. "Are you Oliver Jones, come to rescue your momma?"

He walked slowly toward the limousine. It was bigger and more beautiful than anything he had ever seen, with long ribbed chrome pipes snaking out from under the hood and through the fenders, stand-alone golden headlights, and a white tonneau roof made of real leather. "My name's Oliver," he affirmed.

"Then you're my man. Please get in." She winked and held the door open. When the door closed, the woman's arm—all he could see of her through the smoky window glass—vanished. The driver's door did not open. She did not get in. The limousine drove off by itself.

Oliver fell back into the lush suede and velvet interior. An electronic wet bar gleamed silver and gold and black above a cool white-lit panel on which sat a single crystal glass filled with ice cubes. A spigot rotated and waited for instructions. When none came, it gushed fragrant gin over the ice.

Oliver did not touch the glass.

Below the wet bar, the television set turned itself on. Passion and delight sang from small, precise speakers.

"No," he said. "No!"

The television winked off.

He edged closer to the smoky glass window and saw dim streetlights and headlights blur past. A huge black building trimmed with gold ornaments loomed on the corner. All but three of its many windows, outlined in red, were dark.

The limousine descended into a dark underground garage. Lights throwing huge golden cat's eyes, tires squealing on shiny concrete, it snaked around a slalom of walls and pillars and came to a smooth, quick stop.

The door opened.

Oliver stepped out.

The same chauffeur grinned and doffed her cap. No sense asking questions now, he'd never stop.

"Thanks," Oliver said.

"My pleasure," she replied.

The car had parked beside a big, thick wooden door set into an arch of hewn stone blocks. Fossil bones and teeth were clearly visible in the matrix of each block. Glistening ferns in dark, kidney-shaped pools flanked a wooden bridge leading to the door.

Oliver heard the car burble away and turned, but did not see whether the chauffeur drove this time or not. He walked across the wooden planks and tried the door's black iron handle. The door swung open at the first brush of his fingers. Beyond, a narrow, red-carpeted staircase with maple rails carved into rose canes—buds, flowers, thorns and all—ascended to an upper floor. The place smelled of cloves and mint and, somehow, of what Oliver imagined dogs or horses must smell like—a musty old rug sitting on a floor grate. (He had never owned a dog and never seen a horse without a policeman on it, and never so close he could smell it.) Nobody had been through here in a long time, he thought. But everybody knew about Miss Belle Parkhurst and her place. And the chauffeur had been young. He wrinkled his nose; he did not like any of this.

The dark wood door at the top of the stairs swung open silently. Nobody stood there waiting. Oliver tried to speak, but his throat itched and closed. He coughed into his fist and shrugged his shoulders. Then, eyes damp and hot with anger and fear, he croaked, "I'm Oliver Jones. I'm here to get my momma!"

The door remained unattended. He looked back into the parking garage, dark and quiet as a cave; nothing for him there. Then he ascended quickly to get it over with and passed into the ill-reputed house of Miss Belle Parkhurst.

The city extends to the far horizon, divided into quarters by roads or canals or train tracks, above or underground; and sometimes you know those divisions and know better than to cross them, and sometimes you don't. The city is broader than any man's life, and it's worth more than your life not to understand why you are where you are.

The city encourages ignorance because it must eat.

The four quarters of the city are Snowside, Cokeside (where few sane people go), Sleepside, and Sunside. Sunside is bright and rich and dangerous because that is where the swell folks live. Swell folks don't like intruders. Not even the police go into Sunside without an escort. Toward the center of the city is uptown, and in the middle of uptown is where all four quarters meet at the Pillar of the Unknown Mayor. Outward is the downtown and scattered islands of suburbs, and no one knows where the city ends.

The Joneses live in downtown Sleepside. The light there even at noon is not bright, but neither is it burning harsh as in Cokeside, where it can fry your skull. Sleepside is tolerable. There are good people in Sleepside and Snowside, and though confused, the general run is not vicious. Oliver grew up there and carries it in his bones and meat. No doubt the Night Metro operator smelled his origins and knew here was a young human crossing a border to go where he did not belong. No doubt Oliver was still alive because Miss Belle Parkhurst had protected him.

That meant Miss Parkhurst had protected Momma, and perhaps lured her, as well.

The hallway beyond the stairs was lighted by rows of candles held in gold eagle claws. He passed slowly between the claws and the candles, unable to summon enough spit to whistle, let alone talk. At the end of the hall, through another open door, he stepped into a broad, wood-paneled room decorated with lush green ferns in brass spittoons. The Persian rug in the center of the room revealed a stylized garden in cream and black and red. Five black velvet-upholstered couches curved around the far end, unoccupied, expectant, like a line of languorous women amongst the ferns. Along the walls, chairs covered by white sheets asserted their heavy silhouettes.

Oliver stood, jaw open, not used to such luxury. He needed a long moment to take it all in. Miss Belle Parkhurst was obviously a very rich woman, and not your ordinary whore. From what he had seen so far, she had power as well as money—power over cars and doors, and maybe over men and women.

Maybe over Momma.

"Momma?"

A tall, tenuous, white-haired man in a cream-colored suit walked across the room, paying Oliver scant attention. Oliver watched him sit on a sheet-covered chair. He did not disturb the sheets, but sat *through* them, as if they were not there. Leaning his head back reflectively, he lifted a cigarette holder without a cigarette and blew out clear air, or perhaps nothing at all, and then smiled at something just to Oliver's right.

Oliver turned to look.

They were alone.

When he looked back, the man in the cream-colored suit was gone.

Oliver's arms tingled. He was in for more than he had bargained for, and he had bargained for a lot.

"This way," said a deep female voice, operatic, dignified, easy and friendly at once. He could not see her, but he squinted at the doorway, and a small, imposing woman entered between two fluted green onyx columns. He did not know at first that she was addressing him; there might be other gentlemen, or girls, equally as tenuous as the man in the cream-colored suit. But this slight woman, with upheld hands, dressed in gold and peach silk that clung to her all smooth and quiet, was watching only him with her large, dark eyes. She smiled richly and warmly, but Oliver thought there was a hidden flaw in that smile, in her assurance. She was ill at ease from the instant their eyes met, though she might have been at ease before then, *thinking* of meeting him.

She had had all things planned until that moment.

If he unnerved her slightly, this woman positively terrified him. She was beautiful and smooth-skinned, and he could smell the sweet roses and camellias and magnolia blossoms surrounding her like a crowd of familiar friends.

"This way," she repeated, gesturing through the doors.

"I'm looking for my momma. I'm supposed to meet Miss Belle Parkhurst."

"That's me. I'm Belle Parkhurst. You're Oliver Jones . . . aren't you?"

He nodded, face solemn, eyes wide. Under her steady, languorous gaze, he nodded again and swallowed.

"I sent your momma on her way home. She'll be fine."

He looked back at the hallway, biting his lip. "She'll have to take the Night Metro," he said.

"I sent her back in my car. Nothing will happen to her."

There was a long, silent moment. He realized he was twisting and wringing his hands before his crotch and he stopped this, embarrassed.

"Your momma's *fine*. Don't worry about her."

"All right," he said, drawing up his shoulders. "You wanted to talk to me?"

"Yes," she said. "And more."

His nostrils flared and he jerked his eyes hard right, torso and then hips and legs twisting that way as he broke into a scrambling rabbit-run for the hallway. The golden eagle claws on each side dropped their candles as he passed and reached out to hook him with their talons. The vast house around him seemed suddenly alert, and he knew even before one claw grabbed his collar that he did not have a chance.

He dangled helpless at the very end of the hall.

In the far door appeared Miss Parkhurst, her fingers dripping beads of fire onto the wooden floor. The floor smoked and sizzled. "I've let your momma go," she said, voice deeper than a grave, face terrible, smoothly beautiful, and very old, very experienced. "That was my agreement. You leave, and you break that agreement, and that means I take your sister, or I take back your momma."

She cocked an elegant, painted eyebrow at him and leaned her head to one side. He nodded as best he could with his chin jammed against the teeth of his jacket's zipper.

"Good. There's food waiting. I'd enjoy your company."

The dining room was no larger than his bedroom at home, very small, that is, occupied by two chairs and an intimate round table covered in white linen. A gold eagle claw candelabrum cast a warm light over the table top. Miss Parkhurst preceded Oliver, her long dress rustling softly at her heels. Other things rustled in the room as well; the floor might have been ankle-deep in windblown leaves, but it was spotless, a rich round red and cream rug centered beneath the table; and beneath that, smooth old oak flooring.

Oliver looked up from sneaker-clad feet.

Miss Parkhurst waited expectantly a step back from her chair. "Your momma teach you no manners?" she asked softly.

He approached the table reluctantly. There were empty gold plates and tableware on the linen that had not been there before. Napkins dropped from thin fog and folded themselves into swans on the plates.

Oliver stopped.

"Don't you mind that," Miss Parkhurst said. "I live alone in this big old place. Good help is hard to find."

Oliver stepped behind the chair and lifted it by its maple headpiece, pulling it out for her. She sat and he helped her move closer to the table. Not once did he touch her; his skin crawled at the thought.

"The food here is very fine," Miss Parkhurst said as he sat across from her.

"I'm not hungry," Oliver said.

She smiled warmly. It was a powerful thing, her smile. "I won't bite," she said. "Except supper. *That* I'll bite."

The napkin on his plate lifted and spread and placed itself across his lap, and before him, on a fine china plate, leaf by fluttering leaf, appeared a salad. Oliver smelled wonderful spices and sweet vinegar. He was very hungry and he enjoyed salads, seeing fresh greens so seldom in Sleepside.

"That's it," Miss Parkhurst said soothingly, smiling as he ate. She lifted her fork in turn and speared a fold of butter lettuce, bringing it to her red lips.

The rest of the dinner proceeded in like fashion, but with no further conversation. She watched him frankly, appraising, and he avoided her eyes.

They finished eating.

"Come with me, sweetie," Miss Parkhurst said.

Down a long corridor, past tall windows set in an east wall, dawn glowing gray and pink around their faint shadows on the velvet-flocked flowers of the west wall, Miss Parkhurst led Oliver to his room. "It's the quietest place in the mansion," she said.

"You're keeping me here," he said.

"That I am," she said. "I hope you won't mind."

"You're never going to let me go?"

"Please allow me to indulge myself, just this once. I'm not just alone. I'm lonely. Here, you can have anything you want . . . almost . . ."

The door at the corridor's far end opened, as always, by itself. Within, logs burned brightly in a small fireplace, casting a warm and flickering light over a wide bed. The bed's covers turned themselves down. Exquisite murals of forests and fields adorned the walls; the ceiling was a rich, deep blue flecked with gold and silver stars. Books filled a case in one corner, and in another corner stood the most beautiful ebony grand piano he had ever seen. Miss Parkhurst did not approach the door too closely. There were no candles; within this room, all lamps were electric.

"This is your room. I won't come in," she said. "And after tonight, you don't *ever* come out after dark. We'll talk and see each other during the day, but never at night. The door isn't locked. I'll have to trust you."

"I can go anytime I want?"

She smiled. Even though she meant her smile to be nothing more than enigmatic, it shook him. She was deadly beautiful, the kind of woman his brothers dreamed about. Her smile said she might eat him alive, all of him that counted.

Oliver could imagine his momma's reaction to Miss Belle Parkhurst.

He entered the room and watched her face, trembling as he pushed the door shut. There were a dozen things he wanted to say; angry, frustrated, pleading things. He leaned against the door, swallowing them all back, keeping his hand from going to the gold and crystal knob.

Beyond the door, he heard skirts rustle as she retired back along the corridor. After a moment, he pushed off from the door and walked with an exaggerated swagger to the bookcase. Miss Parkhurst would never have taken Oliver's sister Yolanda; that wasn't what she wanted. She wanted young boy flesh, he thought. She wanted to burn him down to his sneakers, smiling like that.

The books on the shelves were books he had heard about but had never found in the Sleepside library, books he wanted to read, that the librarians said only people from Sunside and the suburbs cared to read. His fingers lingered on the tops of their spines, tugging gently.

His eyes drooped, despite his curiosity and fear and slowly receding anger. He decided to sleep instead. If she was going to pester him during the day, he didn't have much time. She'd be a late riser, he thought; a night person.

Then he realized: whatever she did at night, she had not done *this* night. This night had been set aside for him.

He shivered again, thinking of the food and the napkins and the eagle claws. Was this room haunted, too? Would *things* keep watch over him?

Oliver sat on the edge of the bed, his mind clouded with thoughts of living sheets feeling up his bare skin. He lay back, still clothed, tired—almost dead out. Somehow, his eyes closed. He slept.

The dreams that came were sweet and *she* did not walk in them. She had spoken true. This really was his time.

At eleven in the morning, by the gold and crystal clock on the bookcase, Oliver kicked his legs out, rubbed his face into the pillows, and startled up, back arched. A covered tray waited on a polished brass cart beside the bed. His nose twitched. He smelled bacon and eggs and coffee. A vase of roses on one corner of the cart added to the delicious scents in the room. Against the vase leaned a folded piece of fine ivory paper. Oliver sat up and read the note, again written in golden ink in a delicate hand.

I'm waiting for you in the gymnasium. Meet me after you've eaten. Got something to give to you.

He had no idea where the gymnasium was. When he had finished breakfast, he put on a plush robe, opened the heavy door to his room—both relieved and irritated that it did not open by itself—and looked down the corridor. A golden arc of warm sun clung to the base of each tall window. It was noon, Sunside time. She had given him plenty of time to rest.

A pair of new black jeans and a white silk shirt waited for him on the bed, which had been carefully made in the time it had taken him to glance down the hall. Cautiously, but less frightened now, he removed the robe, put on these clothes and the deerskin moccasins by the foot of the bed, and stood in the doorway, leaning as casually as he could manage against the frame.

A silk handkerchief hung in the air several yards away. It fluttered like a pigeon's ghost to attract his attention, then drifted slowly along the hall. He followed.

The house seemed to go on forever, empty and magnificent.

Each public room had its own decor, filled with antique furniture, potted palms, plush couches and chairs, and love seats. Several times he thought he saw wisps of dinner jackets, top hats—eager, strained faces in foyers, corridors, on staircases as he followed the handkerchief. The house smelled of perfume and dust, old cigars, spilled wine, and ancient sweat.

He climbed three flights of stairs to the tall, ivory-white double doors of the gymnasium. The handkerchief vanished with a flip. The doors opened. Miss Parkhurst stood at the opposite end of a wide black tile dance floor, before a band riser covered with music stands and instruments. Oliver inspected the low half-circle stage with narrowed eyes. Would she demand he dance with her, while all the instruments played themselves?

"Good morning," she said. She wore a green dress the color of fresh wet grass, high at the neck and down to her calves. Beneath the dress she wore white boots and white gloves, and a white feather curled around her black hair.

"Good morning," he replied softly, politely.

"Did you sleep well? Eat hearty?"

Oliver nodded, fear and shyness returning. What could she possibly want to give him? Herself? His face grew hot.

"It's a shame this house is empty during the day," she said. *And at night?* he thought. "I could fill this room with exercise equipment," she continued. "Weight benches, even a track around the outside." She smiled. The smile seemed less ferocious, even wistful; she seemed more at ease, and younger.

He rubbed a fold of his shirt between two fingers. "I like the food, and your house is fine, but I still want to go home," he said.

She half turned and walked slowly from the riser. "You could have this house and all my wealth. I'd like you to have it."

"Why? I haven't done anything for you."

"Or to me, either," she said, facing him again. "You know how I made all this money?"

"Yes, ma'am," he said after a moment's pause. "I'm not a fool."

"You've heard about me. That I'm a whore."

"Yes, ma'am. Mrs. Diamond Freeland says you are."

"And what is a whore?"

"You let men do it to you for money," Oliver said, feeling bolder, but with his face hot all the same.

Miss Parkhurst nodded. "I've got part of them here with me," she said. "All of them. That's my bookkeeping, my ledger. I know every name, every face. They keep me company now that business is slow."

"All of them?" Oliver asked, incredulous. "Even the dead ones?"

Miss Parkhurst's faint smile was part pride, part sadness, her eyes distant and moist. "And why not? They gave me all the things I have here."

"I don't think it would be worth it," Oliver said.

"I'd be dead if I wasn't a whore," Miss Parkhurst said, eyes suddenly sharp, flashing anger. "I'd have starved to death." She relaxed her clenched hands. "We got plenty of time to talk about my life, so let's hold it here for a while. I got something you need, if you're going to inherit this place."

"I don't *want* it, ma'am," Oliver said.

"If you don't take it, somebody who doesn't need it and deserves it a lot less will. I want you to have it. Please, be kind to me this once."

"Why me?" Oliver asked. He simply wanted out; this was completely off the planned track of his life. He was less afraid of Miss Parkhurst now, though her anger raised hairs on his neck; he felt he could be bolder and perhaps even demanding. There was a weakness in her: he was her weakness, and he wasn't above taking some advantage of that, considering how desperate his situation might be.

"You're kind," she said. "You care. And you've never had a woman, not all the way."

Oliver's face warmed again. "Please let me go," he said quietly, hoping it didn't sound as if he was pleading.

Miss Parkhurst folded her arms. "I can't," she said.

While Oliver spent his first day in Miss Parkhurst's mansion, across the city, beyond the borders of Sunside, Denver and Reggie Jones had returned home to find the apartment blanketed in gloom. Reggie, tall and gangly, long of neck and short of head, with a prominent nose, stood with back slumped in the front hall, mouth open in surprise. "He just took off and left you all here?" Reggie asked. Denver returned from the kitchen, shorter and stockier than his brother, dressed in black vinyl jacket and pants. He passed Reggie a catsup and mayo sandwich.

Yolanda's face was puffy from constant crying. She now enjoyed the tears she spilled, and scheduled them at two-hour intervals, to her momma's sorrowful irritation. She herded the two babies into their momma's bedroom and closed a rickety gate behind them, then brushed her hands on the breast of her ragged blouse.

"You don't get it," she said, facing them and dropping her arms dramatically. "That whore took Momma, and Oliver traded himself for her."

"That whore," said Reggie, "is a rich old witch."

"Rich old bitch witch," Denver said, pleased with himself.

"That whore is opportunity knocking," Reggie continued, chewing reflectively. "I hear she lives alone."

"That's why she took Oliver," Yolanda said. The babies cooed and chirped behind the gate.

"Why him and not one of us?" Reggie asked.

Momma gently pushed the babies aside, swung open the gate, and marched down the hall, dressed in her best wool skirt and print blouse, wrapped in her overcoat against the gathering dark and cold outside. "Where you going?" Yolanda asked her as she brushed past.

"Time to talk to the police," she said, glowering at Reggie. Denver backed into the bedroom he shared with his brother, out of her way. He shook his head condescendingly, grinning: Momma at it again.

"Them dogheads?" Reggie said. "They got no say in Sunside."

Momma turned at the front door and glared at them. "How are you going to help your brother? He's the best of you all, you know, and you just stand here, jawboning yourselves."

"Momma's upset," Denver informed his brother solemnly.

"She should be," Reggie said. "She was held prisoner by that witch bitch whore. We should go get Oliver ourselves and bring him home. We could pretend we was customers."

"She don't have customers anymore," Denver said. "She's too old. She's worn out." He glanced at his crotch and leaned his head to one side, glaring for emphasis.

"How do you know?" Reggie asked.

"That's what I hear."

Momma snorted and pulled back the bars and bolts on the front door. Reggie calmly walked up behind her and stopped her. "Police don't do anybody any good, Momma," he said. "We'll go. We'll bring Oliver back."

Denver's face slowly fell at the thought. "We got to plan it out," he said. "We got to be careful."

"We'll be careful," Reggie said. "For Momma's sake."

With his hand blocking her exit, Momma snorted again, then let her shoulders droop and her face sag. She looked more and more like an old woman now, though she was only in her late thirties.

Yolanda stood aside to let her pass into the living room. "Poor Momma," she said, eyes welling up.

"What you going to do for your brother?" Reggie asked his sister pointedly as he in turn walked by her. She craned her neck and stuck out her chin. "Go trade places with him, work in *her* house?" he taunted.

"She's rich," Denver said to himself, cupping his chin in his hand. "We could make a whole lot of money, saving our brother."

"We start thinking about it *now*," Reggie mandated, falling into the chair that used to be their father's, leaning his head back against the lace covers Momma had made.

Momma, face ashen, stood by the couch staring at a family

portrait hung on the wall in a cheap wooden frame. "He did it for me. I was so stupid, getting off there, letting her help me. Should of known," she murmured, clutching her wrist. Her face ashen, her ankle wobbled under her and she pirouetted, hands spread like a dancer—and collapsed face down on the couch.

The gift, the object that Oliver needed to inherit and control Miss Parkhurst's mansion, was a small gold box with three buttons, like a garage door opener. She finally presented it to him in the dining room as they finished dinner.

Miss Parkhurst was nice to talk with, something Oliver had not expected, though he should have. Whores did more than lie with a man to keep him coming back and spending his money; that should have been obvious. The day had not been the agony he expected. He had even stopped asking her to let him go. Oliver thought it would be best to bide his time, and when something distracted her, make his escape. Until then, she was not treating him badly or expecting anything he could not freely give.

"It'll be dark soon," she said as the plates cleared themselves away. He was even getting used to the ghostly service. "I have to go soon, and you got to be in your room. Take this with you, and keep it there." She lifted a tray cover to reveal a white silk bag. Unstringing the bag, she removed the golden opener and shyly presented it to him. "This was given to me a long time ago. I don't need it now. But if you want to run this place, you got to have it. You can't lose it, or let anyone take it from you."

Oliver's hands went to the opener involuntarily. It seemed very desirable, as if there was something of Miss Parkhurst in it: warm, powerful, a little frightening. It fit his hand perfectly, felt familiar to his skin; he might have owned it forever.

He tightened his lips and returned it to her. "I'm sorry," he said. "It's not for me."

"You remember what I told you," she said. "If you don't take it, somebody else will, and it won't do anybody any good then. I want it to do some good now I'm done with it."

"Who gave it to you?" Oliver asked.

"A pimp, a long time ago. When I was a girl."

Oliver's eyes betrayed no judgment. She took a deep breath.

"He made you do it . . . ?" Oliver asked.

"No. I was young, but already a whore. I had an old, kind pimp, at least he seemed old to me, I wasn't much more than a baby. He died, he was killed, so this new pimp came, and he was powerful. He had the magic. But he couldn't tame me. So he cuts me up . . ." Miss Parkhurst raised her hands to her face. "He cuts me up bad. He says, 'You shame me, whore. You do this to me, make me lose control, you're the only one ever did this to me. So I curse you. You'll be the greatest whore ever was.' He gave me the opener, then he put my face and body back together so I'd be pretty. Then he left town, and I was in charge. I've been here ever since, but all the girls have gone, it's been so long, died or left or I told them to go. I wanted this place closed, but I couldn't close it all at once."

Oliver nodded slowly, eyes wide.

"He left me most of his magic, too. I didn't have any choice. One thing he didn't give me was a way out. Except . . ." This time, she was the one with the pleading expression.

Oliver raised an eyebrow.

"What I need has to be freely given. Now take this." She stood and thrust the opener into his hands. "During the day, use it to find your way around the house. But don't leave your room after dark."

She swept out of the dining room, trailing musk and flowers and something bittersweet. Oliver put the opener in his pocket and walked back to his room, finding his way without hesitation, without thought. He shut the door and went to the bookcase, sad and troubled and exultant all at once.

She had told him her secret. He could leave now if he wanted. She had given him the power to leave.

Sipping from a glass of sherry on the nightstand beside the bed, reading from a book of composers' lives, he decided to wait until morning.

Yet after a few hours, nothing could keep his mind away from Miss Parkhurst's prohibition—not the piano, the books, or the snacks delivered almost before he thought about them, appearing on the tray when he wasn't watching. Oliver sat with hands folded in the plush chair, blinking at the room's dark corners. He thought he had Miss Parkhurst pegged. She was an old woman tired of her life, a beautifully preserved old woman to be sure, very strong . . . But she was sweet on him, keeping him like some reminder of her youth, a backup gigolo. Still, he couldn't help but admire her—and he couldn't help but want to be home, near Momma and even near Yolanda and the babies, keeping his brothers out of trouble, not that they appreciated his efforts.

The longer Oliver sat, the angrier and more anxious he became. He felt sure something was wrong at home. Pacing around the room did nothing to calm him. He examined the golden-buttoned opener time and again in the firelight, brow wrinkled, wondering what powers it actually possessed. She had said that with it, he could go anywhere in the house and know his way, just as he had found his room without her help.

He moaned, shaking his fists at the air. "She can't keep me here! She just *can't!*"

At midnight, he couldn't control himself any longer. He stood before the door. "Let me out, dammit!" he cried, and the door opened with a sad whisper. Tears shining on his cheeks, he ran down the corridor, scattering moonlight on the floor like dust.

Through the sitting rooms, the long halls of empty bedrooms—now with their doors closed, shades of sound sifting from behind—through the vast deserted kitchen, with its rows of polished copper kettles and huge black coal cookstoves, through a courtyard surrounded by five stories of the mansion on all sides and open to the golden-starred night sky, past a tiled fountain guarded by three huge white porcelain lions, ears and empty eyes following him as he ran, Oliver searched for Miss Parkhurst, to tell her he must leave.

For a moment, he slowed to catch his breath in an upstairs gallery. He saw faint lights under doors, heard more suggestive sounds. But this was no time to pause, even with his heart pounding and his lungs burning. If he waited in one place long enough, the ghosts might become real and force him join their revelry. This was Miss Parkhurst's past, hoary and indecent, more than he could bear contemplating. How could anyone have lived this kind of life, even if they were cursed?

Yet the temptation to stop, to listen, to give in and join in was almost stronger than he could resist. He kept losing track of what he was doing, what his ultimate goal was.

"Where are you?" he shouted, throwing open double doors to a game room, empty but for startled ghosts, more of Miss Parkhurst's eternity of bookkeeping. Pale forms rose from the billiard tables, translucent breasts shining with an inner light, their pale old lovers rolling slowly to one side, fat bellies prominent, ghost eyes black and startled.

"Miss Parkhurst!"

Oliver brushed through dozens of girls, no more substantial than curtains of raindrops. His new clothes became wet with their tears. *She* had presided over this eternity of sad lust. *She* had orchestrated the debaucheries, catered to what he felt inside him: the whims and deepest desires unspoken.

Thin antique laughter followed him.

He skidded on a spill of sour-smelling champagne and came up abruptly against a heavy wooden door, a room he did not know. The golden opener told him nothing about what waited beyond.

"*Open!*" he shouted, but was ignored. The door was not locked, but it resisted his push as if it weighed tons. He laid his shoulder on the paneling, bracing his sneakers against the thick wool pile of the champagne-soaked runner. The door finally swung inward with a deep iron and wood grumble, and Oliver stumbled past, saving himself at the last minute from falling on his face.

Legs sprawled, landing on both hands, he looked up from the wooden floor and saw where he was. The room was narrow, but stretched on for what might have been miles, lined on one side with an endless row of plain double beds and on the other with an endless row of freestanding cheval mirrors.

An old man, the oldest he had ever seen, naked and white as talcum, rose stiffly from the nearest bed, mumbling. Beneath him, red and warm as a pile of glowing coals, Miss Parkhurst lay with legs spread, incense of musk and sweat thick about her. She raised her head and shoulders, eyes fixed on Oliver's, and pulled a black peignoir over her nakedness.

In the room's receding gloom, other men, old and young, stood by their beds, smoking cigarettes or cigars or drinking champagne or whisky. All observing Oliver. Some grinned in speculation.

Suddenly, Miss Parkhurst's face wrinkled like an old apple and she threw back her head to scream. The old man on the bed grabbed clumsily for a robe and his clothes. Her shriek echoed from the ceiling and the walls, driving Oliver back through the door, back down the halls and stairways. The wind of his flight chilled him to the bone in his tear-soaked clothing. Somehow he made his way through the abrupt darkness and emptiness, and shut himself in his room, where the fire still burned warm and cheery yellow.

Shivering uncontrollably, Oliver removed his tear-soaked clothes and in a high-pitched, frantic voice called for his old shirt and pants. But the invisible servants did not deliver what he requested.

He fell into the bed and pulled the covers tight about him, eyes closed. He prayed that she would not come after him, not come into his room with her peignoir slipping aside, revealing her furnace body; he prayed her smell would not follow him the rest of his life.

The door to his room did not open. Outside, all was quiet. In time, as dawn fired the roofs and then the walls and finally the streets of Sunside, Oliver slept.

"You came out of your room last night," Miss Parkhurst said over the late breakfast. Oliver stopped chewing for a moment, glanced at her through bloodshot eyes, then shrugged.

"Did you see what you expected?"

Oliver didn't answer.

Miss Parkhurst sighed like a young girl. "It's my life. This is the way I've lived for a long time."

"None of my business," Oliver said, breaking a roll in half and buttering it.

"Do I disgust you?"

Again no reply. Miss Parkhurst stood in the middle of his silence and walked to the dining room door. She looked over her shoulder at him, eyes moist. "You're not afraid of me now," she said. "You think you know what I am."

Oliver saw that his silence and uncaring attitude hurt her, and relished for a moment this power. When she remained standing in the doorway, he looked up with a purposefully harsh expression—copied from Reggie, sarcastic and angry at once—and saw tears silver her cheeks. She seemed younger than ever, not dangerous—just very sad.

His expression faded. She turned away and closed the door behind her.

Oliver slammed half the roll into his plate of eggs and pushed his chair back from the table. "I'm not yet full-grown!" he shouted at the door. "I'm not even a man! What do you want from me?" He stood and kicked the chair away with his heel, then stuffed his hands in his pockets and paced around the small room. He felt bottled up, and yet she had said he could go anytime he wished.

Go where?

Home?

Did he still want that? He stared at the goldenware and the plates heaped with fine food. Nothing like this at home. Home was a place he sometimes thought he'd have to fight to get away from; he couldn't protect Momma forever from the rest of the family, couldn't be a breadwinner for five extra mouths for the rest of his life . . .

And if he stayed *here*, knowing what Miss Parkhurst did each night? Could he eat breakfast each morning, knowing how the food had been earned, and all his clothes and books and the piano, too? He really would be a gigolo then.

But this was Sunside. Maybe he could live here, find work, get away from Sleepside for good. The mere thought gave him a twinge. He sat and buried his face in his hands, rubbing his eyes with the tips of his fingers, then pulled at his lids to make a face. He stared at his reflection in the golden carafe, big-nosed, eyes monstrously bleared. He had to talk to Momma. Even talking to Yolanda might help.

But Miss Parkhurst was nowhere to be found. Oliver searched the mansion until dusk, then ate alone in the small dining room. He retired to his room as dark closed in, spreading through the halls like ink through water. To banish the night and all that might be happening in it, Oliver played the piano loudly. When he finally stumbled to his bed, he saw a single yellow rose on the pillow, delicate and sweet. He placed it by the lamp on the nightstand and pulled the covers over himself, clothes and all.

In the early hours of morning, he dreamed that Miss Parkhurst had fled the mansion, leaving it for him to tend to. The ghosts and old men crowded around, asking how he could be so righteous. "She never had a Momma like you," said one decrepit dude dressed in black velvet robes. "She's lived times you can't imagine. Now you just blew her right out of this house. Where will she go?"

Oliver came awake long enough to remember the dream, and then returned to a light, difficult sleep.

Mrs. Diamond Freeland scowled at Yolanda's hand-wringing and mumbling. "You can't help your momma acting that way," she said.

"I'm no doctor," Yolanda complained.

"No doctor's going to help her," Mrs. Freeland said, eyeing the door to Momma's bedroom.

Denver and Reggie lounged in the parlor.

"You two louts going to look for your brother?"

"We don't have to look for him," Denver said. "We know where he is. We got a plan to get him back."

"Then why don't you do it?" Mrs. Freeland asked.

"When the time's right," Reggie said.

"Your Momma's pining for Oliver," Mrs. Freeland told them, not for the first time. "It's churning her insides thinking he's with that witch and what she might be doing to him."

Reggie tried unsuccessfully to hide a grin.

"What's funny?" Mrs. Freeland asked.

"Nothing. Maybe our little brother needs some of what she's got."

Mrs. Freeland glared at them, then rolled her eyes in disgust. "Yolanda," she said, "the babies. They dry?"

"No, ma'am," Yolanda said. She backed away from Mrs. Freeland's severe look. "I'll change them."

"Then you take them in to your momma."

"Yes, ma'am."

The breakfast proceeded as if nothing had happened. Miss Parkhurst sat across from him, eating and smiling. Oliver tried to be more polite, working his way around to asking a favor. When the breakfast was over, the time seemed right.

"I'd like to see how Momma's doing," he said.

Miss Parkhurst considered for a moment. "There'll be a TV in your room this evening," she said, folding her napkin and placing it beside her plate. "You can use it to see how everybody is."

That seemed fair enough. Until then, however, he'd be spending the entire day with Miss Parkhurst; it was time, he decided, to be civil. Then he might actually test his freedom.

"You say I can go," Oliver said, trying to sound friendly.

Miss Parkhurst nodded. "Anytime. I won't keep you."

"If I go, can I come back?"

She smiled ever so slightly. There was the young girl in that smile again, and she seemed very vulnerable. "The opener takes you anywhere across town."

"Nobody messes with me?"

"Nobody touches anyone I protect," Miss Parkhurst said.

Oliver absorbed that, steepling his hands below his chin. "You're pretty good to me," he said. "Even when I cross you, you don't hurt me. Why?"

"I've lived a long time and nobody like you's come along," Miss Parkhurst said, dark eyes on him. "I've lived this way so many years, I don't know another, but I don't want any more. You're my last chance."

Oliver couldn't think of a better way to put his next question. "Do you like being a whore?"

Miss Parkhurst's face hardened. "It has its moments," she said.

Oliver screwed up his courage enough to say what was on his mind, but not to look at her while doing it. "You enjoy lying down with any man who has the money?"

"It's something I'm good at."

"Even ugly men?"

"Ugly men need their pleasures."

"Bad men? Letting them touch you when they've hurt people, killed people?"

"What kind of work have *you* done?" she asked.

"Clerked a grocery store. Taught music."

"Did you wait on bad men in the grocery store?"

"If I did," Oliver said swiftly, "I didn't know about it."

"Neither did I," Miss Parkhurst said. Then, more quietly, "Most of the time."

"All those girls you've made whore for you . . ."

"You have some things to learn," she interrupted. "It's not the work that's so awful. It's what you have to be to do it. The way people expect you to be when you do it. Should be, in a good world, a whore's like a doctor or a saint, she doesn't mind getting her hands dirty any more than they do. She gives pleasure and smiles. But in the city, people won't let it happen that way. Here, a whore's always got some empty place inside her, a place you've filled with self-respect, maybe. A whore's got respect, but not for herself. She loses that whenever anybody looks at her. She can be worth a million dollars on the outside, but inside, she knows. That's what makes her a whore. That's the curse. It's beat into you sometimes, everybody taking advantage, like you're dirt. Pretty soon you think you're dirt, too, and who cares what happens to dirt? Pretty soon you're just sliding along, trying to keep from getting hurt or maybe dead, but who cares?"

"You're rich," Oliver said.

"Can't buy everything," Miss Parkhurst commented dryly.

"You've got magic."

"I've got magic because I'm here, and to stay here, I have to be a whore."

"Why can't you leave?"

She sighed, her fingers working nervously along the edge of the tablecloth.

"What stops you from just leaving?"

"If you're going to own this place," she said, and he thought at first she was avoiding his question, "you've got to know all about it. All about me. We're the same, almost, this place and I. A whore's no more than what's in her purse, every pimp knows that. You know how many times I've been married?"

Oliver shook his head.

"Seventeen times. Sometimes they left me, once or twice they stayed. Never any good. But then, maybe I didn't deserve better. Those who left me, they came back when they were old, asked me to save them from Darkside. I couldn't. But I kept them here anyway. Come on."

She stood and Oliver followed her down the halls, down the stairs, below the garage level, deep beneath the mansion's clutter-filled basement. The air was ageless, deep-earth cool, and smelled of old city rain. A few eternal clear light bulbs cast feeble yellow crescents in the dismal murk. They walked on boards over an old muddy patch, Miss Parkhurst lifting her skirts to clear the mire. Oliver saw her slim ankles and swallowed back the tightness in his throat.

Ahead, laid out in a row on moss-patched concrete biers, were fifteen black iron cylinders, each eight feet long and slightly flattened on top. They looked like big blockbuster bombs in storage. The first was wedged into a dark corner. Miss Parkhurst stood by its foot, running her hand along its rust-streaked surface.

"Two didn't come back. Maybe they were the best of the lot," she said. "I couldn't know. You judge men by what's inside you, and if you're hollow, they get lost, you can't know what's in their hearts."

Oliver stepped closer to the last cylinder and saw a clear glass plate mounted at the head. Reluctant but fascinated, he wiped the dusty glass with two fingers and peered past a single cornered bubble. The coffin was filled with clear liquid. Afloat within, a face the color of green olives in a martini looked back at him, blind eyes murky, lips set in a loose line. The liquid and death had smoothed the face's wrinkles, but Oliver could tell nonetheless, this dude had been old, really old.

"They all die," she said. "All but me. I keep them all, every john, every husband, no forgetting, no letting them go. We've got this tie between us, forever. That's part of the curse."

Oliver pulled back from the coffin, holding his breath, heart thumping with eager horror. Which was worse, this, or old men in the night? Old dead loves laid to rest or lively ghosts? Wrapped in gloom at the far end of the line of bottle-coffins, Miss Parkhurst seemed for a moment to glow with the same furnace power he had felt when he first saw her.

"I miss some of these guys," she said, her voice so soft the power just vanished, a thing in his mind. "We had some good times."

Oliver tried to imagine what Miss Parkhurst had lived through, the good times and otherwise. "You have any children?" he asked, his voice as thin as the buzz of a fly in a bottle. He jumped back as one of the coffins resonated with his shaky words.

Miss Parkhurst's shoulders shivered as well. "Lots," she said tightly. "All dead before they were born."

At first his shock was conventional, orchestrated by his Sundays in church. Then the colossal organic waste of effort came down on him like a pile of stones. All that motion, all that wanting, and nothing good from it—just these iron bottles and vivid lines of ghosts.

"What good is a whore's baby?" Miss Parkhurst asked. "Especially if the mother's going to stay a whore."

"Was your mother . . . ?" It didn't seem right to use the word in connection with anyone's mother.

"She was, and her mother before her. I have no daddies, or lots of daddies."

Oliver remembered the old man chastising him in his dream. Before he could even sort out his words, wishing to give her some solace, some sign he wasn't completely unsympathetic, he said, "It can't be all bad, being a whore."

"Maybe not," she said. Miss Parkhurst hardly made a blot in the larger shadows. She might just fly to dust if he turned his head.

"You said being a whore is being empty inside. Not everybody who's empty inside is a whore."

"Oh?" she replied, voice light as a cobweb. He was being pushed into an uncharacteristic posture, but Oliver was damned if he'd give in just yet, however much a fool he made of himself. His mixed feelings were betraying him.

"You've *lived*," he said. "You got memories nobody else has. You could write books. They'd make movies about you."

Her smile was a dull lamp in the shadows. "I've had important people visit me," she said. "Powerful men, mayors, even governors. I had something they needed. Sometimes they opened up and talked about how hard it was not being little boys. Sometimes, after we'd relaxed, they'd cry on my shoulder, just like I was their momma. But then they'd go away and try to forget about me. If they remembered at all, they were scared of me, because of what I knew about them. Now, they know I'm getting weak," she said. "I don't give a damn about books or movies. I won't tell what I know, and besides, lots of those men are dead. If they aren't, they're waiting for me to die, so they can sleep easy."

"What do you mean, getting weak?"

"I got two days, maybe three, until I come to the end of my cord and die a whore. My time is up. The curse is almost done."

Oliver gaped. When he had first seen her, she had seemed as powerful as a diesel locomotive, as if she might live forever.

"And if I take over?"

"You get the mansion, the money."

"How much power?"

She didn't answer.

"You can't give me any power, can you?"

"No," faint as the breeze from her eyelashes.

"The opener won't be any good."

"No."

"You lied to me."

"I'll leave you all that's left."

"That's not why you made me come here. You took Momma—"

"She stole from me."

"My momma never stole anything!" Oliver shouted. The iron coffins buzzed.

"She took something after I showed her my hospitality."

"What could she take from you? She was no thief."

"She took a sheet of music."

Oliver's face screwed up in sudden pain. He looked away, fists clenched. They had almost no money for his music. More often than not since his father died, he made up music, having no new scores to play. "Why'd you bring me here?" he cried.

"I don't mind dying. But I don't want to die a whore."

Oliver turned back, angry again, this time for his momma as well as himself. He approached the insubstantial shadow. Miss Parkhurst shimmered like a curtain. "What do you want from me?"

"I need someone who loves me. Loves me for no reason."

For an instant, he saw standing before him a scrawny girl in a red shimmy, eyes wide.

"How could that help you? Can that make you something else?"

"Just love," she said. "Just letting me forget all these." She pointed to the coffins. "And all those." Pointing up.

Oliver's body lost its charge of anger and accusation with an exhaled breath. "I can't love you," he said. "I don't even know what love is." Was this true? Upstairs, she had burned in his mind, and he *had* wanted her, though it upset him to remember how much. What *could* he feel for her? "Let's go back now. I have to look in on Momma."

Miss Parkhurst separated herself from the shadows and glided silently past him, not even her skirts rustling. She gestured with a finger for him to follow, and left him at the door to his room, saying, "I'll wait in the main parlor."

Oliver saw a small television set on the nightstand by his bed and rushed to turn it on. The screen filled with static and unresolved images. He saw fragments of faces, patches of color and texture passing so quickly he couldn't make them out. The entire city might be on the screen at once, but he could not see any of it clearly. He twisted the channel knob and got more static. Then he turned the knob beyond 13: HOME, it said, in small golden letters.

The screen cleared.

Momma lay in bed, legs drawn up tight, hair mussed. She didn't look good. Her outstretched hand trembled. Her breathing was hard and rough. In the background, Oliver heard Yolanda fussing with the babies, finally screaming at her older brothers in frustration. *Why don't you help with the babies?* his sister demanded in a tinny, distant voice.

Momma told you, Denver replied.

She did not. She told us all. You could help.

Reggie laughed. *We got to make plans!*

Oliver pulled back from the TV. Momma was sick, and for all his brothers and sister and the babies could do, she might die. He could guess why she was sick, too; with worry for him. He had to go to her and tell her he was all right. A phone call wouldn't be enough.

Again, however, he was reluctant to leave the mansion and Miss Parkhurst. Something beyond Belle's waning magic was at work here; he wanted to listen to her and to experience more of that fascinated horror. He wanted to watch her again, absorb her smooth, ancient beauty. In a way, she needed him as much as Momma did. Miss Parkhurst outraged everything in him that was lawful and orderly, but he finally had to admit, as he thought of going back to Momma, that he enjoyed the outrage.

He clutched the gold opener and ran from his room to the parlor. She waited for him there in a red velvet chair, hands gripping two lions at the end of the armrests. The lions' wooden faces grinned beneath her caresses. "I got to go," he said. "Momma's sick for missing me."

She nodded. "I'm not holding you," she said.

He stared at her. "I wish I could help," he said.

She smiled hopefully, pitifully. "Then promise you'll come back."

Oliver wavered. How long would Momma need him?

What if he gave his promise and returned and Miss Parkhurst was already dead?

"I promise."

"Don't be too long," she said.

The limousine waited for him in the garage, white and beautiful, languid and sleek and fast all at once. This time, no chauffeur waited for him. The door opened by itself and he climbed in; the door closed behind him, and he leaned back stiffly on the leather seats, gold opener in hand. "Take me home," he said. The glass partition and the windows all around darkened to an opaque, smoky gold. He felt a sensation of smooth motion. *What would it be like to have this kind of power all the time?*

But the power wasn't hers to give.

Oliver arrived before the apartment building in a blizzard of swirling snow. Snow packed up over the curbs and coated the sidewalks a foot deep; Sleepside was heavy with winter. Oliver stepped from the limousine and climbed the icy steps, the cold hardly touching him even in his light clothing. He was surrounded by Miss Parkhurst's magic.

Denver was frying a pan of navy beans in the kitchen when Oliver burst through the door. Denver stared at him, face slack, too surprised to speak.

"Where's Momma?" Oliver asked.

Yolanda heard his voice from the living room and screamed.

Reggie met him in the hallway, arms open wide, smiling broadly. "Goddamn, little brother! You got away?"

"Where's Momma?"

"She's in her room. She's feeling low."

"She's sick," Oliver said, pushing past his brother. Yolanda stood before Momma's door as if to keep Oliver out. She sucked her lower lip between her teeth and looked scared.

"Let me by, Yolanda," Oliver said. He pointed the opener at her, and then pulled back, fearful of what might happen.

"You made Momma si-ick," Yolanda squeaked, but she stepped aside. Oliver pushed through the door to Momma's room. She sat up in bed, face drawn and thin, but her eyes danced with joy. "My boy!" She sighed. "My beautiful boy."

Oliver sat beside her and they hugged fiercely. "Please don't leave me again," Momma said, voice muffled by his shoulder. Oliver set the opener on her flimsy nightstand and cried against her neck.

The day after Oliver's return, Denver stood lank-legged by the window, hands in frayed pants pockets, staring at the snow with heavy-lidded eyes. "It's too cold to go anywhere now," he mused.

Reggie sat in their father's chair, face screwed in thought. "I listened to what he told Momma," he said. "That whore sent our little brother back here in a limo. A big white limo. See it out there?"

Denver peered down at the street. A white limousine waited at the curb, not even dusted by snow. A tiny vanishing curl of white rose from its tailpipe. "It's still there," he said.

"Did you see what he had when he came in?" Reggie asked. Denver shook his head. "A gold box. *She* must have given that to him. I bet whoever has that gold box can visit Miss Belle Parkhurst. Want to bet?"

Denver grinned.

"Wouldn't be too cold if we had that limo, would it?" Reggie asked.

Oliver brought his momma chicken soup and a carefully trimmed orange. He plumped her pillow for her, shushing her, telling her not to talk until she had eaten. She smiled and let him minister to her. When she had eaten, she lay back and closed her eyes, tears pooling in their hollows before slipping down her cheeks. "I was so afraid for you," she said. "At first, I didn't see her. Just her voice, inviting me in over the security buzzer, letting me sit and rest my feet. She seemed nice. I didn't know what she would do. But I knew where I was . . . was that bad of me, to stay there, knowing?"

"You were tired, Momma," Oliver said. "Besides, Miss Parkhurst isn't that bad."

Momma looked at him dubiously. "I saw her piano. There was a shelf next to it with the most beautiful sheet music, even big books filled with music. Oh, Oliver, I've never taken anything in my life . . ." She cried freely now, sapping what little strength the lunch had given her.

"Don't you worry, Momma. She used you. She *wanted* me to come." As an afterthought, he added, not sure why he lied, "Or Yolanda."

Momma absorbed that while her eyes examined his face in tiny, caressing glances. "You won't go back," she said, "will you?"

Oliver looked down at the sheets folded under her arms. "I promised. She'll die if I don't," he said.

"That woman is a liar," Momma stated unequivocally. "If she wants you, she'll do anything to get you."

"I don't think she's lying, Momma."

She looked away from him, a feverish anger flushing her cheeks. "Why did you promise her?"

"She's not that bad, Momma," he said again. He had thought that coming home would clear his mind, but Miss Parkhurst's face, her plea, stayed with him as if she were only a room away. The mansion seemed just a fading dream, unimportant; but Belle Parkhurst stuck. "She needs help. She wants to change."

Momma puffed out her cheeks and blew through her lips like a horse. She had often done that to his father, never before to him. "She'll always be a whore," she said.

Oliver's eyes narrowed. He saw a spitefulness and bitterness in Momma he hadn't noticed before. Not that spite was unwarranted; Miss Parkhurst had treated Momma roughly. Yet . . .

Denver stood in the doorway. "Reggie and I got to talk to Momma," he said. "About you." He jerked his thumb back over his shoulder. "Alone." Reggie stood grinning behind his brother. Oliver took the tray of dishes and sidled past them, going into the kitchen. He washed the last few days' plates methodically, letting the lukewarm water slide over his hands, eyes focused on the faucet's dull gleam.

He had almost lost track of time when he heard the front door slam. Jerking his head up, he wiped the last plate and put it away, then went to Momma's room. She looked back at him guiltily. Something was wrong. He searched the room with his eyes, but nothing was out of place. Nothing that was normally present . . .

The opener.

His brothers had taken the gold opener.

"Momma!" he said.

"They're going to pay her a visit," she said, the bitterness plain now. "They don't like their momma mistreated."

It was getting dark and the snow was thick. He had hoped to return this evening. If Miss Parkhurst hadn't lied, she would be very weak by now, and perhaps tomorrow, she would be dead. His lungs seemed to shrink, and he had a hard time taking a breath.

"I've got to go," he said. "She might *kill* them, Momma!"

But that wasn't what worried him. He put on his heavy coat,

then his father's old cracked rubber boots with the snow tread soles. Yolanda came out of the room she shared with the babies. She didn't ask any questions, just watched him dress for the cold, her eyes dull.

"They got that gold box," she said as he flipped the last metal clasp on the boots. "Probably worth a lot."

Oliver hesitated in the hallway, then grabbed Yolanda's shoulders and shook her vigorously. "You take care of Momma, you hear?"

She shut her jaw with a clack and shoved free. Oliver was out the door before she could speak.

Day's last light filled the sky with a deep peachy glow tinged with cold gray. Snow fell golden above the buildings and smudgy brown within their shadow. The wind mournfully swirled around him, sending gust-fingers through his coat as if searching for any warmth that might be stolen. For a nauseating moment, all his resolve was sucked away by a vacuous pit of misery.

The streets were empty; he wondered what night this was, and then remembered it was the twenty-third of December, but too cold for whatever stray shoppers Sleepside might send out. *Why go? To save two worthless idiots?* Not that so much, although that would have been enough, since their loss would hurt Momma, and they *were* his brothers; not that so much as his promise. And something else.

He was afraid for Belle Parkhurst.

He buttoned his coat collar and leaned into the wind. He hadn't put on a hat. The heat flew from his scalp, and in a few moments he felt drained and exhausted. But he made it to the subway entrance and staggered down the steps, into the warmer heart of the city, where it was always sixty-four degrees.

Locked behind thick glass in her metal booth, wrinkled eyes weary with night's wisdom, the fluorescent-pale clerk took his money, then dropped tokens into the steel tray with separate, distinct *chinks.* Oliver glanced at her face and saw Belle's printed there instead. This middle-aged woman did not spread her legs for money, but had sold her youth and life away sitting in this cavern. Whose emptiness was more profound?

“Be careful,” she warned vacantly through the speaker grill. “Night Metro coming any minute now.”

He dropped a cat’s-head token into the turnstile and pushed through, then stood shivering on the platform, waiting for the Sunside train. It seemed to take forever to arrive, and when it did, he was not particularly relieved. The bull-headed operator’s eyes winked green in their deep pits as the train slid to a halt. The doors opened with an oiled groan, and Oliver stepped aboard, into the hard, cold glare of the train’s interior. At first, he thought the car was empty. He did not sit, however. The hair on his neck and arm bristled. Hand gripping a steel handle, he leaned into the train’s acceleration and took a deep, half-hiccup breath.

Oliver first consciously noticed the other passengers as faces gleaming in silhouette against the dim lights of passing stations. The riders sat almost invisible, crowding the car; they stood beside him, less real than a chill breeze, and watched him through glassy eyes, bearing no ill will for the moment, perhaps not yet aware that he was alive and they were not. They showed no overt signs of their wounds, their sins, but how they had come to be here was obvious to Oliver’s animal instincts.

This train carried holiday suicides: men, women, teenagers, even a few children, delicate as expensive crystal in a shop window. Maybe the bull-headed operator collected them, culling them and caging them as they stumbled randomly onto his train. Maybe he commanded them, used them . . .

Oliver tried to sink into his coat. He felt guilty, being alive and healthy, enveloped in strong emotions; the others were so flimsy, with so little hold on this reality. He muttered a prayer, then stopped as they all turned toward him at once, showing glassy disapproval at his reverse blasphemy. Silently, he prayed again, but even that seemed to irritate his fellow passengers, and they squeaked among themselves in voices that only a dog or a bat could hear.

The stations passed one by one, mosaic symbols and names flashing in dim puddles of light. When the Sunside station approached and the train slowed, Oliver moved quickly to the door. It opened with a sigh. The other passengers sighed as well; they could not leave. Their hands reached for him, but he stepped onto the platform, turned—and backed up against the dark uniform of the bull-headed operator. The air around the operator stank of grease and electricity and something sweeter, perhaps blood. He stood a bad foot and a half taller than Oliver, and in one outstretched, black-nailed, leathery hand he held his long silver shears, points spread wide, briefly suggesting Belle Parkhurst's horizontal position among the old men.

"You're in the wrong place, at the wrong time," the operator warned in a voice deeper than the train motors. "Down here, I can cut your cord." He closed the shears with a slick, singing whisper.

"I'm going to Miss Parkhurst's," Oliver said, voice quavering.

"Who?" the operator asked.

"I'm leaving now," Oliver said, backing away. The operator followed, hunching over him. The shears sang open, angled toward Oliver's eyes. At a wave of the operator's other clawed hand, the crystalline, raindrop dead within the train passed through the train's open door and glided around them. Gluey waves of cold shivered the air.

"You're a bold little bastard," the operator said, voice descending below any human scale—and yet still audible. The voice shivered Oliver's bones, and the white tile walls vibrated as well. "All I have to do is cut your cord, right in front of your face"—he snicked the shears inches from Oliver's nose—"and you'll never find your way home."

The operator backed him up against a cold, moist barrier of suicides. Oliver's fear could not shut out curiosity. Was the bull's head real, or was there a man under the horns and hide and bone? The eyes in their sunken orbits now glowed ice-blue. The scissors arced again before Oliver's face again, even closer; mere hairs from his nose.

"You're *mine*," the operator rumbled, and the blades closed on something tough and invisible. Oliver's head exploded with pain.

He flailed back through the dead, dragging the operator after him by the pinch of the shears on that something unseen and very important.

Roaring, the operator applied both hands to the shears' grips. Oliver felt as if his head were being ripped off. Suddenly he kicked out with all his strength between the operator's black-uniformed legs. His foot hit flesh and bone as unyielding as rock and his agony doubled. But the shears hung for a moment in air before Oliver's face, and the operator slowly curled over. He moaned—and his fingers loosened.

Oliver grabbed the shears, spread the blades, and released whatever cord stretched between himself and his past, his home. Then he pushed through the swarming dead. The scissors reflected long gleams over their astonished, watery faces. Suddenly, seeing a chance to escape, they spread out along the platform, some ascending the station's stairs, some fleeing to both ends of the platform.

Oliver ran through them up the steps—

And stood on a warm evening sidewalk. He was back in Sunside. From the station's entrance wafted a sour breath of oil and blood, and a faint chill of fading hands as the dead evaporated in the balmy night air.

A quiet crowd of well-dressed onlookers had gathered at the front entrance to Miss Parkhurst's mansion. They stood vigil, waiting for something, pinched faces shiny with a sweat of envy and greed. Oliver did not see the limousine. His brothers must have arrived by now; they were inside, then.

Catching his breath as he ran, he slid around the corner of the old brownstone, found a tight alley, and looked for the entrance to the underground garage. On the south side, he found the ramp and descended to slam his hands against the corrugated metal door. Echoes replied.

"It's me!" he shouted. "Let me in!"

A middle-aged man regarded him dispassionately from the higher ground of the sidewalk. "What do you want in there, young man?" he asked.

Oliver glared back over his shoulder. "None of your business," he said.

"Maybe it is, if you want in," the man said. "There's a way any man can get into that house. It never refuses gold."

Oliver pulled back from the door a moment, stunned.

The man shrugged and walked on.

Oliver still held the operator's shears. They weren't gold, they were silver, but they had to be worth something. "Let me in!" he said. Then, upping the ante, he dug in his pocket and produced the last cat's head token. "I'll pay!"

The door grumbled up. The garage's lights were off, but in the soft yellow glow of the streetlights, he saw an eagle's claw thrust out from the brick wall just inside the door's frame, supporting a golden cup. Token in one hand, shears in another, Oliver considered. To pay Belle's mansion now was no honorable deed; he dropped the token into the cup, but kept the shears.

A faint crack of light gleamed under the stairwell door. Around the door, the bones of ancient city dwellers glowed in the compacted stone, teeth and knuckles bright as fireflies. Oliver tried the door; it was locked. Inserting the point of the shears between door and catchplate, he pried and twisted until the lock was sprung.

The quiet parlor beyond was illuminated by a few guttering candles clutched in drooping, tarnished eagle's claws. The air was thick with the blunt smells of stale cigars and old, stubbed-out cigarettes. Oliver stopped, closing his eyes and listening.

There was one room he had never seen in the time he had spent in Belle Parkhurst's house. She had never even shown him the door, but he knew it had to exist—and that was where she would be, alive or dead.

Where his brothers were, he couldn't tell, and for the moment he didn't care. He doubted they were in any mortal danger. Belle's power was as weak as the scattered candles.

Oliver crept along the dark halls, holding the shears before him as a warning to whatever might try to stop him. He climbed two more flights of stairs, and on the third floor found an uncarpeted hallway, walls bare, that he had not seen before. The dry floorboards creaked beneath his shoes. The air was cool and still. He could smell a ghost of Belle's rose perfume. At the end of the hall was a plain panel door with a tarnished brass knob, also unlocked. He sucked in a breath for courage and opened it.

This was Belle's room, and she was indeed in it. She hung suspended above her plain iron-frame bed in a weave of glowing threads. For a moment, he drew back, thinking she was a spider, but it immediately became clear she was more like a spider's prey. The threads reached to all comers of the room, transparent, binding her tight.

Belle struggled to face him, eyes clouded, skin like washroom paper towels. "Why'd you wait so long?" she asked.

From across the mansion, he heard echoes of Reggie's delighted laughter.

Oliver stepped forward. Only the blades of the shears caught on the threads; he passed through unhindered. Arm straining told hold on to the shears, he realized what the threads were: the cords binding Belle to the mansion, connecting her to all her customers. Every place she had been touched, there grew a tough, glowing thread. Thick twining ropes of the past shot from her lips and breasts and from between her legs; not even the toes of her feet were free.

Belle had not one cord to her past, but thousands.

Without thinking, Oliver twisted and thrust out the operator's silver shears and began snipping. One by one, or in ropy clusters, he cut the cords away. With each whispering snick of the blades, some of the cords vanished. He did not ask himself which was her first cord, linking her to childhood, to the few years she had lived before she became a whore; there was no time to waste worrying about such niceties.

"Your brothers are in my vault," Belle whispered, watching, hoping. "They found my gold and jewels. I crawled here to get away."

"Don't talk," Oliver said between clenched teeth. The strands became tougher, more like wire the closer he came to her thin gray body. His arm muscles knotted and cold sweat soaked his clothes.

She dropped inches closer to the bed. "I never brought men here," she said.

"Shh!"

"This was my place, the only place I had."

There were hundreds of strands left now, instead of thousands. He worked for long minutes, watching her grow more and more gray, watching her eyes lose their feverish glitter, her one-time furnace heat dull to less than a single candle. For a horrified moment, he thought cutting the cords might actually weaken her; but he hacked and swung at them regardless. They were even tougher now, more resilient.

Far off in the mansion, Denver and Reggie laughed like fools, followed by a heavy thudding, clinking sound. The floor shuddered.

Dozens of cords remained. Oliver had been working at them for an eternity, and now each cord took all the strength left in his arms and hands. He thought he might faint or throw up.

Belle's eyes had closed. Her breath was undetectable.

Five strands left. He cut through one, then another. As he applied the shears to the third, a tall man appeared on the opposite side of her bed, dressed in pale gray with a widebrimmed gray hat. His fingers were covered with gold rings. A small gold eagle's claw pinned his white silk tie.

"I was her friend," the man said. "She came to me and I helped her out, and she cheated me."

Oliver stared up at the gray man through beads of sweat. Eyes stinging, he held out the shears out as if to stab him.

"Who are you?" he demanded.

"I put her to work right here—but she cheated me. That other old man, he hardly worked her at all."

"You're her *pimp.*" Oliver spat out the word.

The gray man grinned.

"Cut that cord," he said, "and she's *nothing*."

"She's nothing now! She's dying."

"She shouldn't have messed with me," the pimp said. "I was a strong man with lots of friends, lots of influence. What do you want with an old drained-out whore, boy?"

Oliver struggled to cut the third cord, but it writhed like a snake in the shears.

"She would have been a whore even without me," the pimp said. "She was a whore from the day she was born!"

"That's a lie," Oliver said, almost doubled over with exertion.

"What you going to do with her? She give you a pox and you need to finish her off, personal?"

Oliver's lips curled and he flung his head back as he brought the shears together with the last of his strength, boosted by a killing anger. The third cord parted and the shears snapped, one blade singing across the room and sticking in the wall with a spray of plaster chips.

The gray man vanished like a double-blown puff of cigarette smoke, leaving a scent of onions and stale beer.

Belle now hung awkwardly by two cords. Which was her link to life itself? He couldn't see any difference.

She moaned. "Do it!" she murmured. "Finish it!"

Swinging the single blade like a knife, Oliver swiftly parted one more cord. The last drew itself out thin as a thread, glowed brilliant white, then vanished—and Belle dropped back to the bed. Exhausted, Oliver fell across her, feeling her cool body for the first time. She could no longer arouse lust. She might as well be dead. "Miss Parkhurst," he said, and examined her face, high cheekbones pressing through waxy olive flesh. "I don't want anything. I just want you to be all right." He lowered his lips to hers and kissed her lightly, dripping sweat on her closed eyes.

Far away, Denver and Reggie cackled with glee . . .

Followed by silence.

The entire house grew quiet. All the ghosts, all the accounts received, had been freed, had fled.

The single candle in the room guttered out, and Oliver and Belle lay alone in the dark. Oliver finally got up, fumbled his way to the door, and went searching through the mansion for his brothers.

When he returned, he lay back beside Belle and, against his will, dropped into an exhausted slumber.

His breath synced with Belle's.

Cool, rose-scented fingers brushed his forehead.

Oliver opened his eyes and saw a girl in a red shimmy lean over him. She was young, barely his age. Her eyes were big and her lips bowed into a smile beneath high, full cheekbones.

"Where are we?" she asked. "How long we been here?"

Late morning sun filled the small, dusty room.

Oliver glanced around the bed, looking for Belle, and then turned back to the girl. She vaguely resembled the chauffeur who had brought him to the mansion that first night, though even younger, her face more bland and simple.

"You don't remember?" he asked.

"Honey," the girl said, hands on hips, "I don't remember much of anything. Except that you kissed me. You want to kiss me again?"

Momma did not approve of the strange young woman he brought home, and wanted to know where Reggie and Denver were. Oliver did not have the heart to tell her. His brothers lay cold as ice in a room filled with mounds of cat's head subway tokens, lips parted in frozen laughter—bound by the pimp's magic. They had dressed themselves in white, with broad white hats; dressed themselves as pimps. But the mansion was empty, stripped during that night of all its valuables by the greedy Sunside crowds.

Reggie and Denver were pimps imprisoned in a whorehouse without whores. As the young girl observed, with a tantalizing touch of wisdom beyond her apparent years, there was nothing much lower than that.

"Where'd you find that girl?" his momma asked. "She's hiding something, Oliver. You mark my words."

Oliver ignored his mother's misgivings, having enough of his own. The girl agreed she needed a different name now, and chose Lorelei, a name she said "Just sings right."

He saved money, lacking brothers who borrowed but never repaid, and soon had enough to rent a cheap studio on the sixth floor of the same building. The girl came to him sweetly in the rented bed, her mind no more full—for the most part—than that of any young girl. In his way, he loved her—and feared her, though less and less as days passed.

Lorelei played the piano almost as well as he did, and they made plans to pass out fliers and give lessons.

All they had taken from the mansion that last night had been a trunk filled with old sheet music and books. The crowds had left them that much, and nothing more.

Momma did not visit their apartment for two weeks after they moved in. But visit she did, and eventually the girl won her over. "She's got a good hand in the kitchen," Momma said. "You do right by her, now."

Yolanda made friends quickly and easily with Lorelei, and Oliver saw more substance in his younger sister than he had before. Lorelei helped Yolanda with the babies. She seemed a natural.

Sometimes, at night, he watched her while she slept, wondering if there still weren't stories, and perhaps skills, hidden behind that sweet, peaceful face. Had she forgotten everything?

In time, they were married.

And they lived—

Well, enough.

They lived.

GENIUS

"Genius" was developed for the television show "Outer Limits" in 2000, but was never aired.

TEASER

FADE IN:

EXT. CAMPUS OF BURLINGTON UNIVERSITY - EVENING

POV: CUBIST PERSPECTIVE. The campus seen from all angles at once, like a PICASSO PAINTING. This REARRANGES VISUALLY into DAN SHAEFFER walking at sunset to a large brick building. Dan is tall, thin, mid-thirties. He looks middling handsome, feckless, and harried, and carries a box overflowing with papers, and balanced on top, a laptop computer.

SUPERED OVER: Burlington University, Washington State

INT. FUSION REACTOR LAB - NIGHT

SUPERED OVER: DOUBLE PULSE FUSION REACTOR LAB

CONTROL VOICE

Desire and loneliness are not limited to humans, or to the familiar coordinates of Earth. For some, space and time are playgrounds of the mind, a game, an opportunity . . .

Fluorescent lights, bulletin boards, scuffed linoleum: a hallway in a typical university building. Dan encounters ANDREA, a tall, jeans-clad post-doc.

ANDREA

(In passing)

You're late.

DAN

Thanggg . . . you.

ON DAN, trying to push box and computer through a doorway.

CONTROL VOICE

For others, infinite dimensions are a reminder of failure and isolation.

INT. LAB OFFICE - LATER

A SMALL OFFICE, Dan and laboratory director MATT DAUBE sitting on opposite sides of the director's desk. Blueprints and color photos of spectacular (though sub-atomic) explosions cover the walls. Matt is in his early forties, dark-haired, plumpish, with rumpled clothing but an air of frustrated authority. He pores over stacks of documents at the desk. Dan is typing madly on a laptop computer. He leans back, rubs his neck.

DAN

This is it, then—we go with a fifty-four degree internal beam angle.

(Turns laptop screen to Matt)

The first laser pulse hits the pellet, the bottle shapes the plasma into a spinning torus.

THE SCREEN shows a strange bottle-shape, what we will

learn later is a KLEIN BOTTLE (sketch 1), looking like a twisted bagpipe, or a swan, if the swan were to tuck its neck under its wing. The bottle is in blueprint format: a cross-section of the DOUBLE PULSE FUSION REACTOR VESSEL. Dan's finger traces the animation graphic as he explains.

DAN (CONT'D)

We push the second laser through the quantum tunnel at the new wavelength, pump the plasma energy from the inside . . . And we get a continuous and stable plasma at double the density. Should bring us plenty of return energy.

Matt has a headache. He squeezes the bridge of his nose.

DAN (CONT'D)

It's a fundamentally different approach.

MATT

It all looks the same . . .

(Beat)

I don't see the difference.

DAN

We reset the beam angle and change the laser frequency. It's completely new.

Dan closes his laptop with a CLICK. Matt is not happy..

MATT

I'm getting a storm of crap from the university and from our investors. They've given us a pretty good run for the last year, without results. I just don't see how this is any better than the design on the last shot.

DAN

It will work, Matt.

CINDY—twenties post-doc, small, with spiky, short blond hair—pokes her head into the office.

CINDY

We're ready, Dr. Daube. Dr. Shaeffer.

Cindy withdraws.

MATT

What we need is a gusher of sheer genius. I've relied on you from the beginning. But I have to admit, I'm having second thoughts, Dan.

OFF DAN TO:

INT. FUSION REACTOR LAB - NIGHT

A brightly lit warehouse-sized lab, filled with equipment. A COUNTDOWN is underway. Ceiling lights flash, COMPUTER DISPLAYS run blue bars down to zero. Matt and Dan, a grad student JOHN, and the two female postdocs, Cindy and Andrea—surround the massive REACTOR VESSEL, a stainless steel and chromium ovoid with a swanlike curved neck doubling back on one side—just like the blueprint cutaway on Dan's laptop.

MATT stands tensely with arms folded.

COMPUTER VOICE (V.O.)

Twenty seconds to compression. First step: plasma maintenance and measurement. Charging for pulse.

DAN stands beside Matt. He looks worried, even a little ill.

COMPUTER VOICE (V.O.) (CONT'D)
Stored energy at maximum.

MATT
(Low)
It's a fifty million dollar pile of scrap if we don't get out more energy than we put in.

COMPUTER VOICE (V.O.)
Hold for plasma oscillation buffer. Plasma in chamber.

A CHUFF and HUM fill the lab. The lights dim.

MATT
My ass is on the line here.

DAN
Very confident.

COMPUTER VOICE (V.O.)
Lasers fully charged. Quantum tunnel open for internal beam spread.

A high-pitched but ethereal WHINE fills the room. Dan grimaces. His headache is really intense. Matt presses his fingers to his temples. ALL show paleness, exhaustion.

COMPUTER VOICE (V.O.) (CONT'D)
Plasma rotating.

ALL tense.

CLOSE on a QUARTZ BOX suspended on the reactor's "neck," almost hidden by clumps of thick wires. Within the box, a spiraling twist of RED LASER BEAMS pass from one portion of the neck, through the box, and briefly forms a brilliant PINK KNOT inside the box.

CU Matt, PAN to Dan. Dan eyes Matt nervously.

COMPUTER VOICE

Inserting laser pulse through quantum tunnel.

A LOUD BANG. The vessel SHAKES and big steel bolts holding the vessel to concrete piers shed thin drifts of powder. Lights studding the vessel exterior now glow WHITE.

The computer displays flash RED, RED, RED. Instruments chatter in frantic despair.

We hear a HOLLOW THUD, the reactor shudders once again on its foundation, then, a FORLORN, DECLINING SIGH of dropping power fills the lab. No go.

ON MATT. He's really and truly disgusted.

COMPUTER VOICE (V.O.)

Plasma collapse. Experiment concluded.

The team has had it. They fold their notebooks, pocket their pencils, shrug, and scatter, except for Matt and Dan, and Cindy, who checks out the vessel.

MATT

Let's call it a night. A year. Let's call it a goddamned frustrating year.

Matt turns, as if dancing, holding out his arms, driven to something like delirium.

DAN

It should have worked, Matt! The math is undeniable.

MATT

Each one of these tests costs the university fifty thousand dollars. And so far, all we're getting is a hot fart of deuterium gas.

(Laughs, then deadly serious)

Who's going to save us, Dan?

DAN

We're funded for two more runs.

But he doesn't sound convinced. Cindy is pulling equipment out of the crystal cube.

MATT

I'm out of patience, out of aspirin, and I'm just about out of my mind. It's over. I'm pulling the plug.

DAN

We still have funding!

MATT

What, to burn like kindling? I owe these people some sense of responsibility. I need to be big enough to admit our failure.

Cindy approaches the two men, carrying the QUANTUM TUNNEL. It's about two feet long, a series of stainless steel donuts held together by quartz rods. The inside is blackened.

CINDY

We crisped the tunnel again. It'll take three days to re-line.

DAN

We have the money, give me . . . Three days? Three days I'm sure it's simple. It might just be engineering.

CINDY

Don't blame us!

MATT

Every time we shoot this thing off, my head feels like it wants to split.

DAN

It's the flu. It's got us all down. I know we're close!

He looks to Cindy for support. She's ticked about the prior comment, but she swallows it, for the good of the project, the team.

CINDY

Dr. Shaeffer is right. Let's rebuild and try again. The figures looked promising.

MATT

I'm taking the weekend off. You've got five days . . . no, make that a week. Our last shot. I need <u>genius</u>, Dan.

Matt stalks off.

DAN

You won't regret it!

CINDY

(Low, a narrowed eye on Dan)

We *hope*.

DISSOLVE TO:

INT. A BOY'S BEDROOM - NIGHT

TREVOR BOURNE is 10 years old, small for his age, with pale features and a focused expression. He's lying on his stomach, straight-legged, on the floor, drawing with a crayon on a large piece of construction paper. The ROOM is filled with geometric drawings, beautifully abstract Lego models. Geometric paper cut-outs hang from the ceiling: dodecahedrons and a HYPERCUBE (see sketch 2).

We see that Trevor is very organized, very neat, the room is neat as a pin. But there's something about his expression . . . distant. And very ALONE.

CONTROL VOICE

Some are unlikely pioneers. In the invisible reaches they explore new frontiers . . . A new kind of jungle, filled with terrible dangers . . . Tigers from which they cannot flee.

ANGLE ON TREVOR'S DRAWING.

A KLEIN BOTTLE (SKETCH 1). It also resembles the FUSION REACTOR VESSEL we've already seen. It's surrounded by MATHEMATICAL EQUATIONS, really high-level, complex . . . And all in thick crayon.

We tour the room. Shelves of high-level math texts: TENSOR CALCULUS, ANALYTICAL GEOMETRY, etc.. Cartoon books, too. Strange young fellow, but not out of our range of sympathies. Trevor will grow on us; he's a bit of an alien, but with an indefinable something that makes him a little bigger than the people around him.

Trevor looks up, scans the corners of the room. He SEES SOMETHING, leaps to his feet, and hides the drawing behind his back. We HOPE that the room is empty, but then . . .

OFF HIS SHIFTING EYES . . . The corners fill with POOLS of shadow. The shadows creep down the walls. They take on shapes suggestive of fingers, claws, tentacles .

Trevor averts his eyes, shakes his head, as if in answer to some query. And again. He removes the drawing from behind his back, holds it up, for approval, tense, afraid. His hair LUFFS in a breeze, and he squints. A loop of DARKNESS slices the drawing down the middle, sharp as a razor.

A BLACK, SERPENTINE SHADOW pythons around the walls, wrapping Trevor in coils of darkness. Books, models, FLY OFF THE SHELVES, Legos DISINTEGRATE, hitting Trevor. The coils release him, playing with him. He hides behind raised arms.

A SPIKE-COVERED TENTACLE drops from out of empty air in front of him, rotates, twists, begins to SPIN at blinding speed, then JERKS around the room like a TWISTER, scattering everything! He tries vainly to strike out with his fists.

Trevor CRIES OUT, his voice odd, strangled, as if he is not used to talking.

TREVOR

No more!

He tries to grab at his prized paper models as they fly past him, but they are TORN UP, scattered. Two spiked tentacles lift the pieces of his bottle drawing and finish shredding them, then SHOVE him back onto his bed. DEBRIS drifts through the air.

ANGLE ON THE DOOR.

It's PADDED. As the door OPENS suddenly, all the shadows and the tentacles WHIP AWAY and VANISH, and JANINE KALB stands there, dismayed. She's in her thirties, formally pretty, tied-back hair, wearing a white doctor's coat. From her POV, we see Trevor standing in the middle of the mess, papers falling, books cascading off the shelves. Trevor refuses to meet her eyes.

JANINE

Oh, my God, Trevor. Not again.

She's not very surprised. Trevor goes to a corner, squatting on his haunches.

We PULL BACK, through the open door, past MICHAEL, a burly male nurse leaning on the jamb, and see the door is made of steel. Beyond is a sterile white brick hallway, institutional tile: A HOSPITAL. Trevor is in a LOCKDOWN ROOM.

WE SWING BACK, FLY AROUND JANINE, ZOOM IN ON HER FACE. SHE AND ALL AROUND HER MORPH INTO A CUBIST PERSPECTIVE, as if from several angles at once, Picasso-style.

END OF TEASER

ACT ONE

INT. LAB OFFICE - MORNING

Alone in the office, Dan is pulling up sheet after sheet of reactor design sketches, referring them to the schematic on the laptop. Frantic.

DAN

Why can't I see it? It's got to be simple. Genius is always simple, really.

The phone rings. Dan swears under his breath and picks it up.

DAN (CONT'D)

Shaeffer. Oh. Hello . . .

The expression on his face changes to astonishment as he listens.

DISSOLVE TO:

INT. OLIVE GROVE RESTAURANT - DAY

It's middle-class university town dining, clean, with a few potted plants and faux stone paint. Janine Kalb sits at a two-person table near the window, looking over her menu. Given more time with her, we see a pretty but discontented woman in her thirties, almost as formal without her doctor's coat. She LOOKS UP.

Dan is standing by the window, looking in. He meets her eyes, gives a small, cautious smile—very small, very cautious—and pushes through the door. He drops his coat on the back of the chair and sits across from Janine. They're like two teenagers, stiff and uncertain.

DAN

Janine. You look wonderful.

JANINE

Dan . . . Thank you for coming. I know you're busy.

DAN

Very. And you . . . How's the clinic?

JANINE

We're managing. Where are you working now?

DAN

At the university. Consulting. Design work, actually.

JANINE

Sounds important.

DAN

You could say that.

She hands him a menu. He opens it quickly, biting a nail self-consciously, catches himself, drops his hand.

DAN (CONT'D)

I still chew my nails.

JANINE

I see.

TOGETHER:

DAN

What's good?

JANINE

I'm having the salad.

Her steady, appraising look makes him feel guilty.

DAN

There's nothing more to talk about, is there? It's settled. Been a year.

JANINE

A lot of broken crockery.

DAN

You invited me, remember?

JANINE

I'm sorry. My work is tough on manners.

(Beat)

I could use some advice. .

DAN

From me? That's a switch.

Why does he stay? This hurts. But it's apparent he still has a little hope that they might have something to give each other . . . to mean to each other.

JANINE

Where to begin! Burlington is a small town. I don't know any mathematicians but you, Dan. There's a boy in my care. Trevor Bourne is his name. He's twelve years old. Autistic. Do you know what that means?

DAN

Out of touch.

JANINE

Untouchable is more like it. And violent at times, self-destructive. But so very, very intelligent. We have so few resources in the clinic. He deserves better care than I can give.

DAN

I'm sorry.

JANINE

Trevor is withdrawn around people, but when he's alone, he sketches and writes all the time, geometry, math . . . diagrams. Equations. Ideas I can't begin to understand. He has his father's books, high-level math texts. He treasures them. His father is dead.

Dan raises his eyebrows, still not clear on why he's here.

JANINE (CONT'D)

His mother abandoned him six months ago. The state put him into a foster home, but they couldn't deal with him. When he came to the clinic, I used reward conditioning, and he's made progress, but lately he's become extremely reactive. Violent, self-destructive—and quite the little escape artist. I'm at

my wit's end, Dan. I can't even talk
with him now.

DAN

You think I can?

The waitress arrives for their drinks order. Dan orders coffee, Janine iced tea.

JANINE

I'd like you to meet him, see what he
does. I think he could be brilliant. A
genius.

There's that word again. Dan scowls as if at a bad memory.

DAN

He sounds like a hard case, and I'm not
trained. I'm extremely busy—

JANINE

Call it instinct. You could talk to the
boy, draw him out. Ask him what he's
really doing, deep inside that very, very
lonely mind.

Dan smiles. He's aware of the manipulation.

DAN

You still know how to pull my strings.

JANINE

It might do you good.

DAN

Kill two birds with one stone? Help your

patient, and humanize your self-serving
schmuck of an ex-husband.

ON JANINE. Tight-lipped.

DAN (CONT'D)

What's the boy's name again?

JANINE

Trevor.

DAN

So . . . he's the dysfunctional son we
never had?

This stings. Janine pulls her napkin out of her lap, twisted into knots, and flops it on the table.

JANINE

I should have known. My instincts have
always been bad.

Off this last line, the waitress delivers their drinks and looks at Dan. He glances back, *What?* The waitress departs. Then Dan leans forward, intimate, intense.

DAN

How brilliant?

Janine stares at him, non-plussed.

DAN (CONT'D)

How brilliant is he?

She has him. She plays him.

JANINE

Exceptionally.

DAN

Will this reduce my bastard quotient . . .
in your eyes?

JANINE

It'll be a mitzvah.

DAN

I'm not Jewish.

JANINE

Neither am I. If you don't help, I don't
know anyone who can.

We hold ON DAN, he's skeptical, but she's shot home her point, and then

CUT TO:

INT. THE GLORIA P. DUNHAM CLINIC - LATER

Janine signs them in at the station at one end of the clinic's lockdown wing. There's an attempt here to go beyond the institutional-pastel colors, flowered wallpaper, palms—but it's not a success. Efficient rather than homelike. But it's no dump, either. Here, people care, but it's painful to care too much..

Dan stares at a cork board with drawings attached: PUPPIES, SCARY TREES, SMILING FACES, etc., and an UNFOLDED HYPERCUBE, like a cross with four bars. (Sketch 1)

DAN

Trevor did this?

JANINE

Dozens of them. Is it religious?

He plucks the drawing off the board and carries it with him. She takes an electronic key from the guard behind the counter and Dan follows her down a long hall.

DAN

No. It's a tesseract. The three-dimensional unfolding of a four-dimensional hypercube. Well, actually, Salvador Dali thought it could be religious. A cube is made up of six sides, each side a two-dimensional square. Unfold it and you get a kind of cross made of squares. A four-dimensional cube—a hypercube—has sides made up of three-d cubes. Unfold it, and you get this.

JANINE

(Not her thing, really)

Oh.

DAN

As Barbie once said, 'Math is hard.'

Janine gives him a "spare me" look.

DAN (CONT'D)

Seeing any one?

JANINE

(Prim)

My patients.

At Trevor's door. She applies the key.

JANINE (CONT'D)

I have boxes of drawings we've removed from Trevor's room. Stacks. He always makes more. I think, inside, he's a very sweet little boy.

This seems to be a kind of warning. She opens the door as Michael, the burly attending male nurse, joins them, a precaution.

JANINE (CONT'D)

Michael, we'll go in alone this time.

Michael stays outside.

INT. TREVOR'S ROOM

All the lights are on. There are no windows, no doors. There's a sound, a hint of motion, and we PAN to catch Trevor in his corner, squatting down, arms up across his chest like a mummy, staring at nothing. A sheet of construction paper completes its FALL, and a crayon ROLLS OFF the thick-legged desk, which is bolted to the floor AND COVERED WITH RUBBER PADDING.

And—was that a shadow retreating into the upper corner? How could Trevor have knocked these objects off the table and made it to the corner in time?

Dan reluctantly follows Janine into the room.

JANINE

Hello, Trevor. I'd like to introduce you to a friend. Trevor, this is Dan. Dan, this is Trevor.

The boy doesn't acknowledge them. He rocks, squeezing

his fingers into fists, then unsqueezing them, over and over. He is covered with bruises and scratches. Some bandages hang loose from his arms, showing scabs. Dan is unprepared for this.

JANINE (CONT'D)

Trevor, would you like to say hello to Dan? It's worth a Jolly Rancher.

She dangles a wrapped hard candy. Trevor pays no attention.

JANINE (CONT'D)

(To Dan)

Reward therapy. Could you just stay with Trevor, here, for a while? Keep him company? I'll be back.

Janine smiles and backs out, closing the door behind her. Dan is stunned.

INT. HOSPITAL CORRIDOR

Janine glances at the startled Michael, holds her finger to her lips. They both listen at the door.

INT. TREVOR'S ROOM

Dan gapes like a fish, glancing between the padded door and Trevor, and then looks around the room.

DAN

Hello, Trevor.

Fist, no-fist. Fist, no-fist.

Dan moves around the room, avoiding the boy's corner. He examines the models, the sketches, and the equations on the desk, bends to pick up the paper on the floor, reaches up to touch a cut-and-paste DODECAHEDRON—a twelve-sided polygon.

DAN (CONT'D)

Great stuff. Made these yourself? They let you have scissors?

Makes a wry face; that wasn't cool. He pulls out a random sheet of paper packed with equations, then looks up at the shelf of books, all battered, but neatly arranged once again. He turns the paper around, TRACING the spiral of equations with his finger. (Will provide). Now he's very impressed.

DAN (CONT'D)

You did this? Very cool.

Goes to the shelf and takes down a thick book: *ADVANCED n-SPATIAL GEOMETRY*.

DAN (CONT'D)

Your dad was a mathematician?

Trevor looks at the shelf, then back into the corner.

DAN (CONT'D)

You do hear me. I'll bet he was a good one, Trevor.

He kneels a long pace away from Trevor, uneasy.

DAN (CONT'D)

I'm a mathematician, too.

(Beat)

Mind if I just sit on this chair . . . woops!

The chair is bolted to the floor.

DAN (CONT'D)

It doesn't move. I'll sit and wait for Janine. For Dr. Kalb. May I borrow some paper?

No answer. Dan pulls out a sheet of paper and takes up a crayon.

DAN (CONT'D)

Getting nowhere at work. Might as well be here, with you, right? . . . Talking. Shooting the breeze, as they say. But enough about me.

He jabs at the equations on Trevor's paper.

DAN (CONT'D)

You've made an error. This . . . does not lead to this. Let me write out what I think the solution is, OK?

He writes quickly on his sheet. Holds it up. Trevor does not look.

CU ON DAN. This is really getting to him. He swallows and looks around the room, then stands and goes to the door. Trevor gets up and sidles over to the desk, take his sheet, RIPS IT IN TWO, then THROWS it away and returns to his corner.

DAN (CONT'D)

It wasn't that bad. It was mostly right.

He stoops and picks up the halves of the sheet.

DAN (CONT'D)

Don't be so hard on yourself. You'll see the answer more clearly if you graph it. Visual aids are always good, at least for me.

Dan blinks. Just as he's about to pound on the padded door, it opens, and Janine returns.

JANINE

So how's it going? Trevor?

Fist, no-fist, rocking. Janine gestures to Dan, leans over to drop the Jolly Rancher candy on the table, then escorts him from the room. They walk down the hall.

JANINE (CONT'D)

Did he react?

DAN

He doesn't like criticism.

JANINE

He reacted! That's wonderful. Maybe you have the touch.

DAN

How do you stand it?

JANINE

He's a charmer, really. Compared to others.

She smiles at Dan with new respect.

JANINE (CONT'D)

So—you'll come back? Trevor needs time

to get to know you. Persistence is the key.

ON DAN. This does not appeal to him. He shakes his head.

JANINE (CONT'D)

I understand.

DAN

I have a hard enough time dealing with people who talk. You of all people know that.

Janine's expression is tight, controlled; she expected too much.

DAN (CONT'D)

And frankly, there's enough stress in my life right now. I tried . . . I failed. Thanks for thinking of me.

CUT TO:

EXT. THE GLORIA P. DUNHAM CLINIC - DAY

Dan leaves through the front door, descends the steps in a rush at first, hands in pockets, then slows and stands in the bright sun, staring up at the sky. He wipes his eyes with the back of his hand.

DAN

Shit.

DISSOLVE TO:

INT. DAN'S BEDROOM - LATE AT NIGHT

The clock says 3:00. In bed in the dark, asleep. He JERKS.

P.O.V. DREAM

FLASH on Trevor STARING at us with a quizzical expression. Clouds of BLACK SMOKE like squid ink fill the space behind him.

INT. DAN'S BEDROOM

Dan sits up in bed with a strangled SHOUT, eyes wide. Swings his legs over the edge of the bed, sits up.

CUT TO:

INT. DAN'S BATHROOM

He taps a couple of aspirin tablets into his palm, slugs them back, chases them with a glass of water, stares at himself in the mirror owlishly, accusingly.

DISSOLVE TO:

INT. LAB OFFICE - MORNING

Dan paces. He can't work, can't think.

DAN

Leave me . . . all . . . the hell . . .
ALONE!

He pounds on the corkboard that holds pictures of the reactor. The board falls off the wall and Dan stares at it, bends to put it back, fiddles with tacks, pictures. There are diagrams of donut shapes (toruses), within the Klein bottle; he pins one up, then,

MEDIUM on Dan, tossing a tack in one hand, lost in thought. Sudden resolve: he goes to the phone, punches in a number.

DAN (CONT'D)

I'd like to speak with Janine . . . with Dr. Kalb, please.

END OF ACT ONE

ACT TWO

INT. OFFICE SUPPLY SUPERSTORE - AFTERNOON

Dan is shopping for calculators, examining scientific models with graphing capability, opening instruction manuals, as a young CLERK stands nearby, hoping he won't ask any questions.

CUT TO:

INT. THE GLORIA P. DUNHAM CLINIC - MORNING

We drop into the middle of a conversation. Dan and Janine walk past the front desk. Janine is carrying files and a clipboard and appears very busy. Dan is carrying a package—the calculator—and tags along, eager for the answer to a question we haven't heard.

JANINE

I should have known commitment is hard for you.

DAN

I said I'd like to try again . . . What do I have to do?

She stops and confronts him.

JANINE

You have to care!

Dan pulls back.

DAN

I care.

JANINE

You have to care _a lot_.

Dan squeezes his temples with one hand.

DAN

I had a dream about Trevor last night.

Janine is not impressed. Her face takes on a funny, pained expression. There's a conflict inside her.

JANINE

(With growing intensity)

I have dreams about Trevor every night. Nightmares. He dies, alone, because this is a very small town and if I don't help him, who will? _Who will care_?

(Beat, pulls herself together)

You joked that maybe Trevor was my dysfunctional child. I have a number of them . . . But Trevor just breaks my heart.

More manipulation, but it's very effective.

DAN

I'd like to try again.

Janine gives him a very hard, examining look.

DAN (CONT'D)

He gets under your skin.

Janine sighs, gives in.

JANINE

(Ironic)

Oh, he's a charmer all right.

She marches him back to the desk.

JANINE (CONT'D)

Sign in. Trevor's in hydrotherapy, but he'll be back in his room in ten minutes. What about your work? I thought you were extremely busy.

Dan is caught between being defensive and being honest.

DAN

I am my own master. I work when brilliance strikes, and not before.

JANINE

No new ideas?

DAN

Dead in the water.

JANINE

(Lightly—or not?)

Maybe Trevor can help.

OFF DAN'S REACTION, he's dubious, we

CUT TO:

INT. TREVOR'S ROOM - MOMENTS LATER

Janine and Dan enter the room. Trevor is in a swimsuit, squirming and fighting as Michael, the male nurse, very gently towels him down.

JANINE

Pat him lightly, Michael. Don't rub.

Michael nods and finishes, folds the towel, and raises an eyebrow at Janine as he leaves. Trevor retreats to his corner, still in his swimsuit, and assumes his crouch.

Dan lays his package on the table. He looks up at Janine, pleading for a little help this time, and she stands with her back against the padded door, watching.

A beat or two. Trevor gets to his feet, shivering. Dan watches. As if they are not there, the boy goes to a stack of paper and pulls one off the top, then slaps it on the table, an angry gesture, though his face is blank, and he never looks at Dan or Janine. Back to his corner. Dan picks up the paper, reads the extensive equations written on it. He's pleased.

DAN

You've been thinking about this, haven't you? I brought something to help.

He TAPS the package. Trevor does not react. Dan peels open the paper and pulls out a beautiful new scientific calculator with a big display.

DAN (CONT'D)

Real fancy. Wish I'd had one when I was

your age. Algebraic, reverse Polish
notation, graphing functions, hundred
stack memory, math library, differentials,
integrals.

JANINE

What did that cost?

Dan brushes this off, HOLDS UP THE CALCULATOR and Trevor turns slowly, tracking this MARVEL with his eyes, but when Dan brings the calculator IN LINE WITH HIS FACE, Trevor TURNS AWAY abruptly.

Dan opens the manual and reads from it.

DAN

"Congratulations! As the proud owner
of a programmable DC Industries DC-2000
graphing scientific calculator, you now
have the power to explore the infinite
worlds of mathematics." Who writes this
stuff, huh?

Trevor LOOKS at the calculator again. Dan lays it on the table. Trevor's eyes FOLLOW. No games. Dan backs away and stands beside Janine, arms folded. It's like waiting for a wild animal. Trevor WANTS THE CALCULATOR, but it might be too much to go for . . . with people in the room. But he REALLY WANTS IT.

TREVOR

(To the wall, voice flat)

I want to know . . .

ON JANINE. Painful hope. PAN to Dan, shocked that this is working.

DAN

Yes?

TREVOR

I can't talk with you. It hurts. But I want to know.

Janine is very pleased.

Trevor side-steps to the table and grabs the calculator, then flees back to the corner.

TREVOR (CONT'D)

(Agitated)

Come back later. Show me how it works.

DAN

Thank you, Trevor. You set the pace.

This is too much of an effort, and Trevor starts to tremble. Janine TOUCHES Dan's shoulder, and they leave, closing the door behind.

INT. THE CORRIDOR OUTSIDE

Intense, excited. Dan and Janine try to figure out what has just happened.

JANINE

My instincts weren't wrong!

DAN

I got through to him, didn't I?

They break into excited laughter and hug. Then . . . They break, Janine is embarrassed, has to keep her dignity.

JANINE

He'll be ready tomorrow. You do have the time?

Dan is amazed that she's touched him, and that he's done something right for a change.

DAN

I'll make time.

DISSOLVE TO:

INT. TREVOR'S ROOM - THE NEXT DAY

Dan DROPS a stack of cards on Trevor's table. Trevor sits facing away from Dan, fists near his face, opening and closing. He touches his cheek occasionally, looks up at a corner, looks back . . . at nothing.

DAN

Let's see what you're most interested in, Trevor. Algebra, logic, analysis, and of course geometry . . . All ripe for a brilliant young mind, no? Dr. Kalb tells me you've read all your books over and over . . . What do you understand?

Trevor moves closer to the table.

DAN (CONT'D)

Set theory. Godel's theorem.

(Pronounced gerr-del.)

Non-Euclidean geometries. The Riemann hypothesis.

Trevor raises his hand to the top of his head and pats it swiftly, almost painfully. Dan tries to interpret this.

DAN (CONT'D)

Which was it? Riemann, Non-Euclidean—

Trevor pats his head once more and leans to one side, then returns to opening and closing his fists.

DAN (CONT'D)

Okay. I'm sure you know all about Euclid. Let's talk about Hilbert and Riemann and the rest of the gang. I'll flash these cards at you—basic learning tools for the subject you've chosen.

He riffles through the cards and pulls out a banded set, slips off the rubber band.

DAN (CONT'D)

Shall we?

With a flourish, Dan shuffles the flash cards and deals them out on the table.

DISSOLVE TO:

MONTAGE OF VARIOUS SETTINGS IN THE CLINIC- THREE DAYS

Dan working with Trevor, with flash cards, the calculator, the books:

IN TREVOR'S ROOM

AROUND THE SMALL INDOOR POOL

IN THE LUNCH ROOM OVER SANDWICHES

Janine watches with a serious expression, then smiling

approval, but it's usually just Dan and Trevor and perhaps Michael passing by.

We see Trevor becoming more and more responsive, stopping his fist behavior, sitting closer to Dan. The cards and books and equations flash by, Trevor works intently with his calculator and his crayon, he is absorbing, growing, emerging from his shell.

DISSOLVE TO:

INT. THE POOL ROOM - MORNING

Dan, as our MONTAGE ENDS, is in the pool swimming around Trevor as Michael watches from the side. Dan splashes Trevor, who takes it stoically, and even grins, though still not making eye contact. In the middle of the splashing, Trevor SHOUTS:

TREVOR

I want to know!

Dan stops splashing. Janine walks into the pool room with a robe for Trevor. It's time to get out, but Trevor walks to the side of the pool, avoiding her.

DAN

What do you want to know?

TREVOR

(Still loud, flat)

I want to know, is a donut the same everywhere.

(Beat)

The same as a cup with a handle.

Janine is puzzled. Dan is not.

DAN

A donut, a cup with a handle . . . they're the same. You can mold one into the other without making a cut or a second hole. That's the study of the properties of shapes in space, basic topology.

TREVOR

(Impatient, even a little rude)

I know that. But are a cup and a donut the same everywhere.

Trevor points, then waves his finger around the room, without looking at Dan or Janine.

DAN

It's worth thinking about.

Janine gives them both a cautious smile.

JANINE

Time to get out, Trevor. You'll be all pruny.

DISSOLVE TO:

INT. FUSION REACTOR LAB - MORNING

Dan walks past the Double Pulse Reactor Vessel in the main lab, carrying books and rolls of blueprints. Cindy and John are working around the neck of the vessel and the QUARTZ BOX. Conduits, wire harnesses, and other equipment litter their workbench, and the two post-docs are grimy and sweaty.

ON THE WORK BENCH: the QUANTUM TUNNEL, stacked donuts supported by three steel braces . . . as in Trevor's sketch.

Cindy WIPES HER FOREHEAD, looks up, and sees Dan heading out the exit.

CINDY

Dr. Shaeffer . . . Can we talk?

DAN

I'm late.

CINDY

Cat's away, Dr. Shaeffer.

DAN

What?

CINDY

We have two days to get this right. You aren't around much.

Dan approaches, trying for a little authority, but also to mollify.

DAN

You're re-lining the quantum tunnel, right?

CINDY

That's finished.

She taps the quantum tunnel lightly with a finger.

CINDY (CONT'D)

Now we're balancing and aiming the

internal laser. The donut and the cup,
Dr. Shaeffer.

Dan is taken aback.

DAN

I beg your pardon?

CINDY

(Fast and clear)

We need you to give us a proper angle for the injection beam. When we inject the laser through the quantum tunnel, basically, it takes a detour in another dimension through the skin of the torus, never touches it—and comes out inside, doubling the plasma density. Boom! Extra energy. That's how it works, right? Basic 4D geometry.

DAN

Yes. So?

CINDY

(Tartly, irritation growing)

So is the plasma really a torus, a donut, or is it a cup, or is it a bottle with two holes in it? That should all affect beam angle. I'm just trying to jump-start some answers here, Dr. Shaeffer, because we all think you're kind of slowing down on us.

Andrea joins the group, carrying a small bottle of pills, and with arms folded, they all stare at him. They are so young, with pierced nostrils and short hair and radical clothes, and so smart. And very accusing.

DAN

The beam angle is critical, of course.

The vessel looms over them, shiny and ominous. Dan looks at the assembly they've removed from the quartz box, picks up a beautiful, jewel-like red rod mounted in a steel gimbal, and twists the rod back and forth experimentally.

DAN (CONT'D)

Funny you should ask about a donut and a cup.

He hands the assembly to John, then departs, and shouts over his shoulder,

DAN (CONT'D)

I'm on it! 24 hours a day.

He leaves. The post-docs regard each other with severe doubt. Andrea holds out a bottle of Tylenol, the object of her errand, and pours two apiece into Cindy's and John's OUTSTRETCHED HANDS. They swallow the pills, swig from a runner's bottle of water, then get back to work.

CINDY

Smell that?

ANDREA

What?

CINDY

The stink of a good mind going to waste.

ANDREA

His, or ours?

JOHN

How long does flu last?

CINDY

In hell, forever.

CUT TO:

INT. TREVOR'S ROOM - EVENING

Trevor is in his corner, humming to himself and rocking. He clutches the calculator as if it is a soothing Teddy bear. He looks incredibly vulnerable.

We HEAR A SOUND in the room, papers SHUFFLING. Trevor LOOKS OUT OF THE CORNER. The papers are arranging themselves on his table. A crayon is MOVING, SCRIBBLING, gripped by an isolated curl of shadow with a faint, pearly gleam. Suddenly, the crayon FLIES OFF THE PAPER toward Trevor's face, where it HANGS SUSPENDED.

Trevor FLINCHES, but he is not in the least surprised. He reaches up, takes the crayon, and the curl of shadow VANISHES. The boy walks to the desk, SIGHS, this is dull but familiar, and goes to work. He crudely sketches stacked donuts supported by three braces—we recognize the QUANTUM TUNNEL.

Janine looks in on him. Trevor pauses in his work until she leaves then LOOKS BEYOND THE CAMERA, with his own kind of PATIENCE and COURAGE.

END OF ACT TWO

ACT THREE

INT. THE GLORIA P. DUNHAM CLINIC - AFTERNOON

Dan is checking out blunt scissors from the desk. Michael signs them out.

MICHAEL

Don't leave them in the room.

Dan walks down the hall. Janine comes out of her office and hurries to catch up with him.

JANINE

Wait up! How are the lessons?

DAN

Fine. I hope we're not going too fast.

JANINE

It's up to Trevor.

They're at the door.

JANINE (CONT'D)

I think it's time to tell you more about Trevor.

(Glances at her watch)

I'm busy all afternoon. Dinner tonight?

Janine unlocks, Dan smiles tentatively at her. An overture?

JANINE

Professional . . . dinner.

DAN

Ah. Of course. I need to be back at the lab by eight.

DISSOLVE TO:

INT. TREVOR'S ROOM - MOMENTS LATER

Dan has cut a long strip of paper. Trevor sits halfway between the table and his corner, glancing now and then at what Dan is doing. Trevor clutches the calculator.

DAN

I'm sure you know about a Moebius strip. My favorite trick. Let's say you're a little two dimensional insect, right?

Dan takes a shiny ANT ON A STICKER and places it on the strip of paper. Trevor sniffs.

TREVOR

Ant.

Dan takes the strip, gives it a half-twist, daubs one end with glue, and sticks the ends together. He holds it up, then lays it on the table. Trevor takes the paper in his hands.

DAN

The ant walks around the paper.

Trevor traces his finger all the way around the strip of paper, starting with the ant, ending with the ant—and no edge.

TREVOR

He can see his own butt.

DAN

(Laughs)

You do know this, don't you? It's now a one-sided piece of paper. The ant can walk all the way around, over and over again, and never cross an edge. It's like a closed, two-dimensional universe. A loop.

TREVOR

The ant shines a flashlight. It goes all the way around and lights up his butt.

DAN

Exactly right. Big round of applause!

He claps his hands. Trevor can't take this. He shreds the Moebius strip and retreats into the corner.

TREVOR

Sorry.

Trevor shakes his head, hides his face.

DAN

Should I go now?

Trevor shakes his head vigorously.

TREVOR

Don't go.

DAN

What should we do, Trevor?

TREVOR

Stay with me.

DAN

I'm staying.

He folds his arms and waits. A couple of beats, silence in the room.

TREVOR

No more simple stuff.

Trevor makes large circles with his free hand.

TREVOR (CONT'D)

I want to solve tough problems. Like what you do. What's a Klein bottle?

DAN

You're the man, Trevor.

Dan leans forward. He draws a Klein bottle (sketch 2, already familiar to us).

DAN (CONT'D)

It's a kind of bottle whose inside is continuous with its outside. Like a Moebius strip, but in three dimensions. Except where the neck passes through the bottle's wall and connects with the inside . . . We have to cheat a little and slip that through the fourth dimension. Just as we twist the Moebius strip in the third dimension.

TREVOR

I know. Like a door.

Trevor looks up. Shadows are pooling in the ceiling corners behind Dan, as if they're EAVESDROPPING. Shapes hover and merge and separate in the air—SEE SKETCHES. They are completely SILENT. Dan is unaware, focused on Trevor—and used to his wandering and intent gaze, as he avoids looking directly at people. But we know that Trevor is tracking something else.

DAN

Right. I have some problems nobody knows the answers to, about bottles like this, and how an ant can crawl through the door and shine a flashlight on his own butt.

TREVOR

I know.

DAN

I hope you do. They are very important problems.

Trevor watches the shadows grow. They almost fill the space behind Dan. Dan wrinkles his brow at the DIMMING of the light, and WHIPS HIS HEAD AROUND to stare at the wall, but it's bright and innocent again.

DAN (CONT'D)

(Laughs nervously)

Whoa. Felt like someone was watching me for a second there.

TREVOR

(Flat)

I'm supposed to help you.

DAN

That would be great.

Michael opens the door and breaks the spell. He looks a little suspicious.

MICHAEL

Time for bath and snack in five minutes, Trevor.

Dan is vastly irritated. Trevor shakes his head and pushes the papers away. He flings his hand at the door.

TREVOR

Go.

Dan gets up.

DAN

Tomorrow morning?

TREVOR

(Loud)

Go.

CUT TO:

INT. THE CORRIDOR OUTSIDE - MOMENTS LATER

Dan confronts Michael as the nurse folds towels on a rolling cart.

DAN

We were making good progress. Why bring it all to a screeching halt?

MICHAEL

(Guarded)

The boy has his routine. He needs his rest.

He walks away. Dan won't let it go so easily.

DAN

What, something wrong, you don't approve?

Michael returns Dan's look, but will not be baited.

DISSOLVE TO:

INT. OLIVE GROVE RESTAURANT - LATER THAT NIGHT

Janine is dressed simply but less severely, and has let her hair loose . . . a little. Dan is wearing a tweed jacket, professorial. He's picking at a plate of pasta. Janine's plate is still full. She's doing the talking so far. Her words are sensitive, but there's a professional matter-of-factness about them. She shows little actual passion.

JANINE

I hope you understand how unusual Trevor is. Autism is a horrible affliction. It affects how you process your world. You focus on things, not people or situations. Comparisons and metaphors are difficult, sometimes impossible, but you can have an intense focus on particulars. Sometimes you get so overloaded with stimulus, any stimulus, that you have to scream or hide or just withdraw. His baths . . . Michael . . .

DAN

Rubs him the wrong way?

JANINE

Rubbing, scraping, can be awful. But Trevor enjoys steady pressure, a deep massage. I've seen Michael have Trevor completely relaxed on a table, happy . . . as happy as Trevor can ever be. Michael cares, he's good with the boy, but Michael is like furniture to Trevor. Trevor is actually talking <u>with</u> you. That is a wonderful accomplishment, Dan.

DAN

(Proud)

Without candy.

JANINE

Without candy.

Dan leans forward, elbows on the table, and holds up his hands expressively.

DAN

What about his brilliance? Where does that come from?

JANINE

Not all autistics are brilliant or even smart. They're just people, after all. Trevor has a special talent, and I don't think it's connected with his affliction. He could be a kind of savant, with one area of his mind compensating for weakness in other areas. That . . . and his love for his father.

DAN

I thought autistic children had a hard time connecting.

JANINE

Some love differently, but they still love. Trevor never talks about his father. But those books are his prized possession. He's probably read them all a hundred times. You don't know how pleased I am you can talk with him. Be there for him. He needs a person he can connect with. A man.

DAN

Is something else bothering him? Is it just autism?

JANINE

Why?

DAN

(Shrugs)

Have you told Trevor anything about my work?

JANINE

No. How could I? I don't know anything about your work.

DAN

Just this funny feeling today, before Michael interrupted us.

Janine puts out her hand and takes his, rubs his fingers.

JANINE

We're all protective of Trevor. But you're doing just fine.

DAN

Is it okay if I challenge him?

JANINE

That's why I asked you.

He rubs her hand in return, and she slowly disengages, withdraws. Dan alerts a waitress.

DAN

Do you have any aspirin? I'm fresh out.

WAITRESS

Acetaminophen. Will that do?

DAN

Fine.

(To Janine)

Sinus, flu . . . It's hit the lab. All around town, I hear.

JANINE

I got over it weeks ago.

(Afterthought)

I hope it's not too bad.

Dan shrugs; just par for the course. The waitress brings him tablets and a glass of water. He takes the pills. Now's the time to understand some things.

DAN

Janine . . . I want to—understand where we are.

Janine is suddenly in a hurry.

JANINE

It's almost eight. You need to get back to the lab, right?

The moment passes. Dan might be afraid to learn the truth.

DAN

Right.

CUT TO:

EXT. OLIVE GROVE RESTAURANT - MOMENTS LATER

They stand at the curb, waiting to part. Janine is fidgety. Dan has his hands deep in his pockets and is obviously in pain.

JANINE

Are you sure you're all right?

DAN

I can hardly see straight.

JANINE

Can I drive you home?

DAN

It'll pass.

JANINE

(Relieved, fragile)

A brave man.

DAN

I wouldn't go that far.

She takes his face in her hands, too intense, like a scared deer.

JANINE

(Forced)

Good with children.

DAN

(Laughs nervously)

Oh, Lord. Not that.

JANINE

No. This.

She kisses him square. His eyes wander for a moment in surprise, then focus. He kisses her back, walks his lips across her face, hungry. Abruptly, she breaks and gives him a look of distress.

JANINE (CONT'D)

No! I won't do it! I have to go.

And before he can answer, she's running down the street toward her car. Dan is AT A COMPLETE LOSS.

DISSOLVE TO:

END OF ACT THREE

ACT FOUR

INT. TREVOR'S ROOM - AFTERNOON

Trevor is alone in his room. He works intently with his calculator, writing answers on the papers on his table. We do not know if he is happy; Trevor's affect is FLAT unless otherwise indicated.

ON THE PAPERS. Masses of very complex equations (will provide).

Dan enters with a clutch of blueprints under his arm, smiles sunnily at Trevor. Trevor looks up, though not at Dan, and stops writing. He puts down the crayon, crosses his arms in a NORMAL fashion, not mummy-like, and waits.

DAN

Good morning, Trevor. Yesterday's work was excellent. We're making real progress.

He puts down the blueprints and unrolls one on the table. It's THE REACTOR VESSEL, a Klein bottle. Trevor glances at it from the corner of his eye.

DAN (CONT'D)

I really feel a little embarrassed, coming to you like this, but I must confess you're the better mathematician.

TREVOR

Thanks.

Dan purses his lips in appreciation. This is a breakthrough.

DAN

You are welcome! Wow. All right. Let's get down to the brass tacks, as the engineers say.

TREVOR

Thanks.

DAN

(Again)

You're welcome.

He unrolls another blueprint, the QUANTUM TUNNEL.

DAN (CONT'D)

We're in the quantum tunnel now. Our angles are going to get very strange here.

TREVOR

I know.

DAN

And because the angles and timing are so critical, we have to adjust the laser frequency for a kind of shift in spectrum, depending on our angle. Right? This is what we did yesterday. The beam has to be several places at once, and we explained that, right?

TREVOR

I know.

Dan lifts a piece of paper and cuts two quick holes with the scissors, a finger's-reach apart.

DAN

The geometry is simple, the math is not. We say this paper is our three-dimensional space. My hand is the laser.

He squeezes his index pointing fingers together, making a kind of gun, which he jabs.

DAN (CONT'D)

We run it through the tunnel, where it is boosted to a higher dimension, 4-space.

TREVOR

Right.

Trevor runs his finger over the tunnel in the blueprint.

DAN

It's just one laser, but in 4-space it can be made to act like two.

He separates his fingers and jabs them through the paper, then taps his wrist.

DAN (CONT'D)

One laser.

And wriggles the fingers on the other side, where they look like two worms.

DAN (CONT'D)

Now two.

TREVOR

Can I say something.

DAN

Of course.

TREVOR

You aren't the only one.

Dan lifts his eyebrows.

DAN

There's Dr. Kalb, and Michael, of course. I'm in a bit of a hurry here, Trevor. We have a test later today . . . My boss is back in town.

TREVOR

Okay. Don't be mad.

DAN

I'm not in the least mad.

TREVOR

Here's the right answer.

And he takes out a fresh piece of paper, scrawling a large equation quickly. He slides the paper to Dan. Dan looks at the equation in wonder.

DAN

That was fast. I'd have never thought of it that way. Unique. Unique insight.

OFF TREVOR, eyes shifting,

DISSOLVE TO:

INT. FUSION REACTOR LAB - LATER THAT AFTERNOON

The postdocs Cindy and Andrea and John are working under Dan's direction, in the shadow of the reactor vessel. Cindy is assembling the quantum tunnel on a work bench, inserting the gimbaled red laser guide. Andrea and Dan are conferring, and John is listening in, while he holds a large wire harness.

DAN

We should do a dry run.

ANDREA

Dr. Daube won't be back until tomorrow.

DAN

Then let's surprise him.

ANDREA

I don't think that's a great idea.

Dan types in a few keystrokes on his laptop on the test bench, and shows the screen to the postdocs. Cindy kneels in front of the computer and critically assesses the results.

CINDY

It looks like a new approach.

ON DAN. He's tense, perhaps guilty? No trace of crayon here.

CINDY (CONT'D)

You came up with this all by yourself?

DAN

How about a little respect here?

The postdocs are not impressed.

DAN (CONT'D)

That's why they pay me the big bucks.

CINDY

Yeah, right.

ANDREA

(Studying, she's encouraged)

Still, it is a new approach. It could work..

DAN

It will work. Let's do it.

DISSOLVE TO:

WIDE SHOT. FUSION REACTOR LAB - HOURS LATER

The equipment is up and running, everyone is sweaty and stained with grease. Dan is in his element.

CU on the quartz box, with its red laser beams pulsing.

DAN

No plasma this time. Let's see where the beam goes first. Charging.

Dan stands by the CONTROL BOARD, adjusting dials as the REACTOR COMPUTER DISPLAY shows status of all elements is GREEN. Dan types in an instruction, and we hear a low, grinding WHINE, like a wind of TINY BALL BEARINGS blowing out a STEEL PIPE.

DAN (CONT'D)

Quantum tunnel open.

ON CINDY and ANDREA. They wince at the painful SOUND. PAN TO JOHN. He's irritated, as well.

JOHN

That's new. Where's it coming from?

DAN

The laser guide, I think. It's nominal for this configuration. Everything's green.

CINDY

Let's go, then.

COMPUTER VOICE

Charging internal laser. Test shield is in place.

DAN

Firing!

SIMULTANEOUSLY, the BALL BEARING WIND noise reaches a CRESCENDO.

CU on the quartz box, and within the TUNNEL, the lasers form a brilliant pink KNOT.

RAPID CUTS:

CINDY and ANDREA clasp their hands to their ears and SCREAM.

The QUARTZ BOX CRACKS, and ONE PANEL SHATTERS.

Dan ducks behind the control board.

A thick shadow like INTELLIGENT SMOKE whirls around the room, and GETS SUCKED BACK INTO THE REACTOR through THE OPEN BOX with a SOUND LIKE AGONIZED VOICES.

The LIGHTS DIM, BRIGHTEN. Then . . . SILENCE.

A beat. Dan and Matt get to their feet. John is kneeling beside Cindy.

ANDREA

Is she all right?

JOHN

I don't know. She's out cold.

Matt stares at Dan. Cindy comes to and sits up, holding her head.

CINDY

Did you see what I saw? Like . . . faces?

JOHN

You were hit pretty hard.

CINDY

By what? All the debris went over that way. Something really creepy is going on.

John inspects the area around the shattered quartz box.

Dan is in shock. He wanders around the console.

JOHN (O.S.)

Hey, the guide and tunnel are intact.

DAN

We should check the computer record..

JOHN

The tunnel isn't even burned.

DAN

But did it work? DID IT WORK?

Andrea is at the console, calling up the test record. Cindy backs off; she's had enough.

ANDREA

We got a strong internal laser pulse, and it split into two. But the beam angles were wrong. They blew out the shields. If we'd had a plasma in there, it would have destroyed the bottle.

John circles and looks at Dan suspiciously.

JOHN

Someone has it in for us.

ON DAN. He's concealing RAW ANGER and his jaw is working.

DAN

How long to fix?

Cindy is really spooked. Andrea frowns, shakes her head, looks at John, who is none too enthusiastic, either.

ANDREA

A day? Cindy?

Cindy shakes her head, does not answer.

DAN

I'll re-check the figures.

JOHN

Dr. Daube should be here for the next one, don't you think?

PAN PAST ANDREA TO CINDY. This formerly bold post-doc is scared. Cindy looks up at the reactor vessel.

OFF CINDY'S UNCERTAINTY AND FEAR,

DISSOLVE TO:

EXT. THE GLORIA P. DUNHAM CLINIC - THE NEXT DAY- MORNING

Dan takes the steps slowly, pauses at the door, shakes his head. Very grim.

CUT TO:

INT. THE CLINIC - MOMENTS LATER

Dan is signing in at the desk, a RECEPTIONIST watching benignly. Janine exits her office and sees Dan. He

LOOKS UP, avoids her eyes, and walks down the hall to Trevor's room.

JANINE

Dan . . .

He stops in the hall. Janine is almost apologetic; she may be trying to mend fences. Dan is wary around her; she's not exactly predictable.

JANINE (CONT'D)

We had a bad night last night. Michael is straightening things. Trevor is in the sunroom, playing by himself.

DAN

(Very stiff)

I can come back later.

JANINE

He'd miss not seeing you. Some time outside the clinic would be terrific for him. Trevor's been looking forward to a visit to the park. Would you like to take him?

DAN

If that's all right.

JANINE

I apologize about last night. I behaved a little strangely.

DAN

Par for the course.

JANINE

I beg your pardon?

DAN

Maybe you wanted to twist the knife a little . . . for revenge?

JANINE

That's ridiculous. I am . . . revising my feelings. We do have a history. Please allow me some confusion?

DAN

And please allow me some dignity.

(Beat)

I'm ready whenever Trevor is.

CUT TO:

EXT. BELLINGER PARK - LATER

Dan and Trevor walk side by side. Trevor clutches two of his books to his chest. It's a gorgeous day. Trevor walks with a deliberate, quick boy's gait, to match Dan's stride. Dan doesn't seem to be paying the boy much attention; he's lost in thought.

Trevor glances in Dan's general direction. Dan doesn't react. Trevor sees a bench and runs over to it, sits, wriggles, aims his face at the sun with his eyes closed. Dan joins him. His anger is about to spill over.

DAN

Why did you give me the wrong answer, Trevor?

Trevor winces, hides his face.

DAN (CONT'D)

I trusted you. Why would you want to cause trouble for me?

TREVOR

I don't mess up my room. I'm very neat.

DAN

I need the right answer this time, no fooling. I relied on you, Trevor.

ON TREVOR. He's trembling, and this is cruel, but Dan is past being sensible.

DAN (CONT'D)

My whole career could be ruined. <u>My life</u>.

TREVOR

I want to tell you. Doctor Kalb says I have an imaginary friend.

DAN

What?

TREVOR

But I think I have an imaginary enemy.

DAN

Don't go all nutty on me, Trevor.

TREVOR

It gets mad at me when I don't do what it wants. It messes up my room.

DAN

I don't have time today.

Trevor swings his arm <u>out there</u>.

TREVOR

It tries to get into people's heads. It makes their heads hurt.

DAN

Great. Gives us all headaches?

Trevor's words seem to strike a chord. Dan thinks about this for a second.

DAN (CONT'D)

All right. I'll bite. What sort of imaginary enemy?

(Satirical)

It lives in your room, right, under the table?

Trevor takes a piece of paper out of the book and places an ANT STICKER on it. Then he pokes the crayon through the paper around the ant, four holes, and sticks four fingers through the holes, poking them up around the ant sticker, wriggling them for Dan's inspection.

As Trevor demonstrates, and explains, we see a THORNY SPHEROID appear in the air behind Dan. It BREAKS UP INTO THREE, then FOUR.

TREVOR

It lives where I can't point. In the fourth dimension. It can be lots of places at once, but it's just one thing. Sometimes I can see it. Sometimes I can't.

Dan looks down at the paper with some surprise. THE

SPHEROIDS FORM SERPENTS, circle behind DAN, but he still can't see . . .

TREVOR (CONT'D)

I think it's lonely.

END OF ACT FOUR

ACT FIVE

EXT. THE PARK - CONTINUOUS

WIDE SHOT ON TREVOR AND DAN, AND THE SPHEROIDS, we resume:

TREVOR

If the reactor works, if you open the tunnel all the way, more will come here. They want to live in us, like . . . what are those crabs that live in shells?

CLOSER. THE BOY GRIPS HIS ARM. Dan GRIMACES at the pressure.

DAN

Hermit crabs?

TREVOR

Yeah.

Trevor looks very forlorn, as if he's about to betray a confidence.

TREVOR (CONT'D)

It gets inside Dr. Kalb and then she hurts me.

This is incredible, and Dan is in no mood.

DAN

Forget about "imaginary enemies." Dr. Kalb would never hurt you, Trevor.

Trevor LOOKS RIGHT IN DAN'S EYES.

TREVOR

It makes her.

DAN

(Very stern)

I know you can give me the right answer. If you don't, I'll tell Dr. Kalb that I can't visit you any more.

Trevor is devastated. He struggles to explain himself.

TREVOR

Please don't make it mad. Sometimes it moves me around. It peels me off, like this . . .

HE LIFTS THE ANT STICKER OFF THE PAPER, stuck on the end of HIS FINGER, and waves it in the air, then sticks it on the bench.

TREVOR (CONT'D)

That's how I escaped before.

Dan stands up from the bench. He's angry and disgusted at this nonsense.

DAN

This was a bad idea from the beginning. We're going back.

Trevor is in a PANIC. He gets up and HOLDS ON to Dan as if his life depends on it.

TREVOR

NO! They will find other people to live in. They will hurt them!

His eyes track something on the SIDEWALK and he LETS DAN'S ARM GO.

A RIPPLE IN THE SIDEWALK, a kind of WAVE, advances and BREAKS AGAINST DAN'S FEET. He feels the pressure and looks down, seeing only rough concrete. His CELL PHONE CHIMES. Distracted, he pulls it out of his pocket and answers.

DAN

Shaeffer. Yeah . . . He's back? Tell him to wait for me. Yeah. No.

(Heated)

That was a dry run. It did not cause substantial damage!

P.O.V. FROM THE TREE

LOOKING DOWN ON DAN AND TREVOR. In the branches and leaves, SOMETHING IS MOVING. We see a SILHOUETTE, some DETAILS . . . It could be a kind of SNAKE, floating there, with a head like a LAMPREY, circular teeth OPENING AND CLOSING. The leaves and branches TREMBLE and RUSTLE. It HOVERS within the thick branches, supported by nothing but air. Then it separates . . . into TWO SNAKES.

ON TREVOR. Trevor grabs a piece of paper and writes furiously, darting glances up at the tree, the SHAPES behind Dan. The SHAPES VANISH.

DAN (O.S.)

Andrea, I don't care if he hired another consultant. Don't start it up until I get there. We have a contract—he can't just fire me! I'll be there as soon as I can!

Dan CLICKS the phone shut, furious, then swivels on Trevor. Trevor holds up THE PAPER for Dan's inspection.

DAN'S P.O.V. He takes the paper, covered with equations, and reads it, obscuring his (and our) view of Trevor.

FROM BEHIND TREVOR: Another LAMPREY-SNAKE morphs out of thin air, latches on to TREVOR'S BACK. TREVOR JERKS, FREEZES. HE VANISHES.

DAN

This reverses the polarity on the tunnel. Still not right, damn it! It would suck in—like a vacuum cleaner.

He LOWERS THE PAPER. Trevor is nowhere to be seen. Dan looks around, glances at the books and papers scattered around the bench. SOMETHING RUSTLES in the tree, and Dan turns, looks up at THE TREE. We see A SHADOW, then . . . nothing.

DAN (CONT'D)

What in hell? Trevor!

He walks, then runs, looking for the boy.

DAN (CONT'D)

TREVOR!

CUT TO:

INT. THE CLINIC - MOMENTS LATER

Michael wheels a cart full of Trevor's shredded books and papers, stacked on top of a broken chair and parts of the table, past the main desk, where the receptionist is giving Dan a shrug and a blank look. Dan is frantic.

DAN

I didn't see him leave! He could be anywhere.

MICHAEL

What's up?

RECEPTIONIST

Mr. Shaeffer came back without the boy.

MICHAEL

Dr. Kalb took Trevor out of his room, ten, fifteen minutes ago.

DAN

That's impossible! He was with me!

MICHAEL

I saw them. She looked pretty upset, but she definitely had Trevor with her.

The pressure is off—for the moment, but not the mystery. Dan scans the mess on the cart. He picks up a broken chair leg, bolts dangling.

DAN

Jesus!

MICHAEL

Quite a night for our young man.

DAN

Is he that strong?

MICHAEL

(Shrugs)

Something is.

Dan picks up a book. It's badly damaged, covers ripped, pages torn.

DAN

Must have been bad, for him to rip his father's books.

MICHAEL

His father's?

DAN

Janine said they belonged to his father. They came with Trevor when he was sent here.

MICHAEL

You must have heard wrong. Dr. Kalb brought Trevor to the clinic. Nobody knows who his father is. She bought him these books because she wanted to encourage him.

(Beat, his eyes narrow)

I keep my counsel around here, Dr. Shaeffer. But I wonder . . . Do you or Dr. Kalb really care what you're doing to Trevor? Helping him, or using him? Maybe I'm speaking out of turn.

DAN

Why would she lie?

A stack of paper spills off the cart. Michael and Dan bend over it simultaneously. Dan is amazed: in Trevor's crayon, there are dozens of drawings of nearly all aspects of the Double Pulse Fusion Reactor: the vessel itself, the quantum tunnel. He THUMBS THROUGH THE DRAWINGS, realization DAWNING. Their EYES MEET.

MICHAEL

There's a lot of odd stuff happening, Mr. Shaeffer. Do you really think a ten-year-old-boy could rip up heavy furniture like this? I know you're friends with the boy . . . But Dr. Kalb, she works him sometimes day and night, and that isn't right.

DAN

(Fear and resolve)

I've got to go.

CUT TO:

EXT. THE STREET - SECONDS LATER

Dan is in his car, a Miata convertible. He SPINS IT OUT of its parking space, SWINGS ACROSS TRAFFIC, tires SCREECHING everywhere, and the Miata FISHTAILS dangerously back to a straight course down the street.

CUT TO:

EXT. CAMPUS OF BURLINGTON UNIVERSITY - MOMENTS LATER

Dan runs toward the lab building. The BALL-BEARING WIND SOUND comes from the building.

CUT TO:

INT. FUSION REACTOR LAB - MOMENTS LATER

ALL HELL HAS BROKEN LOOSE. The REACTOR is running FULL BORE, shaking, powder drifting down around its concrete piers, making that incredible SOUND. SERPENT SHADOWS dart around the lab, LAMPREY-SNAKE heads merging, flowing. (See sketches)

John, Cindy, Andrea, are sprawled on the concrete floor, INERT. MATT IS STANDING, weaving as if drunk, his face SCRATCHED. He KEELS OVER.

ON JANINE, standing beside the console, in the shadow of the REACTOR. She clutches TREVOR. Their hair is blown back by passing SHADOWS. Janine propels Trevor to the console, forces him into the seat. But Trevor is withdrawing, crossing his arms.

JANINE

Do what it wants!

ON DAN. He enters the lab and sees Janine standing by the reactor. Trevor has withdrawn and sits at an angle, with arms crossed, fist-open, fist-closed, in the console swivel chair.

DAN

What is going on?

JANINE SCREAMS and JERKS.

JANINE

It's in my HEAD, DO WHAT IT WANTS!

We see a STAIN OF SHADOW outline her head, her torso, FAN OUT as SHADOWY TENTACLES.

DAN

JANINE!

JANINE

You opened the door! Your machine let it in!

Dan tries to pull Matt back from the chaos, manages a few yards, but it's useless. He turns as if to run away.

JANINE (CONT'D)

DON'T LEAVE US HERE!

ON DAN. He's terrified, his courage is nothing like Trevor's.

DAN

I don't understand, there's nothing I can do!

JANINE

Trevor kept giving you the wrong answers, to break the machine!

Her entire demeanor CHANGES from fear to RAGE, then to GLOATING TRIUMPH.

JANINE (CONT'D)

I tried to tell him how stupid that was! It's given me such <u>power</u>. It's showed me how I can change my life! It takes me wherever I want to go, around the world . . . instantly!

Janine's shadow aura BRIGHTENS and she is MOVED INSTANTLY to stand beside Trevor at the console.

JANINE (CONT'D)

I can have jewels, money, lifted from all over the planet. I can live like a Queen in a world filled with servants! No more taking care of broken people—no more dealing with losers! All I have to do is arrange for its friends to cross over.

ON DAN, kneeling beside Matt. He can't believe what he's hearing.

DAN

Why Trevor? He's just a boy!

JANINE

(Absolute zero chill)

Because you're the only other mathematician I know . . . and I loathe you! We need a bigger door, Dan. Fix it! If you don't do what it wants, I'll have it kill Trevor . . . and then kill you!

Dan makes his decision. He rolls Matt over, takes the CONSOLE KEY from Matt's hand. A shadow BREEZES past his head, nearly knocking him over, and wrestles with his arm, but he breaks free and RUNS past Janine to the console.

Dan SPINS Trevor around in his chair, then shouts to the shadows, to Janine.

DAN

Don't hurt him! I'll do it!

The shadows GATHER around Dan and Trevor, expectant, pulsing. Dan pulls Trevor to him and whispers in his ear.

ECU ON DAN AND TREVOR.

DAN (CONT'D)

Let's do it right this time! Like you showed me in the park!

The shadows SPIN UP like slugs mounted on a wheel, distracting him.

DAN (CONT'D)

Damn! How can you tell how many there are?

Trevor opens his eyes, STARES DAN IN THE FACE. Dan PRESSES THE KEY into Trevor's HAND, then guides it to the console LOCK. Trevor TURNS THE KEY. Dan types into the console, biting his lower lip in concentration, distracted by the shadows . . .

ON JANINE, taking a step toward them, WATCHING with deep concern.

DAN (CONT'D)

How about a little reversed polarity? Let's suck all the genies back into the bottle.

Dan initiates his—and Trevor's—change.

DAN (CONT'D)

(Shouting)

HERE IT COMES! BRING ALL YOUR FRIENDS!

The SOUND ramps up into an even harsher GRIND. The reactor's vibrations BLUR its contours.

The SHADOWS AND SHAPES slow their spinning, STOP . . . REVERSE

ON JANINE. Her rage becomes puzzlement, then SHOCK. She steps forward to wrestle Dan away from the console. THEY STRUGGLE.

ON TREVOR. He pulls himself together, types in an additional simple instruction, and

ECU Presses the ENTER key.

The QUARTZ BOX EXPLODES, scattering shards all over the chamber.

THE SOUND REVERSES, and the SHADOWS AND SHAPES DEFORM. They struggle against an incredible pressure that is SUCKING THEM into the open area where the quartz box was. One by one, the SHAPES contort, lengthen, and are VACUUMED UP into the reactor bottle with weird cries of RAGE AND PAIN.

ON JANINE, as Dan breaks free. Her face shows PANIC. Her SHADOW AURA elongates toward the reactor, and she is DRAGGED ALONG with it. She REACHES for DAN.

JANINE

Help me!

Dan tries to grab her hand, but the fingers slip through.

TREVOR WATCHES.

And Janine is SUCKED IN WITH HER SHADOWY MASTER.

The reactor SHUTS DOWN. The SOUND DROPS IN PITCH, STOPS.

The CONSOLE DISPLAY blinks RED, RED, RED.

THE DISPLAY, in a BLACK SQUARE, flashes: *Experiment concluded.*

THEN, *Reactor offline.*

Dan HUGs Trevor, who grasps his arm and turns his face into Dan's shoulder.

DAN

You're a brave boy. A very brave boy.

HOLD ON THIS, PULL BACK and BACK until we take in the entire lab, smoke drifting, the reactor knocked from its concrete piers. Out of action. A mess. The post-docs and Matt slowly come to, get on their feet, disoriented, surveying the damage.

DISSOLVE TO:

INT. THE GLORIA P. DUNHAM CLINIC - MORNING

Trevor walks down the hall carrying an old, battered suitcase. He's still Trevor, still an autistic boy, but his step is quicker, livelier, and his manner less stiff.

Michael WATCHES and smiles as Trevor walks past.

MICHAEL

See you around, Trevor.

Trevor gives a sideways nod. He SEES SOMEONE. His FACE BRIGHTENS.

It's DAN. He takes Trevor's suitcase, and holds the boy's hand. Together, they walk past the main desk.

CUT TO:

EXT. THE CLINIC

Dan and Trevor descend the steps.

CONTROL VOICE (V.O.)
The mystery of knowledge is hidden within. We are who we are, and when the nightmares flee, we remain, changed only a little . . .

ON TREVOR, glancing up at Dan. Dan SMILES.

CONTROL VOICE (V.O.) (CONT'D)

In the memory of our survival.

DISSOLVE TO:

INT. A BASEMENT HALL, SOMEWHERE, YEARS LATER

A YOUNG MAN in a rumpled and stained lab coat JINGLES a ring of KEYS as he nonchalantly approaches a big STEEL DOOR. He's carrying a clipboard with a checklist.

THE DOOR is marked *Equipment Storage.*

He unlocks the door and pushes it open with a ghastly SQUEAL of hinges. He grimaces at the sound, then FLICKS a light switch. Far away, hovering over piles of boxes and several big CRATES, a VERY SMALL BULB switches on, providing dim illumination.

He makes a face at the dimness, then steps through and

around crates and boxes, checking against serial numbers and labels on the bigger crates. He TURNS . . .

AND WE SEE A BIG, VERY BIG, FRAMEWORK CRATE. Inside, unmistakable, is our KLEIN BOTTLE REACTOR VESSEL.

The young man has his back to this crate when he finds what he's looking for. He bends over to shift a box.

ON THE REACTOR VESSEL. A hollow, empty MOANING WHINE from within, and the crate SHAKES.

The YOUNG MAN straightens, turns slowly, staring at the crate, LIFTING HIS GAZE to the ceiling, higher and higher, where the crate SCRAPES AGAINST PLUMBING.

THE CRATE SHUDDERS and something BANGS.

The young man drops his clipboard, gives a small SHRIEK and runs for the DOOR—but the DOOR IS CLOSING ON HIM!

IT SLAMS SHUT. The lights go out, and we hear that pulsing, BALL-BEARING WIND SOUND, RISING IN VOLUME.

FADE OUT:

END OF SHOW

ABOUT THE AUTHOR

Greg Bear is the author of over twenty-five books, which have been translated into seventeen languages. He has won science fiction's highest honors and is considered the natural heir to Arthur C. Clarke. The recipient of two Hugo Awards and four Nebula Awards, Bear has been called "the best working writer of hard science fiction" by the *Science Fiction Encyclopedia*. Many of his novels, such as *Darwin's Radio*, are considered to be classics of his generation. Bear is married to Astrid Anderson—who is the daughter of science fiction great Poul Anderson—and they are the parents of two children, Erik and Alexandria. Bear's recent publications include the thriller *Quantico* and its sequel, *Mariposa*; the epic science fiction novel *City at the End of Time*; and the generation starship novel *Hull Zero Three*.

THE COMPLETE SHORT FICTION OF GREG BEAR

FROM OPEN ROAD MEDIA

Available wherever ebooks are sold

Open Road Integrated Media is a digital publisher and multimedia content company. Open Road creates connections between authors and their audiences by marketing its ebooks through a new proprietary online platform, which uses premium video content and social media.

Videos, Archival Documents, and New Releases

Sign up for the Open Road Media newsletter and get news delivered straight to your inbox.

Sign up now at
www.openroadmedia.com/newsletters

FIND OUT MORE AT
WWW.OPENROADMEDIA.COM

FOLLOW US:
@openroadmedia and
Facebook.com/OpenRoadMedia

DA 04/16

CPSIA information can be obtained at www.ICGtesting.com
Printed in the USA
BVOW05s2337270316

441845BV00001B/1/P